WHEN HIDDEN EYES GROW DIM

AARON DICK

ALSO BY THIS AUTHOR:

In this series:

Where The Fields Grow Light

Other books:

Rotten

This is a work of fiction. Names, characters, places and incidents are either the product of the author's imagination or are used fictitiously. Any resemblance to actual persons, living or dead, events, or locales is entirely coincidental.

Copyright © 2022 by Aaron Dick

All rights reserved. No part of this book may be reproduced or used in any manner without the written permission of the copyright holder except for the use of quotations in a review.

First Edition

Book Cover Illustration by Millikodea
Book Cover Design by oliviaprodesign

ISBN 978-0-473-63913-6

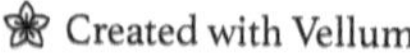 Created with Vellum

This novel is dedicated to Carla,
For asking what happened next.

PROLOGUE

The water is thick and dark. The trees that grow out of this water are tall and twisted; with thick green leaves shedding water in a steady stream of droplets that plummet to the rippling surface below. The water is shallow, and he swims through it carefully, twisting his body to minimise the noise he makes. He grips onto the tangle of roots that pierce the surface, pulling himself out of the water, out of danger. Behind him he hears the water splash as something changes direction. He shivers.

The canopy of branch and leaf above is beginning to reveal the orange light of morning brightening the sky. He can see his surroundings more clearly. He was woken before dawn and brought down to the orchards. He was forced in the water immediately, to swim in darkness. He is grateful for the light.

He pulls himself along the roots, heading higher into the tree he has chosen. He knows others are climbing in the trees all around him, but the thought gives him no comfort. If something were to lunge from the water below, to snatch him down, none of them would pause in their task. The punishments for interrupting their work would be too great. He knows that he wouldn't turn if he heard one of them fall either.

Above him, the tree's flowers are opening in the golden morning light. They are like small purple pods that split open and reveal the tufts within, seeds stuck within the soft white material. He reaches out to pull the pods off the branches, but they are still too far away. He needs to climb higher.

A long low croak breaks the quiet of the morning and he freezes. Something flaps across the canopy, and a shadow passes overhead. He waits, listening for the sound of rushing wind as it swoops, or snapping twigs where it breaks through the trees. No sound comes. Finally, he moves again.

Now, closer, he can reach out and pull the pods and their precious tufts from the branches. He tugs each one free and then reaches over his shoulder to tuck it into the sack buckled around his back. He continues as long as he can, filling the sack until he risks spilling his collection into the black waters below. It is not worth bringing back a half full sack, but each lost pod risks punishment as well.

Another croak and then the rush of wind. He freezes and closes his eyes, his heart racing. But the sound of breaking branches does not come from above him. Instead, a tree to his right is filled with movement and sound as one of the others is attacked. The bird stabs through the leaves with its long thin beak, grabbing another worker, and then thumps its wings and drags them into the clear sky above the trees. He tries not to look, scared that he might recognise the one who was taken. He tries not to hear them crying out from the blue open sky.

Slowly and solemnly he moves down the branches, placing his feet carefully until he reaches the firmer footholds of the roots. Now he must swim back, through the dark muddy waters. He looks at the ripples passing by, trying to determine whether each is caused by wind or current or something else. As he watches, he pulls the sack closed, sealing it against the water. Satisfied, he slips into the water and begins to slide forward.

He hasn't gone far before something breaks the surface behind him. He spins at the sound and sees a dark eye watching him above a long scaled snout full of dull white teeth. He cracks his tail in the water, attempting to move faster, to find some roots nearby that he can clamber onto. As the creature in the water closes on him, he lashes out with his claws, hoping against hope that he can drive it away.

Despite his attempts, the long jaws open and come crashing down.

1

Shanti sat in a curved booth in the corner of the Stout Shelter, a pub near the home she shared with Keema. She was nestled comfortably into the soft velvet seats and watching the others having a drink with her. Her wife stood in front of the darts board, swaying precariously and barely supported by one arm that rested on the shoulder of Bolan. Bolan and Keema had just spent hours arguing over the merits of particular routes from one landmark in the city to another while Shanti laughed into her own glass, and now they were determined to finally discover which of them was the better darts player. Shanti smiled as she listened to Keema berate Bolan for having the unmitigated cheek to score well with his last throw. Bolan laughed and levered Keema off his shoulder.

"But really, you should've, you shouldn't be throwing like that." Keema swallowed. "Because it's dangerous!" She stuck one finger in the air to emphasise her point.

"You're just here to look out for me, aren't you

Keema," grinned Bolan. He glanced over at Shanti and rolled his eyes. Shanti giggled.

"I am! I care about you. You are- you are my friend." Keema staggered a little and Shanti shook her head. *If only Keema could hold her drink as well as she thinks she can.* She took a sip from her tall glass of cider and smiled back at Bolan.

"If you care about me so much, why don't you muck up this next throw of yours, eh?" Bolan bowed and waved Keema towards the board.

"No, it's because, it's because I do care about you, because my friend, that's why, that's why I do so good." Keema staggered to the line, looking over at the dart board. Shanti wondered if Keema could even focus on the small circular target tonight. Keema was wobbling more than the tall trees near Shanti's home village did during storms.

One of the Skuggi, the poor people who lived as best they could in the alleys of Gorduum, was delivering drinks to the table by Shanti.The patrons at the table barely noticed the young boy's presence, but Shanti smiled at him as he turned around. He bobbed his head, but the expression on his face was a grimace. Shanti frowned and returned her attention to her boisterous wife.

Keema lifted her arms and threw her first dart. Shanti couldn't quite see how good the throw was from her booth, but she could see Bolan's shoulders slump and she heard the whoop of triumph from Keema.

"Come on, you're too drunk to make a shot like that!" groaned Bolan.

"I am the master!" yelled Keema. Shanti laughed again and drank the last mouthful of her cider. She smacked her lips as she put the empty glass down on the table in front of her. *Should I have another,* she asked herself. She looked over to where Keema was doing a victory dance, knees knocking and arms jutting from side to side over her head. Bolan was holding a hand over his eyes, and a few of the other regulars laughed from their stools. *Probably better to have at least one of us with a clear enough head to find our way home,* she decided.

Kartee came by, gathering up empty glasses and wiping down the tables with the thick cloth that she wore tucked into her belt. She leaned in closer as she picked up Shanti's empty glass.

"Looks like your young lady is getting a little unmanageable to me," the older woman murmured. Her dark hair was bound up in a bun, with a few streaks of grey beginning to lighten it. Shanti frowned. *I hope Keema hasn't caused too much trouble.* Shanti hated the idea that the people around her might be judging her and her wife for their behaviour. Then she met the pub owner's eyes. It was clear that Kartee was not upset. Shanti nodded.

"I think she has certainly drunk her fill for tonight."

"Mmmm. Perhaps it might be a good idea to take her home now." Kartee raised an eyebrow.

Shanti grinned. "Are you sure you wouldn't like to see how well she leads the bar in a song?"

Kartee grimaced and shook her head. "Not again. It's only been two months since the last time she started bellowing. I need at least six before my ears stop ringing!"

Shanti laughed and slid out of the booth, touching Kartee's shoulder as she walked past. She stepped up next to Keema and put a hand on the other woman's waist.

"What is it? Who?" Keema turned to see who had touched her, one eyelid half closed. She smiled when she saw Shanti standing next to her. "Hey! Did you see, did you, because I did some good darts!"

Shanti lifted a hand to Keema's cheek. "Yes, I saw. You're the best in the world! Now I think it's time to go. Bolan needs a chance to practise, if he's ever going to beat you." Shanti winked over Keema's shoulder at Bolan, who made a rude gesture in reply.

Keema nodded seriously. "Yes. He should. Lots of practise. Yup." She tried to put down her remaining darts on the table nearby, but missed. She had to pause and focus carefully in order to move her hand where she wanted it to go.

"Come on," said Shanti, with her arm around Keema's side, guiding her to the door. "Let me take you home."

THE NEXT MORNING Shanti woke slowly and pushed her legs through the sheets, enjoying the feeling of them slipping along her calves. The sheets were so warm and comforting, and she didn't want to get out of bed before she had to. Perhaps she could steal a few more minutes of comfort before she would have to admit that it was time to get up?

Footsteps approached softly along the floor through the dark room and Shanti rolled over. A tiny dark blue light, with a slowly curling stem and only a few small broad leaves, grew in its pot in the corner of the room. It provided just enough light for

Shanti to make out the outline of Keema, leaning down over the bed. The other woman was already dressed in a tight shirt and dark pants, her hat set jauntily on her sharp hair.

"Good morning Petal," whispered Keema as she leaned over to kiss Shanti's cheek.

"Good morning." Shanti lifted her arms over her head and stretched. "Is it that time already?"

"I'm afraid so. See you tonight."

Shanti lay back on her pillow and watched Keema walk out of the bedroom. She waited until the door to their apartment clunked shut and then sighed and pulled aside the cover. *I guess I had better start my day too.*

Keema had to wake before dawn in order to get out onto the streets and find customers for her taxi, and she would usually not get home until after dark either. Her busiest times were first thing and at the end of the day. Shanti hoped that today there would be a lull in between those times, as there sometimes was, allowing the two a chance to meet up for lunch. It sometimes felt as though that was the only time they were able to spend with each other.

In the meantime, Shanti cut off a large slice of the bread in their cupboard and smeared a good helping of butter across the dark brown hunk. She chewed on it as she got dressed, enjoying the flavour, and then left the small apartment. After she locked the door, she smiled and nodded at some of her neighbours as they passed by in the dark corridor, beginning their own days.

Outside, the streets of Gorduum were already filled with crowds. Carts rumbled over the cobbles in the street and the susurration of hundreds of voices spread through the air. Shanti stood at the top of the steps that led down from her building to the street and took in the view of the lively street around her. *This is wonderful,* she thought, smiling and pulling in a deep breath. Since leaving her small village behind, she had worried that she would feel homesick, or out of place in the massive city that she had decided to make her home. Instead, she had felt more alive and excited than she had ever felt while dusting shelves in her mother's store. The city was tall and bright, and full of new sights and sounds around every corner. In the two years she had spent here, Shanti still hadn't explored it all.

On the street she raised a hand to try and catch the attention of a taxi. Two of the small carts passed her by as she waited, even though the passenger seats were empty. When Shanti had first arrived in Gorduum she would have been surprised or even insulted at being ignored in such a way, but Keema had explained to her that many taxis had regular routes and clients, which left them little time to spare for casual customers. Now she remained patient as they clattered by.

The third cart pulled to a stop in the middle of a swarm of pedestrians, who began to flow around it like fish around a rock in a stream. Shanti looked to her right as she walked over to the cart, careful not to bump into anyone. The people began to move around her in the same way as they avoided the cart.

"Good morning Shanti. How are you?"

Shanti smiled. The driver who had pulled over was Bolan.

"Won't Keema be jealous? Why would you be calling a taxi over when you've got your very own personal chauffeur?" Bolan grinned, his dark eyes twinkling as he reached out a hand to help Shanti climb aboard.

"We'd soon run out of money if I made Keema carry me everywhere I wanted to go in this city instead of letting her go to work," chuckled Shanti.

Bolan spread his hands in innocence. "Are you saying that keeping Keema occupied would open up a vast opportunity for other drivers such as myself? Perish the thought!" He laughed. "Where to, my friend?"

"I have a meeting at Brin Surety in Rinlosh District. It shouldn't take long and then I need to head over to Arfa District to meet with my uncle, if you're interested in a guaranteed fare? He sent three messages to our house yesterday!"

Bolan sucked on his teeth and bobbed his head as he considered the idea.

"Could do, could do. Tell you what, if I'm still outside the building when you come out from your meeting, I've decided to help you out." He winked at her.

Shanti smiled and nodded. If Bolan waited for her she would be glad to pay a friend for his time, but if he decided he had better prospects elsewhere she wouldn't blame him. Hearing about the tight days Keema sometimes had, it was fair enough for a driver to spend their day trying to maximise the routes they were able to travel in order to get the most customers.

Even after two years living in Gorduum, Shanti enjoyed the sights and sounds that she saw travelling through its streets. Bolan took her through the long broad boulevards that wound from the city centre out to small buildings on its outskirts, avoiding the narrow alleys that might have been a more direct route to her destination.

The alleys were safer now. There had been a blight that infected the lights growing along the buildings, leaving the alley in deep shadow. Thankfully the blight had been curtailed, making it harder for thieves to hide in the shadows. However the number of people walking through those narrow passages now made them nearly impossible to travel by cart. The time saved by taking a direct path to her meeting would have been completely undone by the slow movement in the narrower spaces.

She was glad though, as she enjoyed admiring the buildings that were a feature of travelling along the boulevards. They were lined by tall apartments and grander buildings that looked like palaces from the stories she had read in her youth. Heavy columns fronted them, alongside broad stone facades carved with ancient inscriptions. Lush lights grew in thick spirals up the sides of their entrances, shining red and blue and violet, even in the light of the morning sun. Shanti enjoyed looking for signs of the ancient empire that had once been centred on the city of Gorduum.

As they passed through one crossroads full of people, dressed in bright colours that reflected the warm sunlight washing down over them, Shanti admired a ridged spike that stuck up out of the plaza to the height of a four story building. It was a rigid geometric shape, with no curves or signs of what she would consider a human touch. It was like a crystal that had erupted up through the cobblestone and soared into the sky.

Near its base, an oval of darker stone had been inlaid into each of its four sides. Though the ovals looked small from where she was in the cart, Shanti knew that they were actually much taller than a person, having spent time examining them closely during earlier tours of Gorduum with Keema. Golden figures and symbols were set into the dark stone, to dazzling effect.

Shanti sighed as the spire retreated behind Bolan's cart. There was so much to see in Gorduum, and she always felt as though she would never manage to find it all, or to admire it in the detail that it deserved. And yet, she had begun spending more time at the docks and the train station, when she had the time. She would stand at the side of the bustling crowds, taking in the sight of boats and trains, full of cargo and people who had travelled from far off places. It made her smile, and her heart lighten. Watching those vessels loaded up, with people setting off to who knows where, was one of the things she valued most in her days.

2

Rinlosh District wasn't far from Shanti and Keema's apartment, a bit closer to the outskirts of Gorduum perhaps. That position made it easier for traders coming into the city along the wide roads that ploughed through the surrounding valleys towards distant lands, and it was a convenient place for the locals living just outside Gorduum to bring in their own goods for trade. Only certain people wanted the use of buildings in this district, and so the rents were cheaper, which meant plenty of large storehouses lined the narrow streets. Rinlosh was where larger carts and merchants would deliver their own cargo.

There was always a medium sized street market bustling amongst the alleys between the warehouses, constantly shifting its exact locations and stalls around the corners and byways of the district. The market was an opportunity for business that would be beneath the attention of larger companies. Companies would spend their money on train freight as they valued the saved time. The items for trade in Rinlosh District were either very local and cheap, or fragile and expensive. Locals without the means to export, or with products that couldn't survive the journey came to the Rinlosh market. Shanti loved exploring the stalls for hidden wonders.

Bolan guided the taxi up to a small building that looked just like every other building on the street. Barely two storeys tall, and with plaster peeling off narrow red bricks beneath, an observer would have been excused for thinking that the neighbourhood was poor and contained little of value. Shanti knew otherwise.

"Thank you," she said to Bolan as she dropped down to the street from the passenger seat of his cart. She brushed her skirts out and looked around the neighbourhood. It was less busy here than in the streets around her apartment deeper in the city. That made sense. Keema wanted to live where there were plenty of pedestrians so she had enough work each day. Out here it looked as though Shanti's wife would waste a lot of time waiting for someone to reluctantly ask for her services. Keema would have to rely on finding people who had business deeper in Gorduum if she was stuck in these streets.

"Will you wait?" she asked. Her friend pursed his lips and lifted a hand with outspread fingers that he wobbled back and forth like an unbalanced scale.

"It's quiet here. I'll wait a little while."

"Thanks in advance if you are still here when I get out." Shanti looked at the faded sign above the door. Brin Surety was painted on it in green letters. She rolled her shoulders and then walked inside.

The room beyond the door was just as faded as

the outside of the building. A single low desk ran across the end and a middle aged man was leaning so far back on a simple wooden chair that its front legs were lifting off the ground. He had a newspaper in his hands. A young boy, in the worn out clothes of the Skuggi, was sweeping dust into the corner of the room.

"Morning," said the man in the chair without looking up and then turned a page of the paper.

"Good morning. I believe I have an appointment with Ms Fotot?"

The sound of the name made the man turn his head sharply and peer at Shanti over the top of his small spectacles.

"You have, have you? Most people don't know Ms Fotot even works here." The man managed to ask the question without quite crossing a line into presumption.

"That should make it clear that I know why I'm here then, shouldn't it?" teased Shanti.

The man chuckled and folded the paper then placed it on the desk in front of him.

"Won't be a moment," he said as he stood up and walked out through a door behind him. Pale cream coloured paint was beginning to peel off the door in long curls like waves on the river.

Shanti stood in the lobby and looked around the walls. She hadn't been to this office in person before, but it was decorated largely as she had expected from the letters she had exchanged with Ms Fotot. Light brown maps were pinned to most of the walls, interspersed with paintings of groups of people in unusual landscapes. The general run-down and faded nature of the walls and furniture surprised her though. She had thought that Ms Fotot was responsible for a successful business, but that success didn't seem to be reflected in this room.

The young sweeper murmured an apology as he swept around Shanti. She shook a hand at him to let him know no apology was required and then moved closer to examine the paintings on the walls. The landscapes were the most fascinating to her. One was a broad pale canvas, wide enough that she would barely be able to touch both edges with her arms outstretched, broken only by dark blue jagged ice. The painting gave no clue to the scale of the ice and Shanti wondered if she was looking at the detail from a small pond, or great sharp mountains. Another painting was so dark as to be nearly black, but in the darkness Shanti could squint her eyes to make out tall thick trunks, vines, and heavy leaves overhead. There were half a dozen other paintings, each with a strange location depicted in fine detail. Most of the paintings contained between three and five small human figures. After examining the figures more closely, Shanti recognised that one of them featured in multiple paintings.

That figure wore her hair in a distinctive broad tail, bound by what appeared to be golden rings. She wore strong tramping clothing. Shanti had seen such clothes before and expected that they were made of thick and hardy material. However, the painted figure included some patches and belts to help make the outfit stand out, functional but fashionable also. Shanti thought this person would be someone worth sitting and talking to. *The stories that they must have!*

The door opened and Shanti looked over, expecting to see the man coming back to speak to her. Instead she saw a tall skinny man with large eyes coming out the door. He was startled when he saw her.

"Oh excuse me, I didn't realise that anyone was here," he murmured, lowering his eyes.

"It's no concern," said Shanti. "Do you work here?"

"Um," the man smiled awkwardly. "Sort of. Sometimes. Have a nice day!" Shanti liked the brightness in his eyes immediately. Before she could say anything else, the man nodded politely, crossed the room and strode out the front door.

"Good morning ma'am, if you would come through here?" The man from the desk had returned, and was now politely gesturing for Shanti to come through the door at the back of the room.

"Thank you," she smiled as she stepped past him.

Behind the door she found a flight of stairs that was illuminated by a tall thin window on the landing, halfway to the next floor. Its glass was thick with dark grime, but it allowed enough light through for her to climb the steps. Halfway up, caught in a shadowy small space between the threshold of one floor and the next, Shanti paused on the landing with her hand on the bannister. She took a deep breath and closed her eyes for a moment. An unforeseen panic had suddenly blossomed beneath her collarbone. Breath by breath she brought herself under control, calming her breathing, then her heart and finally her memory of another dark stairwell and the nightmare that overtook her there.

Then she breathed out through pursed lips and opened her eyes again, finishing the climb.

At the top of the stairs there was only one door, and she knocked on it.

"Yes, come in Shanti," came a voice from within.

This room was as wide as the one downstairs, and it was occupied by three desks. A large woman sat behind one of the desks, watching Shanti come in. The other two desks were currently empty, but from the piles of letters and documents that covered them, it was clear that they were still actively used.

Shanti walked over to the woman and extended her hand.

"Good morning, you must be Ms Fotot?"

The woman stood, and Shanti blinked. The woman was much taller than her, and broader. It was as though she had been built using slightly larger measurements than everyone else. The woman extended a hand, enveloping Shanti's.Her shake was firm but not tight, and her skin was tough but her touch was soft.

"That's me. And you're Shanti Penpen, the woman who's been writing to me for so long without ever actually making the short journey to meet me."

"I actually came out to Rinlosh a few times earlier in the year," protested Shanti. "You just weren't in Gorduum at the time so I didn't think it was worth stopping by."

Ms Fotot laughed and sat, indicating that Shanti should seat herself in the chair in front of the desk.

"I have been gone for a while this year I must admit. But to business! In your letters you suggested that we undertake a different task to our usual. What inspired that?"

"I did some asking around, and everyone said that if I wanted the services of someone trustworthy who would travel to the ends of the world, yours was the company to seek."

"We aim for that level of trust." Ms Fotot sniffed. "But we don't usually fetch things. We specialise in accurate cargo and risk assessments. My accountants are geniuses with numbers."

"I appreciate that." Shanti nudged the satchel that she had placed by her foot, noting the weight that it held. "And the unusual nature of the task is part of the fee we negotiated."

"How did you even know that we would be able to get it? And how do you know that we aren't inflating the price?"

"Technically, I suppose I don't. But like I said, everyone said your company was the highest word in trust."

Ms Fotot grunted. She sat behind her desk, with her elbows resting on the surface and her hands clasped in front of her face. Her eyes bore down on Shanti. Finally she shook her head and sat back.

"I have to admit, it was such an odd request that I had to take it to the end." She reached down behind the desk and lifted a simple wooden box into view, setting it on the desk between them. Shanti reached over and ran a hand over the lid. It wasn't carved, or polished, it was just a simple wooden box. There was a name stamped onto the top: Kechooka.

"Wow. It looks so much plainer than I might have thought."

"Go on then; what is it?"

Shanti sat back in the chair, surprised. "You didn't open it?"

"No." Ms Fotot frowned and narrowed her eyes. "You didn't give us instructions to open it. Just to get to Chechezuk and ask for any items marked Kechooka and this was all that was there."

"Other people must have sent agents sooner," Shanti murmured, still watching the box. "I wouldn't have minded if you had looked inside, but it is nice to see just how reliable your company is. It is a scroll."

"A scroll?" Ms Fotot's eyebrows twisted and she glared at the box, as though it was some sort of insult to her. "It's just a scroll?"

"A scroll written by Kechooka, who is one of the foremost astronomers in his country. He died a year ago, and any of his work that was available would be very valuable to certain contacts of mine."

"Does it have some sort of spell written on it, or a treasure map that uses the stars, or..." The large woman's voice trailed off. She was clearly confused by the scroll entirely.

Shanti spun the box towards herself and prised the lid open. The hinges creaked and the lid moved slowly, stiffly, but it opened. Sitting inside, on a bed of hay to cushion it from damage, was a wrapped scroll, still sealed by a large blob of yellow wax. The shape of a thin bird was pressed into the wax. Its beak was a long narrow spear poking forward from the circular blob of its head. An equally long curved neck extended from its small body, while stick-like legs jutted out underneath. *That must be Kechooka's crest,* thought Shanti as she examined the scroll. It was yellowing and cracked on the edges. She hoped that it wasn't quite as fragile as it appeared.

"Did my estimates prove accurate?" she asked.

"Actually, yes, quite precisely! Our agent was surprised." Fotot drew a document from one of the piles on her desk and slid it forward next to the wooden box so that Shanti could see it. Shanti leaned over to read the record more closely. As the woman said, the recorded price on the document was very close to the amount Shanti had said items that had belonged to Keechooka might fetch.

She leaned down to her satchel and dug out her purse. Inside was a bank note of credit that she signed in front of Ms Fotot.

"That should cover the bulk, and..." She counted out some very weighty coins, feeling relieved to be leaving them in the possession of this woman rather than continuing to carry them through the streets of Gorduum. "That should cover the rest."

Ms Fotot quickly counted through the coins, flicking them to one side with her fingers as she did. She smiled as she finished.

"Wonderful. Now, that invoice shows that you provided us more in the initial retainer than you actually needed to, so you can keep these." She pushed a selection of the coins back across the desk towards Shanti.

"You have been so easy to work with, please keep it as a bonus," Shanti replied.

The older woman raised an eyebrow and then nodded slowly.

"Did you use your contacts in the shipping industry to get someone to carry it for you? I was never sure how you would fulfil the task, aren't your people normally pencil pushers and paperwork experts?" asked Shanti.

"It's been a pleasure doing business with you

Miss Penpen," smiled the other woman without answering the question. "Will you join me in a cup of tea?"

3

─────────

After she left Brin Surety and the office of Ms Fotot, Shanti was pleased to see that Bolan had decided to remain. She was surprised to see him though, as she had sat and conversed with Fotot about her journeys for more than an hour. The stories had excited Shanti and she was in a decidedly pleased mood as she climbed back into Bolan's cart.

"How was the wait?" she asked.

"It was quiet," muttered Bolan as he flicked the reins and got his horse moving. "Not even a casual conversation with any loaders or shifters."

"Did you consider taking on a different passenger?"

"I did," allowed the man. He shrugged. "But really there was no-one around here who wanted to go anywhere near the centre of the city at this time of day. They all wanted to go back and forth a street or two. I did actually run two of them around the block, and I was still here in time for you."

"At least it wasn't a total waste for you then,"

Shanti hoped. Bolan sniffed, but he didn't look too put out thankfully.

"Yeah, it's fine. To your uncle's is it?"

"Please."

The ride to Arfa District and her uncle Dunin's apartment was pleasant and quiet. Neither Shanti nor her friend felt like talking. Bolan must have settled into an introspective state of mind as he waited outside Brin Surety, and Shanti leaned back into the cart and enjoyed watching the buildings on either side pass her by. In some ways it was like watching the tall trees of the forests near her home pass by when she had travelled as a child. The sounds of the city were like water rushing between rocks to her now, and the heat of the sun beating down on her face from the blue sky above made her wish that she could take a nap.

It was unusual for Bolan to be so quiet, honestly, but Shanti didn't want to think about that for long. She often found herself caught up worrying about what was going on in other people's heads. She was trying to get better at allowing them to think whatever they wanted and to focus on her own needs. She had been worrying about this delivery for weeks, and the stress of carrying so much coin through the city had kept her shoulders taut all morning. She hoped that her friend was not too upset about the lack of work, but she needed to try and relax.

"Here you are," came Bolan's voice all too soon, and Shanti sighed as she paid him and started walking into the apartment building. *There's always something else that needs doing,* she thought. *No matter how many errands are completed, somehow there seems to be just as many more still to go.* Up a narrow flight of stairs, beneath a curling lightvine that wound along the ceiling, Shanti headed towards her uncle's apartment, the space from which he ran his various investments and opportunities.

She paused in the hallway outside his apartment. Shanti mentally prepared herself to speak to her uncle. Somehow Dunin never asked too many details about herself and Keema, but she took care to avoid spending much time on the topic of her wife. Luckily, her uncle was a very stern businessman, and he tended not to wander in his conversations with her. He knew that Keema was in her life, but so far Shanti had managed to avoid insulting him by confirming that she had not even invited him to witness their marriage. Hopefully that meant he hadn't told her mother back in Graama either. He just about never sent letters back home, she was probably safe on that front. She blew out a long breath and then knocked on the door.

A moment later, it was pulled open by a tall young man with soft eyes and curly hair.

"Good day Gunin," said Shanti as she walked in. He smiled and took her satchel, hanging it on a hook just beside the front door to the apartment.

"Hello miss. He's been in his office all morning, and I've heard him growling. I think he's had some bad news. Shall I make some tea?"

"That would be lovely. Is there anything to eat?"

"There may be a few things," grinned the young man, and he bustled off into the kitchen to prepare something. Gunin had been Dunin's lad for a few years now, and Shanti had become quite good friends with him in that time. He was a good cook, and he kept Dunin's apartment clean. She wondered whether she should ask him to come to the pub with Keema and her one night.

"Hello Dunin," Shanti said as she found him down the hallway.

"What's good about it?" he grumbled in reply from his desk in the small room he called his office. A narrow shelf next to him was stacked with books and documents and letters, and even a few small sculptures. Dunin was sitting staring at a piece of paper on the desk in front of him, with one hand rammed against the side of his head, propping it upright. His fingers curled into his flesh and he moved his lips as he read the paper.

"I've had a good meeting already, so that's one good thing at least," chuckled Shanti as she shifted her skirts and settled into the chair opposite him. While he tried to process whatever was on the document in his hands she used the time to pluck some lint from his sleeve.

"You've done what?" he asked as he pushed the document off to the side, face down.

"I had a good meeting. It turns out that Brin Surety are quite trustworthy, and can perform more tasks than they advertise."

"Oh yes? Do you think there's any opportunity there?" Dunin lay against the back of his chair, with his fingers interlaced on his stomach.

"Nothing immediate, but they retrieved a fairly valuable item for me, and provided me with an invoice and were prepared to return the excess value that I had paid in deposit. I told them to keep it as a bonus, seeing how quickly they had been able to retrieve the item. It looks a fair price, and they managed to arrange the delivery in less than two months, even though it came from Chechezuk. That sounds useful to me!"

"It is." Dunin sniffed. "Clearly they have some very efficient messenger services. I wonder if there's anyone who could start sending me some information on bumper yields or low years." Dunin began murmuring through the ideas for himself.

"But I didn't come here to tell you that," said Shanti, with a raised eyebrow.

"Hrm?"

"I came here because you wanted me to visit. You told me the other day that you thought there might be an opportunity to follow up on. And you sent three messages by runner yesterday!" Dunin would have had to pay the small children who had passed on his messages through the streets, and Shanti knew how much he hated letting go of his small coins.

"Oh! Oh yes!" Dunin leaned forward again and began to rummage through the papers and cardboard folders on his desk. Eventually he found a broad but flat package, wrapped in thick waterproof paper and held closed by a red string that wrapped around a brass pin. The deep green wax seal that had held the string was broken. Dunin passed it over to Shanti.

"Check out this letter."

Shanti unwound the string and opened the thin pouch, pulling out a folded piece of paper within. She spent a minute running her eyes along the curled handwriting then looked up at her uncle.

"This contact of yours thinks that Chechezuk has a new source of tuft?"

"Exactly!" Dunin grinned.

"Are they reliable? Do you think this new source will pay off?"

"I'm not sure, but I am curious and more than a little optimistic about the report. That's why I decided that you should head down to the docks as soon as you can!"

Gunin came in and placed a tray on the desk between them. Shanti smiled at the lad and he nodded in return as he left. Steam rose from the teapot, and Dunin handed out cups and saucers, before pouring the tea himself.

"Okay, why do I need to go to the docks? What do the boats have to do with this opportunity?" asked Shanti as she lifted her cup to her lips.

"Because I know a captain who just shipped in from there, and I think you might be able to find out whether or not we follow up. See if he knows anything about the situation. If there's a chance we can invest early, the returns could be well worthwhile!"

Shanti fingered the rough material of the letter as she folded it and slipped it back into its pouch. Something was bothering her about what it said.

"This letter seems to claim that we might be seeing a ten-fold increase in the tuft supply from Chechezuk, yes?"

"Yeah."

"You don't see a potential problem with that?" Shanti slid the pouch back across her uncle's desk.

"You're worried that the prices will fall if we bring in too much," Dunin said. He nodded and smiled. "It's a fair concern. But I think that, if it really is such an effective new supply, we can ride it up and then try to influence the supply to maintain. I mean, you're very persuasive, that's why I think you should get involved! Everyone loves sweet young Shanti!" He spread his arms, gesturing at his niece.

"Hmmm. It may only be that they like me more than grumpy old Dunin," Shanti demurred, narrowing her eyes slightly. Dunin was encouraging her more and more to build contacts and make her way in the city, and he had helped her collect some quite lucrative deals. But she was never quite certain whether he was hoping to build up his own reputation alongside hers for his own benefit. And even if he was, she wasn't sure whether or not it was a problem.

"Is tuft really the sort of market that we want to be involved in anyway?" she asked.

"Do we want to be involved in it? Are you mad? Of course we do! Tuft is worth its weight in gold!" Dunin rolled his eyes as he considered the statement he had just made. "Okay, tuft doesn't really weigh anything, but you know what I mean! This stuff is amazingly valuable."

"It's really only used by the highest of society ladies though," pressed Shanti. "People talk about it being so expensive because it takes such a long time to collect, and the process of deburring it and spinning it, just to get a single thread..." Shanti pursed her lips and shook her head. "Even if this is correct, and the supply is going to rise dramatically, are we really doing anything of value? We're just making more dresses for fancy ladies."

"Those fancy ladies do like to pay good money for their fancy dresses."

"Sure, we can make money." Shanti looked up at the ceiling and pushed her hands along the sides of her head, pulling the hair back towards the braid at the back. "But when I first came to Gorduum, you were trying to invest in inventors. You were looking to support people who were going to make everyone's lives better."

"I invested in them because I expected to make money when they succeeded," he interjected.

"But what's the best possible outcome here? The price drops from oversupply and some more women can afford nice dresses?"

"You wouldn't like to be able to afford a nicer dress from time to time? What about Keema?"

"Don't you try to change the subject!" Shanti felt her heart skip as the conversation unexpectedly wound too close to her relationship.

"Look, I know what you mean, but you saw the people I was working with back then. Some of them were less philanthropic than they seemed."

Shanti pressed a hand to her stomach and swallowed hard. The sensation sank down her throat like a rock. Memories crept out of the shadows in her mind, like wolves bearing down on a flock at night. She was all too familiar with how awful some of her uncle's previous investment partners had been.

"Sorry," said her uncle as he saw her expression stiffen. "I didn't mean to-"

"Yes." Shanti cut him off and tried to move the conversation on. "Well, I'm just trying to see if this is really a worthwhile opportunity."

"Here, these are the details for my captain," said Dunin, leaning forward with another letter. He smiled resignedly at her. "If you get a chance to visit the docks today, let me know. Otherwise I'll go to see him tomorrow."

"That sounds fair," agreed Shanti, taking the document and putting it into her satchel alongside the wooden box that she had collected from Brin Surety. *If I have time I have time, and if I don't then I don't,* she said to herself as she finished the tea in her cup.

Bolan had moved on by the time that Shanti came out of her uncle's apartment onto the packed streets. He must have found many paying passengers now that he was back in the middle of the city. She couldn't blame him for leaving. She shielded her eyes and looked up at the sky, examining the angle of the shadows near the upper stories of the buildings that lined the busy street.

She placed a hand on the satchel, pressing to feel the corners of the wooden box inside, thinking of her friend Darsat, at the university. She intended to give the box to him. *Is it worth trying to give him this right now? It's after noon already,* she thought to herself. *And it's the middle of the week.* She frowned, causing a nearby young girl wearing a large floppy cap and carrying a bundle of newspapers under her arm to jump and quickly alter her direction. Shanti sighed. *He'll be in a lecture for sure, and his wife Dulku sees her social club this afternoon. He would love to see it now, but perhaps tomorrow will be better.*

Shanti lifted her hand from the satchel, pulling out the letter that her uncle had passed over. *This lead had better turn out to be worthwhile, that's all I can say.*

4

The docks of Gorduum spread along the banks of the Naatat River, which flowed wide and deep and dark through the centre of the city. The Naatat grew out of converging streams and smaller rivers that cascaded down from hills and distant mountains, then wound through the farms and orchards and groves that provided Gorduum with so much of its food and, more importantly, grew the lights that were the source of the city's wealth. These waterways interlaced and wove together like strings being bound into a thick rope, forming one broad river, the Naatat. By the time the water left the city on the far side, it cut a straight channel through the plains until it reached the coast.

Large merchant ships stowed their sails as they manoeuvred into the many docks and wharfs that studded the shoreline, as wide banks of oars slipped out of their locks and into the constantly swirling surface of the busy river. Smaller vessels skipped across that surface like insects, shipping people and smaller cargo from one district of the city to another.

A variety of different docks served the various markets along the Naatat, and Dunin had sent Shanti to one that she hadn't visited often. It was downriver of the city, and as Shanti walked towards the main pier she was able to look along the river out into the plains that led to the coast. The city's buildings grew smaller and smaller along that end of the river, until broad clear fields separated one set of buildings from another. She found herself wondering how the inhabitants decided when any one cluster of homes and stores was a district of Gorduum, and when it was its own town or village.

The sky spread out like a pale blanket over this view, wide and coloured a light blue that was nearly white. The day held only a few small puffy clouds which reminded Shanti of the tuft that she was being sent to investigate.

What an odd substance, she thought as she neared the pier. So small and light, who would have believed that it could be wound into such a strong material? Wool was much easier to collect from the flocks of sheep and goats that the people in the hills had bred for generations, but she had to admit that it could be scratchy. Whereas the light tuft-cloth felt much nicer on the occasions where she had been able to run her fingers along any. Even the finest linen couldn't seem to match it.

But who could afford so much mola for something so slight and small? It made for good detailing and decoration in the dresses of the upper class, and she had seen some of the richer men in Gorduum wearing entire shirts of tuft-cloth. Even now, as she walked through the docks, Shanti shook her head at the indulgence of it. Maybe dropping the price would actually be a positive thing she could do for the people of the city after all. Then some of the less extravagantly wealthy citizens would be able to afford some fine and tough clothing. Dunin would probably be upset at the idea of losing so much money if the price did fall though.

I wonder what this captain will be like. Where is his ship?

The pier was lined with large ships, all roped tightly to sturdy wooden bollards. Sailors were crawling over each one, like birds in a fruit tree, and Shanti smiled at the sight. More than one sailor waved to her as she walked past, but she made do with a quick smile if needed and kept looking for one ship in particular. She had a purpose to her visit that must come first.

The ship she was looking for was the fifth one tied to the pier, near its end. It was slightly longer than the others, and not as tall on the sides. A broad white line had been painted horizontally along the entire length of the ship. Between ropes as thick as train rails that pulled the ship to the pier, two gangways were set up. Shanti put her hand on the railing and her foot on the ramp, but was instantly halted by a voice from the top of the gangway.

"Who are you and what do you want?" came the curt call. Shanti peered to the top of the ramp, trying to see who was talking to her. An old man with a thick grey beard stood there in a tightly buttoned jacket, though the day was very warm.

"Good afternoon," she began, taking another slow step. She wasn't sure if she should climb up so that she didn't have to call out quite so loud, or if she should wait on the wharf. "I was hoping to speak with Captain…" She peeked back down at the document from Dunin. "Captain Karikar. He knows my uncle I believe?" She was now only a metre or two from the top of the gangway, able to look through a gap in the railing at the broad deck inside. Three youths were crouched down on the planks, scrubbing at the wood with large brushes.

"Do you have an appointment with the captain?" asked the old man with a scowl.

"No," said Shanti. "My uncle, Dunin, thought I'd be able to see the captain easily enough. I'm sorry, I'd be happy to make an appointment if he's busy."

The old man grunted and scrunched up his nose, but he shook his head.

"Wait here while I go and ask him." He set off across the deck with a slight limp, pausing only to grouch at one of the youths to work harder. All three started scrubbing much faster.

Shanti looked around the ship, taking in the sights. Three huge masts rose like trees from the deck, and there was a higher section of the ship at the back, where the grumpy man had walked off. It was a big enough structure to contain her and Keema's entire apartment. The grumpy man had disappeared through a black and gold door in the side of the structure. *That must be the captain's quarters,* though Shanti. She looked back the other way. *So where does everyone else on board stay?*

Like the other boats tied up to the wharf, this ship had many sailors climbing through the spider's web of ropes that seemed to be necessary to the running of a ship. Shanti watched them for a while as she waited, enjoying the sight of their activity in the same way as she enjoyed watching birds sing and flutter in a tree.

"Alright," called out the grumpy man. Shanti blinked and turned her head to see where he was. He was leaning around the door and waving her closer. "Captain says he'll see you."

Shanti smiled and started across the deck. The grumpy man gave her a half-hearted smile in reply as she walked past him and through the door.

He sniffed. "Through that door there," he said, pointing a finger as gnarled as an old piece of wood to a door on the right of a short corridor. Then he closed the door behind her. Through circular whorls in the diamond panes of glass in the door, Shanti could see him stumping back to his post by the gangway.

She paused outside the door that he had pointed to. After two years working with her uncle in Gorduum, she was much more comfortable attending these sorts of meetings. Sometimes she was able to walk inside without even thinking about it. But something about being on this ship, being in such a small space by herself, was making her feel uncomfortable. With the door to the deck closed, it was dark in this space. Something was waiting on the other side of a door, and her heart was beginning to race. Old memories reached out from the darkened corners of her mind.

With a great effort, Shanti forced herself to close her eyes and take deep breaths in through her nose, breathing out through her mouth. She held a hand to her chest, trying to feel her own heartbeat. After a minute she could tell that it was slowing again. She blew out one last breath and then made herself smile, stretching the tension out of her cheeks. She knocked on the door.

"Yes, please come in!" came a warm voice from within. She opened the door.

THE ROOM inside looked much as every other office she had ever had a business meeting in, which surprised her. For a moment she felt as though she was no longer onboard a large trading ship. A desk filled much of the space, and two chairs were set up in front of it. However, the chairs were bolted to the wooden plank floors, which made Shanti blink as she sat down in one of them. The desk was against the side of the room, instead of facing the door she had come in by. To her left, now that she was sitting, she noticed another door.

"That's my actual quarters. No one needs to see where I sleep."

The man who must be the captain was sitting behind his desk. He had half risen as she entered, but his chair must be bolted into place as well, and so he was unable to stand to his full height easily. He sat back down just after Shanti, and smiled.

Shanti tried not to stare at his pale features. His skin was the palest skin that she had even seen. As he smiled, his teeth blended into the rest of his face. Only the darker pink of his lips helped mark them out. On top of that, his hair was the same red as fire. It was tied into thin braids that hung like a cluster of ropes to his shoulders.

"Tozan says you are Shanti, Dunin's niece? Your uncle mentioned you in some letters."

Shanti coughed to clear her throat and blinked rapidly. "Uh, yes, Dunin's niece. And you are Captain Karikar?"

"You can call me Zekeka. It's a pleasure to meet you." The captain smiled again and Shanti found herself staring once again. This time the captain chuckled and bit his lip while looking down. "You've never met someone from Chechezuk, have you?" He looked back at her, small creases of amusement crinkling the corners of his eyes.

"I have to admit, no," murmured Shanti, feeling embarrassment spread across her cheeks.

"That's alright. I know I stand out in Gawaalti lands! That's why I like to let Tozan stand the gangway and be my first face to passers-by."

"Oh. Are people judgmental?" Shanti hoped that she had not added to the captain's burden, with some sort of unintended rudeness.

Zekeka shook his head. "Just surprised. People who have dealings with me know what to expect, so everything works out fine. People like your uncle," he finished, emphasising the connection.

"Yes, sorry." Shanti shook her head slightly, trying to return focus to her thoughts. "He sent me to find out what you know about new business developments in Chechezuk."

"New developments? What does he want to know about the wood carvers?"

Shanti was about to correct the captain, but then his words caught up with her thoughts.

"Wood carvers?"

The captain laughed.

"You know nothing about my city, do you! The carvers are our pride and joy! Does Dunin want some art for his home? Or is he planning to build something and needs the finest artisans in the world to ensure it is most beautiful when complete?"

"No, it wasn't to do with wood carvers at all."

Zekeka leaned forward and narrowed his strange pale eyes slightly.

"Perhaps it is something more devious that your uncle has in mind, hmm?" He flicked a thin braid of his hair back over his shoulder. "I know how your uncle thinks."

"He wasn't trying to pry," protested Shanti, though she wondered whether he had already tried to uncover as much as he could before passing the task onto Shanti. Perhaps he thought that her cheerful smile would dig out more secrets than his wheedling. "He has heard that there might be new opportunities in tuft, and wonders what rumours you can share."

Zekeka leaned away from the desk and tilted his head.

"New opportunities? What sort of opportunities."

"I don't know, he showed me a letter that he received."

"Who sent it?"

"I don't know that either." Shanti began to notice heat in her cheeks. Perhaps she had stumbled into this meeting without preparing properly and now she felt as though she was going to embarrass herself. "I don't need you to tell me about tuft itself, but have you heard anything? My uncle seems to think you are the sort of man who knows what is going on."

The captain looked away from her for a moment

while he thought. Then he reached down below the desk and there was a sound of wood scraping before he pulled up a squat thick-glass bottle. Dark brown liquid sloshed inside it, and the man pulled out a pair of small glasses which he placed alongside.

"Would you care for a small nip of this?" the captain asked, raising an eyebrow at Shanti as he held up the bottle.

5

Shanti frowned but nodded. It was usually better to go along with the whims of those she met in these sorts of meetings. She accepted the small glass and took a sip. The drink burned at her throat, but left a warm muddy scent in her mouth.

"There are rumours," began the captain as he looked at the thin smears of liquid left on the sides of his glass. "These are only rumours, mind, nothing to be known for sure!" He jabbed a finger at Shanti briefly. "But some are saying that one of the tuft orchards has found a way to harvest the tuft at a greatly reduced cost."

"My uncle suggested ten times more tuft than usual would be coming. That seems extraordinary." Shanti drew a breath through her nostrils and was amazed as the smell of the drink rushed through her head still.

Zekeka nodded slowly. "Perhaps as much as that, if the rumours are at all to be believed."

"How could costs be reduced so far so quickly?" Shanti wanted to find out how likely this fortunate change in circumstances was. "Are the exaggerations of lonely people being taken as Writ?"

Zekeka snorted and looked down. He paused. Shanti could see that he was weighing up a decision, and it was one that took some time to consider. Eventually he lifted his gaze again.

"You seem like a nice young woman," he said. "And your uncle, for all his flaws, does keep his word. He might try to convince me to change a deal from time to time," he laughed. "But if I refuse, he holds to the bargain. I'll share something with you."

He leaned forward again, resting his elbows on the desk. Shanti leaned forward as well.

"I'm the vessel of choice for a man named Kayzark. The rumours claim that someone has reduced costs in the orchards? It's Kayzark that has done it."

"Do you think so? Why?"

He shook his head.

"I don't think anything of the sort. I know. I'm selling off the last of this cargo load and then I'm returning to pick up the first full shipment of tuft. Your uncle might like to get in on the ground floor. He could be my distributor here in Gorduum." The captain spoke so casually about the possibilities, but Shanti could see a gleam in his eyes as he watched her. She knew that he was testing her.

"I think he'd be interested, but we did have a few things we wanted to ask about." She tried to keep her voice calm, but she was concerned that her racing heartbeat would be loud enough for the captain to hear by itself. "Number one, that letter my uncle received says that the supply could increase ten fold. If you think Kayzark is to be so successful, won't that drive the price down?"

Zekeka pursed his lips. "I mean, it could." He rubbed his hands together. "But I don't think you're going to be facing a lot of sources of tuft, just the supply from Kayzark. And there are a lot of people who want it. The demand is there to support much more tuft, by my reckoning. Besides, if we find that the supply is making too much of a difference, he'll make sure things slow down."

"It's just one source then?"

"Even all the other groves combined can't match the output that he is beginning to see."

"That sounds remarkable."

"It's quite impressive." Zekeka turned his head and smirked.

"I would have to see it for myself," said Shanti.

"WHAT?" The captain blinked and thin braids danced at the sudden jerk of his head. Shanti's heart felt as though it was about to explode. She was sure that the captain could see through her eyes down into her core, where he would see the nervous girl inside her. She just knew that he would declare it impossible for her to come and see the operation in Chechezuk; then she would have to hold her face calm while she tried not to show how disappointed she was. She didn't even quite know why she had said it. But as soon as the words had left her lips, she had felt a burst of excitement and hope that she knew she had to nurture. The chance to travel beyond Gorduum, beyond any of the Gawaalti lands, was too fantastic to pass by without trying.

"Are you asking for passage?"

Shanti nodded. Her throat felt tight.

"Sure, if you like. The journey takes about a month, in good weather."

She felt as though a hole had opened up in her stomach. She was dizzy.

"Just like that?"

The captain shrugged slightly. "If you can pay for passage, I'm happy to take you."

Shanti controlled her breathing. *Payment, of course.* She shouldn't have been surprised. The captain was running a business after all. But he hadn't dismissed her out of hand. She began to wonder whether or not she would be able to convince her uncle to invest in her adventure. A small flame of excitement began to allow itself to grow in her chest.

"A month each way," she said as she processed what was happening. "I couldn't be gone for so long."

"A month is nothing! I'm planning to head back in a day or two, if this cargo shifts, and it'd be helpful to say we have a contact in Gorduum ready to handle the influx. If you come along with the authority to make an agreement on behalf of yourself and Dunin, I think it could be effective." He paused and watched Shanti for a quiet moment before adding "We have other places that we could be delivering this supply to, but I told my friends that Gorduum was the trading centre of the world. We'd get the best prices here, and you know Dunin will want to be part of that." He pulled a scrap of paper out of the drawer in his desk and scratched a number on it. "That'd be the cost of a return passage."

Shanti nodded slowly and placed her fingers on the paper, drawing it over to her side of the desk. "I'll have to talk to my uncle, but I think you're right. This sounds like something he will want to be part of." She reached up and ran a hand across her forehead. "At least two months away from home, I just don't know." She didn't want to pull back from this chance, but the reality of the journey did make her pause.

Zekeka leaned across the desk with his pale hand stretched out to Shanti.

"If you're back onboard when the tide is right, I'll take you with me. If you're not, well..." He made a sucking sound against his teeth. "Then I'll go looking for some other places that might want this supply. As I said, I have options."

There was the hook. While he was making her a tempting offer to be part of the upcoming boom, he could just as easily keep her out of it. Their experience in the city would be helpful for him, but they were not unique. How could she allow such an offer to fall away unclaimed? Shanti wasn't even certain that this supply would turn out to be as impressive as her uncle or this captain were claiming. But wouldn't that be the point of the journey, to investigate and ensure the deal was worthwhile?

Shanti reached out and took his hand, squeezing it firmly and meeting his eyes. "If I'm not back here within two days, then you are welcome to look for other partners."

He smiled and stood, awkwardly manoeuvring his way out from the bolted-in-place chair behind the desk. He used one hand to guide Shanti to the door.

"It was a pleasure to meet you young lady." Shanti looked at his bright red hair and pale face. *He can't be much older than me*, she realised. *I hadn't noticed, because I was so caught by surprise, but he has barely any wrinkles or any signs of weathering like the sailors on deck had.*

"You too, young man," she replied as she left.

AFTER THE MEETING-FILLED DAY, Shanti made her way back to the small apartment she shared with Keema. The late afternoon meant that the streets between the tall city buildings were shaded, only a narrow band of sunlight was left to illuminate their very tops. Birds chattered as they dove from one perch to another. Shanti always wondered why they became so active as dusk came on in the city. Each ledge was just as convenient as another to her mind. What was the reason for so much effort, only to end up exactly where you had started? Surely, one place was just as good as another really?

As Shanti and her wife lived down a smaller side street, there were none of the usual large streetlights growing along the middle of the lane, with thick stems woven through tall iron poles. However, each building in her lane had a lightvine looped over its entrance, and the residents made sure to prune them and feed them regularly. Shanti had been surprised by how well kept the lights in this street were when she arrived. However, it took expert knowledge to truly nurture them, and she had begun to teach some of the local children a few tricks and secrets as well. The vines were getting thicker already. She remembered quite a lot from her lessons with

Sudru, the gardener who had been training her back in the village she had grown up in. A pang squeezed her stomach. *I wonder how they are all doing back home?*

She had left Graama so quickly, barely waiting for the last trellis to be taken down from the Festival before packing as many of her belongings as she could and getting on a train back to Gorduum, with no chaperone this time. Her parents hadn't had much of a chance to argue, after she had told them about the dangers she had encountered and survived during her first visit to the city. She had discovered a clandestine plot to sabotage the city's lights, after going dancing with the evil-minded man behind the plan, as well as attending a dinner in his home. A simple train ride alone was nothing to worry about for her now.

I'll have to write them a letter tonight, she told herself. *When did I send the last one,* she pondered as she climbed the steps and went inside. She placed one hand on the railing of the stairs that led up to the higher apartments. *Maybe a month ago? No more than six weeks, surely. I shouldn't have let it get so long! Yes, I definitely need to send a new letter!*

She unlocked the door to their small apartment and dropped her satchel next to the front door as she entered. The sight of the tiny living space always made her smile. It was hers. She moved into the kitchen and picked up a thick ceramic jug. She wobbled it from side to side, listening to the splash inside. *Hmm, not much,* she thought. She lifted the jug up onto her shoulder and turned to walk outside and fetch some water for the evening. Just as she did, the door swung open, and Keema walked inside.

"Hello Sunshine," Shanti greeted her with her smile and tried to lean forward for a kiss. Keema barely looked at her, though she did bob her head in for a peck on the lips, before trudging past and slumping onto one of the chairs in the kitchen.

"Is everything alright?" asked Shanti.

"Yes, everything's good, it's just been a long day," muttered Keema. She rubbed the side of her face, then scrunched it up as if testing that all the muscles still worked. "For some reason no one was in a good mood today. Try as I might to offer a pleasant con- versation, I got nothing in return, and I got no tips at all." She began to loosen her collar, unbuttoning the top of her shirt. "Is there any tea?"

"I was just going to get some water."

"Oh. Oh!" Keema's eyes widened as she noticed that Shanti was standing by the door with a jug in her hands. Keema pulled herself to her feet. "I can do it!"

Shanti giggled. "It's alright. My day was much better than yours by the sounds of things, you sit for a while. I'll be needing you rested enough to be smiling by the time we go to Temple tonight."

Keema froze.

"Is something wrong?" asked Shanti with raised eyebrows.

"No," said Keema, stretching the syllable out like a strand of honey on a spoon, stuck to the side of the jar. "It's just that... I had forgotten about Temple tonight, and-"

"Did you make other plans?" Shanti frowned and shifted the jug on her shoulder.

"No plans." Keema lifted her hands to push aside the possibility. "I just was rather hoping we could stay in tonight." Her voice lifted in a hopeful questioning tone.

Shanti paused. *Would it matter if I missed Temple tonight?* She looked at Keema, standing a metre or so away with questioning and pleading eyes. *But when did I last go? It's funny how life seems to get in the way of the things I know are important sometimes.*

"I'll think about it. Let me go and get the water and I'll make us some tea."

"Fair enough," nodded Keema, and she sat back in her chair as Shanti left.

6

Shanti considered the idea of staying at home for the evening as she walked out onto the street. Children were chasing each other along the broad and rutted paving stones, skipping around the occasional cart that trundled by. Men and women were leaning at the entrances to each building, catching up with their friends and neighbours. Shanti wasn't the only one carrying a jug to the fountain near the corner, a broad semicircular basin beneath a spout carved into the shape of a small child carrying a jug of their own. Water spilled from the child's jug in a thin constant stream. Some people swung their vessels through the basin, scooping up water, while Shanti waited behind a young man who was holding his own jug directly under the stream. She prefered to get her water that way too.

She looked around at the life of the street as night closed in over the top of them. The lights over each entrance were glowing well now, and the street felt alive. Laughter and smiles surrounded her, and what she could see of the main road was even brighter and noisier.

She needed connection, she decided. She looked at the people around her and knew that she would be able to chat with anyone here, there were many familiar faces, but she also knew that she wanted to make some of those connections at Temple. The Masked God watched over everyone, especially in a street like this, where no-one was ever truly alone. But Shanti wanted to be reminded of their presence, to hear stories and lessons of how she could best be their Eyes.

Thinking of the Masked God's Hidden Eyes made Shanti miss her family. She walked back towards her apartment, the heavy jug of water balanced on her shoulder as she passed the other people from the neighbourhood, and their faces took on faces she remembered from Graama. The children running past her could be the same ones that bundled over the rough stone walls of the fields around her village, chasing cats and one another in games that made no sense to outside observers. That man and woman who smiled at her as she passed could be the mayor, or the innkeeper. That woman with the harried face, who scurried along half hunched over could be Sudru the gardener of Graama, always worried that some vine or light would be over-watered or strangled by weeds, rushing through the village streets to check on her charges.

Shanti felt a tear beginning to form at the corner of her eye, but she drew in a deep breath and blew it out slowly. Who was watching over them? Who was making sure that her younger brother Fellbin wasn't causing any trouble that he couldn't get out of? How was her mother? She shook her head, trying to throw off these thoughts, as she climbed the stairs inside her building. She balanced the jug on her hip and reached behind her so that she could carefully open the door to the apartment and ease through without bumping the water filled vessel. She walked in and filled the heavy black kettle sitting on the squat iron stove in the corner. Then she put the jug down on the bench and turned to Keema, who was still in the same chair, with her eyes closed. She had a piece of paper in her hands.

"What's that?" asked Shanti.

"Hrm?" mumbled Keema as she sat up straighter. "This? Just a letter from your mother. It was on the table here." She placed it back on the small kitchen table. Shanti swallowed hard, wondering if Keema had read it again while she was waiting. Shanti still hadn't found the right way to tell her family that she had married Keema so soon after returning to the city. She didn't know how to explain to them that she had decided to undertake such an important event in her life without them, in a small office in the town hall instead of Temple. She wanted to be able to let them know in the same letter that would invite them to a proper celebration of the marriage. In the meantime Shanti knew that there was no mention of Keema in that letter from the table, and Shanti wondered whether her wife noticed. There was a quivering in her chest as she felt guilt leak through her veins.

"We are definitely going to Temple tonight," Shanti declared.

.   .   .

WHEN SHE HAD RETURNED to Gorduum, it had taken a while before Shanti managed to find a temple that she was comfortable with. Many of the well-known temples on the main roads were too large, and they were open all day every day, which she found strange. When Shanti had walked in to them she had sat on elaborately embroidered cushions that were tied down in loops across the open hall, so far from the priest that she could barely hear their words as they read from the Writ. She certainly couldn't see the priest's face. It was the same in each of the next five temples that she located, down to the hum of genial conversation around her as the parishioners caught up with their friends but paid little attention to the stories that were supposed to be teaching them.

Then, after two months, Shanti had found this small temple. It was quieter, and only opened its doors for evening services and in the morning once a week. Unlike many of the larger temples, its cushions were plain, or even patched. What she liked most was the way a simple green lightvine grew in a spiral on the ceiling that centred over the priest. Priest Komom was quiet and kind and when she read from the Writ, the whole temple paid attention to what was being said. It made Shanti feel like she was at home.

Shanti and Keema walked in for the evening service. They were a little early and there was still time before the reading was to begin, so they split up. They made their way in opposite directions around the circular hall to greet familiar faces. Shanti had hugs to give and receive, children who wanted to show her new tricks that they could do, and older faces that deserved checking on. On the far side of the hall, Keema was bursting into laughter, surrounded by the dusty waistcoats and weathered faces of other drivers, builders, and the like. The crack of their enthusiastic handshakes echoed over to Shanti.

The friendly atmosphere reminded Shanti of what she had left behind in Graama, and she missed it again. Although this temple was as close as she had been able to find in the city, this was not her childhood village. She and Keema had many many new friends among the parishioners, but they were not the people she had grown up with. *Maybe I should just go home,* she wondered. *Rather than write a letter. It might be easier to tell my family in person.*

They met again at the far end of the hall opposite the doors they had entered by, and Shanti was pleased to see the grin that Keema was now wearing.

"Happy that we came?" she asked as she stepped into Keema's waiting arms.

"Absolutely my petal," grinned Keema, leaning down to kiss Shanti on the forehead. The pair turned to find a place to sit, Keema's arm around Shanti's waist and Shanti's head resting on her wife's shoulder. "Sounds like there's going to be a darts competition this week, and the gang are all trying to get some bets going."

"Oh? Are you thinking of betting on someone?"

"Yeah, me!" Keema laughed. "I'm the best around, you know that!"

Shanti laughed too, and bumped Keema's side with her hip. They settled down onto a pair of cushions halfway between the seats that lined the wall and the podium where Priest Komom was standing, the Writ held closed at her side. All around them the parishioners were hushing one another politely and sitting as well. Before long, the room was silent.

"Welcome everyone," began Priest Komom, turning her gaze around the room to take in as many of those seated on the cushions or around the edge of the room as she could. "It is always such a pleasure to see so many of you present for a lesson from the Writ. May the Masked God watch over you all."

"And you," came the murmured response from the congregation. Shanti glanced at Keema, and was pleased to see that Keema had mouthed the response. Keema had never been a regular parishioner in her youth, and Shanti knew that she found it a little awkward to fit into the traditions of Temple sometimes.

"I thought that today would be a good day to read one of the earliest stories that the Writ tells us. Not one of the first stories in the Writ, but one that we know must have been among the first ever told. Followers of the Masked God would have shared this story when the God was unknown, sharing the God's wisdom with those who had not yet heard of them"

The woman bowed her head slightly and drew a deep breath. Silence flowed out from her as the congregation stilled and all attention was focused on her.

"All of you know how the Masked God helps us," and with this comment the people gathered on the cushions surrounding the central podium giggled softly, "but I think it always pays to remind ourselves of how they help everyone else as well.

There was a small village. The Writ does not record where this village was, though some believe it was not far from Gorduum. Some believe it may have been Gorduum herself, in the many years before even the Gaawalt Empire. I personally think this is just our local temples and priests trying to make themselves feel important. The village could have been anywhere."

More soft chuckles. Priest Komom turned slightly, to address another section of the congregation.

"What is important to know about the village is that the Masked God was there. Everyday the people would gather in the town square to present the Masked God with their conflicts and problems. The Writ describes the seat that the God sat in. It sounds very nice! Tall and strong and covered in gold and carvings."

Priest Komom glanced from side to side as though looking for eavesdroppers, and then stuck her head forward slightly.

"I rather think the descriptions of the seat are the same as saying the village became Gorduum. People can't help but want to make things special, rather than true." She spoke in a false whisper, making it seem as though she was confiding in each member of the crowd alone.

"But special or true, the location of the village and the decoration of the chair don't really matter," she concluded in her normal voice, making the crowd lean back, startled.

"The Writ tells us many of the problems that the villagers brought to the God and I'm sure you have heard many of those parables. They often become children's stories and are shared by families over meals."

Shanti remembered hearing many of the parables herself. The way the priests in Graama had told those stories had made them feel alive, dressing the children in robes and prompting them to recite simple versions of the lines. It had been a lot of fun.

"Please would someone bring me back my dog?" had been the one that Shanti had enjoyed delivering the most when she was a child, as it was followed by a sad gasp from the villagers watching her. All her parents' friends had come to her afterwards and exclaimed over her talent in performing the role. It wasn't until she had grown older that she had reread the parable for herself. A sad story where a child loses a puppy, and nothing can be done. The Masked God comforted the child, but Shanti had often wondered what lessons their followers should take from it.

She saw others in the crowd nodding and smiling and she knew that they were all sharing similar memories at the same time. Then Keema glanced at her, met her eyes, and shrugged with an apologetic smile. Shanti raised an eyebrow and Keema frowned and shrugged again. Shanti reached over to pat the other woman's shoulder. *She really didn't spend much time at Temple while she was growing up, poor thing. I'll have to share some of the parables with her,* she decided.

7

———

"I'm not here to share those parables again right now," continued Priest Komom. "Though I can see many of you will have favourites in mind already. Those stories show us the wisdom of the Masked God, and remind us that their decisions come from a place of deep understanding. The villagers all appreciated the God, all respected the God, all knew that the presence of the God was a good thing for them; even if sometimes the God would direct them to a harsher path or judgement than they would have wished. They saw time and time again that the God showed no preference.

This is why the God wore the Mask, of course. Did you know that?"

Priest Komom turned further, pointing with a hand as though jabbing the question into those listening to her. Many heads jerked from surprise at the movement. Shanti pondered the question. She had never really thought about why the God wore a mask, they simply did. It was like asking why water was wet.

"The Mask covered the God's identity so that no one in the village might bribe them, or threaten them. The Mask ensured that those who came before the God would not recognise if even their own mother was sitting on the chair in judgement over their problems! Some scholars have even suggested that, at first, the God was not a god, but someone from the village, possibly even different people taking turns!"

There was a murmur of shock amongst the audience. Shanti herself felt her jaw drop open at the idea. She had never heard anyone suggest such a thing! Priest Komom raised her arms for quiet, drawing the congregation's attention back to her.

"I know it is a daring thought, but do not concern yourselves with it now. The rest of this story shows that, whatever the origin of the Masked God, they had become something so much more than that already.

You see, after years and years of this situation serving the village very well, the Writ tells us that the Masked God stood up in their chair at the end of one afternoon, exactly as they did every day. But, instead of turning and heading inside the God's temple, the Masked God announced that they would be leaving the village. They explained that there were other villages that needed the wisdom of the Masked God, other people who fell into arguments and indecision too often, and their villages suffered. The Masked God asked the inhabitants of the village if it was fair to keep help from others who needed it, if you knew that you could improve things for them. Though the villagers wished that they could keep the God for themselves, they agreed.

And so, that very night, the Masked God walked out of the village and out of sight. That night was one of the longest nights that the villagers had ever known. They heard the wind blowing through the streets and thought that it was a colder wind than they had ever heard. They saw a crescent moon shine down and thought it was the sharpest moon they had ever seen. Large, strong men tossed and turned in their beds, and children woke, whimpering.

The next day passed slowly for them all. Everyone was taking care not to create a problem, because they were terrified that they would not know how to resolve it without the Masked God. Everyone was studiously polite, and children in the street would bow for passers-by. But many days passed, and slowly the people of the village forgot to be careful of one another.

The Writ names the people who fell into an argument," continued Priest Komom. "It says that Posco was a well liked man, who allowed children to play in the creek behind his house. But, on the day in question, Posco came rushing out into the street, pulling a young boy by his elbow.

'What is going on,' cried the villagers who saw this. They were shocked, you understand. They did not expect to see Posco treating a young boy this way, and they assumed something awful must have happened. Posco looked very angry, and the boy was crying.

'This disrespectful child has broken the statue to my wife that was built in the corner of my garden,' declared Posco. This was a great crime, as Posco's wife had died a year earlier, and the statue was his way of remembering her.

'How dreadful,' replied the villagers.

'And now I will take him home to his mother where she must punish him severely!' "

Priest Komom paused and looked out over her congregation. She sighed and nodded slightly.

"You understand of course? The boy would have to be punished. The villagers all agreed, and they followed Posco as he dragged the boy to his mother's house. But when they arrived, the boy's mother frowned.

'How do you know that the boy broke the statue?' she asked. 'Did you see him? Was it an accident?'

'I found him standing alone in the garden, next to the broken pieces! Of course he broke it!' declared Posco. The crowd behind him nodded. Posco was a kind and well-respected man. He would not lie about such things.

And then the boy's mother knelt down, so that her head was at her son's height, and she put a hand on his shoulder, and she asked him, 'What happened?'

The boy sniffled and coughed, his face wet with tears.

'A rabbit was eating the vegetables in Posco's garden,' he began. 'I came into his garden to scare it away, but then a fox jumped through the fence and chased it away. They ran past the statue and knocked it over. I had no time to do anything, and then Posco came out and grabbed me.'

The crowd was quiet. That was a possible explanation. The animals from the woods were not uncommon sights in the gardens of the village. Was it true?

Posco's face grew dark. 'Preposterous! The child simply wishes to excuse himself so that he is not punished!'

The boy's mother stood up. 'Maybe. Did you ask him what had happened when you came out?'

'The very idea!' blustered Posco. 'I am a respected man of this village, and I demand that a punishment be served for the destruction of my extremely important property.'

What to do? Who to be believed? In days past, the villagers would have taken Posco and the boy to see the Masked God, and the God would have levelled a decision that all would have accepted, even if it was difficult. But what could they do now that the Masked God was gone?

As the crowd stood in the street, talking to one another and trying to determine what could be done, a small girl walked forward.

Her eyes were on her feet as she shuffled through the dusty street, and her shoulders were hunched. She twisted her fingers together in front of herself. She was clearly very shy, and did not want to be noticed. But she stepped up to Posco and the boy, and she murmured something.

'What was that?' asked Posco.

'I said, I saw what happened,' repeated the girl softly. The crowd went silent again.

'What did you see?' asked Posco kindly. For after all, he was a kind man.

'I saw the rabbit and the fox. What the boy said was true.'

Posco stood shocked. The crowd drifted away,

back to their chores around the village. In the end, only the four of them were left.

Posco knelt down and apologised to the young boy. The young boy nodded and was comforted. They all thanked the girl for her bravery in stepping forward with what she knew, even though she was shy, even though she had to contradict a respected man of the village who had been so angry."

Priest Komom tucked her hands together and bowed her head. The congregation began to shift and whisper to each other. It was a good story, and it had a happy ending. Shanti had heard the story of Posco and the young boy before, and it was one of her favourites because of that happy ending. She had never realised that the story happened as it had because the Masked God had left the village.

Priest Komom lifted her head again and parishioners stilled. Was she going to say something else?

"What happened next?" asked Priest Komom.

What does she mean, thought Shanti. *That's the end of the story. I've heard it so many times before.* Clearly Shanti wasn't the only one who was confused, she could see people seated all around her exchanging shrugs and wrinkling their foreheads.

"The Writ carries on with more stories of the village living without the Masked God among them. You will have heard many of those parables also. But I want to refer to a much later passage, when the Masked God returns. How many of you have heard this passage, or been studious enough to read it yourself?"

Shanti had only ever glanced through the Writ by herself. It was usually printed into such a large and impressive looking book, and the text printed in such small letters, that she felt self conscious moving through the pages. As such she had only ever really read the stories and sections that she had already heard, the parts that she knew, or even just whatever was on the page before her when she opened it. She had never heard of the Masked God returning to the village.

"Yes, I can see a few people who are unfamiliar with this. After nearly a year, the Masked God returned to the village and sat on their seat in the middle of the village. The villagers walked up as they had before, but they had no disputes for the Masked God to settle. The God stood from their seat and surveyed the villagers, asking why there were no arguments to solve.

The villagers realised that they had learned to solve their problems themselves, with even the smallest amongst them standing up to share what they had seen when it was needed to help. The biggest and strongest had learned to help others in the village when times were tough, as it led to fewer problems later. And now they did not need their own god."

Shanti shifted on her cushion. She had not heard this part of the story of the Masked God, and it made her uneasy. She could tell that she wasn't the only one. All around the crowd, people were adjusting their shoulders. How could anyone not need the Masked God? Even now Shanti knew that she needed the Masked God to keep their Eyes on her, and all her family.

"Many of the villagers began to explain what they had been doing, and how they had begun to solve their own problems. They were proud, and the

Masked God nodded to acknowledge their good work towards one another. Then the God beckoned a small girl forward. It was the same small girl that had spoken up to Posco, and had told him that he was wrong.

The girl approached the seat and the God leaned down so that she could whisper past the mask to where their ear would be. The mask nodded again. Then the God stood straight.

'You have become so proud that you were able to work together to solve your problems when I was gone! I am pleased for you. But I never left you.

Wherever any one of you goes, you watch over each other for me. Whenever one of you sees injustice, you speak up in my place. You all know that whatever you do, my Hidden Eyes are keeping watch.'

The girl beside the seat turned to face the crowd. Her eyes shone like the sun and many in the crowd had to turn away.

'I was here with you from the first raised word, and whether or not you see me, I will be with you hereafter. Be my Hidden Eyes, and know that your actions are weighed by those around you. You are so proud to have worked together instead of coming into conflict. You should be! Continue to build your connections with your neighbours, and I will see you again in the future.'

And then the Masked God walked out of the village again. The girl's eyes faded and she fell into a sleep that lasted two days. The villagers who had been there did not see the Masked God again in their lives, though as we know, the God has returned many times."

8

Priest Komom paused and watched the crowd looking at her. Shanti felt less uneasy now. The story was unfamiliar, and she had felt as though the priest was trying to say that the Masked God was not real, or that the parishioners did not need to know about the God. She was relieved to discover that the story emphasised the need to follow the Masked God's teaching and wisdom.

"That is why we use the phrase Hidden Eyes," said Priest Komom. "It is the first time in the Writ that the Masked God let us know that we embody the God for each other."

This time the murmur around the room was one of wonder and surprise, instead of confusion. Shanti found herself smiling. Keema's hand reached over and took hers, giving her a gentle squeeze. She turned to look at her partner. Keema had lowered her brow and mouthed the words "Are you okay?"

Shanti sniffed and realised that there were thin streaks of tears running down from the corners of her eyes. Just one or two drops of water, but she wiped them away and nodded to Keema. "I'm fine," she mouthed back. *Which Eyes are watching over my family back in Graama,* she thought to herself. Then she felt her shoulders tense. How long had it been since she had thought of the village she grew up in as Graama instead of as Home?

The rest of the temple meeting passed quickly. A shared song of celebration filled the hall with voices, some of which were even lovely to listen to, but all of which held devotion and raised it to the ceiling. A time of discussion with the people sitting nearby allowed Keema and Shanti to talk about the idea of Hidden Eyes with some young families. The parents of the families, holding infants to their shoulders, and trying to keep tiny toddlers from charging off and climbing on strangers, expressed their gratitude for Eyes helping watch their children. Keema said that she hadn't really realised what Hidden Eyes might mean as she grew up. The streets of Gorduum could be dangerous and she had always felt alone when she walked them. After being pressed by Shanti, she did acknowledge that she had friends who taught her how to handle herself, and who had helped her out of tricky situations more than once.

Priest Komom read more of the Writ, focusing on a story that described how councils of trusted people had become the traditional method of leading villages and towns that believed in the Masked God; groups of people that had to demonstrate their reliability in front of the people that they led. Shanti thought of the council that ran Gorduum, with leaders of various industries and classes meeting regularly in order to set the rules for the city. Hearing stories of the council and the rules that they declared always made Keema laugh. Keema said that the council had no idea what actually happened on the streets of the city outside their mansions, and most of the people in the city weren't inclined to educate them. Shanti remembered a burning building, and a woman with fierce eyes, and a solution that had had nothing to do with the council and their rules. *Yes, the council should stick to themselves,* she decided.

After they left Temple, Keema sat up straight watching the driver closely as they rode home in a late-night taxi. Shanti leaned on her wife's shoulder and, with her feet tucked up on the seat next to her, they spoke in soft voices about what the near future held for them.

Shanti explained that she was going to visit the university in the morning, to see Darsat, an old friend, and wondered if Keema would be able to join her. Keema shook her head, there was too much work to be done, too many bills to be paid. Keema kept flicking her eyes back to the driver.

"Is something wrong?" whispered Shanti.

"Yes," answered Keema softly right next to Shanti's ear. "She's holding the reins all wrong, it's going to irritate her horses and she'll get less out of them." Keema tightened the arm around Shanti's shoulders. "It's alright, I'm not going to say anything." But she frowned and glared at the back of the driver's head. Shanti giggled.

"There's something else I wanted to tell you," she said, with her eyes lowered and her voice muffled by Keema's shoulder.

"What's that Petal?"

"I'm thinking of going on a business trip. To Chechezuk."

Shanti could feel Keema's whole body stiffen. She risked a peek up at the other woman's face. Keema's brow was furrowed and she was staring back down at Shanti.

"Chechezuk? That's... that's forever away, isn't it?"

"Sort of." Shanti found it hard to admit. "It's a month by boat, so I'd probably be gone for just over two months."

"Two months?" Keema's voice hissed. Shanti worried that the driver would turn around and see what was going on but the young woman didn't seem to notice. From what Keema had told her in the past about how much she could hear her passengers, Shanti was glad that their driver had good self control and was pretending to ignore them.

"Two months." Keema repeated softer. "Wow, that's a long time."

"Yes. But I was thinking, maybe you could come with me?" Shanti had not considered the idea fully yet, but it was the obvious thing in her heart as she spoke. She couldn't imagine being so far from her wife for so long.

Keema didn't answer. She slowly raised an eyebrow at Shanti.

"We've always talked about going on more adventures, leaving Gorduum and seeing the world. This would be our chance!" Shanti couldn't help the excitement that crept into her voice. She had spent years exploring Gorduum and it was a fascinating place, with many corners still left for her to dig into, but the idea of going beyond the city and seeing brand new places made her heart brighter than anything else. She sat up next to her partner and clutched the other woman's shoulder with a tight hand. Keema lifted a hand to cover Shanti's and sighed.

"When would you be leaving?"

"The captain of the ship I was thinking of travelling on said I would have to show up within two days to meet his schedule."

Keema shook her head. "Two days? Two days to sort out our apartment, to figure out who will take care of my horse and cart, to find out how we can even afford to-" She pinched the bridge of her nose. "Shanti this is too much. I don't know how we could do it."

Shanti felt her chest tighten. "I know it's a lot. Maybe it's too much. I still have to see if Dunin is even willing to invest in it, so I can explore his new prospects. I might just tell him that the idea doesn't suit us." She leaned back down onto Keema's shoulder. Her wife still felt as stiff as stone, and her hand on Shanti's was less of a comfort than usual. Keema sighed softly and then they rode the rest of the way back home in silence.

THE NEXT MORNING Shanti woke to an empty apartment, as usual. She ate her breakfast slowly, wondering what she should do about the opportunity that lay before her. The chance to travel to a distant country, somewhere brand new, was something that appealed deeply to her. The chance to be linked to a successful new business (or at least, an old business that was about to undergo a huge change) was potentially very interesting to her uncle, and that was the only way she would be able to afford the journey. But leaving Keema behind for over two months? That was something that left her cold. She gathered up her belongings and walked outside, walking along the street to the larger main road before she signalled one of the many taxi carts that trundled through the crowd.

She watched the sky as the cart took her to her destination. When she had first arrived in Gorduum, she had been taught to watch the paths that the taxi drivers took closely, to be wary in case they were going to drift close to dangerous alleys, or take her somewhere that she didn't know. She was warned that they may take a long route to a nearby destination, just to justify a large fee. But after many long and amusing nights with Keema in the workers' pubs she knew most of the drivers, by face if not name, and Keema had taught her so many of the routes through the city so well that she felt more comfortable relaxing during these rides.

The sky was grey this morning, and the lights growing up their tall metal posts in the centre of the street illuminated more than usual for the time of day. Shanti wondered if it was going to rain.

The driver took her through the tall gates of the university and into the wide cobbled plaza beyond. He smiled and tipped his cap as she paid and climbed down, then he flicked his reins and led his cart back out into the boulevard and disappeared into the passing stream of people. Shanti looked up at the tall building. When she had first arrived in the city, she had been overwhelmed by it, it was so huge and intimidating. But now that she knew it was full of funny little men and women whose whole lives were focused on the minutiae of their odd little interests, she could not help but smile every time she looked at it.

She walked confidently through the long hallways, stepping around the Skuggi who were sweeping them out or dusting marble busts that sat on display here and there. She nodded at various preoccupied passers-by heading in the opposite direction to her, and rushed through a garden full of workers pruning and clipping the various bushes and flowerbeds. Quickly, Shanti found her way to the office of her old friend Darsat.

"Shanti! I am so happy to see you, it has been such a long time!"

"Has it?" asked Shanti as she closed his office door behind her and walked over to him. He rose from his desk and took her hands in his own, leaning over to give her a peck on the check as a welcome. In direct opposition to how he had presented himself when they first met, his cheeks now bristled with white hairs that poked out on either side of his face like whiskers. He had taken to trimming his chin clean, emphasising the effect. Shanti wondered if he was trying to look like a cat on purpose.

"I don't think I've seen you since you came to dinner at our home two weeks ago!" he declared as he moved over to the side of his office and began rummaging in a cupboard. He returned with two tall glasses of pale yellow juice, and a pile of crackers. "Here, enjoy!"

"Thank you." Shanti lifted one of the glasses and

sipped at the juice. It was cool and refreshing. *I've seen more of this man than I have of my own father,* she realised as she picked up a cracker. *And I still haven't written a new letter home! They must be worrying about me. And I should be worrying about them! How is mother's store coping without me taking shifts? I know that she said she had hired one of the other village girls, but that expense must be making things difficult.*

"And how is your charming young lady?" asked Darsat, sipping at his own juice.

"She is very well."

"I do enjoy conversations with her. She is always willing to put forward a new perspective for me! It is like when I was young enough to dance without my legs hurting. Turning in new directions at all times!" He leaned back in his chair for a moment. "You've found a good one!"

"I know! And how is Dulku?"

"My own wife is full of passion! She has begun to learn something of carpentry, which has been a surprise to me! She carved this small thing for me to remember her while I am here in my office."

He picked up a small wooden frog that was sitting on his desk. It was roughly shaped, but the colours of the wood suited the curves of its pudgy body, and just looking at it brought a smile to Shanti's cheeks.

"That is lovely. Has she been working at that for long?"

"Not long. She decided that she wanted to learn how to repair a chair from our dining room barely a fortnight ago, and then she enjoyed turning the wood so much that she found a tutor. Now she creates beautiful animals, and wishes to rebuild all our furniture!" He laughed and placed the frog back on his desk. "So my dear, is this a simple visit to say hello, or is there something more important that brings you here today?"

9

"Actually, there is something very important that I've come here for, sorry" Shanti told Darsat, blushing as she admitted that she was not simply there to enjoy his company. She lifted her satchel onto her lap and reached inside. The older man's curiosity pulled him forward, trying to peek down into the bag to catch a glimpse of what she was pulling out. When he saw the wooden box he frowned slightly.

"Is this a gift?" he asked, his voice unsure.

"It is!" grinned Shanti, placing the wooden box that Brin Surety had retrieved for her on his desk. She carefully turned it around so that it was facing him, within his reach. His eyes widened.

Darsat reached over and ran stiff fingers along the sides and corners. He traced the name imprinted on the top. His frown deepened.

"Kechooka? Didn't Kechooka die a few months ago?" He raised an eyebrow at Shanti. She nodded.

"Five months ago."

"I was just writing him a new letter when I heard," murmured Darsat, and Shanti coughed slightly. *The first thing I am going to do when I am done here,* she resolved, *the very first thing I do when I get back home, is to write a letter to my family.*

"What were you writing to him about?" she asked.

"You know me, I am always interested in new theories. He had some ideas about the orbit of Sereetha that were intriguing. He thought that the irregularities in the rhythm could be explained by another planet, one even further away from us; so far that we could not see it!"

Shanti laughed. "That sounds impossible! How would we have missed a whole planet spinning around out there?" She leaned back and gestured towards the ceiling.

"Yes, it is a difficult proposition to take seriously, is it not?" Darsat lifted the box, so that he could examine the underside of it for a moment. "And yet, he was so sure. I wanted him to send me more of his calculations, so that I might try and track Sereetha myself, to verify if I saw the same movements." He placed the box back down and pressed an open palm down on top of it's lid. He looked into Shanti's eyes with his own, widening them in excitement. "So what is contained in here!?"

"To be honest, I'm not really sure," admitted Shanti. "I knew that you and he were admirers of each other's work, you talk about your correspondence all the time. So I thought it would be worth sending an agent to purchase anything of his. I did try to encourage them to find his scholarly work rather than keepsakes. I'm hoping this scroll is something interesting for you."

She decided that Darsat didn't need to know that

she was also investigating the effectiveness and reliability of Brin Surety. She and her uncle had believed that the way the company worked would make it useful for other errands, and they had been proven correct with the retrieval of the small box. Although it claimed to be a shipping insurance company, she and Dunin suspected that they occasionally sent passengers on ships to confirm proper precautions were being taken onboard. Possibly those agents could be used to deliver messages, retrieve items, or investigate events that might affect Dunin's investments. The purchase and delivery of this box had proven that, regardless of the specifics of how they operated, Brin Surety could be used for other expertise as well.

"Let us not keep ourselves waiting," said Darsat, a massive smile splitting his face and revealing his shining teeth, his eyes glinting just as brightly above. He lifted the lid of the box. The raised wood hid his expression from Shanti momentarily, and she shifted sideways in her chair to see his reaction. She was pleased to see his eyes still wide, and his jaw dropping in awe.

"As you say, it is a scroll! And so old! Was this one of his pieces, or is this his reference?" murmured Darsat, reaching forward with both hands to cradle the fragile object and slowly lift it out of the box. Shanti opened her mouth to answer him and then realised that he was talking to himself, not her.

"Exquisite," he breathed. He placed the scroll on to the only clear space in front of him on his desk, a small square of bare wood. Then he pushed the wooden box further out of the way. He leaned in closer to examine the wax seal.

"Yes, this is Kechooka's seal. He used it on letters to me also. I wonder why he sealed this?"

"Maybe he didn't want others to steal his ideas?"

Darsat chuckled. "Maybe. Or maybe he had finished reading this one, and wanted the reminder to leave it aside?"

He opened a drawer and pulled out a small thin knife, then slipped the blade under the edge of the scroll and slowly eased it through the solid wax. The wax split and cracked, and some parts simply separated from the scroll, leaving a small discoloured patch. Darsat began to push the curled material open.

Shanti stood and came around her friend's desk, looking down over his shoulder. The revealed section of scroll was covered in tiny writing of a language that she didn't recognise, with letters made of sharp angular lines, like a series of small trees. Diagrams made of circles and ovals carved out spaces on the scroll as well.

"What do you think?" she asked, leaning closer and resting one hand on the older man's shoulder.

"It's wonderful!" exclaimed Darsat. "I'm not very good at reading Zukian though. It is hard for me to be sure what it is saying. But I think this is an ancient record of a transit, which is remarkable!"

"Really?"

"Yes, it would have taken some careful knowledge to track such a thing, and I cannot imagine what equipment may have been required! I hope the scroll includes details that allow me to tell how old it is, and how they accomplished this. Oh, I wonder if this helped Kechooka establish the irregularities he describes in Sereetha's orbit?"

"It all sounds very exciting," said Shanti, heading off Darsat's explanation before she was completely lost. "This scroll is from Chechezuk?"

"Of course." Darsat turned in his chair to look up at her, his brow furrowed. "But you know this. You arranged for it to come from there?"

"I did, but I didn't know if the scroll was from there, or just had ended up in Kechooka's possession there." Shanti returned to her seat, and Darsat closed the box so that he could see her clearly.

"I wondered if you had ever been to Chechezuk yourself?" she asked, straightening her skirts across her legs.

"I'm afraid that it is one place that I never managed to get to," he admitted sadly. "Why is this?"

"I have an opportunity to go there. For business." Shanti reached up and rubbed her lower lip between her thumb and finger. "And you know how much I have always wanted to go out to see as much of the world as I can."

"But this is wonderful also," declared Darsat. "You will love to go on such an adventure!"

"Yes, but it would have been helpful if you could have given me some idea of what to expect. I am a little bit nervous about the idea." She sniffed. "And Keema isn't sure if I should go."

"Oh, I see. That makes things more difficult." Darsat stroked a hand across his chin, pulling his whiskers down and not seeming to notice as they sprang back afterwards. "Well, let me think. What do I know of Chechezuk?" He pulled at his lower lip with his teeth and made a sucking noise as he rummaged through his memories to find anything useful he could pass on to Shanti.

"It is a cooler country, but much more humid. When it is hot there, the damp air makes you feel very hot, but when it grows cold, you will feel much colder. I understand that their cities are spread out, made of smaller buildings than our own. Oh, and they have canals everywhere!"

"Canals?"

"Yes! You know how you sometimes will take a ferry on the river, to travel through Gorduum?"

"Of course."

"In Chechezuk, their cities are full of waterways like this! It is much more common to take a boat from one place to another!"

"And what are the people like?" asked Shanti. Darsat's description of the distant country was renewing her excitement to see it for herself. It sounded so unlike anything that she had seen before in her life, and the old desire to travel and find new things was rising in her veins.

"That, I am not sure. Kechooka wrote wonderful letters, very polite, and I would say that we became friends. But we wrote to each other based on reputations, we never actually met each other." His large eyebrows drooped. "I was so sad when I heard that he had passed away. I never actually got to shake his hand."

"Oh Darsat, I'm sorry." Shanti rose from her seat and moved around the desk to put an arm across her old friend's shoulder. He frowned and told her not to bother, but she felt his shoulders shake as she stood by him, and saw a tear move down his nose. She placed a hand on his shoulder in sympathy and wondered what sort of people she would meet in Chechezuk.

. . .

DESPITE REALISING that she had decided in her heart that she would travel to the distant port, Shanti knew that it would be meaningless if she didn't have the backing and financial support of her uncle. Because of this, she immediately went to his apartment after leaving the university.

As she climbed the stairs to his home, Shanti tried to rehearse what she would say to him in her head. *I'll have to really stress how important it will be to our getting involved in the tuft market,* she told herself. *If I just tell him how much I want to go on an adventure, there is no way he'll be willing to contribute any money towards it.* She pressed a hand to her stomach. *And I simply cannot think of any way to convince him to help pay for Keema to accompany me! But I can't just leave her behind, can I?* The idea of holding this discussion was making her jittery, and she struggled to keep her hands still.

Gunin opened the door and smiled as he greeted her. She returned the greeting warmly and followed him to Dunin's office, where he announced her. Shanti stood in the doorway while her uncle finished rummaging through the papers in front of him.

"You're lucky I'm here," he grumbled as he gestured at the chair on the other side of his desk, clearly suggesting that she take a seat. "I was about to go and meet with Darnaan, he's finally come around on the Gutun farm and if we buy up the debt then I think they'll have a bumper year next year and we should share in the yield." He looked up at her and shook his head slightly. "Of course, that's not really important right now. What do you need?"

Shanti took a deep breath and licked her lips. She walked into the office and pulled the quote from Captain Karikar out of her stachel and placed it in front of her uncle and then sat in the chair by his desk. He looked down with a wrinkled brow and then snorted.

"What is this number?"

"That's the cost of passage to Chechezuk," replied Shanti. She tried not to wind her fingers together. She didn't want to show how nervous she was.

"It is, is it? And why would you be showing that number to me?"

"Because you are the one who thinks that a ten fold increase in tuft supply is imminent and you are also the one who thinks it would be worthwhile for us to invest in that now."

Dunin crossed his arms. Shanti was used to her uncle's gruff demeanour now, and so she was not intimidated by the glare that he directed at her. She knew that he typically emanated waves of grumpy displeasure, and let them wash past her. All his lessons from the last two years in how to survive a business meeting were coming to her mind, ready to use against him.

"What's that got to do with passage to a foreign land?"

"The captain said that he knows the man who is going to be responsible for the increase in tuft, and he's willing to introduce me to him." Shanti waited as her uncle's eyes widened. She could see them begin to shine as he considered the wealth that such a meeting might lead to. "So, if you can cover the cost of my passage, then I can make a deal to import the tuft to Gorduum and distribute it without flooding the market. More importantly, I can see the orchards and decide whether their plans actually live up to their hopes."

Dunin narrowed his eyes and leaned back. Shanti could see the machinery turning in his mind as he weighed the costs of investment versus the likelihood of a return. Shanti controlled her breathing as she waited, determined not to be the one who broke the silence.

10

———

The silence felt like a blanket that was pressing down heavier and heavier as Shanti waited for her uncle to speak. Finally Dunin leaned forward again.

"What about Keema?" he asked.

"What?" Of all the answers she had prepared herself for, that was not one she expected. "Keema?"

"Yes. Your wife?" Shanti could feel her cheeks blush as she was reminded again that even her uncle had not been present at the office where she and Keema had signed the legal papers that meant they were married. She had just about convinced herself that he didn't know, they spoke so little about it. Dunin raised an eyebrow. "Are you simply going to leave her behind for all that time?"

"I... There are..." Shanti wasn't sure what to say. She shrugged. "If I have to leave her behind I suppose I might, though I wouldn't wish to." She didn't want to seem too eager to have Keema join her. That would give some power in this negotiation back to Dunin, and lessen the chance that he might contribute to Keema's passage. "I guess I believed the captain. I think you were given good information, there really is something important happening in Chechezuk and we might be able to be part of it." If she could emphasise the potential reward of this trip, it might encourage him to be more generous in his offer.

Dunin nodded slightly.

"Let me tell you this," he muttered. "The last two years have been... very successful for me." He rubbed his chin. "People take a liking to you, and it means that we've signed a lot more deals than I managed on my own. You say you have a feeling that this one is a good one?" He paused and looked into her eyes. Shanti nodded. He sniffed and nodded himself. "Alright. Then I think it's only fair that I invest into this deal enough for you both to go."

Shanti tried to remain composed but a squeal of joy leaked out of her mouth. She lifted her fists to her chest and shivered in excitement. Dunin laughed and stuck out a hand.

"Alright, alright, but I'll recover half the cost from the profits if this deal goes through! When would you leave?"

"The captain said he's planning to return to Chechezuk tomorrow."

"Fine. I'll draw up a document authorising you to make deals on my behalf as well, and you two can go and have a bit of the adventure you keep talking about, on the way."

Shanti jumped out of her chair and rushed around the desk to gather her uncle into a hug. She planted a kiss on his cheek.

"Thank you so much!"

"Hurumph," he said, though he was smiling. He

patted one of her arms. "Go on, you'll have a lot to do to be ready in time. Pick up my letter when you go."

Shanti went back to the apartment she shared with Keema and spent the evening at the table, sipping a cup of tea. The light through the window from the street outside was fading, leaving the apartment dim, lit only by a few tall thin lights in their terra-cotta pots in the corners.

The door banged open and Keema came striding into the room. Her face was long, with dark circles under her eyes. She threw herself down into the seat on the opposite side of the table to Shanti.

"Phew, what a day. I have to say, the streets are getting grumpier this month." Keema shook her head and ruffled her short hair with one hand. "It seems everyone is on the downs, and for some reason they want to blame me for their bad situation. Like it's my fault? I'm just taking them home in the evening, or dropping them at whatever destination they wanted to get to! You know, there was one boy, right, barely an adult, you could still see the fluff on his cheeks, but he told me that he was going to a party celebrating his best friend's engagement. You'd expect him to be happy right?"

Shanti nodded, with a small smile touching her cheeks.

"Right! But no, he spent the whole journey telling me that his best friend was getting engaged to this girl that he had been sweet on for years! And what's worse, as he got out of the cart, he told me that he was disappointed that I hadn't been sympathetic enough, and he wouldn't want to ride with me again!" Keema's eyes flashed with anger and she sat up straighter, suppressed fury making her whole body twitch.

"Sounds dreadful Sunshine. At least you're home now though," said Shanti, reaching one hand across the tabletop. Keema grimaced and reached over to squeeze Shanti's hand, nodding and slowly allowing a smile to grow on her face.

"It is good to be home," she admitted.

Shanti licked her lips and then drew a deep breath. *Here goes nothing,* she thought.

"I've decided that I do want to follow the opportunity in Chechezuk."

Shanti couldn't bring herself to look up. She felt the roughness of Keema's fingertips clutched around hers. She was sure that she could feel the other woman's gaze on the top of her head, and it made her scalp feel as though it was about to burst into flame from the attention. Shanti drew her lower lip between her teeth. *What is Keema going to say? Will she hate me?*

"You've decided that you really do want to leave Gorduum for two months." Keema's voice was flat. Shanti couldn't tell if she was angry, or upset, or even whether she was happy at the news. Shanti had to peek up to try and see Keema's face, to meet her eyes and figure out what was happening in her mind.

Her wife sat on the other side of the table with slightly drawn brows, and lips set in a firm line. Shanti squeezed Keema's hand again.

"I know that this is a complicated situation, but I just think that it's a great opportunity."

"For your uncle?" asked Keema.

"Yes, it could be very profitable for us to establish a connection with this business," Shanti began, but Keema shook her head.

"Profitable. You could make a business deal from Gorduum if you really wanted. No, there's more to this." Keema slowly slid her hand back to her side. "Are you tired of living like this?"

"What?" Shanti felt as though someone had reached into her chest and grabbed her lungs in both hands. All the air was driven from them in one burst.

"It's okay, I wouldn't blame you. I know we're only just managing to scrape by, and you wanted more when you came to live in Gorduum. You had seen your uncle's home, you'd been taken out to balls by academics and wealthy contacts in the city, you weren't expecting to have to make yourself comfortable in two rooms in a poor district." Keema turned her head away, and her shoulders slumped. "I knew a taxi driver's money wasn't going to keep a woman like you in the lifestyle she deserved. I knew this was going to happen. Not to mention you keep talking about going on adventures far from here."

"What?" Shanti was trying to organise her thoughts so that she could respond, but Keema's voice kept coming. Shanti lifted a hand and started shaking her head. "No no no! I'm not trying to say that I'm sick of this place!" She reached across the table, trying to catch Keema's retreating fingers. "I know that it will be strange for me to go for so long, I just wanted to tell you that it was important to me. I really want to go. But I definitely want to come back." She finally caught her partner's fingers and looked into Keema's eyes. She curled her fingertips around Keema's. "I'll come back to Gorduum. With you."

Keema looked down. "But you'd be gone for two months. What am I supposed to do for two months?"

"You'd come with me though," Shanti declared. She felt hope open in her chest as she said the words, hope that Keema would understand how much she needed her with her. But Keema's face twisted in confusion and the hope shrunk like a wilting flower.

"Come with you?" Keema looked absolutely bewildered, as though Shanti had just explained that she knew how to fly and was about to take Keema to the moon. "I couldn't just come with you!"

"Why not?"

"Why not? Why not? Like I said last night, what about my horse? What would happen to Breenar? I couldn't just leave her wandering around the streets of Gorduum."

Shanti had an image of Keema's horse, plodding through the streets and chewing on any plants that were managing to poke their way through the cobbles and stone of the city. She covered her mouth with one hand as she giggled. *Breenar would be chewing on the street lights before an hour was out, the sly glutton!*

"Couldn't one of the other drivers take care of her?" she asked.

"They'd charge me," grumbled Keema. "And that's just one of the bills we'd still have to pay. I'd be paying for the stable where I put up Breenar, and we'd be paying the rent for this apartment. How could we manage all of that?"

Shanti nodded. *It was true, there's so many things that we would still have to deal with, how could we manage? Someone would want to be paid for taking care of Breenar, and probably even more if they had to take care of her all day. What could the solution be?*

"Dunin agreed to cover the cost of your travel," volunteered Shanti, hoping that the goods news would encourage Keema.

Her wife snorted.

"That's good, but it's not everything." She paused and scratched the back of her head, fingers digging into her short spiky hair. "Actually..." Keema began slowly, then frowned. "No, that's too unlikely."

"What is it? Do you have an idea?" asked Shanti.

"I just... I was talking to some other drivers, and I do know that there are a few who are lodging together at the moment who wish that they weren't."

"You think that one of them would pay the bills on our apartment? If we said that they could stay here?"

Keema tapped her lips with a finger. "Obviously it would be a tough ask, but if they took my cart out and made their own money..."

"Yes! I'm sure there has to be someone who needs some time to learn how to drive or get into the trade, and if they used your equipment for a few months, that would be worthwhile for someone!"

Keema leaned back and snorted. "Well, it's an idea. And it would mean that I could come with you. But there's no guarantee that I'll find someone who is keen on the idea and ready to go at such short notice."

"No guarantee but there's a chance." Shanti stood and came around the table, leaning over to wrap her arms around Keema and pressing closer to kiss her cheek. "I can't wait for you and I to go out into the world and have an adventure together!"

"Yes, well, maybe." Keema lifted her hands to hold onto Shanti arm's, turning to kiss her fully, drawing her close. "If we're lucky."

11

The next afternoon Shanti was standing with Keema on the wharf, with her arm around her wife's waist. Slowly rising and falling on the river next to them was the ship they hoped would carry them to adventure in distant Chechezuk. The Tide's Daughter was tall, like a curved building floating on the surface of the Nataat. Three masts strove towards the sky. Shanti couldn't help but smile as she realised that she would be spending weeks onboard this ship, travelling further than she ever had before.

Keema was shuffling from one foot to the other and kept turning to glare at passing sailors and workers, as though she thought that they were about to snatch her travel trunk from where it sat beside her and go darting off with her belongings. Shanti placed a hand on her shoulder.

"Relax Sunshine. Let's get on board and put our things somewhere safe so that you can unwind."

"Hmmmm." Keema made a sound that indicated that she was willing to go along with Shanti's idea, but that she wasn't convinced that the plan would actually lead to her relaxing. She grabbed the handle to her trunk, while Shanti took her own. The pair moved to the gangway and began heaving them up the ramp.

At the top, Shanti smiled at Tozan, the grizzled old man who was in charge of all the sailors on the Tide's Daughter and whose glaring eye surveyed everyone who came aboard. He was standing in exactly the same position that he had been the first time she came aboard a few days earlier, planted firmly on deck to the side of the gangway, arms crossed. The broad man grunted in return then raised an arm and snapped his fingers. A young sailor came rushing over and bobbed his head when he saw Shanti and Keema standing at the top of the gangway.

"Yes sir?"

"As you can see, we've got a couple of passengers joining us. Show them to their quarters would you?"

"Yes sir."

The sailor jumped forward, grabbed both of their trunks, and began walking towards the far end of the deck, where a set of stairs led below. Shanti was impressed at how easily he moved the wooden travel luggage, and nudged Keema.

"He must be quite strong," she whispered.

Keema shrugged. "I don't think mine was particularly heavy." She staggered to one side and grabbed Shanti's shoulder, then looked around. "Did you feel that?"

"Feel what?"

"The whole ship moved." Keema narrowed her eyes at the sailor leading the way, as though he was to blame for whatever had occurred.

"I didn't notice, sorry."

"Well it did," said Keema. Shanti opened her mouth but could think of nothing to say, and after a moment's pause they both kept walking.

The area below the deck was a small dark space, full of sailors moving around and packed tightly with boxes. Keema elbowed Shanti to get her attention and then leaned closer to whisper a question.

"What's in all the boxes? I thought you said that this ship brought goods from Chechezuk to Gorduum?" They passed one box that had been pried open and saw that it contained Gorduum glass, cups and fashionable plates, all packed into thick straw to protect it. "Oh," Keema said, her cheeks flushing. "It takes cargo from us back to them, doesn't it?"

Shanti nodded, trying not to laugh.

"I should have realised that," sighed Keema. "I just feel like my head is full of oil sloshing about at the moment."

"You'll be okay Sunshine." Shanti squeezed closer to Keema and kissed her cheek.

The sailor that they were following moved through the narrow spaces and darkness like a cat in an alley. Shanti felt that he was moving easier through the maze with both of their trunks then she and her wife had been able to get through the open streets of the city on their way here!

Shanti felt her breath catch as she and Keema had to turn sideways and edge around large sailors, men and women with stern faces and solid muscles. *It's alright,* Shanti told herself, running through the same mental list that she did whenever these feelings overtook her in cramped dark spaces. *Keema is here. There is no reason to think these people are going to be dangerous. Just because it is dark, doesn't mean that I am unseen. Keema is here. There is no reason to think these people are going to be dangerous. Just because it is dark, doesn't mean that I am unseen.* The thoughts circled around her mind, and she struggled to keep her eyes open and focused on where she was going.

The space was lit by small lanterns. Their thick glass and heavy metal banding obscured the light that flickered inside them. *Flickering lights,* wondered Shanti. *That's unusual?* The plants that lit Gorduum and the towns and villages it supplied did not flicker. They shone at different levels of brightness, but it was a steady and clear light. Flickering was unheard of. Shanti looked closer at one of the lanterns as she followed the sailor past a thick support beam. *It's got a flame inside! They are using actual fire as light.* Shanti hadn't been in a place that was lit by candles or lamps in over two years. *It's amazing how quickly I got used to the lights being absolutely everywhere,* she realised.

Towards the rear of the space, there was a narrow doorway in the wall. The sailor who had manoeuvred their trunks through the cramped boxes of cargo dropped them on the wooden boards and opened the door for Shanti and Keema. The inside of the room was just as claustrophobic as the area outside, but it also had a set of bunks built into it on either side.

"You strap your luggage under the bottom bunks, so that it can't move around," the sailor told them, pointing out the leather straps and tarnished buckles that were bolted to the floor below each bunk. "Unfortunately you'll have to share the quarters. We don't have enough space to provide you with anything more private."

Keema nodded, but Shanti paused and frowned.

"Is that appropriate? Will you at least introduce us to the sailors who will be in here?"

"Sailors?" The young man blinked and then smiled. Shanti couldn't help but notice that he was missing quite a few teeth. "No miss, sorry for the misunderstanding. You'll be sharing with some other passengers on their way to the same port. This is all the bunks we have."

Shanti twisted her lips and sighed, crossing her arms as she stood in the tiny doorway, surveying the bunkroom.

"These are the only bunks?"

"Yes ma'am."

"Where do the sailors sleep then?"

"We set up hammocks out here." The sailor walked over to the side of the dim space they had passed through and pulled out a sheet of thick brown material. He held it out towards Shanti and showed her the heavy loops at the corners, then slung it up onto hooks set into the beams that made up the structure of the space. This created a long narrow shelf of material that he somehow twisted and jumped into, ending up laying out on the sheet.

"Is that comfortable?" Shanti asked, unconvinced.

"As comfortable as I need," grinned the sailor. He leaned over and dropped out of the hammock to his feet. "And it tucks away while we're working." He demonstrated the speed that he could stow the material back into its pouch on the wall.

"Leaving the bunks for the passengers. Sounds

good to me," said Keema from behind Shanti. "Come on Petal, let's get packed in."

"I'm still uncomfortable that others will be here with us, sleeping in the same room, people who we don't even know," Shanti said to the other woman as they pushed their trunks under two of the lower bunks, the sailor having returned to his duties up in the fresh air.

"I understand why," said Keema. She sat on one of the lower bunks and tried to bounce, grimacing as her bottom struck the remarkably solid mattress. "But it looks to me as though we just have to get used to close quarters on this boat."

"I'm pretty sure that ones this big are called ships," said Shanti.

"Whatever it is. There's no space, we're going to be on top of each other a lot, and we're going to be out at sea with no one else around for nearly a month." Keema shrugged. "We just have to trust that everything is going to be okay."

We have to trust that the Masked God is watching, Shanti told herself. *And the best way to ensure that, is to make sure that we are watching others for them.* She lay down on her bunk, and Keema lay down on hers, their heads ending up next to one another. Shanti turned to look at Keema's upside down face. It made her smile, and she leaned over to kiss Keema, then turned to look up at the wooden slats of the bunk above her. The fluttering in her stomach was calming down. *Yes, if I am one pair of the God's Hidden Eyes, then there must be others watching over me as well.*

· · ·

SHANTI WATCHED the sailors as they rushed over the ship like insects on a rotten log. She enjoyed trying to figure out what the sailors were doing, but between seeing small teams shifting heavy crates, tying ropes, folding thick canvas, then watching other teams coming and reshifting, retying, untying, and unfolding she was extremely confused. She had no idea what their tasks were for.

She was also intrigued to see some of the sailors folding their fingers into strange little shapes occasionally while they worked. It didn't seem to have anything to do with the task they were undertaking, as they had to flex their fingers back out before they could continue each time. *I wonder what's going on there,* she thought.

It had been two hours since she and Keema had claimed the first beds in the passenger quarters, and others had arrived over that time. There were now two other couples in the bunkroom. One was an older married couple who wore their finest clothes and sat on the lower bunks opposite Shanti and Keema. The man had long white hair that was tied back into a neat ponytail, while the woman's curls were arranged into a pile on her head that resembled a cloud. They both looked around the room with curled lips and flared nostrils, as though they could smell the wooden structure of the room and were not pleased by it. Clearly they had not realised what travelling on the Tide's Daughter would be like.

The second couple were two young men, one with a long pointed beard and who wore loose cream and gold coloured clothing. The other was taller and broader but seemingly shyer. The second man stood with slightly hunched shoulders and a bowed head, often stepping behind his partner. Keema moved over to talk to them immediately, gripping the bearded man's hand tightly and breaking into loud peals of laughter. The older couple in their well-embroidered clothes flinched at the sound.

Shanti decided to leave the bunkroom. There was so little space inside that if the occupants weren't actually sitting on the bunks that they had claimed, then they wound up standing on one another's feet. Instead she wove her way back out to the stairs and up on to the deck where she could pull her shoulders back and breathe deeply in the fresh air.

The sailors rushing about on the deck glanced at her often, so she tried to wedge herself into a corner near the front of the ship where there were no ropes and she could stay out of everybody's way. She watched as ropes were tied, slung, looped. The sails were rising on masts that towered over her, and the breeze that cut across the railings felt damp from the river. She closed her eyes and lifted her face into the cool air. She wondered if it was salt that she could smell on the breeze as well. She'd been told many times about the salt of the ocean, but she had never experienced it for herself.

After a few minutes of watching the activity on the ship, she turned her attention to the wharf that they were still tied to. Sailors and merchants from other boats and ships were moving about on the wharf, much more calmly than the ones onboard with her. But then she saw someone running from far away down the nearby streets. She shifted over to the railing on that side of the ship to try and get a clearer view of the rushing figure. It appeared to be a man, running with a large canvas bag bouncing over his shoulder. His long thin legs swung in huge bounds along the broad weathered planks of the wharf.

12

———

The tall thin man reached the gangway to the Tide's Daughter and spun to race up it, skidding on the wharf as he did, leaning precariously over. The gangway bounced under his feet as though it was a sheet being shaken out before being used on a bed. Shanti felt her own fingers grip the railing in panic as she watched him almost be thrown from the narrow plank. He grabbed the railings at the top of the gangway to stop himself flying out onto the deck and was pushed off balance by the sack pressing against his shoulders. He stopped and stumbled then pulled himself back upright. Tozan was in his regular position at the top of the gangway, and Shanti could see that the old mate was amused by the skinny man.

The newcomer immediately began talking to the older man, leaning in close and gesturing rapidly with his spare hand. Tozan scowled but looked as though he was listening. Shanti expected the grumpy old man to turn the newcomer back straight away, but he didn't. Perhaps she had misjudged him. She tried to sidle closer to hear what was going on, but their voices were still too low. She decided to raise a hand, to try and catch Tozan's attention. He scowled when he noticed her, but he beckoned her closer..

"What is it?" he asked.

"I assume this is another passenger for Chechezuk?" she asked as she drew up to the pair. Now she had a chance to look at the newcomer closer. He was nearly a full head taller than her, though remarkably skinny. His nose was large, and his throat bulbous, but his eyes were as large as plates, and they shone with humour and kindness. Shanti recognised him immediately. She had seen the same young man briefly before her meeting with Brin Surety only a few days earlier.

"Aye, this lad is coming with us. Though he nearly didn't make it, we are due to raise the gangway already."

"Hence the running," panted the man as he nodded.

"My name is Shanti," she said to him, extending a hand. "What's your name?"

"Felldan," he replied, grabbing her hand and pumping it up and down, then releasing it and hauling his bag back up his shoulder.

"It's a pleasure to meet you. I think I saw you at Brin Surety recently?"

The man spluttered and pounded on his chest with one hand. "Yes, possibly, I did ask them to take care of some items for me." It took some time to settle the cough in his chest.

"How about I lead him to the bunkroom," Shanti explained to Tozan as Felldan sniffed. "That way none of your sailors will have to be interrupted."

The old man grunted and frowned, but he nodded. As Shanti and Felldan began to head back to the stairs, the grouchy old man called for the gangway to be raised and declared that they were leaving.

"Let's be quick," Shanti grinned at her companion. "I've never been on a ship voyage before!"

"Yes, we'll get you back up here as soon as we can. It's quite a sight," agreed the tall man.

In the bunkroom Shanti was unsurprised to find Keema sitting cross-legged in the middle of the room, shaking a handful of dice and tossing them to the wooden floor. The bearded man was crouching down near her and there was a pile of small coins in front of him, while his partner lay on a top bunk watching them. The older couple were still sitting on their bunks with knees pressed closely together and hands in fists resting on top of their legs. Their knuckles were turning white. *I wonder why they are so nervous,* Shanti thought.

Keema glanced up and winked at Shanti as she came back in.

"You've started already, have you?" Shanti asked Keema. She turned to the bearded man and raised an eyebrow. "Do you know what you've got yourself into here?"

He laughed. "I'm sure that Keema is a very devious customer!" He smiled broadly, his teeth shining from behind the thick black hair on his face. "But these are my dice!" And it was his turn to wink.

Keema laughed and picked up the dice, ready to roll again. "I got triple fives, so let's see what these three give me."

Shanti motioned Felldan forward from the doorway. "This is the last passenger who will be joining us. This is Felldan." He waved at the others in the room. "I'm Shanti, and you all know my wife Keema it seems." Keema pushed the hair back from her eyes and smiled.

"My name is Gudan," said the man with the beard. He jerked a thumb towards the bunks behind him. "My husband is Taadin, though he often needs to get used to people before he's comfortable with conversation." He smiled up at his husband as he spoke.

Shanti and the others turned to the two older people. The man blinked and his mouth gaped like a fish.

"I, uh, well, my name is, uh, my name is Rahit, and this is, um, this is my wife Lorku," he managed to stammer, his eyes bulging slightly. His wife shrunk on the bunk next to him.

"Have you two travelled by ship before?" asked Gudan, with narrowed eyes.

"Uh, no," admitted Rahit. He shuffled a little from his perch, licking his lips and glancing around the other passengers. "It is... smaller... than we had expected."

Gudan and Keema laughed and the young man leaned over to nudge her shoulder.

"I don't mean to laugh at you, but you must see that it looks quite amusing from the outside!" said Gudan to Rahit.

Lorku frowned and her head sank down beneath her shoulders. Shanti felt sorry for the couple and walked over to sit next to them. Felldan looked around with large eyes and then blew a breath out from his lips as he stowed his bag beneath the bunks and climbed up into one of the only remaining spaces.

Shanti reached over and patted Lorku's hand, hoping that it was a comforting gesture.

"Where are you going?" she asked.

Lorku glanced at her and then away again.

"Chechezuk," was the quietly whispered reply.

"Yes, that is where I am going too," said Shanti, inserting an extra dose of cheer into her words, to try and encourage the older woman to relax a little. She tried not to let her frustration at such an obvious answer show. "I have a business opportunity to follow up. That, and I have always wanted to go and see the world, so this was a fantastic chance for me." She could feel the smile bending her cheeks a little further than she normally would. She hoped that she looked friendly and cheerful, and not too intense. It was honest joy that was driving her. The realisation that she was really on this adventure made her so happy that she made no attempt to rein it in. "Why are you travelling there?"

"My husband is treasure hunting," scowled the woman. Her voice was low, but Rahit clearly heard. His shoulder jumped and he turned to look at Shanti and his wife with his own lips pursed. He held his tongue though.

"Treasure hunting?" asked Shanti cautiously. "What do you mean?"

"He is sure that Chechezuk has vast supplies of gold that, somehow, no one else has noticed yet."

"No, that is not what I said. I am quite sure that the inland areas have spices that could be extremely valuable," muttered Rahit, leaning over to add his contribution. Lorku snorted. "Well, that's a very different proposition to gold!" he insisted. "The internal landscape of Chechezuk is a tangle of swamp and thick jungle, why wouldn't there be groves and spices there that no one has claimed yet? Much easier to transport than gold too."

"Because people have lived there for centuries, and would have known," grumbled Lorku, but her heart wasn't in it. Rahit glared and then turned back to the rest of the cabin, while Lorku focused her eyes on the floor below her feet. Shanti sighed and patted the back of the woman's hand again. *This could be a very long journey.*

Felldan hopped down and walked back over to stand in front of Shanti. He held out his elbow towards her.

"I'm going to go and watch the city fall behind us as we head downriver," he said with a broad smile. "Would you like to accompany me?"

"Yes, please," Shanti began to reply, but then she looked over at Keema to check what her wife was doing. The other woman was still rolling dice with Gudan, her brow knotted as she tried to calculate odds. "Would you like to come up with us too, Sunshine?"

Keema looked up from the game with a smile. "I would Petal, but we have nearly finished this game. I just need to get one more roll and I'll have him!"

Gudan cackled. "If you're blindingly lucky maybe!"

Keema smirked. "Okay, maybe not one more turn, but it's close. I'll come up as soon as we're done, okay? You should go and enjoy the view though."

Shanti and Felldan stood at the front of the ship, leaning on the railings with crossed arms. Shanti had ridden on ferries from one district to another across the Naatat many times, and even once on a pleasure cruise up and down the river with a bottle of wine and Keema. The Nataat was the broad dark river that looped lazily through the middle of Gorduum, decorated with the low ferries and boats that transported the citizens from one district to another. But all of those boats had been much smaller than the ship she was riding on now. Standing at the railings gave her a sense of flying, moving along at such speed and from such a height over the rippled surface of the river.

She looked across the wide dark water to the shore, with the wind pushing strands of her hair across her face, and the sound of the sails creaking above her. Walls and small jetties lined the edge of the river, small waves lapping up against them. Boats moved like insects around the ship, darting out of its path if they got too close. Shanti was reminded of times that she had been in a ferry that had to adjust its course to avoid a ship like this. They looked so huge from down low on the river, like huge wooden walls passing by in an eerie silence. From up here it was so easy to forget the smaller craft in the river unless she deliberately cast her eyes down.

The passing buildings and pale cloudy sky above drew the eye much more easily. Tall orange buildings covered in terracotta tiles dominated her view, but apartment blocks peppered with tiny windows were noticeable too. From the middle of the river, the crowds walking between the buildings were a collection of small dots and speckles, shifting like sands in the wind.

As the ship continued to sail down the river, Shanti noticed the buildings began to change. The massive block-like buildings that filled the centre of Gorduum became less and less common. Instead smaller and less well-constructed buildings began to appear, built on awkward angles and with extra supports holding them up. The sky grew larger as the buildings hiding it shrank. Before long, muddy spaces were opening up between the buildings also, though the swarm of people trudging in those lanes grew no less. Shanti turned to look further ahead of the ship and gasped. She could see the end of the city, and the landscape around Gorduum was opening up around her.

On the downriver side of the city, the land was like a bowl, surrounded by low green hills with the city in the middle. The river ran almost perfectly straight towards the only break in those hills, though distance made the view between them hard to determine. The hills were mottled with dark clusters of trees, and divided into a patchwork of fields and fences. Shanti knew that there must be villages and farmhouses in those fields, but they were distant enough to be invisible to her. She wondered if the fields were light orchards, and whether these hills would glow at night as the upriver hills and ranges did.

The city began to fall behind them, though there was no clear line where Shanti could say that they had sailed beyond Gorduum's edge. There were just fewer and fewer buildings, each smaller and more humble than the last, and then the Tide's Daughter was moving through broad fields and the river held no other craft than them. A flock of birds swirled like dust in the air then looped towards a copse of trees near the river's edge, settling into the branches and twittering and singing like the chorus at a play. The sky was darkening, and the first stars were beginning to appear through small holes in the clouds.

13

———

A hand touched Shanti's shoulder and she jumped. She spun around from the railing of the Tide's Daughter in panic. She had been lost in her memories and the hand was a sudden intruder. She raised her hands to push away whoever it was, to throw them back from her before she was hurt. Then she realised it was Keema who had come up behind her, with a happy face that was being shocked into a guilty grimace. Shanti sucked in a calm breath and leaned forward into her wife's embrace.

"I've told you not to sneak up on me," she grumbled into Keema's shoulder as she slid her hands around the other woman.

"You have, I'm sorry," admitted Keema. She rubbed Shanti's back softly, soothing her. "You looked so calm and peaceful, I just forgot."

"Hrmmm."

"You reacted far more strongly to a hand on your shoulder than most people," said Felldan from where he was leaning his back on the railings. His eyebrows were raised in surprise. She felt somehow offended by the way he spoke, but she tried to ignore the feeling. When she was in a moment like this, she often felt more upset than she would normally.

"Shanti went through some terrible times a few years ago," said Keema to answer his unspoken question, but then she closed her mouth firmly and squeezed Shanti. Shanti was glad that her spiky haired partner didn't say anything else. She felt exposed when people discussed what had happened then without her input, and the Masked God knew that she didn't want to talk about it herself. The three of them stood at the railings of Tide's Daughter, watching the night fold in overhead, until they all returned to the bunkroom and sleep.

The next morning Shanti came up the stairs to discover that they had already left any sight of land far behind. She walked onto the broad wooden deck and saw grey clouds overhead and dark green waves lifting and falling slowly around them, but there was nothing else in sight as far as she could see. The view was simultaneously horrifying and uplifting. There was absolutely nothing other than water that she could see. It was as though the Tide's Daughter was the only thing that existed in the entire world now. Keema stepped up behind her and put an arm around her hips.

"Wow."

"I know, right?"

"It's... overwhelming." Keema turned in a slow circle to get the full impression of the sight, and then stumbled as the ship shifted sideways. "What was that?"

"Just a lateral swell," answered a sailor who was passing by. She sniffed and stepped closer for a moment. "When a wave is pushing into our side, sometimes the ship gets shoved a little. It's not a problem, thank the Currents." The woman nodded once and then continued on. *There is something strange about the way she described the ocean,* Shanti thought as she considered what the sailor had said. Keema staggered a second time.

"Are you alright Sunshine?" asked Shanti, putting out a hand to steady her partner.

"Yeah yeah, I'm just..." Keema staggered again. "Blinded Eyes!' she swore loudly.

"Keema, please!" said Shanti. She hated it when Keema used such language around her.

"Sorry. I just-" she wavered slightly, lifting a hand to her head. "Would this thing just stay still!"

"Come on, let's get you back to the bunkroom, you can be more comfortable there."

Keema spent the rest of the day lying in the bunkroom while the others explored the ship as best they could. By the middle of the day they all realised that there wasn't a lot to see, and most of the passengers retreated back to their bunks, trying to stay out of the way of the sailors. None of the sailors had complained, or even sent an accusing glance their way, but it was clear that the passengers were making daily chores more difficult.

Keema tried to come out and see the ship with Shanti after the others returned. Shanti offered her elbow to her wife, and Keema frowned but took the support. After one turn around the deck, Keema stumbling and tripping most of the way, Shanti escorted her partner back to the bunkroom.

"This is ridiculous," muttered Keema as she landed on her mattress and gripped the thin blanket as though it were a vine over a cliff's edge. She clung to it as the only way to save herself from falling.

"I agree, you do look ridiculous," joked Shanti as she leaned over to kiss the top of Keema's head.

"Oi," yelped the other woman from her safe perch, swiping a hand at her partner. Shanti smiled but she was beginning to get concerned about the drops of sweat that she could see forming on Keema's forehead.

"Should we see if there's a ship's doctor on board?" asked Felldan from the bunk above. He was peering over the edge in the same way birds in Gorduum peered over roofs at pedestrians eating in the streets.

"Yes, I think that might be a good idea," said Shanti.

The two stepped out of the room and examined the dim space between them and the stairs. The hold was filled with boxes and ropes, nets securing various objects in place, and a few hammocks slung up across the pathways. Sailors moved through the chaos like ferries around the docks of the Naatat.

"Who can we ask?" asked Shanti. "They all look so busy."

"Mmmm," agreed Felldan, scratching the back of his head. "Maybe we just interrupt someone anyway?"

"That seems like it would be quite rude."

"Maybe, but how worried about your lady are you?"

"Are you trying to imply that I don't care about Keema enough?" asked Shanti.

Felldan laughed and pushed her shoulder. "Of course not!" He crossed his arms as he examined the shifting madness. "Maybe we could talk to one of the people in the hammocks?"

They wound through the narrow spaces below the decks and edged closer to a collection of three hammocks. The cloth sides of each were pulled up high, forming a cocoon that hid each sailor within from sight. Felldan reached over and grabbed the edge of the nearest hammock, ready to pull down, but was interrupted by a sailor who raced up from behind them and slapped his hand away. Her dark hair was bound into a bun at the back of her head.

"Oi, don't wake them. They've been in the rigging all night, and we need them rested for this evening as well." The sailor's eyes were narrow and angry.

"I'm sorry!" said Felldan. "We just need some help with one of the other passengers and-"

But the sailor had sped away as soon as she was convinced that they weren't going to wake the sailors in the hammocks. Felldan sighed and turned to Shanti then shrugged.

"We can try above deck instead, I suppose?" she suggested.

They made their way to the stairs and up to the deck. The sails above them creaked and groaned in a wind that had grown stronger since she had last come up. Shanti had to press her hands to her legs to keep her skirts under control and Felldan was pushed along the deck by the wind.

"It's a little more blustery than I might have expected," he said, offering a hand to Shanti to help her keep her feet. She held it gratefully as they approached the structure at the back of the deck. Tozan was standing outside the door, with arms crossed and his usual glare plastered across his face. A gust pushed Shanti as they arrived, and she had to clutch at Felldan to stop from falling over.

"What?" asked Tozan when it became clear that the pair were approaching him.

"We were wondering if there is a doctor on board?" asked Felldan, raising his voice over the wind. Shanti glanced behind them at the sky, worried that a storm was coming. But, although the sky was grey and full of clouds, she didn't think that they looked black and threatening as a storm might. No one above decks acted concerned at all either.

"Why?" came the curt response. Shanti looked back at the mate.

"My wife is looking quite sick. She's having trouble standing too."

Tozan snorted and his lips twitched back towards a grin. "Ten to one she has cobblefeet."

"She has what?" Shanti lifted a hand to her mouth, her eyes widening. A cold fear bubbled inside her. "What is that?"

"It's nothing." Tozan shook his head and turned to the door. "Cobblefeet means she is too used to walking around on settled stones, she has no head for the rhythms of the ocean. Come in." Shanti and Felldan followed him through the door he had been standing in front of. Once they were out of the wind, Shanti felt much steadier. His tone also settled her fear about Keema back down momentarily.

But then Shanti's pulse raced faster in the dark hallway, just as it had the last time she had come to meet with the captain, Zekeka. The small dark space was not the sort of place that she wanted to spend much time. Half-remembered sensations of being trapped kept bubbling to the surface of her mind. She clutched Felldan's arm a little tighter, and he patted the back of her hand.

Tozan knocked on the door to the captain's room and waited until his voice called from inside. "Come in!"

They found the captain bent over his desk in his office, one hand on a pile of papers and keeping them in place as the ship shifted and rolled. The movement was not large enough to send anything flying off his desk, but clearly he didn't want to risk the papers scattering across the floor. He raised his blue eyes from the map spread out in front of him. *Look at them,* thought Shanti. *They shine like my mother's own lights.*

"Yes?"

'One of the passengers seems poorly and these two have come to ask for someone to look her over. I think it's cobblefeet, but defer to you." Shanti was impressed at how deferential Tozan was to the captain, and how he described what was going on without judgement. She would have expected him to be gruff with the other man, and to sneer about Shanti's concerns. *Maybe I was wrong about him,* she thought. *Perhaps that gruff exterior isn't the full measure of the man.*

Zekeka nodded and pursed his lips. "Find Kechak and ask her to take a look."

"She might be busy," suggested Tozan.

"Even so. If this woman is sicker than we suspect,

then the whole ship might be at risk." Zekeka lowered his gaze back to the map and waved them out of the room. As Shanti led Tozan and Felldan back out to the deck, she asked Tozan who Kechak was.

"She's got a few roles onboard, she's proven herself very capable. But what matters for you is that she is the closest thing to a doctor that we have on the Tide's Daughter."

The three of them stood near the door that they had just come through. Above, the clouds were beginning to thin, looking more white than grey, and there were even some small patches of blue peeking through the cover. The wind still blew heavily against them though, and Tozan had to cup his hands around his face and bellow to be heard by the sailors working nearby.

"Where's Kechak?!"

Heads turned and popped up over railings to find the source of the yell. Just as Tozan was lifting his hands to his face again, a pale face appeared from among the sails towards the front of the ship. The face was shockingly light to Shanti, just as the captain's had been, making the distant figure extremely difficult to distinguish from the cream coloured sails. As they began to move around the masts towards Tozan, Shanti was able to see more of the figure. She was short and broad, but clearly very fit, and as she approached, Shanti could see that her hair was like a cluster of tightly wound golden wool, cropped short across her skull.

Shanti could hear the woman muttering something angular as she approached. When no one replied, the woman shook her head and shouted again, louder this time.

"You called?" she said as she drew close.

"Indeed. We need you to come and take a look at one of the passengers."

14

———————

Tozan led the way back below decks and into the bunkroom, followed by Kechak, then Felldan, with Shanti at the rear. She found herself often glancing forward to the woman that Tozan had summoned, captivated by the way her skin was as pink as a cat's nose.

In the bunkroom, Keema was still lying on her mattress with her eyes closed. Shanti moved past the others to take her hand, though it was difficult given how many people were now crowding into the tiny room. Up close she was relieved to see that her wife looked much more settled now that she was lying in bed. Shanti reached over and brushed the back of her fingers across Keema's forehead.

Shanti thought of how her father Neeran would take care of her when she was a small child back in Graama. When she felt ill, he would tuck her into bed and fetch a small ceramic bed warmer from the kitchen. He would have filled it with water boiled on the cast iron stove in the kitchen. He would sit next to her bed, stroking his fingertips through her hair, slowly and rhythmically, while he murmured comforting nothings to his daughter. As she ran her fingers through Keema's hair, Shanti wondered what he was doing right now, whether he was warm and safe, whether her brothers were well. It had been so long since he had comforted her.

"How are you feeling Sunshine?"

"Much better now," murmured Keema, moving a hand to touch Shanti's leg. "But I can't believe that you're still walking around. Don't you feel like the whole boat is trying to knock you over?"

"It's a ship," grumbled Tozan.

Kechak stepped up and placed the back of her hand on Keema's forehead. Then she leaned over and instructed the other woman to open her eyes. After Keema did, Kechak reached down and pulled the other woman's eyes open further, staring into Keema's eyes closely. Shanti found the contrast between Kechak's skin and Keema fascinating, made so clear by the pale hand of the doctor resting on the darker face of her wife. Then Kechak stood up.

"I think Tozan is right, it's a bad case of cobble-feet. That said, let me know how she goes over the next few days. If it gets worse then I may be wrong, but I don't think we are in danger of anything spreading to anyone else on board." The woman's accent was thick and spiky, like the captain's.

"We're going to be at sea for nearly a month, aren't we?" Shanti asked.

Kechak stopped in the doorway and turned back, making no attempt to hide the way she rolled her eyes. "Obviously. Ships can't fly, can they?"

Shanti flinched and frowned. "But then, does that mean that Keema is going to feel this awful the whole time?"

Kechak smirked.

"She might. But honestly, the waves are rough at the moment and the weather should calm. Some people just need more time to get used to it. I'm sure she'll be up above decks with the rest of us before long, should the Wind and Stars share their gifts with her."

The strange pale woman winked at Shanti and then spun out the door. Tozan nodded and left without another word. Shanti sat on the end of Keema's bunk, stroking her partner's hand.

Keema fell asleep eventually, though she still let out quiet moans as the ship shifted in the ocean. Shanti wished that there was something more that she could do for Keema, but she had watched over her and sought the only aid that had been onboard. The Masked God knew that there wasn't much else that she could do.

"How is she?" asked Gudan, who came over to sit on the bunk next to her. The short man still had a wide smile behind his sharp beard, though his eyes were sympathetic.

"Sleeping, so I hope that helps," replied Shanti, stroking Keema's forehead. "But I don't know how she will make it through the rest of the journey."

Gudan tilted his head sympathetically. "How did you two meet?"

"Keema was one of the first people I met in Gorduum," said Shanti with a wide smile. She explained that Keema had been the first taxi driver who had given Shanti a ride when she arrived in Gorduum. Shanti had been so keen to explore the city for herself that she had rushed away from the older couple who were supposed to be chaperoning her. But the city's size had been intimidating, until Keema had caught her with her bright eyes and wide smile.

As Shanti's her first visit to the city had grown more and more dramatic, with rich young men whisking her away to fancy balls, and the shockingly dangerous uncovering of a plot to kill off the lights that made the city famous and wealthy, she had grown closer and closer to the spiky haired taxi driver with the fast mouth.

"You had something to do with the Blight back then?" Gudan's smile faltered and his eyes grew large.

Shanti pressed her mouth closed. That was an area of her life that she preferred would stay undiscussed. The emotions that would swim to the top of her mind could overwhelm her.

"More importantly, Keema and I spent time visiting someone I knew at the University, and she showed me around to some of the places she spent her free time. When I came back to Gorduum, I knew we had to be together."

"Ah, true love," smiled Gudan. His cheeks dimpled as he glanced across the room to his partner Taadin. "We got married quickly too."

"We didn't get married that quickly," Shanti hurried to say. She felt embarrassed at the idea that she would have rushed into such a relationship. She didn't want a stranger to think that she was the sort of person who did not think through the consequences of her actions.

Gudan raised his hands. "No need to explain yourself to me," he said placatingly. "I know what it's like to have everyone watching you, making judgements about your every action." He leaned back on the bed. "We've been together for three years now, but after our wedding, all the comments about it being too soon vanished immediately."

"What do you mean?"

"We got married in Temple in a little town just outside Gorduum, where Taadin's family come from. He was wearing his best suit. You can imagine how good he looks in a fresh shirt and tie, can't you?" They both looked over at the large bald man. He saw them looking and frowned, and then ducked his head lower, blushing.

"That does sound lovely."

"Yes, and the priest was this lovely old man who had known his family forever. There were light bouquets around the temple, and everyone came. It was stunning. I think even those who thought we were rushing into things could admit that we were at least taking it all seriously after that, right!" He laughed and leaned over to nudge Shanti. "And three years later we've proved our point, I'd say! How about you two, how was your wedding?"

Shanti swallowed and nibbled on her lower lip. She didn't want to admit that she and Keema had gone to the town hall to get a marriage licence privately. None of the people in the city that Keema knew were present, and Shanti hadn't even told her family about it, let alone invited them to make the journey from their village of Gramma. She hadn't even asked Dunin, her uncle.

"We just knew that we wanted to be together, and thought that it would be easiest to be married," she said, trying to speak as lightly as possible.

"Oh yes, I see," Gudan nodded.

"Yes. That meant that we were able to find an apartment together quickly, and no one questioned how we support each other." Shanti patted Keema's sleeping shoulder as she spoke, and tapped her foot.

"Of course, very sensible." Gudan sucked in a deep breath and patted his hands on his legs. "I think perhaps I'll just go and see how Taadin is doing. It'd be terrible for more than one person to come down with cobblefeet on this journey."

"Of course."

Shanti sat in silence after Gudan left. He and Taadin left the bunkroom and went for a walk around the Tide's Daughter. She felt as though he had judged her more in his silence than if he had snorted and decried the decisions she and Keema had made.

What would he know about their situation anyway? After Shanti had rushed back to Gorduum she had not taken long in tracking down Keema, and they had instantly developed a very strong relationship. But Shanti was staying with her uncle, and she knew that he wouldn't put up with that for long. Instead of trying to find two places to live, she and Keema had decided that it would be easier to find one space for them both. But if they were to move in together, they would have to be married first.

Shanti recalled the conversation, as they sat next to one another in the Stout Shelter, the pub that Keema and her colleagues enjoyed spending their free time in.

"Maybe we could find a place together?" Keema had suggested, looking up at Shanti with nervous eyes.

"Together?" Shanti's heart had skipped at the

idea. She knew that she would love to live with Keema already, so safe did the other woman make her feel. But there was no way they could move in unmarried. Shanti tried to imagine what her parents would think. Or, worse, what would the people in Graama think? They had only known each other for weeks! "It's so soon. Our reputations would be..." She trailed off.

"I know, I know." Keema sipped at her beer and then cleared her throat carefully. "We could make it official though?"

"What do you mean?"

"You know what I mean." Keema squeezed Shanti's hand.

Shanti gasped. "Are you asking me to marry you?"

Keema shrugged awkwardly and blushed. "I'm sorry, it's not romantic enough, and you don't really know me."

"Yes." Shanti sat straight in her seat and spoke in a strong clear voice. She smiled. "Yes, I would love to marry you." Her heart was ready to explode from the sudden emotion that was building inside her. Her head felt as light as air.

Keema grinned and gasped, struggling to find words. She leaned forward and grabbed Shanti in her arms, before kissing her.

Shanti allowed herself to fall into the sensation, ignoring the small voice that was trying to tell her it was too soon, that it was not a sensible decision. In that moment, all Shanti had felt was the joy that flooded off Keema and filled her.

Keema broke off and leaned back. "We can send letters to your family tomorrow, and-"

"No, let's just go to the town hall tomorrow instead!" Shanti felt a tight ball begin to form in her stomach.

"You don't want to let your family know?" Keema's brow creased.

"Of course! But let's get things sorted out so we can find a home. We'll celebrate later with them!" The ball clenched.

Keema leaned away. Her eyes showed her confusion. "If that's what you want. Shall we send a messenger to your uncle?"

Shanti shook her head. "No, he's so grumpy that he wouldn't be interested anyway. He'll just be glad that I'm out of his hair."

It was simply a matter of speed, Shanti thought to herself in the bunkroom on the Tide's Daughter. *We needed to make things official so that we could find a home quicker. Maybe it meant that we didn't have everyone in attendance that we would have liked. And maybe it meant that we didn't have time to make it into a big celebration. But there was no other way.*

She wished that she had managed to send a letter home, before they had climbed on board the Tide's Daughter. Maybe it would have finally been the right time to tell her family what she had done. She swallowed thickly at the thought that her parents may have been disappointed in her actions. But Keema understood. It was just how things had to be. One day they would do it all again, and then they would have a chance to celebrate with everyone they loved. She slid her fingers through Keema's hair. One day they would be able to celebrate.

15

The couple who had worn their best clothes to travel on the Tide's Daughter, Lorku and Rahit, were delighted to discover that passengers were invited to dine privately with the captain every night. The meal was served in a cabin through one of the other doors in the cramped hallway outside the captain's office. The dining cabin was not large, compared to the rooms that Shanti was used to in Gorduum, but space on board was limited. Every centimetre of the ship that could be used for cargo or stowing equipment generally was, so even this small room with a long table was luxury.

Shanti sat between Felldan and Tozan, and eating was a matter of carefully timing where to put your elbows without banging them into your neighbour's. It was like dancing, each member of the table taking a mouthful in alternating unison.

The first night at the table was a festive affair, with all the passengers enthusiastically telling their tales to one another. Through small diamond shaped glass panels in a broad window that opened onto endless rolling waves and encroaching clouds, they could watch as the sky darkened. Without being able to see the stars above, the cabin soon felt like a cave. It was lit at either end by more of the heavy lanterns, and Shanti asked Tozan why they didn't use lights on board.

"After all," she added after swallowing some richly buttered bread. "Lights are so much clearer than the dim flames trying to make themselves noticeable through all that metal and glass."

"Unfortunately, lights are blindingly expensive," growled Tozan. "You live in Gorduum, and you are used to lights being everywhere."

"I grew up in a small village though, we had far fewer lights there." Shanti didn't like the way Tozan was dismissing her entire experience so simply.

"Indeed, and how many was that? Every other house had one growing outside? Perhaps a few were hanging on posts in the streets. I bet you even had special days where the whole village got dressed up in fancy lights and everyone walked through it all going 'Ooooo' and 'Ahhhh'." He grinned at her, his eyes lit up like a cat that had seen a mouse. Shanti didn't reply. She scooped up a spoonful of red spiced rice and stuck it in her mouth without looking at the mate. He laughed and returned to his own meal.

"Exactly. Lights are expensive, and even though you grew up in a village, it was not a poor one. We run these ships on the lowest costs we can. The more we save on buying lights, and employing gardeners to keep the unseen things alive through months of shifting weather, the more profit there is at the end of the journey."

"It's very common to use lanterns like these on

ships," said Felldan from Shanti's other side. His tone was low. "They are built thick and with a special reserve of water, so that they are unlikely to break and even if they do the water should douse any flame."

"Oh good," said Shanti. "That eases my mind." *They must think I'm worried about the danger of having a flame on a wooden ship. I wish that had occurred to me before, then maybe I wouldn't feel so embarrassed.* Shanti knew that Tozan was right, and she had just become so used to lights that she expected them everywhere she went. But she also knew that such expectations were not really reasonable. She had spent years learning how to tend the fragile light-plants while she grew up in Graama, and she knew how difficult they could be to coax illumination from them, even when conditions were steady and suitable. She looked around the table and felt as though everyone was staring at her, in pity or judgement, looking at her without seeing her intentions and thoughts and feelings. She wished Keema had felt well enough to join them at dinner.

As the journey progressed, these evening meals quickly grew quieter. There was less to talk about, less that had happened in the day, less unknown about one another. Shanti found that the feeling of being unseen was growing in her. Every day she spent most of her time avoiding getting in the way, as though she were no more than a stray cat. She would try to encourage Keema to leave the bunkroom, but on the few occasions that she was successful, the other woman quickly grew unsteady and nauseous. Once or twice Shanti tried to stay with Keema, curling up next to her on the bunks.

But the hours passed so slowly in the dim cabin, with Keema in no condition to speak, that Shanti would soon make excuses and head out to the decks. *Better to be ignored in the fresh air than effectively alone in the cramped cabin,* she reasoned.

Shanti tried to find things to do on board the ship that wouldn't get her in the way of the sailors who would appear in every shadowed corner of the ship. This was how she discovered that Felldan made a good companion. He knew a lot about the running of a ship, and they would sit together in the lee of a railing while he would explain why the sailors were scurrying about in the ropes and sails, or what a particular gust of wind meant.

"You must have done a lot of travelling," said Shanti after Felldan explained a passing sailor's comment. Felldan shrugged and looked down.

"I've been around boats a lot of my life," he admitted. "My father was a ferryman on the Naatat, so I spent a lot of time at the river."

"Were you ever a sailor?"

"No." He sighed. "I tried to get onto a few ships' crews, but they always said they didn't need me."

"What do you do now?"

"I find my way," he smiled, but she could not get any more details out of him.

Instead, he offered to help teach her some of the language that was spoken in the city that they were travelling to. Shanti clapped her hands at the suggestion and asked if he would teach her to understand the commands that the sailors called out to one another from around the boat.

Felldan coughed. "Uh, no, I don't think that's a good idea."

"Why not?" Shanti asked as one of the calls chattered overhead.

"For example, they just asked someone to tie a certain rope."

"What's wrong with that?"

"They added some colourful descriptions of the person they were talking to, the rope they were talking about, and also the type of knot that they think it should be."

"What sort of colourful descriptions?"

"Um. Put it this way. Imagine the worst words you can think of."

Shanti blushed and blinked. "I don't-"

"No, of course you don't know any words like that, a woman like you." Felldan winked.

"So, how much of what they just said was…?" Shanti let the question trail off.

"Basically everything except 'Tie' and 'Rope'," he answered.

Shanti put a hand over her mouth.

After a week at sea, Shanti was feeling more and more alone. Despite filling much of her days onboard with Felldan, practising the language of Chechezuk and learning what he could teach her about sailing, there were still long hours of time where she had nothing to do. Early in the journey Shanti tried to catch a glimpse of the short-haired broad woman, Kechak. She felt sure that there was a spark in that woman that would be worth the time to find out more about.

But somehow the ship hid its workers in a way that Shanti could not understand. She saw Kechak moving past the bow of the ship while she and Felldan were practising at the base of the main mast, but by the time she was able to excuse herself the woman was gone. Each evening, as the shifts changed and sailors unrolled themselves from their hammocks below deck to swap places with the weary eyed men and women coming down, Shanti looked for Kechak. Every evening she could not spot her.

Then one day, as the sun hung directly over-head, behind a faint mist of thinly drawn clouds, Kechak came to Shanti while she was leaning on the railing and looking out over the mottled ocean.

"How is your friend?" said the woman in her clipped accent.

"What?" said Shanti, caught by surprise. She swallowed thickly as Kechak's eyes pierced into her own. "Oh, Keema? She is still very unwell." Keema still found it impossible to leave her bunk, and spent most of her days drowsing.

"That is a shame. Perhaps she should not have come on a ship, if she cannot survive it." Kechak held out her left hand and made a small gesture with her fingers, tucking two in by her palm and then rolling her wrist. Shanti was surprised to hear the woman speak so bluntly.

"You think she will die?" she gasped.

Kechak blinked and then laughed. "No! But she is so sick! Maybe it would be better if she had not come." Her eyes looked wide and bright.

Shanti frowned. "I thought it would be good for her to come. I've always wanted to see new places."

"Has she wanted this?" asked Kechak."Or is it you who has wanted it?" She raised an eyebrow and smirked. Then she patted Shanti on the shoulder and walked away, to complete some task that Shanti would never understand. Shanti watched her go, watched the way she walked so firmly on the gently swaying deck, the way her strong arms caught hold of a rope as she pulled herself up and onto a railing. A shiver passed across Shanti's skin..

Shanti shook her head and tried to put Kechak out of her mind. She moved to her accustomed position near the front of the ship, watching the life of a sailing vessel happen around her, but separated from it. For a week the sky had been full of dark clouds, pressing low. So low that she was sure that their soft yet threatening presence would reach down far enough that the mast of the Tide's Daughter would pierce them, and allow whatever it was that weighed them down to tumble out. She had nightmares that the clouds were giant sacks of rocks and stones that would rain down like an avalanche upon them, smashing the ship and sending the entire vessel, crew, and passengers sinking to the bottom.

I can't keep on like this, she realised while wrapping her arms around herself to try and stay warm in the damp wind that whistled across the deck. *I know what I'm missing.* She had an idea of what might help.

She went to speak with Tozan about the idea, to find out whether or not he would allow it, and whether there were any supplies on board that she would be able to use to bring it to fruition. Unsurprisingly he scowled at her in response, but then he nodded and said that he would find space for her. He took her into the same cabin that they used for their dinners, and showed her a small cabinet in the corner of the room, which he unlocked with a key from a large iron ring that was attached to his belt.

"I'll unlock it when you want to get in and lock it again after," he growled at her, but he motioned her forward. Inside the cabinet were a few books, bound in thick hard leather and board. She saw what she needed and drew it out, and then Tozan shut and locked the cabinet again. "You can have it for the afternoon, so that you're prepared, but mind you take extra care of it. Any damage, and we'll charge you."

"Of course," smiled Shanti and then she hurried below decks to find a quiet spot out of the weather where she could begin reading.

At first she headed towards the bunkroom, but then she slowed and stopped. She would feel self-conscious reading in front of the passengers still inside. Gudan and Taadin spent a lot of their time in the cabin, playing all sorts of dice games, and she knew that they would have a lot of questions for her. Instead, she looked around the cramped storage space until she found a spot between two large crates and beneath one of the heavy lanterns. She wedged herself into the narrow gap and propped the book open in front of her, ready to read. She was surprised at just how comfortable it felt to be held by the firm wood on all sides.

And now, she told herself, *I need to find a good reading for tonight.*

16

———

Tozan kept his word and made sure that the crew cleared a space for Shanti near the rear of the boat as night began to fall. After she had decided on the reading that she would use, she spoke to the other passengers, explaining her plan to them all. She mentioned it to some of the sailors who had asked her why she was stuck between crates with a book, and hoped that word would spread among the crew. She explained her plan to Keema, though unfortunately the slim woman was not able to pull herself upright long enough to make the journey out onto the deck. But the idea of all those faces, people that she did not know, watching her while she attempted to do something she had never tried before was making her more and more nervous as the moment approached. So when she found that Felldan, Lorku, Rahit and two sailors she didn't know were the whole of her audience, she was quietly pleased.

"Good evening," Shanti began. "I am so glad that you decided to join us here. I was worried that no one would show up and that I would be left standing here by myself!" She chuckled and was relieved to see that her small audience smiled at the joke.

"I have felt cut loose from the rest of the world while we are out here in the ocean," she began, gesturing with one arm at the endless rippling water that stretched from horizon to horizon around them. "I have felt as though we are so far away from everything that I knew in my life, that I couldn't understand how to fit in. I have felt as though that whole world might vanish if I don't purposely maintain my memories of it. I'm not sure if that is something that you recognise as well?"

She paused, to check if the other five agreed. Lorku nodded slightly, but the sailors just glanced at one another. Shanti took a deep breath. Even as she was speaking to them, she was realising that these feelings were caused by more than just her time at sea. These were feelings that had begun to grow while she lived in Gorduum as well. She was so far from her home, so disconnected from the memories that she had made. What could she do to regain what she had lost?

"In any case," she continued, straightening her shoulders. "I thought that a good way to maintain my connections, to feel seen again, would be to hold a reading from the Writ of the Masked God. I hope that you are here because you want to be seen as well." This drew small nods from the sailors, which encouraged Shanti. "May the Masked God watch over you all. I chose this story to begin with because it is short, and simple, and I think it shares an important message for us all to remember."

She pulled the Writ that she had borrowed from

Tozan out from under her arm and opened it to the passage she had marked with a scrap of cloth. She coughed to clear her throat, and held up the heavy book in both hands, rotating on her feet slightly to catch the last rays of light from the sun so that she could see the words on the worn out pages. The copy that had been kept safely in the private cabin was large and clearly expensive. Shanti felt like a priest as she ran her fingers along the thin pages, ready to read aloud.

The story that Shanti had chosen was one of the most famous stories of the Masked God. It told of an orphanage run by a kind woman and her husband. The couple took in children and made sure that they grew up well cared for. But then the woman's husband died, and she began to grow bitter at her situation, no longer caring for the children of the orphanage. She blamed them for eating all her food, and taking up all her time.

"The children grew hungry," she read aloud, "and were not allowed out of the orphanage. They became frightened of the woman, and they grew lonely with only one another for company.

A storm crashed against the orphanage one evening; screeching winds and walls of rain blasted past the orphanage. A passerby banged on the door and called desperately for a dry warm bed. The old woman was sour but she knew that if she treated the passerby poorly then the stranger might go on to tell others, perhaps the locals who lived nearby, and the old woman would be shunned in the village. And so the old woman put the passerby into a small but comfortable room.

The orphans were instructed to remain out of

sight, and to be quiet so that the passerby would not know that they were there. Tired and fearful, the orphans did their best to obey. But the youngest one, hungry and thirsty, pulled open the door. The sound of the hinges creaking alerted the stranger and she came down the hall to investigate. She immediately discovered the orphans.

'What is this?' she asked when the old woman came rushing down the hall as well.

'These are my curse,' replied the old woman with twisted lips. 'I said that I would take care of these wretches many years ago, but since my husband died they have eaten all my food and they make a mess that I spent all my days cleaning. They are the least grateful beings in this good land.' "

Shanti paused the story here. She could feel herself on the edge of tears. The story of the orphans was one of the first stories that children were told about the Masked God. Every time she heard it in Temple she was reminded of the feeling that had burrowed deep into her stomach when she first listened to her father telling it. She had been such a small child, and hearing about the orphans trapped in their room without food or water had terrified her. She had wondered what it might be like to be trapped somewhere like that with her brothers, especially her younger brother Fellbin, who had been so tiny then. He had been barely more than a baby.

Even now, standing on deck with this group of tough sailors and strangers, Shanti felt tears prick at the corners of her eyes. She sniffed and cleared her throat, and then continued the reading.

She read out that the passerby had been grateful to the old woman for being taken into her home in such awful weather, and had no reason to doubt the woman's story. These children were wild-eyed and bedraggled, and it was easy to believe that they would cause mischief and chaos if left to wander through the house.

"But," said Shanti, a blossom of light unfurling in her heart as she read the words aloud. "The Masked God was watching all this through the stranger's eyes which had begun to glow like molten gold, like the dawning sun reflecting off the still waters of a lake, bright and clean and pure. The old woman had recoiled from that light, and then the Masked God's voice spoke from the stranger's throat, in tones like the tolling of a bell.

'Be ashamed old woman,' the Masked God said. 'I have seen how you treat those who are vulnerable to you, and it is unworthy.' The light from her eyes grew until neither the old woman nor the children could make out the figure of the stranger through the halo that spread around her. The light moved through the house, tearing locks off doors and flinging open each window. Outside, the rolling black storm clouds retreated in a widening circle of clear night sky, covered in stars. 'It is the duty of all of us to watch one another, to provide for one another when we need help. Those who will not keep eyes on their neighbours for me, will find they have no neighbours at all.'

There was a flash and then the orphans were standing alone in the house. The stranger had gone, as had the old woman. The kitchen cupboards were full of food and skins containing wonderful things to drink, and the orphans held a feast in celebration of their new-found freedom. And as they grew up, watching out for one another and helping one another, they became favourite faces in the village and they were watched from above each night by the hundred starry eyes of the Masked God."

Shanti closed the Writ and bowed her head, letting the feelings that had bundled up in her chest and throat dissipate into the cool air. Now the night had completed its take over of the sky, and when the small congregation looked up they could see glimpses of stars through the clouds.

"Good timing," murmured one of the sailors.

The other sniffed and nodded and then sighed. "Been a long time since I've heard from the Writ." she said.

"Would anyone like to say anything else?" offered Shanti. She knew that this small meeting on the deck of a ship wasn't like really attending Temple, but following the same process as Temple made her feel more connected to the world that she was used to back on land.

The sailors shook their heads. Lorku lifted a hand up and then stepped forward to stand near Shanti and turned to face the others.

"I'm sure you've all heard the story of the orphans before as well. That story is especially important to me, because I was actually an orphan while I was young."

Shanti pressed a hand to her stomach. *Oh dear, was this too much for her? I hope that I haven't sparked bad memories for her.*

"I remember hearing this story while I lived in an orphanage, and it gave me hope. Hope that someone was watching me, even when I felt as though no-one in the world noticed me." She smiled. "It was a good orphanage, they tried to be kind to us, but it is difficult to cope with that many youngsters." She turned to Shanti. "Thank you for that reading, I hope it reminds us all to keep eyes on each other, and to help where we can."

The sailors nodded again, and Rahit clapped for his wife, though he soon looked around and stopped when he realised that he was the only one doing so. He coughed.

"Thank you all for coming. It really makes me feel like we are all in this together. I am hoping that the mate and captain will allow me to do more readings at least once a week until we reach our destination. I hope to see you again for those."

After the others moved away, Felldan was still waiting. He stepped closer to Shanti.

"That was a very good reading," he told her. "Your voice was clear and you were easy to listen to."

"Thank you," said Shanti, blushing a little.

"I mean it!" he grinned. "I've heard priests who couldn't read a simple passage that nicely, and it's always torture."

"I just thought it was a good place to begin." Shanti squeezed the heavy cover of the Writ in both hands and tucked it against her hip. "I have to take this back to Tozan now."

"I'll accompany you," said Felldan.

They walked without speaking over to the doorway to the internal rooms at the back of the ship. Tozan was sitting on a stool in the hallway, the first time Shanti had seen the gruff old man at anything approaching a relaxed condition. He blinked and raised his head as the two approached.

"Ah yes. Thank you young lady," he said, taking

the copy of the Writ from Shanti and standing up. He rolled his shoulders and Shanti could hear the bones cracking and creaking. He groaned. "I've been sitting here too long. I think this old hand needs to get to bed." He set off to return the Writ to its cabinet and waved Felldan and Shanti back out the door. "Good night you two."

Shanti shivered as she walked back towards the stairs and the dark warmth of the bunk room. Sailors moved through the rigging as she listened to sails slapping and wood creaking around her.

"Are you alright? Would you like my coat?" asked Felldan.

"No, thank you, I'll be okay. We're nearly there," Shanti reassured him.

Once they were back in the bunkroom and Shanti was settling on to her mattress, she reached out for Keema as soon as she could. Her hand patted on the soft mattress and burrowed through the sheets until she ran into a hard rock covered with fluff. *There she is,* laughed Shanti to herself as she ran her fingers through her wife's hair, recognising the swirls of it as she did. She heard Keema's breathing and then felt the other woman's hand reach up and take her own. Hand in hand, lying in the darkness among strangers, Shanti joined Keema in sleep.

17

───────

Shanti didn't know whether or not to be pleased by the uneventful journey of the Tide's Daughter across the sea. While the quiet days meant that her wife grew no iller than she was in that first week, and the gentle movement of the ocean made Shanti feel that she would reach their destination safely, it also left her alone with her own thoughts for a long time.

After the poor weather of the first days, the sky cleared somewhat, and the rising swell of waves rolling past the ship began to calm and still. She even saw gigantic creatures swimming at a distance from the ship, pausing at the rail to point them out to Felldan. A passing sailor said that the whales were wary of ships because some people hunted them, but he thought they were just as impressive as the passengers did.

Kechak remained difficult to track down. Shanti tried to follow the woman more than once, but every time the short-haired woman seemed to vanish among the ropes and sails and boxes that filled the ship. Shanti wanted to find out more about what life as a sailor was like, and the brief conversations she did manage with Kechak made her feel re-energised, despite their brevity.

Shanti continued her readings once a week, as much to give herself something else to think about as for the enlightenment of the others onboard. She was pleased to find more sailors coming by to listen to her each evening. She spent much of her time between these events sitting in the passenger bunkroom reading through the Writ and looking for something that she thought would appeal to the crew, something that might impart an important message to them. Keema would lie with her head in Shanti's lap, and Shanti would read while running her fingers through Keema's hair and stroking her ears. Keema never made it above deck to one of the readings, but she would listen as Shanti practised the reading in a whisper to her, and offer her thoughts and encouragement with eyes closed.

The sailors began to share their ideas after each reading, and Shanti was thrilled at the discussion. They spoke about how they supported each other on the ship, and who was responsible for each other in the case of danger. Shanti tried to contribute her own thoughts on the matter, but found that the sailors tended to nod politely and then continue their own discussion. Some of them spoke of the way the winds watched them, or the currents sped their passage. Shanti found this a little odd, but she supported everyone's contribution. She hoped that she was providing Eyes for the Masked God amongst the crew.

Felldan's lessons in the language of Chechezuk continued, and Shanti tried to practise her new grasp of the words with the sailors after the readings. Sometimes they laughed at her simple attempts, but she was proud of her progress by the time they neared the end of their voyage. No one was willing to translate the calls between the sailors still, and their curses remained completely opaque. However, she did start to hear other words that were spoken often while climbing high amongst the sails, or pulling ropes to tie along the railings. She was surprised to see the sailors making shapes from their fingers when they spoke, even as they tried to hold the ropes secure.

"Wind carry this line."

"Fibres bind."

"What are they saying?" she asked Felldan one afternoon as they were walking across the deck towards the dining cabin.

He patted her hand where it rested on his elbow.

"They are asking for help from the spirits that they believe guide the ship."

Shanti found the idea hard to believe. What spirits were there here? How could these people tell? She looked around and saw a sailor standing near the ship's rail, his hand outstretched against the evening sky. He was squinting at his own fingers.

"Stars bring us home," she heard him murmur before Felldan pulled open the door for her.

On the second to last night at sea Tozan joined the reading. They were due to arrive in Chechezuk in little more than a day, and Shanti had chosen a reading that was about celebration and supporting others in their achievements, as the Masked God would want. Tozan stood at the back of the crowd, and Shanti wasn't sure if the crew saw him there, leaning on a railing with his arms crossed. His usual scowl was in place on his weathered face, but she saw him nod once or twice as she was reading.

As had become routine, the men and women who had come to listen to Shanti's reading began to discuss the ideas that had been raised by the story she chose. One voice quickly elbowed its way to the centre of the discussion.

"Why are we even listening to these stories though?" it asked. "We are in the waters of Ocean, pulled by Tide and pushed by Wind. When we exist as part of the woven fabric of the world, does some god in a mask matter?"

Shanti was taken aback, and tried to spot who had spoken so harshly about the Masked God.

"The Masked God only asks that we look out for one another," she said as she looked around. "I don't think that is so bad is it?"

Some of the sailors shook their heads, and then a figure from near the back moved forward. Now Shanti could see who had complained, and it surprised her. The pale woman with short tight curls of yellow hair, and large blue eyes. Kechak, who had unceremoniously declared that Keema would remain bedridden for the voyage.

Kechak crossed her arms. "Sure, no harm to it. But we have our own ways of doing things, we are part of the fabric together, bound together." She held out her hands with palms out and her fingers interlaced. "I think that has kept us well enough in Chechezuk and we don't need your God telling us what to do."

Shanti felt a strange conflict in her heart. As she watched the short broad woman, she wished that

Kechak would understand why the Masked God was so important to her. She wanted to reach out and place her hands on Kechak's strong shoulders and lean close to explain the Writ to her. She felt as though she would fall into the woman's eyes as they found a way to understand each other.

So it hurt that Kechak was dismissing the Masked God out of hand, so easily discarding something that Shanti felt so strongly about. Shanti wished she knew why this outburst affected her so much more than the sailors who had simply chosen not to attend. Why would Kechak have come to this reading, if she felt this way?

Kechak turned to leave, and Shanti was saddened to see some of the other sailors followed her lead. She also saw Tozan shift back into the shadows, as though he did not want to be singled out as Kechak led her fellows away over the deck. *Why doesn't he say anything,* she wondered. *Either to rebuke Kechak for her anger, or to agree with what she says about the spirits of Chechezuk? Instead he stays silent and hidden.*

The conversation was awkward after Kechak left, and Shanti wrapped it up quickly, letting everyone go back to their beds.

"What do you think that was about?" she asked Felldan as they headed back to the bunkroom.

"What do you mean? I think Kechak has her own beliefs, and that's all."

"No, I understood that, even if I didn't understand her being so rude. I meant, Tozan. He was just watching them all, and he didn't want to be noticed."

"Do you think so?" Felldan grunted as he considered the point. "Maybe so." The tall man sniffed and his lips twisted. He turned to glance back at the stairs they had just descended. "Maybe he's never really heard of the Masked God?"

"It's his copy of the Writ that we are using," said Shanti. She wished she knew what was going on with the mate, and Felldan looked pensive.

The next day Shanti spent all her time at the front of the ship, with the wind whipping past her. It pulled at her braid, untangling loose hairs that began to dance around her nose and lips, tickling her and making her flinch. She had to constantly raise her hands to try and pull them back into place.

The sea spread like a mottled grey blanket all around the Tide's Daughter, mostly smooth but unsettled. Seagulls drifted high above the boat, little more than specks in the sky, but occasionally diving low enough that she could see their white wings spread wide to catch the wind. Their croaking calls whispered down to the ship from the heights.

The spray that kicked up from the prow of the ship spattered up to her face, droplets carrying like mist and then falling again. Now that she had grown used to the wet air and the strong winds, Shanti enjoyed standing out on the deck, letting the weather of the ocean push around her. It made her feel small and surrounded by something large and powerful, and yet in that vulnerable space there was a sense of freedom. The ocean was mighty and huge and if it turned on her then she would not last long. That was clear. But it was impersonal, it was not malevolent.

If something did go wrong, if a storm ransacked the ship, then she took comfort knowing that it would have stormed for anyone and everyone would be affected equally. When she thought of the dangers she had faced on her arrival in Gorduum, she felt differently. Those dangers had come from people, from individuals who were seeking out people who they could hurt. She had been hurt, and others had been hurt worse, and that was difficult to cope with. Why had she passed through those storms when others hadn't? The wind drove against her face and she felt her eyes watering.

"Land!" came the cry from high in the masts. Shanti opened her eyes wider, staring to the horizon, trying to find a glimpse of what they had seen. But there was nothing to see yet.

Felldan walked up to the railing next to her.

"I feel like you've been waiting for this moment pretty much since we left," he laughed.

"I love arriving somewhere new," said Shanti. "I love seeing something I have never seen before, and knowing that it is a whole world, where people have lived their whole lives. Could there be anything more amazing?"

"I suppose not," he smiled at her.

They kept their eyes pinned to the horizon.

"There!" yelped Shanti, thrusting out an arm. A smudge of deeper grey was beginning to appear slightly to the right.

"Where is it?" asked Felldan. He leaned over to her, near resting his head on her shoulder. He tried to look along her arm to see what she was pointing at, and she leaned a little closer, adjusting her arm to try and compensate for his eyeline.

"Can you see it? It's just a tiny smear right now." Even as she spoke they could see the dark shape was growing in the distance. His head was so close to hers. She felt her breath catch in her throat.

"No, I don't... Wait, yes!" Felldan lifted his head away and turned to Shanti. He reached out and took her shoulders in both hands. "We're here! How do you feel?" His smile was broad and filled Shanti with warmth.

"We're not here yet, " she smiled in return. Then she let her lips spread into a grin and she bounced up and down with her hands on the railing. "But it's pretty exciting all the same!"

Over the next few hours the dark smudge grew larger and larger, extending over the horizon into a rough lump of shadow. Clouds were melting away in the sky overhead and Shanti could see the pale blue of midday beginning to shine down on the land in the distance. She could see that it rose up in a short jagged peak and then sank bank toward the ocean again. She frowned.

"It seems smaller than I expected," she murmured, turning a questioning glance to Felldan. He smiled.

"It's just one island. Chechezuk has a lot of islands."

It was true. As the Tide's Daughter continued closer, Shanti saw more islands appearing over the horizon or beginning to peek around from behind the ones she saw at first. They sailed by the first island, the one she had seen earliest, and Shanti stared at it in wonder. The island looked so small in the distance, but by the time they sailed by she realised that the rocky peak was at least three times taller than the ship at its highest point.

The island was shaped into a rough cone, as

though some mighty hands had gathered up huge jagged rocks and let them tumble into a pile. Sharp outcrops jutted out from in between the plants that grew over the island, rocks that were broad and flat and ragged at the end, like broken planks of wood. The plants were difficult to get a good view of from this distance, but their leaves seemed wide and deep green. Small shapes flitted from one tree to another, looking to Shanti like swarms of gnats. She wondered how big the birds would really be if she got a chance to come close to them.

"I have to get Keema," Shanti declared.

"But what if you miss something?" Felldan objected, his hand still on her shoulder.

"She will miss all of it otherwise," she replied before racing back to the stairs as fast as she could. She didn't want to miss any more of the islands than she had to, but she couldn't imagine creating this memory without Keema at her side.

18

In the bunkroom Keema was asleep, but Shanti thumped down onto the mattress beside her and began shaking her by the shoulder. The sharp faced woman stirred and groaned as she rubbed at her eyes. They were sunken and darker than usual. Shanti wished Keema had not suffered so much during the long voyage.

"What?" asked Keema in a rough voice. She had to pause and cough to clear her throat immediately.

"We are nearly there. There are islands all around us, and it is beautiful! You have to come and see."

Keema grumbled but she swung her legs out and put an arm around Shanti's shoulder. Together the two women moved to their feet. Shanti gasped as she took Keema's weight. She had to hold on tight so that the other woman wouldn't topple over straight away. It felt as though Keema was completely unable to support any of her own weight, and was leaning fully on Shanti.

"Are you alright?" she asked.

"No." Keema replied curtly. She clutched onto

Shanti's shoulder and took in a deep breath. "But I think I'm better than I have been for a while. Come on, let's see these islands that you're so excited about." Together they began to stagger out to the stairs.

Back on deck, Felldan was waiting by the top of the stairs. He held out a hand to help Keema up the last few steps and then gestured beyond himself and over the railings.

"Welcome to Chechezuk," he said, his smile broad and bright.

The Tide's Daughter had turned into the channels between the islands and they were surrounded on all sides now by imposing piles of stone and green leaves. The water between the islands was calmer here, the swelling bulk of the ocean broken apart into many smaller ripples. Waves lapped at the rocky shores of the islands, and large brown creatures reclined on the grey rocks, their dog-like faces turning to watch the ship as it passed by. Shanti put both hands to her lips and tried not to squeal.

"Look at them! What are they?"

She dashed to the railing and turned to see if Felldan was able to tell her more. He was still standing by the stairs, with one arm around Keema's shoulder and one arm in front of her, which she was clutching.

"Oh goodness, I'm so sorry," exclaimed Shanti and she rushed back to help bring Keema over to the railing as well. "I was just so excited," she tried to explain. Keema scowled at her, a sight that was all the more imposing given her sweaty face and blood-shot eyes. "I'm sorry," she said again.

Once they were all leaning on the railings,

Shanti watched the creatures that she had seen before. They were nearly as big as a person, and looked like dogs, but they had heavy fins like fish. As Shanti was watching, some of them wriggled back and forward across the rocks and then dove off into the water, slicing into the blue liquid with only the smallest splash. The water was so clear that Shanti could watch the dark silhouettes of the creatures speeding along, spinning and spiralling around one another, diving completely beneath the ship and out of sight.

"They're incredible."

"Yes. To answer your earlier question, these are seals."

The sight of the odd animals darting through the water, weaving around one another and the ship, reminded Shanti of her youngest brother Fellbin. If there was an animal that embodied the way he would look straight at you with his large dark eyes, full of sincerity and mischief, just before diving off the edge into trouble, it was these seals. She watched them bouncing amongst the waves and thought of Fellbin ducking and hiding through the low stone walls of their village. He was always looking for something that he thought was fun, and somehow his fun always involved annoying the other inhabitants of Graama.

Shanti wondered what trouble he had been getting into since she was gone. So much of her life in Graama had been taken up by trying to soothe egos and make sure that Fellbin didn't leave any permanent damage to his reputation amongst their fellow villagers. But she hadn't been home to find out how he was doing recently.

They watched the creatures in silence, the only sounds the clap of the heavy sails and the creaking ropes that stretched across the boat behind them. Gentle slaps of waves striking the hull of the ship echoed up to them also.

Shanti slowly allowed herself to look away from the seals and to examine the new islands that they were passing. Most were smaller than the first she had seen, but many of the islands in these narrow passages rose up in sheer cliffs from the surface of the water. Their tops were covered in trees that curled over the edges and dangled towards the waves below. More birds were visible now, in many colours.

"They are so bright," she breathed.

"Yes. There are all sorts of birds in the jungles around Chechezuk."

Yellow and red birds spun from island to island overhead, and seagulls hovered on the air above them all. Some other birds that looked like black seagulls with long thin necks dove from the air into the water, reappearing moments later with thin silver fish clutched in their beaks.

"What do you think Keema?" asked Shanti, looking over at her wife. Keema had both arms crossed on the wooden railing and was lying her chin on them with her eyes half closed. *At least she isn't throwing up,* thought Shanti.

"It is all very colourful and beautiful," murmured Keema. "I wish I was feeling well enough to take it in." She swallowed slowly and licked her lips. "It's like riding my cart through the streets of Gorduum, but totally different." She smiled weakly.

"I know what you mean," said Shanti. And she

did. The islands rose around the ship like buildings lining the streets in their city, and the water beneath the ship was the cobbles that they rode on. Instead of the bustling life of the city, made of people rushing about their errands, here the birds and seals were the commotion. She moved closer to Keema and put her arm around the thin woman's waist. Keema leaned closer to Shanti as the ship continued between the many islands.

"And here is Chechezuk the city," said Felldan, standing at the railing of the Tide's Daughter. The tall man had a note of pride in his voice, as though he had built the city himself and was keen for Shanti and Keema to see how well he did.

The city revealed itself from behind a cliff of pale rock as the Tide's Daughter turned past a head-land, accompanied by the sound of creaking wood and calls from the sailors behind the trio. Tozan's voice rang out, bellowing instructions. Shanti stood taller, as though she could see more of the city if she only rose to the tips of her toes.

She was impressed at the sight, but also slightly confused. The city was shorter than she had ex-pected. The buildings were generally a storey high, although she could see one or two structures that reached a second level. They were all built of dark wood, and even with the distance still left for the ship to travel, she could see the ends of logs poking out from some of the walls. She couldn't see any people though, which was odd. The buildings clus-tered right down to the edge of the estuary, and she couldn't make out any sand or mud lining the bank.

"It is wonderful to see, " she said. "But..."

'But? What but?" asked Felldan.

"It's lower than I thought it would be." Shanti watched the city approach them. The rocky islands that they had passed through were less numerous here, and there was a wide bay full of waves that rolled in to the edge of the city.

"Where is the river?" she asked.

"What river?" asked Felldan.

"We are travelling by boat. I assumed that would mean that there must be a river for us to sail into the city?"

"Oh, like there is in Gorduum!" Felldan nodded and rubbed his chin. "Yes, I see why you might expect that. In Chechezuk, there is no river." He grinned. "Or maybe we could say that the city is all river?"

Shanti looked back at the buildings. They were much closer now. The ship was heading towards the solid walls at a much faster speed than she had expected. She could see that the buildings clustered down to the water's edge and there were no docks or wharfs extending from them.

"Then, where is this ship going?" Shanti gripped the railing a little tighter as she spoke.

Felldan chuckled. "I'm just teasing you. There is a river, but it is much further inland. It barely resembles the sort of rivers that you would think of from Gaawalt, I am sure! But the delta is full of marshy land and small offshoots of that main river. The city is built on that."

"Oh." Shanti paused and looked down the bay. The low wooden buildings stretched to the horizon, following the water's edge. "But then where is this ship going?"

"There will be a poler soon enough."

As Felldan had said, a small boat was rowing out to the Tide's Daughter within minutes. It drew alongside the large ship and a rope ladder was unfurled to allow someone on the small boat to climb aboard. They saluted Tozan when they reached the top and Shanti saw that the newcomer had long yellow hair pulled into a bun on the back of her head, and the same pale skin that she had seen in many of the ship's crew, such as the captain and Kechak.

Tozan saluted the newcomer and led her off to speak with the captain at the back of the ship. Shanti watched their conversation until Zekeka nodded and then began calling out instructions, which were relayed via the bellowing voice of Tozan. Sailors began adjusting the ropes and sails above them and the ship lurched to one side. Keema groaned.

"Just when I thought it was safe," she grumbled.

The Tide's Daughter began to adjust its course, heading further left than it had originally been. Shanti watched the buildings of Chechezuk get closer and closer and began to worry that the vessel was going to ram into them. Her fingers were tightening on the rail.

Suddenly her perspective shifted, and what had looked like a small alley between one building and its neighbour twisted and resolved to reveal a narrow passage of water between the buildings.

"It really is like a street," Shanti gasped. She remembered what her friend Darsat from the University in Gorduum had told her about the canals, the streets of water that were used to travel through this city. She had never pictured that they would be large enough to accommodate this entire ship!

"Yup!" replied Felldan cheerfully. "I think you are going to be quite enthralled with this city."

Other small boats scudded through the waves near the buildings, like a swarm of insects walking across the surface of a pond. They slipped backwards and forwards criss-crossing the bay, and now Shanti could make out small figures crouching inside each one. As they sailed closer to the watery street, Shanti tried to get a closer view of the city within.

It looked very much like the view she already had of the city, just long walls of wooden buildings reaching up from the water. There were no paths covered in pedestrians, nor riverbanks or docks with boats tied up. Shanti noticed some small outcrops that the smaller boats were heading to and from. She assumed that these must be how the casual water-goers got on and off their boats, but it was strange to not see the people of the city filling the space between the buildings.

The Tide's Daughter turned into the passage and began drifting along it. Below the railing, small boats moved to the side of the water, out of the way. Shanti looked down on one boat and saw a woman in a broad hat, shaped like a cone woven out of thin leaves. She was standing at the back of the boat and leaning on a pole that stabbed into the water. The woman looked up at Shanti with a scowl. *What did I do?* Shanti wondered.

Shanti watched the buildings that lined the passage and grew worried.

"Won't the ship scrape into them?" she asked.

The wooden planks and logs that made up the buildings alongside the passage were so close that she could reach over and pluck a splinter from their surface. In her mind she could just imagine the destruction that such an accident would bring, and it soured her stomach.

"It shouldn't," said Felldan.

Keema stood up, leaning away from the shockingly close building. Her face was clearer now that they were so far from the rolling open ocean.

"Are you feeling better now that we're in a city?" Shanti asked her.

"Are you sure this counts?" chuckled Keema as she rubbed a hand over her forehead. She raised her eyebrows at the rough wooden walls that they were passing, clearly unimpressed in comparison to the solid stone and brick of the buildings in Gorduum.

19

Shanti stepped closer to Keema, reaching out to take her hand. Keema squeezed Shanti's fingers and slipped her other arm around Shanti's waist. Shanti leaned into her partner. It felt good to be close to her again, but standing up now instead of slumped along a bunk bed.

A pale bridge filled the space above the water ahead of them. The bridge was supported by two tall blocky towers, one on either side of the water. They rose up taller than many of the buildings that Shanti could remember in Gorduum even, made of dark wood and with thick ropes extending down to hold the structures in place. The bridge itself looked strangely geometric between the towers. It consisted of a gently sloped section on either end, and then each side turned at a corner into a level section that connected them. As they drew closer, Shanti was able to see that the bridge was decorated with carvings that were full of bulging curving shapes. They twisted and rolled over one another like clouds, or a school of fish.

"What is that made of?" Shanti asked.

"Wood," said Felldan. "The whole city is made of wood. Stone and brick would get too heavy and sink into the estuary."

"Wood? But look at it! It curves so smoothly! And it's all bright white! That can't be wood."

"It is. Wood that's been painted. These people pride themselves on their woodcarving techniques."

As the ship continued closer Shanti leaned further into Keema's embrace.

"We're going to hit it," said the other woman in a soft voice.

Shanti was about to agree when shouts tolled out from the rigging of the Tide's Daughter, to be echoed from the towers. Ropes stretched between the bridge and its towers began to shudder and shift then pull and Shanti gasped as the entire middle section of the bridge shuddered to one side. The wood complained as it rose, a low shriek beneath the rumbling sound of the rope moving. The Tide's Daughter passed beneath the section of bridge as it was still pulling up into the air, reaching impossibly high into the sky above them.

Shanti could see the bridge much closer now. The first thing she saw was that Felldan was right; the bridge was made of wood. Now that some sections were moving, she could see the exposed worn out edges and hidden beams that supported its structure. She could even get a closer glimpse of the white curving shapes that had been carved up the sides of the bridge. They wrapped around and over one another along the railing and outcroppings. This close, it was much easier to see that the shapes were figures, mostly human but all slightly unreal. One was a powerfully muscled man with thick rolls of hair that somehow spread out behind him like a billowing cape, and his beard swept up into it. In one hand he clutched a stick that was capped with a broad leaf. Another figure was a woman in a snug outfit with a long sleeved top, pants, and a high collar. Her mouth was broader than seemed possible, but her eyes conveyed a dangerous intelligence. Shanti had to admit, the carvings were amazing.

She wished that she had some way to show her older brother Taanin these carvings. He had always been the one with an eye for the beauty that could be found in such things. She knew how to look at them and enjoy them, but he considered the way that an artist would have had to draw the shapes from the wood with their hands and tools. She knew that he would want the ship to stop if it could, and stay beneath the bridge while he traced his fingers over the carvings and imagined how he could create something even half as wonderful.

The second thing that she saw was the crowd, still waiting on the side of the bridge that had been disconnected from the raised section. There were about twenty or thirty people waiting there for her ship to pass by and for the section to be lowered again. All of them had the pale skin that she had discovered in the captain and some of the crew onboard. *Natives of Chechezuk,* she thought to herself. The crowd were watching the ship pass by with the same level of curiosity and animation that a herd of cows might use to watch a merchant's cart passing along a country road, slowly chewing their grass. It was something to occupy the eyes, but certainly not worth thinking about.

"We're so close!"

Shanti jerked away from the voice at her side, then turned to see that Rahit was leaning over the railing with a disturbing leer pulling his mouth to its widest. She was surprised that there was no drool dripping from his lips. His eyes were on fire. He turned to stare at her.

"I can't wait to get off this ship and into the jungle!" he declared. His eyes were wide and shone with an intensity that shocked her.

"I'm sure it won't be long," she stuttered.

"Pah!" He spun on his heels and rushed off to the stairs.

"What happened to him?" Shanti asked Keema and Felldan. "He has been so quiet and calm. He came to all my evening readings."

"He's here to make his fortune," sighed Felldan. "A lot of travellers come to new places expecting to find a way to make their money quick. It seldom works out."

Shanti didn't respond. Felldan's comment made her think about her own situation. Her entire purpose for travelling to Chechezuk was to make easy money also. *But I'm not reacting like him, like a child with no sense of manners or restraint!* She brushed the front of her skirts straight and resolved not to stare at the buildings that were so close, or the elaborately carved bridge that was now passing behind them.

Another half an hour passed as the Tide's Daughter followed the instructions of the pilot who had climbed aboard earlier. Shanti was surprised to discover that the buildings they squeezed through were only a narrow island in the city. They soon emerged from its far side into a large watery expanse. All around they could see other islands, covered to the edge in short wooden buildings.

"The pilot will guide the captain through the shallow water here. The channels shift constantly," explained Felldan. Some of the islands were close enough to be connected by more bridges, shaped in the same bright white and graceful curve they had seen in the last one. Some of these also had tall towers to the sides, though others did not.

"How many islands are there?" asked Shanti.

"It's not worth counting them," laughed Felldan. "Some islands have been paved over, so that the only hint that they were once separate is a dark tunnel somewhere beneath the paths."

The pilot led the ship through the open rippling expanse, and then down another narrow watery lane. Shortly after they entered this passage, the Tide's Daughter emerged into a space that Shanti would have called a plaza if she had seen it in Gorduum. It was broad and open, and buildings faced into it from all sides. People were thickly scurrying around the edges, carrying boxes and setting ropes. But the difference with this plaza, and it was a big difference, was the fact that the people were hurrying around its edges on the only path, a semicircle around its edge. The rest of the space was dark still water that the Tide's Daughter carved through on its way to one of the heavy mooring posts that jutted up near the edge.

The ship was roped on to the post as they drifted in. Behind the passengers at the rail, the sails had been taken in now to reduce their force. Shanti expected the rope to snap or the post to pull itself out of the water, but instead there was a jerk and the ship stopped moving. Sailors threw down heavy ropes to secure the other end of the ship and keep it from slowly bobbing back out into the lagoon.

As Shanti and her companions moved away from the railing, to prepare for disembarking, they met the captain sweeping across the deck towards them, his arms spread wide beneath a massive smile.

"My friends, what do you think? This is Chechezuk!" He spun around, looking up at the buildings lining the broad lagoon.

"It's so much more than I had imagined," said Shanti. "There's so much water, I can barely see any streets!"

"Yes, it is wonderful, isn't it?" asked Zekeka, falling in beside the small group as they walked away from the railings. "There is nothing like the feel of the air in a city on the ocean." He drew a deep breath, motioning towards his stomach in swirling gestures, as though he could actually bunch up more of the air and stuff it towards his nostrils.

"I don't know about that," muttered Keema. "My stomach is still not really recovered from that journey, and this smell isn't helping."

Shanti sniffed, and actually considered the scents that she was noticing. She hadn't thought about the way the air smelled much in her life up to this point, but she had to admit that there was a strange smell here, something rotten or mouldering. But it was faint. It didn't overpower her, or leave her feeling sick.

"What is that?" she asked, just as they arrived at the stairs that led below deck.

"Just the smell of the ocean," said Zekeka, before

he turned away and headed off to yell orders at the sailors.

Back beneath the deck, Shanti and her companions were confronted with a maelstrom of sailors engaged in their work. Shanti felt her pulse race as she was bustled to one side of the cramped space while huge crates were wrapped in lengths of rope and hooks before doors were opened on the deck and the crates were hoisted out.

Sailors yelled and grimaced and ran from one piece of cargo to another, and Shanti was worried that she and her companions would be crushed amongst it all. She clutched onto Keema's arm and could feel the other woman was holding on to her just as hard. She realised that her wife must still need support in order to stand comfortably, and especially to move through the difficult passages under the deck. Shanti was grateful for Felldan's help, and the way he kept a firm hand on her shoulder to stop her getting stuck behind a crate where no one might see her.

She breathed out with relief when they reached the bunkroom with no more incident than a snapped instruction to step lively. They gathered their belongings, trying not to get in one another's way as the other passengers did likewise. Rahit was standing at the door to the bunkroom, bouncing on his heels and constantly leaning his luggage over before pulling it upright again, ready to move. He was quivering with impatience as Lorku realised that she had forgotten to pack yet another small item of clothing that was waiting on her bunk. Shanti stared at the two and wondered how well they would

manage in the jungle that they planned to visit, beyond the edge of the city.

Rahit kept his collar buttoned tight and had
spent many mornings brushing his hair until each
curl was in the right place. Lorku had more lace trim
on her clothing than Shanti had ever before seen in
one place. The land here was wet and wide, and
from the way these two had been surprised by the
plain bunkroom, Shanti doubted that they knew
what they were getting themselves in for. None-
theless, Rahit and his wife were the first to leave the
bunkroom, with barely a word of farewell for the
others.

"Typical, yeah?" said Gudan, pointing at the
doorway they had just vacated. He grinned, and
Shanti smiled back. He crossed the room to give her
a huge hug, and then stepped over to do the same to
Keema, lifting her off the floor for a moment.
Taadan smiled too, but stayed on his side of the
room and made a small waving motion with his
hand.

"I don't know if we will see you in Chechezuk,
but I hope that you find what you came for!" said
Gudan, and then he took Taadin's hand and the pair
left.

20

———

"Do you need a hand?"

Felldan was waiting for Shanti and Keema next to his bunk. He had even tucked in the simple sheets that had been provided, so that his bunk looked square and tidy, as though no one had ever slept there. Shanti thought that he was very practised at it. *I wonder why?*

"Actually, I think I do," admitted Keema sheepishly. Shanti knew that she would have hated to reveal that. Keema was so independent and proud of her ability to manage in any situation. She watched as her wife pursed her lips and took a deep breath, but accepted the help that Felldan was offering. The tall thin man picked up her case and the three of them began trying to make their way off the boat.

When they arrived back above deck, Shanti felt as though she was in the middle of a storm. Figures were moving everywhere and the shouts and calls of workers trying to unload the ship's cargo filled the air, louder than the cries of seagulls that lined the rooftops nearby.

The captain was standing near the mast, leaning

over to speak instructions into the ears of Tozan, who lifted a long thin whistle to his lips and blasted strange repetitive notes on it in response. Shanti began to walk over to them, and Keema and Felldan followed.

In a lull between whistle blasts, Shanti leaned closer to Zekeka.

"Where should we go?" she asked.

"What?" said Zekeka, his brow creasing.

"I said, where should-" began Shanti in a raised voice.

"No no," Zekeka cut her off with a chopping gesture. "I heard you. I just don't know what you mean?"

Shanti was taken aback. *What does he mean he doesn't know what I mean?*

"We're in the way here," she said slowly. The captain nodded. "So I thought we probably shouldn't stay on board."

"Of course not!" exclaimed Zekeka.

Shanti tried not to frown. *I don't want him to know he's confused me so.* She felt as though her vulnerability was on display, and it made her want to walk away and hide somewhere.

"So where should we go?"

"That's really up to you," he said.

Shanti drew a slow breath and tried to calm herself. *He just doesn't quite understand what I'm trying to ask,* she decided. *I'll try saying it a different way.*

"I came here to speak to your contacts, about the tuft supply they are hoping to bring to Gorduum."

"Yes."

"I assumed you would need to know where I am, for that to happen?"

"No," Zekeka chuckled and crossed his arms. "You need to know where I am for that to happen. And you do, I'll be right here, on the Tide's Daughter. You're the one who is looking to get something out of this."

Shanti felt a prickling along the backs of her arms. *I didn't plan this properly,* she realised. *I'm so used to having others include me in their plans, I didn't think of how I might not be in the captain's plans. I'm so stupid!* Keema reached out and put a hand on Shanti's shoulder.

"It's fine Petal, we'll find somewhere to stay and we can come back to speak to the captain once they have finished shifting all this cargo."

"See, your lovely lady understands," grinned Zekeka. He nodded at them all and then returned his attention to the commotion that filled the ship. "See you later!" he called without looking at them.

Keema and Felldan led the way off the ship and onto the broad dock below. Shanti followed with a furrowed brow, dragging her case behind her. She felt completely off balance, a feeling which was only made worse by the fact that the dock was not moving now that she had grown used to the ship shifting under her feet over their weeks at sea. She was so unsure of what to do that she didn't look up as they walked, keeping her eyes on the feet and legs of the others. How had she ended up here? Shanti walked along the streets of Chechezuk without paying attention to her surroundings. What was she going to do now?

"Petal, isn't this amazing?"

Keema's voice struck at something deep in

Shanti, straightening her back and clearing her eyes. Now she looked at where they were.

Felldan and Keema had led her down one of the many lanes that had opened onto the broad semi-circular path that edged the lagoon and doubled as a dock. These streets were narrow and Shanti was only protected from the buffets of the crowd by Keema and Felldan leading the way. She looked higher, examining the wooden walls that sheltered them on either side.

The walls were dark and plain, with rectangular holes that marked doorways as the only interruption to the flat planks. It seemed Chechezuk did not bother with windows to many of their buildings. The crowd moved with purpose around Shanti and her friends. Very few people lingered on the streets. Shanti was entranced by the pale skin and unfamiliar clothing that surrounded her, though she tried not to stare. The people wore broad conical hats and both men and women wore light long-sleeved shirts and pants, in simple colours but with detailed embroidery around the cuffs and collars. The collars were tall and stiff, and created a fifth sleeve for the occupant's neck.

Shanti slapped at her neck. Something had landed and pinched at her skin. She pulled her hand away and looked at what was there. Smashed under her fingers was a remarkably long, thin black insect. She flicked the pieces of the insect away and shuddered. Felldan slapped the back of his arm too.

"It's beautiful," she said. "But are the insects common?"

"Unfortunately, yes, they are a part of life here," answered Felldan. Keema slapped her neck.

"Is that what the collars are for?" asked Keema. "To protect their necks?"

"Could be," allowed Felldan. "I hadn't thought of it, to be honest! I always just thought that it was Chechezukian fashion."

"Where are we going?" asked Shanti. She had realised that their small group was walking with purpose through the crowds, but she had no idea of the destination that they were searching for. *Keema surely wouldn't be leading the way, she couldn't have made plans that I don't know about could she? Does Felldan have a plan? Or is he just walking through a familiar city?* She turned to see if she could still find her way back to the Lagoon and was surprised to see that the gentle weaving of the narrow lane had already hidden it from sight entirely.

"I know a small place near the Plaza. I figure it's the best place for us to settle ourselves."

"Ourselves?"

"Weren't you listening?" asked Keema. "We've been talking about this since we got off the boat. Felldan's been here before and suggested we stay at this place he knows, just as he was going to anyway. Did you want to look for somewhere else?"

"No, that sounds fine." *I can't let myself get caught up in negative thoughts,* Shanti scolded herself. *If I stop paying attention to the city, I could get in trouble. Keema taught me that on my first day in Gorduum!*

Felldan led the way through the narrow lanes between the buildings. A few other streets appeared between the buildings, but when Shanti looked down them she saw that most of them ended in water only a short distance from the crossroads. The watery passages looked like small streams in the middle of the city, but there was no ground or banks visible to either side of them.

"What are those streams?" she asked Felldan.

"Canals is the word that they use in Chechezuk. The whole area is marshy land, and the city has been built into the silt, and raised above. The moisture is channelled through the canals, and the people use them for travel."

As if he had arranged for it to happen on cue, a thin boat appeared moving along the canal to their right. Two people sat in the front of it, older men with long grey beards. Large baskets full of bread and vegetables filled the boat between them. A young woman with the golden yellow hair that Shanti had seen on many of Zukians stood in the back of the boat, pushing it along with a long pole.

"That must take a lot of strength," she said. *Of course. This is what Darsat meant.*

Keema glanced over at her as the boat disappeared past the corner of the next building.

"I could do it," she said.

They turned down some of the avenues that did not end in drops into the water, walking across low humped bridges over the canals and into new lanes on the far sides. At the peak of one bridge, Shanti turned to look along the waterway and saw that the canal looked exactly like another of the lanes. Although it had no path for people to walk along, she could see doors into the buildings that lined its sides, and many more of the thin canal-boats navigating their way past one another. While she watched, she saw a young girl walk out of one building with a basket of bread. The girl stepped into one of the thin boats that was waiting for her, and then the man standing at the back of the boat began to push on the long pole he was holding and moved it out into the main waterway. It seemed that Chechezuk barely noticed the difference between water and dry land underfoot.

With Felldan's explanation in mind, it became much easier to see that the buildings were all sitting on foundations that stretched down into the water. Most of the time the thin boats in the canals sent small ripples washing against the dark walls that sank under the water's surface, but in some places the buildings sat on massively thick posts instead and those ripples vanished into the shadowy space beneath. Shanti wondered if people ever used those passageways.

Shanti was surprised to hear a constant quiet whispering in the streets as they moved. At first she thought that it was the sound of the breeze amongst the low buildings, or the lapping of small waves in the canals nearby, but then she saw an inhabitant of the city walking towards them with their lips moving, and fingers fluttering. As the woman passed, Shanti was able to catch a few of the words she was saying.

"Stinger?" she asked once the woman had gone by. Felldan turned to her.

"What do you mean?" he asked.

"She was saying Stinger over and over, and some other words I couldn't understand yet."

Felldan's confusion cleared and he smiled.

"Yes, she was asking the spirits of these insects to pass her by."

"The insects understand her language?" Keema sounded shocked.

"No!" laughed Felldan. "She is calling on the spirits of the insects, so that she will not be bothered by them. You heard how the sailors called on the tides to keep the Tide's Daughter on course, and saw that the spirit of the trees was carved onto the bridges to hold it up? It is like that."

"I see." *So those were the spirits of the trees on that bridge? How fascinating!*

Felldan's destination turned out to be a tall narrow building that appeared even taller and narrower because of the way it was squeezed on either side by others. It was three stories tall, which meant it stood out dramatically against the single story buildings that surrounded it.

"Do they find that that impressive, do you think?" asked Keema with a small sniff. "It's pretty average height compared to back home."

"Mmmm," Shanti replied noncommittally. She was very aware of how many of the city's inhabitants were pressed around them. Though they were not staring at her, she could feel their curious glances running over her and she didn't want to attract any negative attention. "Are there any quieter streets?" she complained as they pushed their way in through the door.

"No," said Felldan. "There's no space to spare in Chechezuk, so this is what it is like everywhere."

"How are we going to get back to the Tide's Daughter?" asked Keema. She had narrowed her eyes as they entered the small dim room beyond the door. Dark red and green wall hangings decorated the sides of the room, and small copper bells dangled from threads along the bottom of each. Whorls of embroidery looked like eyes staring out from the walls at them.

"You'll find it easily enough, there's not actually that many options on the streets. I'll give you some directions anyway."

Felldan led the way forward, towards a small bench constructed of deep brown wood. A little bell was sitting on the top. Felldan lifted it up and rang it.

21

A harsh voice responded in Zukian from somewhere in a room nearby. The voice sounded crackly and jagged. A short little man with the same light skin everyone in the city shared, pushed his way in, past one of the wall hangings, which jangled riotously. He squinted at them over a spiky orange beard. Shanti saw him roll his eyes when he saw them. *What was that about,* she wondered.

"What? Are you booked in?" he said in Gawaalti. He had a much stronger accent than Captain Zekeka had. Shanti found that the rhythm of his speech was more poetic than she expected from his gruff face.

"No, but I was hoping you might have space anyway?" asked Felldan, smiling broadly.

The short man sniffed and looked at Shanti and Keema and then back at Felldan.

"How many rooms exactly?" The man narrowed his eyes.

"Two," said Keema quickly.

Felldan nodded.

"Two, you say," murmured the man, pulling a

wide book bound in red leather out from somewhere behind the desk. He dropped it open with a heavy thunk and ran his finger down one page. "Yeah, alright, I've got a bit of space on the top floor." He slammed the book shut and motioned for them all to follow him. "Through here."

They all pulled their luggage through the small gap next to the desk. Keema took a bit longer as she had to try and rotate hers enough for it to get through, and eventually had to lift it up and over the dark wood desk. The host pulled aside the hanging that he had come through and Shanti found a very small hallway and some extremely steep stairs lay beyond.

Sitting on the floor near a door at the back of the hall was a gigantic lizard. It was like the small ones that scuttled through gardens back in Gorduum or her home village, but as long as her leg. Half of its body was a long thin tail and it sat staring at them as they walked in, its head held slightly sideways to keep them in view of one large watching eye. Unlike the lizards back home, it was mostly a dark orange colour, with large patches of mottled green covering its back. Long spikes rose in a crest on its head and ran down its spine. Shanti swallowed as she looked at the massive animal, and wondered whether she should be afraid or curious. The short man aimed a kick at it as he passed, but he didn't connect and the lizard showed no sign that it had noticed him at all. Shanti blinked and then decided to try to ignore the creature.

The man looked around the small space and snapped something in his sharp language. Shanti could not recognise the word and turned a quizzical eye to Felldan. He shrugged.

"It's a name," he whispered. "I think he's calling for a servant."

The man rattled off a string of curses that Shanti recognised from the sailors on the Tide's Daughter. She didn't know what each snipped syllable meant, but she blushed at the clear intent behind them. He turned back to the three visitors and clipped out one more phrase.

"He's explaining that his worker must be shirking. He's not pleased about it," translated Felldan.

The man growled and then began to climb up the incredibly steep stairs. Shanti let her gaze drift up the flight, examining the dark rectangular spiral above.

"That's a ladder not a staircase," she exclaimed. "How are we supposed to get these up there?" She hefted her luggage at her side.

"I can take it for you and then come back for mine," offered Felldan. "Seeing as his worker isn't here."

Keema stepped forward. "She'll be fine, I'll make sure she gets it up there."

Felldan shrugged and began climbing after their host, dragging his case up each step with a rhythmic clunk.

"Why did you say that?" asked Shanti. She turned to look at her wife with a puzzled expression. "I don't know if I'm going to be able to do this."

"You'll be fine. Felldan's a nice lad, but we don't want him to think he's the best thing in the city, do we?" Keema grinned, and her eyes sparkled.

"I suppose, but this is really going to be tough."

Keema followed her up the stairs, pushing Shanti's luggage higher before pulling her own up to the next step. She huffed and wheezed with each step, but refused Shanti's attempts to help.

Shanti whispered back down to her wife. "Did you see that lizard?"

"Of course. How do you expect me to miss something that huge?"

"Do you think it's dangerous?" Shanti felt a flicker in her stomach, as though flies were buzzing around inside it.

"If it was dangerous, Felldan would have said something. The local guy might be used to it, but Felldan has been pretty good at letting us know what we need to know," Keema grudgingly acknowledged Felldan's help.

"Yes, I suppose that is true," agreed Shanti as she reached up for the next step. "He is a very useful man to have around, isn't he."

Keema didn't reply to that.

When they were nearly at the top of the steep flight, a small boy came out of a room with his arms full of tangled pale sheets. Their host paused to berate the youth and Shanti blushed again without quite knowing why. She was able to figure out some of what was said this time, even without Felldan translating for her.

It seems cruel to tell the boy off for not carrying our things, she thought with a frown. *He was clearly carrying out some other task that he was supposed to be doing.* The host snorted, putting Shanti in mind of a bull, and then continued to lead them even higher into the building. She tried to smile at the boy with the sheets as she passed, but his eyes stayed on the floor of the small landing he stood on.

The rooms they were shown to were very small and Shanti felt a little self conscious that Felldan would be sleeping right next to the one that she and Keema would share. There was just enough space in their room for the two of them to stand up straight next to the worn out mattress, so long as they didn't mind bumping into one another. Keema pushed their luggage into some racks on one side of the room, and Shanti sat on the bed, grimacing as she sank lower and lower into its overly soft surface. Through the thin wooden walls they could hear the creaks and footsteps of Felldan in his own room.

"What do you think so far?" Shanti asked.

"What do you mean?" Keema was pulling some clothes out of her case and holding them up against her. She looked down at the top and shook her head slightly.

"Is this city what you thought it would be?"

"No." Keema tucked the top back into her case and then pulled out two more. "It's damper than I expected, and those insects are infuriating. But at least I'm not feeling sick any more."

"That's good." Shanti bit her lower lip. She hoped that Keema wasn't too upset by the journey, when it had been so hard to convince her to come in the first place.

Keema sat down on the bed next to her, the movement making the mattress heave and shift as badly as the Tide's Daughter had done in high winds. Keema stretched an arm over Shanti's shoulders and Shanti leaned in closer to her, leaning her head on the other woman's shoulder. She could feel Keema's short hair brushing against her ears.

"Do you like it?" whispered Keema.

"I do," replied Shanti, in a low voice. She wanted to be truthful with her wife, but she didn't want Keema to think that she liked Chechezuk more than Gorduum already. She felt just like when she had first travelled to Gorduum. While overwhelming and sometimes worrying, Shanti could think of nothing that excited her more than the discovery of a new place. She loved seeing how different it looked, and finding out the little differences in the way the people behaved. But she didn't want to act too effusive. She was worried that Keema would think less of her. "I love seeing how they have built on the water. It's so unusual."

Keema lifted a hand to stroke Shanti's hair off her face. "Then this city is beautiful, insects and all." She leaned in to kiss Shanti, her soft lips drawing out Shanti's anxiety. Together they lay back onto the mattress. Shanti thought of Felldan in the next room, and the creaking of the poorly made rooms, but then those thoughts fled and she allowed Keema to occupy her totally.

Outside the window, perched on the sharp gable, another lizard perched. Its tongue flickered out to taste the air and it shuffled to get a better grip on the wooden tiles.

THE NEXT DAY, Keema and Shanti woke slowly. Shanti enjoyed the feeling of Keema's legs wrapped around hers, the arm that was draped over her. Although the pillow was shockingly hard and the mattress had sunk down so far that she could feel the wooden slats it was lying on, laying with Keema alongside her instead of head to head as they had been in the bunks on the Tide's Daughter was a treasure she wanted to hang on to.

Footsteps banged on the landing outside their door.

"Are you two decent?"

Shanti stretched and heard Keema mumble something.

"We can be soon," she called.

"I thought I'd show you around for breakfast, and show you how to get back to the ship."

Shanti jutted an elbow backwards and heard Keema grunt.

"What?" groaned the other woman.

"Felldan wants to show us around. What do you think?"

"Of course he does, that preening pigeon. He wants you to love his city."

Shanti pursed her lips. "What's that supposed to mean?"

"Nothing, nothing." Keema leaned forward and kissed Shanti's cheek, then crawled out of the blankets over the top of her. "You're a sweet girl, and I love you, but I'm not sure about him." Shanti was about to ask why Keema was unsure about the man after saying he was reliable only a day ago, but then Keema grabbed some clothes off the top of her case and began pulling them on. As her head poked out of the top of a shirt and she began to tie it closed properly, Keema noticed Shanti watching her with a small grin.

"What?"

"Watching you get dressed is as much fun as the other way around," giggled Shanti.

"Oh hush!" laughed Keema, grabbing her trousers off the floor and flinging them at Shanti, who squealed.

The pair got dressed and came out of the room. Felldan was standing on the top steps of the steep flight that led down past two other identical landings. He was leaning against the wall with his arms folded, looking up at the ceiling which rose to a point above them.

"Ready?" he asked as the women came out. Shanti nodded. "Then let's find something to eat!"

Back in the narrow lane outside their lodging, he directed them to the left, which Shanti immediately realised was the direction that they had arrived from the day before. Although the walls of the streets were largely undecorated and identical, she did recognise the slim doorways to various shops. The shops had signs, and colours decorated the frame of their doors, which helped her keep her bearings.

After walking over one of the short but high arched bridges, Felldan led Keema and Shanti into a small plaza. Here the shops were open and the space was filled with wooden poles supporting thin canvas shelters. Benches criss-crossed the stones. People sat and chatted on the benches, holding food that was nearly falling out of thin bread pouches.

The three ordered their food from a shop operating out of the walls of the Plaza. Shanti was thrilled to take the opportunity to try out what she had learnt of Zukian from Felldan. She couldn't really see what made the food in one shop different to another, but there were definite preferences amongst the crowd. One shop had a long queue of people waiting next to it, all talking to each other as they waited to get their food, while a few of the others had no one waiting. The keepers at those shops leaned on their elbows and watched the crowds as morosely as a cow in a field. Occasionally someone would stop and look at the bowls of food in these stalls, resting on coals to keep them hot, but they usually moved on before the keeper could straighten up.

22

———

Shanti, Keema and Felldan sat together and ate the food they had ordered, pouches of heavy bread filled with meats and rice, thick brown sauces dripping down their chins and fingers. Shanti licked at the back of her hand to try and catch it all, and Keema reached over to wipe a drop off Shanti's lips and then sucked it off her own finger.

"This is a good place to come to get food," said Felldan once he had finished chewing. "The Plaza stays this busy most of the day, and it's close to our rooms."

"It's a good place to come for dinner, do you think?"

"Yes, and there're often musicians around in the evenings." He slapped at a bug that was crawling on his sleeve, looking for a way in. "And this is also a good place to get your bearings for the lagoon where the ships are moored." He twisted in his seat and pointed. On the far side of this plaza, between two of the taller buildings lining its side, was a lane leading out. There was a simple peaked arch built over this lane, and the building on the left rose into a spire two or three storeys higher than any of its neighbours.

"See that street? That's the main path and it will take you pretty much directly to the lagoon. There might be a couple of turns along the way, but you can just keep checking that the canals are on your right, and you should get there."

Shanti nodded. She felt a familiar tingling in her stomach as she considered whether or not she would be able to find her way through the city. It was an adventure, the sort of excitement that she always said that she wanted to experience, but it was a little scary. To be on your own in a new place, to not know what risks potentially lie around every corner. She blew out a breath. "I think I can handle this."

Felldan smiled. "I think that you can too. In any case, my business takes me away from the lagoon today, so I will have to bid you lovely ladies a good day. I hope I find you this evening!"

"Goodbye Felldan," said Keema with finality.

Shanti glanced at her partner but then said her own farewell. She turned to Keema as Felldan walked away.

"What was that?"

"What?" Keema sniffed.

"You were rude to him."

"That wasn't rude. I just said goodbye. He had other places to be. Can I help it if I'm looking forward to actually spending some time with you?"

"I like spending time with you too." Shanti reached over to hold Keema's hand. The other woman smiled back.

"But we are here for a purpose. Let's go back to

the ship and see when the captain can introduce us to his contact."

After finishing their food, Shanti and Keema set off through the arch that Felldan had pointed out. However, they had only gone a few steps into the street before Shanti felt lost. Her stomach was doing flips and she could feel sweat building between her shoulder blades. She searched the walls of the lane for any hint of direction to follow, a sign on a wall, a landmark peering over the top of the dark buildings, but found nothing.

"Are you alright?" asked Keema.

"Sure," breathed Shanti, pressing a hand to her stomach.

Keema paused and put a hand on Shanti's back. Shanti felt as though she couldn't draw enough breath.

"It's not a big deal Petal. The food plaza is right there."

Shanti looked back and realised Keema was right. The archway to the Plaza was barely twenty metres away. A couple of dark shapes were crawling along the wooden crossbeam, lumpy creatures crawling up to the height of it. She could see orange mottling and realised they must be more of the lizards that had been in their lodging house.

"I guess I'm just worried about getting lost here." Shanti was surprised at the wave of anxiety that had come over her. It reminded her of being in small dark hallways, and the memories that such places called up. But she was not in such a place now. Why would those old concerns rise up here?

"No need to panic," laughed Keema. "You're here with one of the suavest and cleverest drivers that the jewel of the continent ever saw! I can get you through, no worries."

With that pronouncement she hooked Shanti's arm in her own and started striding along the street, dodging around the crowd of pale-skinned native cityfolk. Shanti followed along, letting Keema turn her down side streets and over more of the small hump bridges, but she wished that she could understand how Keema knew where to go. *Didn't Felldan say that I was supposed to keep the canals on the right? Why have we crossed two of them? Surely that means we must be going the wrong way?*

But her fears turned out to be unfounded. Keema led her out into the lagoon after a brisk walk. Together they stood watching the sunlight glinting off ripples that bounced back and forwards along the water's surface.

"Thank you," Shanti murmured with her eyes low.

"Any time Petal," laughed Keema as she squeezed Shanti's hand.

The Tide's Daughter was still tied up where they had left her, and the gangway led up to the deck as it had in Gorduum. Tozan stood in his position at the top, and nodded when he saw Shanti and Keema about to walk up it.

"Good timing," he called down. "Wait there, the captain was hoping to leave soon anyway."

Zekeka joined them at the bottom of the gangway. He was wearing the same light material that Shanti had seen on the inhabitants of Chechezuk, with embroidery at the cuffs and around the tall collar. He waved away a pair of droning insects that were hovering near his face.

"Come along, I will introduce you to my friend."

"So soon?" Shanti stuttered.

"Why not? It is why you have come all the way to this city is it not? I am going to see him anyway."

"Yes, but I was not prepared for a meeting today." Shanti pressed her hands against the sides of her dress, wondering whether it was formal enough to meet with a potential business partner. *What will I need to find out,* she thought. Suddenly she wished she had spent more time on the journey to this city planning out what she needed if she was to make a decision about this business.

Shanti didn't have time to make any further objections, as it turned out that the captain's friend worked behind a door on the side of this lagoon. Within a few minutes the small group were standing outside the door, with Zekeka smiling and waving them inside. Shanti looked at the wall around the door, hoping for a sign or some indication of the type of business that was inside. Perhaps the name of the person she would be meeting. Like all the buildings she had noticed in Chechezuk so far, there were no windows and practically no decoration on the outside. The only thing that differentiated this door from any other that they had walked past was a symbol painted in black on the door itself. This symbol was a spiral with a serrated edge that curled in on itself. Shanti wondered if it represented the captain's friend, or just the building they were to enter.

Once inside, Shanti was impressed. The building was mostly taken up by a room that was incredibly broad, though the roof was low over their heads near the entrance. After a short distance the roof lifted sharply to the height of the second floor, leaving room for a landing that ran around the huge square room and looked down to the level they were standing on. Holes in the floor beneath their feet revealed dark water sloshing below the building, a sight that made Shanti feel less secure. Plants grew out of large ceramic pots in the corners of the room; tall green leaves that reached up into the air before curling over. A few of the insects that kept harassing everyone were humming through the space, but people sitting in easy chairs all around the room held broad fans that they used to waft the insects away whenever they approached.

Brown-clothed workers moved hurriedly along the landing, occasionally descending a broad staircase to either side of where the captain had led them in, so that they could scurry over to one of the plump chairs and lean down to speak into the ear of its occupant. Zekeka led Shanti and Keema to one of the chairs on the far side of the room. As they crossed the middle of the room, Shanti looked up at a chandelier that hung down from far above them. *That chandelier looks like it could be bigger than Keema's cart!* It was difficult to tell, but the construction appeared to be made of small white shells strung together and supported by curved thin struts. Dozens of candles burned in its depths, illuminating the huge room.

"Here you are," said Zekeka, bowing to the man in the chair they had arrived next to. Shanti wasn't sure if his comment was directed at her or at the man.

"Welcome to Chechezuk," replied the large man, speaking with the same spiky accent that she had heard from other inhabitants of the city. His cheeks were broad, and he had a full bushy beard that was the colour of fire. His hair was long but lank, and stuck to his scalp. He stood up and Shanti was surprised that he was about her own height. He gave the impression of being much taller, as though his personality was already trying to push beyond the limited space that his body took up.

"This is Shanti Penpen," Zekeka introduced her to the man. "Shanti, this is Kayzark. He's been a big part of many successful businesses here, and now he's looking into tuft."

The big man chuckled and rolled his eyes.

"I'm sure this lovely woman has much more experience in the world than I, coming all the way from Gorduum to our little town." His small blue eyes glittered like the sea. "And you came all this way just to speak with me?"

He sat back down in his large chair. Shanti was about to ask where she should sit when she realised that some of the servants, who were in constant motion through the building, had appeared behind her and the other new arrivals, carrying comfortable stools for them all. She settled down and smoothed out her skirts on her legs.

"I did come to see you, but your business opportunities weren't my only incentive." Shanti smiled at him, leaning forward and crossing her legs. "I've been wanting to get out and see the world my entire life! I've always wanted to find out what new adventures await beyond the horizon." She grinned. "Chechezuk has certainly opened my eyes already!"

The man laughed loudly with a wide mouth. His shoulders shook like mountains. "I'm glad you have enjoyed the experience! Please, enjoy the morsels that we have here, while I speak to my old friend for a moment."

Kayzark stepped away from the large soft chairs with Zekeka, hanging one arm around the taller man's shoulders. The two murmured to each other, though their faces seemed cheerful. Shanti looked at the small table that a servant had placed in between the chairs. Arranged neatly across the top were a series of small round pastries, with intricately woven spirals pressed into patterns on their tops. She picked one up and bit into it curiously. A burst of sweetness erupted from behind the thick pastry and Shanti hummed happily, then nodded at the table to Keema.

"You have to try these!" she said, trying to keep crumbs from tumbling out her lips.

After they had each devoured two of the pastries, the men returned and Kayzark settled himself back into the plush chair he had been sitting in before.

"I see you have both enjoyed our sweet treats! I hope that you will find much of Chechezuk to your liking. But you are here for business too I hope?"

She nodded. "Absolutely. Zekeka has worked with my uncle many times in the past, and he said that you have found a way to practically monopolise the supply of tuft? I know my uncle would love to be the conduit for you to bring that into Gorduum."

"Excellent, shall I bring you a contract?" He raised his eyebrow and began to lift a hand, as though extending it to her for them to shake. Shanti could see the lines of servants moving around the balcony overhead change directions, preparing to respond to their master's whims.

23

"I'm sure I would like to see a contract eventually," Shanti said, laughing herself this time. "But first I would like to know about how steady and reliable this source of yours is. I understand tuft is normally so expensive because of the extreme difficulty in collecting it?"

Kayzark leaned back in his chair. It was broad and green, stuffed thick with padding, and still it creaked as he shifted. He held his hands together in front of his face, fingertips touching in a sharp crest.

"How much do you know about harvesting tuft?" he asked.

Shanti shrugged. "I believe it is grown? I don't know much more than that."

Kayzark nodded and pursed his lips. "I think you should come out to the orchards with me. I was going to go out to them tomorrow anyway, and it would be a great sight for you to add to the others you have already found on your journey. Then I can show you the reason I am so confident in my sources."

"That sounds excellent, thank you so much!"

Keema coughed beside Shanti. Shanti turned to her with creased brows.

"What?" she whispered. Why would Keema be interrupting right now? She knew that this was an important connection for Shanti to establish, and it wouldn't pay to be rude to him.

There was a pause as everyone looked at each other. Then Keema sighed and asked "Would it be alright if I came along?"

Kayzark turned back to Shanti with a questioning look.

"This is my partner Keema. Would it be alright if she joined us tomorrow?" asked Shanti. Keema coughed and Shanti tried not to glare at her. *She's going to ruin this meeting if she keeps disrupting things!*

"I see! Yes, of course, I think that would be a great idea. You will enjoy the experience also." He turned his broad smile to Keema.

The conversation continued, beginning with Kayzark's recommendations of where to go in Chechezuk if they were there long enough, further instructions about how tomorrow's trip would go, and some hypothetical questions and comments about the contract that Shanti would sign, should everything meet her expectations. By the time they left the massive room and were out on the edge of the lagoon again, it was much later in the afternoon.

They walked with Zekeka back to the Tide's Daughter. When he asked if they would like to share in dinner on board, as they had during the journey, Keema shook her head before Shanti could accept. Shanti was surprised. She would have liked to stay to share a meal with the captain and find out what she could about Kayzark and how reliable he was.

But, before she could say something, Keema took Shanti's hand and tucked it through her elbow, said a pleasant farewell to the captain, and began pulling Shanti towards the lanes that led out of the lagoon and back to their rooms.

"What was that about?" asked Shanti.

"What do you mean?"

"Rushing me away so quickly? Dinner with Zekeka on the Tide's Daughter would have been a nice way to spend the evening."

Keema kept walking without looking at Shanti. She led the way down one of the streets, and Shanti tried to glance around to figure out where they were. She couldn't tell if they had walked along this road earlier or not.

"Would it have been? I wouldn't know, I never had dinner with the captain."

"What?"

"I never got to the dining cabin, I was sick all the time."

"All the more reason to join him tonight then. We could have shown you what it was like."

Now Keema did look at Shanti, but it was with a disdainful glance. They walked the rest of the way in silence, as Shanti tried to figure out what had happened. She was very confused by the way Keema was suddenly acting so grumpy. *She really didn't like the idea of dinner with Zekeka, thought Shanti. Maybe she's jealous of him? Actually, that does make sense. If she thought that I was attracted to him, maybe she doesn't want me to be around him too much! I bet that must be it.* Shanti thought it was sad that Keema would be so distrustful of her. And then, as they kept walking, she grew annoyed with her partner, for not telling her that she felt that way. *It's no way for us to solve a problem, to just be grumpy at one another. What if I hadn't worked it out? Then we'd be stuck walking in silence for the rest of the night!*

She pressed her lips tighter together as they moved down the narrow streets, with the bare windowless walls watching from either side. Lanterns hung along the streets were beginning to be lit as the afternoon grew dim. It looked to Shanti as though the inhabitants of each doorway were responsible for some of the lanterns nearest it. Young girls were coming out carrying lit tapers and oil jugs that they used to refill the lanterns and light them, their pale skin reflecting the flame and glowing like they had lights from Gorduum growing beneath the surface.

Shanti watched as one girl, with fiery hair bound into a single tail at the back of her head, had to shoo away one of the massive mottled lizards from her lantern. The creature watched the girl approach with its head held sideways, large eyes tracking her every step while the head and body stayed totally motionless. Then, just as the girl waved the taper at it, the lizard blurred and vanished up the side of the building then over the edge of the roof out of sight.

Keema led Shanti back into the Plaza where they had eaten breakfast then released her hand, stepping away a little.

"Shall we get dinner?" she asked, for all the world as if nothing had happened.

Shanti gritted her teeth. *We could have been having dinner already,* she wanted to say. *And it would have been delicious, I'm sure!*

"Yes, let's. Did you want to get something different to this morning?"

"I dunno." Keema spun slowly, looking at all the shops lining the edge of the Plaza. The crowds were still thin this early. "I don't know what some of this stuff is. I reckon we should just stick with what we know."

Shanti nodded, but frowned when she thought Keema couldn't see her face. *We are in a city so far from anything we know, why would you say to stick with what we know? The whole point is to try out things we have never tried before!*

Once they had bought their food, the two women found a table that wasn't being used yet and sat down to eat. Shanti sat opposite Keema, and they smiled at each other before taking a bite and chewing and watching the table between them.

Shanti and Keema ate in silence for a few minutes.

"Do you think that there is a temple anywhere in the city?" Shanti asked eventually.

"To the Masked God?" Keema asked. Shanti nodded. "I wouldn't think so. It looks like this city doesn't believe in the Masked God."

"Some of the sailors did." Shanti thought about the readings that she had held on the Tide's Daughter. If she kept to the same schedule that she had been following on the ship now that she was on land, then she would be due another reading in two nights time.

"You mentioned that, yes, but I think they were from Gorduum, or at least Gaawalt somewhere."

"You don't think people believe in the Masked God here?" Shanti looked around the crowd of people. A small family sat near them, two young children in broad hats laughing as their father made funny faces. *How could they not know about the Masked God,* thought Shanti. *How could they grow up secure, without knowing that the God was watching out for them through the eyes of their neighbours? How could they watch the world around them without wondering how they could embody the God's will?*

More people began to walk into the Plaza, and the hubbub of conversation grew louder and louder. Street musicians began to walk in as well, playing stringed lutes and guitars, some blowing trumpets or flutes. Shanti grimaced a little as their songs tried to compete with each other, first one growing louder and then the next, notes clashing and fouling each other. Then, all of a sudden, the musicians all came together in their sound and the song became something joyful and bouncy. She looked around. None of the musicians were near each other, but they had become one band. All around the plaza, faces were lifting with smiles and bright eyes.

The tables were nearly all full now, and so it was no surprise when a young native woman dropped onto the bench next to Shanti.

"Good evening!" she said in a thick accent.

"Hello," replied Shanti politely.

The woman had a broad face and bright red lips beneath hair so yellow that it looked like the sun had been woven into threads that slipped from her head and around her shoulders. She put her elbows on the table and murmured a word softly. It sounded a bit like she was saying "Fires warm my stomach". Then she lifted her own food to her mouth, taking a gigantic bite. Keema raised an eyebrow.

"You two aren't from the city, are you?" said the woman around a mouthful of meat and bread.

Shanti giggled at the sight. She shook her head. "No. We have come from Gorduum on business."

"Gorduum! Fantastic! I hear that they have strange glowing plants there?" The woman turned on the bench to face Shanti more directly.

"I suppose so," said Shanti. "We just call them lights, but they are plants that glow."

"We have normal lights here," said the woman. "None of your weird plants in Chechezuk. Just good old fashioned lamps and lanterns."

"Yes, so I've seen. But using fire to see what you are doing can be dangerous in the wrong circumstances. You should try to get some lights here." Shanti took a small bite from her food. "What's your name? I'm Shanti."

"Arsook." She held out a hand to shake Shanti's hand. Arsook's hand had small pieces of rice and scraps of green leaf stuck to it by the thick sauce from her meal. Shanti paused at first then reluctantly reached out to shake it. Arsook grinned.

"I'm Keema," said Shanti's wife, leaning over the table with her own hand out. "Nice to meet you."

"Yes," answered Arsook briefly. "So, Shanti, what sort of business brings you to our fine city?"

"I've never been before. When I had the chance to come and see something new, something different, I knew that I had to take the opportunity or I would regret it. And I'm not disappointed! This place is amazing!"

"Thank you! I tidied it up just before you arrived." Arsook's eyes glittered.

Shanti laughed.

"But what sort of business? Myself, I source wood for the carvers."

"I want to see more of the carvings!" said Shanti excitedly. "I saw some beautiful work on the bridge we passed under as we arrived. I have never seen anything that looked so much like a living thing, whether made of wood or stone! They must work extremely hard on the craft."

"They do, but don't talk like that around them or you'll never hear the end of their self-admiration." Arsook rolled her eyes. "I go out into the jungle and find good groves of wood that we can harvest."

"You don't grow it?" asked Shanti.

"Grow it?" Arsook looked confused. "How would we grow good carving wood?"

"By planting trees? In a nursery, or an orchard, or greenhouse, or something like that? The lights of Gorduum are grown in fields and greenhouses."

"I see! Yes, I suppose you could farm the trees." Arsook nodded and tucked her hair over her ear. "The problem is that there isn't a lot of space for growing plants in Chechezuk. You see the canals in the city?"

"Obviously."

"That's just a hint of how much water there is here. The river flows into the estuary, and the city is built on the estuary, but beyond that the land is soft and swampy as far as you can see in any direction. The jungle grows through the water, and what looks like a broad field can turn out to be a tangled mat of jetsam, or a covering of thick algae on still water."

Arsook smirked as she went on. "I go out in my boat with my crewmate and we explore the jungle, looking for trees that might suit a carver. Long, straight, strong trees. Trees that haven't been overrun by lichen and mould and vines. It's a difficult job."

"There are so few trees?" asked Shanti.

"There aren't many that suit," nodded Arsook. "And getting workers out to them to fell them and bring them back can be tricky, especially if the river paths shift. I know the Trees and Rivers respect me, but only because I treat them right. On top of that, there's a lot of creatures out there that can hurt the unwary."

"Creatures?" Shanti swallowed. Hadn't she just agreed to go out into the jungle with her prospective business partner? How dangerous might that be for her? "What sort of creatures?"

24

"Do you know what alligators are?" Arsook leaned closer, with a mischievous light in her eyes.

Shanti shook her head.

"Have you seen the lizards in the city?"

Shanti nodded. There was one waddling across the stones near them now, scampering away if anyone walked close to it, its legs jutting out sideways and flailing it towards the far side of the Plaza.

"They're much bigger than the lizards we get in Gorduum," Shanti said as she watched it.

"Imagine one that is five times as big." Arsook leaned in again, her eyes widening. "Its mouth is as long as your arm, full of teeth like daggers." Her eyes filled Shanti's vision. "They swim beneath the water, barely a ripple showing on the surface. They swim up to your boat. If you have fingers trailing in the water, or if you decide to hop out and wade through it for some reason, then SNAP" She yelled the last word and clapped her hands together in front of her. Shanti squawked and leaned backwards, almost tumbling off the bench. Arsook laughed.

"These are real creatures in the water here?"

"They don't come into the city usually. But yes, I have to watch out for them when I'm looking for wood."

"That must be very scary," said Shanti as she pulled her skirts straight and resettled herself on the bench.

"I'm used to it." Arsook held her head higher, clearly pleased with the story she had told.

The cheerful manner of the young woman reminded Shanti of Fellbin's cheeky smile. It made her warm to the woman faster. Talking with her was a little like talking with her brother, who she hadn't seen in so long.

The three of them kept speaking as musicians played around them in the Plaza, and tall lanterns were lit. Small clouds of dark buzzing insects gathered around the flickering lights at the top of these posts, drawing insects away from the crowds of people eating at the tables. Small groups of people began to dance in spaces between the tables, spinning in pairs with kicks and smiles. People started clapping in time with the music. Laughter bubbled up into the night sky, where stars were beginning to poke their way through the dark-blue dome.

Shanti and Keema left while the half-moon was high overhead, illuminating the streets better than the lanterns. Those poles were shrouded by thick swarms of insects still, the tiny creatures trying to butt their heads into the flames. Keema led the way, as Shanti found it hard to figure out which way to go in the featureless streets. Soon they had returned to the lodging house and climbed their way up the flights of stairs and into their tiny room. As they lay down in the bed, ready to go to sleep, Keema leaned over to where Shanti was settling herself and whispered "I'm here too."

Shanti rolled over and put an arm across her partner, tucking her face against Keema's shoulder. "I know you are Sunshine," she yawned.

DAWN PUSHED through the window beside the two women and Shanti groaned as it's light swept over her eyelids. She raised her head and yawned, moving Keema's arm to the side as she lifted herself up and looked at the light pouring in the window. She smacked her lips and then coughed as she saw a huge lizard watching from the top of the window.

"Ew! Get out of here!" she yelped, waving her hand at the lizard. It had a bright orange belly and it tilted its head from side to side, trying to look at her with oddly bulbous eyes. Then it flickered its narrow tongue and scrambled around before climbing up and out of sight.

"Whatsit?" spluttered Keema as she rolled over and tried to see what was going on. She grabbed Shanti's shoulders.

"Nothing. Just another one of those lizards," replied Shanti as she relaxed.

"Oh." Keema flopped back down onto the pillow and let her eyes close again. "Who cares, those things seem to be everywhere. They're like pigeons."

Shanti sat on the bed for a while longer, watching the window. *Keema's right, they really are everywhere. No one seems to talk about them much.* Shanti wondered how something so big and hard to ignore could become so familiar that no one even mentioned them anymore.

Felldan knocked on the door and waited for them again this morning, walking with them to the Plaza and joining them for breakfast. Shanti told him all about the meeting that she had had the day before, explaining about Kayzark and the room he held his business in, and how he was taking them on a tour of his groves and orchards today. Felldan nodded and smiled as they walked, expressing surprise and delight at all the right moments. Shanti even mentioned that they had met one of the locals while they had dinner in the evening, describing Arsook. They had sat down at a bench by a table before Shanti covered her mouth and gasped.

"But I haven't asked about your day yesterday at all! Have you been making good progress with your work?"

Felldan nodded over a mouthful of bread and rice. A piece of fish, dyed red from sauce, fell to the table and he flicked it away onto the ground. He swallowed.

"Yes, everything is fine for me. I'll be getting on a ship tomorrow I expect."

"Tomorrow? But you just arrived? We haven't been able to spend any time with you!" Shanti said. She could feel her face fall.

"I know. I would love to spend more time showing off the city as well! I have wondered if there's any way that I could extend my stay," said Felldan, leaning closer. "I think that you ladies would benefit from a guide in this city! How far have you ventured into its lanes and alleys so far?"

"Just back to the lagoon for our meeting and

here," admitted Shanti. *This is awful,* she thought. *I just made a new friend and I won't be able to enjoy their company for any decent length of time!*

"You should definitely try to go further afield." Felldan leaned back and took another gigantic bite of his breakfast. "There's a park in the middle of the city that is glorious!"

"A park? With trees and things?" Shanti didn't know what such a place would look like in Chechezuk. The entire city was supported on the water by massive foundation posts and canals cut through it like a web, how could there be a park?

"Sort of. There's this fantastically large tree, with huge tangled roots that rise up out of the water. It's probably four stories tall, and it spreads out enough to cover this plaza completely!"

He spread his hands, flicking small clumps of rice away from one hand as he did. Shanti looked around the Plaza. *That really must be a big tree if it covers this much space.*

"The cityfolk never wanted to cut it down, and so there it sits, in the middle of a ring of buildings. Spectacular sight." He settled down on his elbows to continue eating his breakfast.

"Maybe we could see you again back in Gorduum sometime?" asked Shanti.

"Maybe. But to be honest, I never stay on land long. It's always disembark, check in with the local office, then get onboard and ship out again!"

"Local office?"

Felldan's eyebrows narrowed. "Don't worry about that. Anyway, I've got to go and make some arrangements, so I'll have to see you two lovely women another time. Until then!" He stuffed the last of his wrap into his mouth and stood up, giving Shanti and Keema an overly elaborate bow. Shanti laughed, and tried to pretend that she didn't notice the faces that turned to stare at them from the nearby tables.

As Felldan left, Keema leaned over and placed a hand on Shanti's shoulder.

"You really want to explore this city, do you?"

Shanti reached up and held onto Keema's hand. "Of course! That's part of why I came here in the first place! You know that I've always wanted to travel and see as much as I can of the world. It's just a shame that we won't have time today."

Keema's cheek dimpled as she thought. "I suppose I could look around the streets and find out where this giant tree is? Then I could take you to it if we can find time?"

"Wouldn't that be dangerous? Wandering through an unknown city on your own?"

"You don't think I can handle myself?" It wasn't an angry question, just surprised. Keema's eyes widened.

"Of course I do!" Shanti reassured her wife. "But it would still be dangerous. I wouldn't want you to get into any sort of trouble, even if you can get yourself out of it."

Keema leaned in and kissed Shanti on her lips. "You are sweet, Petal."

Shanti smiled at Keema. "But didn't you want to come with me to see Kayzark's orchards?"

Keema sighed. "Sort of. It sounds fascinating, and I really do want to spend time with you. But I also want to make sure that you get to enjoy this trip as fully as possible. And the God knows, I have never been good at the business talk that you get into with your meetings. Let me know what you want."

Shanti thought about it as she looked into Keema's eyes. The idea of going on this tour without Keema was uncomfortable. It made her feel the same way she would if someone had asked her whether or not she wanted to keep her ears. She simply had never contemplated an alternative situation where they might be missing!

And she certainly would be worried about Keema, in the streets of a new city, alone. Keema had spent a lot of time on the streets of Gorduum taking care of herself, but those were her own streets, streets that she knew. Keema didn't know these streets at all. And that was not accounting for the dangers in the dark waters of the canals.

The idea of her wonderful partner exploring the city without her made her uncomfortable as well. What would it be like for Keema to lead her through the streets and explain to her what everything was, having already had a chance to marvel at it all and to learn its stories? Wouldn't it be better to share that with each other at the same time?

Then Shanti realised that it would mean Keema was in the same position that she had been when they first met. Keema had been the taxi cart driver who had first carried Shanti from the train station in Gorduum through the city and to her uncle's apartment. She had explained about the history of the buildings that they passed and the reason the streets were laid out the way they were, and what each neighbourhood or district was like. Keema had been in her element, expounding on details, making jokes about people Shanti had never heard of. She had also warned Shanti not to be quite so naive as she moved through the city; she had protected Shanti from some of the little problems that arise when someone is new to an area. Maybe she wanted that feeling back?

Shanti knew that she would feel odd going to see Kayzark's tuft business without Keema. But maybe it would allow Keema to be more like the woman that Shanti remembered, instead of the somewhat grouchy person she had been since they decided to come on this trip.

"Alright, why don't you find me this tree. I'll meet you back here this evening after the tour."

Keema smiled. "Sounds good. I love you Petal."

"I love you Sunshine."

Shanti left the Plaza before Keema. She didn't want to sit at the table and watch her partner go strolling off into the strange city without a care in the world, leaving her behind. She knew that was how Keema would have done it too, she was always so quick to get on with new people.

Shanti remembered one evening when she and Keema had travelled across Gorduum, looking for a new restaurant to try out for dinner. They had sat together behind another taxi cart driver, with Shanti leaning close to her wife, head on her shoulder and an arm around her waist. However, once they had found a place and walked inside, Keema had begun a long conversation with the woman who ran it, and then picked up a new conversation with the waiter. Shanti had sipped at a glass of water and listened as Keema and the young man spoke about some sort of tavern competition that they were both interested in until the food had arrived, and then she and her wife had been too busy eating to say much to one another. The waiter had brought them extra glasses of wine with a grin. It wouldn't be any different with this city. Keema would have the whole bustling place eating out of the palm of her hand like an orphaned kitten in an alley by the time she came back to Shanti.

Shanti chewed on her bottom lip. The other problem with Keema leaving, she had to admit to herself, was that now she would have to find her way through Chechezuk on her own.

25

———————

*I*t *can't be that hard,* she told herself. *Keema figured out the path quickly, and Felldan gave me that advice. "Keep the canals on the right, and you'll reach the Lagoon with no problem."* Shanti smiled and stood up, straightening her shoulders and drawing a deep breath. Then she frowned. *Or did he say to keep the canals on my left?*

Shanti left the Plaza in any case, pushing forward through the streets and hoping for the best. Her stomach felt tense but she kept reminding herself that she had managed much more difficult situations than walking through a city. *After all,* she consoled herself. *I could ask for directions if I needed to.* She looked beneath the broad conical hats of the pedestrians around her and received only wide blue-eyed stares in return. *But only if I really have to.*

Shanti kept walking, though the hair on the backs of her arms was beginning to stand on end. She was just about to give in and ask someone for help, and had begun searching the crowd for the kindest face she could find, when she recognised a broken wall at the corner of the building she was walking past. The wood had grown a layer of mould and snapped off in a chunk, exposing the paler wood inside. Probably some collision at some point in the past had led to the feature, but she knew that she had seen it before just by the entrance to the Lagoon. And sure enough, as she rounded the damaged corner, she could see sunlight sparkling on the surface of that water.

Shanti waved a hand through the air, absent-mindedly brushing away some insects that were hovering by her mouth. The Lagoon was busy, but the reflection of the day's light off the water lit the scene with a shifting glow, and a variety of ships slowly lifted and fell at their berths. It was a soothing scene.

Within minutes she was knocking on the door to Kayzark's rooms again.

She was welcomed inside by the endless flow of servants and settled into a comfortable chair. Other seats were sitting around the room, though none were close enough for her to converse with the occupants, and she couldn't see Kayzark. She had a suspicion that the gap between the seats was a deliberate feature of this unusual meeting space. One of the servants came over with a tall glass of a fruity creamy yellow drink. It was extremely refreshing.

As she waited, Shanti tried to hear what some of the discussion in the room was about. She wondered if Kayzark was the only person to use these rooms for his business, or if these others were working with him in some way. Perhaps they were all independent business-people, and they shared the use of the space? Strain her ears as she might, she couldn't catch any words over the endless pattering of feet on the balcony that circled the room above her.

She bit her lower lip and ran her tongue along her teeth, then clenched her jaw and stood up. She paused and stretched her shoulders, taking her time, and then began to leisurely stroll around the room. She could see some servants watching her with confused expressions, but she carefully avoided them, without simply turning sharply aside. At the wall she leaned in to examine the carved columns that divided each panel, while keeping her ears pricked backwards, listening for any of the Zukian conversation that she could understand.

"... late from the Valley, but I'll send another ship and..."

"... took a sip and it was biting lovely, just delicious. I'll certainly be buying..."

"... actually caught it fumbling at the lock, the biting thing. We need to try..."

Only brief snatches of words were recognisable to Shanti. Most of the conversation was in the crunchy native language of the Chechezukians. Although she had come a long way in a short time with Felldan's guidance, there was still so much of the language that she couldn't understand. She kept looking at the carvings, a combination of broad curves and rigid angles that combined to create tall human figures that filled the wooden column dividers. *This is no good*, she decided. *I'm going to have to go and introduce myself.*

She squared her shoulders and turned, then walked over to the nearest group of chairs. There were three, two with their backs to her and so tall that she couldn't see the people sitting in them, which left one facing her. A short man with a long curling moustache sat in it and saw her coming towards them. He straightened up in his chair, making a small gesture with his eyebrows towards her. At first Shanti wasn't sure what he meant, but then she realised that he was indicating her approach to the occupants of the other chairs, whom she could not see. His companions leaned around the edges of their chairs to look at her. Shanti felt her cheeks grow warmer, but she clenched her teeth and kept walking. She forced herself to smile and bowed her head slightly.

"Good morning! My name is Shanti. May I join you?"

The moustachioed man pursed his lips but nodded.

"My name is Chezur," he said as a servant rushed over with a comfortable padded stool for Shanti. The servant had wide eyes, and she suspected that they were worried that she would be offended not to have the same elegant chair as the other three. She tried to smile at the servant, to reassure them, but they rushed off without meeting her eyes.

"It is a pleasure to meet you," continued Chezur, without the faintest hint of a smile passing across his face. He didn't ask any questions, but Shanti could feel one hanging in the air between them. *Why are you here?*

Shanti gulped but kept her smile in place. "I'm in Chechezuk on business, and I was wondering if you would mind assuaging my curiosity for a little while?"

Chezur didn't respond but the woman in the

chair to Shanti's left nodded. She was older, and probably as short as him, with long hair draped across her shoulder like a shawl. It was so yellow and pale that Shanti wondered if she was old enough for the hair to begin turning white. Maybe it already was, with only a few golden strands left of her original colour. Her hair was so pale that it was hard to tell. Despite nodding, the woman did not speak or encourage Shanti in any other way.

"I was just wondering about the tuft orchards. Are you familiar with these?"

Chezur laughed once. "Of course! Most of the business in Chechezuk is related to the tuft. It's a massively valuable export."

"I thought that carving was what the city was known for though?"

"Absolutely." Now the older woman spoke. "However, though the quality and value of our carving is beyond compare, the volume that we sell to other countries is not high."

"More often our carvers are employed by them to complete a piece and then return home," added Chezur

"So tuft is more common? More people are connected to it?"

"Indeed."

"What is it like? When growing I mean. I have never been here before, and the landscape is so strange to me."

"Gathering in the orchards is dangerous work." This was a new voice and Shanti had to turn to look at the speaker from the third chair. This woman was much taller and skinnier than the other two, and her bright yellow hair was cut so short that Shanti could see the pale skin of her scalp at the sides. Spiky hair erupted from the top of the women's head. Her eyes were gigantic and bluer than a summer sky. "There are so many dangerous animals, and the trees themselves are gnarled and slippery." The tall woman's accent was much heavier than any other that Shanti had come across in the city so far, lilting and emphasising odd parts of some words.

"That does sound dangerous. Do people get hurt?"

"Thank you for that Ayzuk," said Chezur. He smacked his lips and turned to Shanti. "Yes, people get hurt. Sometimes workers fall from the trees, which often results in severe injuries, and can easily be deadly if they strike the boughs below. It is only by the forbearance of the Fisher Hawks and Alligators that we can harvest as much tuft as we do."

"And alligators take more than a few workers each year," added the short older woman. "Now that you've reminded us of these tragedies, is there anything else that we can do for you?"

Shanti blinked. *Why was this woman so snippish? What have I done?* Shanti didn't think that she had been rude. She had possibly interrupted a conversation, but they could have politely asked her to move on if that was the case.

"I do have one more question," she said slowly, wondering whether she was being extra rude by asking, or whether it was a reasonable amount of curiosity. "If it is so dangerous to gather the tuft, why does anyone do it?"

Chezur's eyebrows folded and he coughed. His mouth opened and shut as he looked around, as though trying to find some sign that he could recognise in the servants that moved ceaselessly along the balcony, or in the carved panels on the walls. "I don't even... What do you mean? It's very profitable."

"But does the money make up for the danger?"

"Again I..." Chezur frowned and sipped from his glass, a tall thin container of fizzing pale liquid. "Izuk, do you know what she means, I'm lost."

The older woman leaned closer and frowned as she considered Shanti's question, then sat back into her cushions and shook her head. When she spoke, it was directly to Chezur, as though Shanti wasn't even there. *But she's speaking in my language,* Shanti noted. *That means she wants me to understand.*

"I think she is asking why the workers climb the trees for tuft in the first place."

"What? How is that..." Chezur grimaced and then faced Shanti again. "It's not dangerous to us, we don't climb the trees, so of course the money is worth it. And that is why so many of us are involved with it. As for the workers, well..." he waved a hand and leaned back.

Ayzuk took up the reply.

"The workers climb the trees, because if they didn't, what else would they do?"

"But you've just said how dangerous it is," Shanti insisted, not quite willing to let the idea go yet. There was something that she wasn't understanding about the process, but she could not quite place what was making her feel so unsure.

"Better to undertake a dangerous job to earn your pay, than no job and be sure of starving," said Izuk.

Shanti nodded. She had heard business owners in Gorduum talk this way, and it always made her uneasy. *If I was the one making people work by climbing deadly trees in a jungle full of deadly animals, I would feel responsible for their deaths,* she thought. *I would feel as though I had done it to them, and if I was not making sure that they were rewarded for that risk...* She drew a shuddering breath and pressed her hands on the hard knot that was tightening in her stomach.

"Thank you for your answers. Chechezuk is a beautiful city, but I am just so unfamiliar with it."

"Yes yes," Chezur. He leaned over to the older woman and muttered something in their jagged language to her. Shanti stood, her cheeks flaring and walked away from the trio as quickly as she could. They had treated her quite shortly and she did not relish the thought that they were about to become deliberately insulting to her face. As she sat down in the chair that she had been directed to in the first place she realised that she had left her drink by Chezur and his companions, half finished.

Shanti slouched in her chair and sighed. Then a servant arrived beside with another of the drinks she had left behind, holding it out to her.

"Oh! Thank you!"

The servant looked down until she took the glass, and then rushed off without a word. Shanti leaned back in the soft chair and sipped at the drink.

26

"Good morning my dear," said a voice from just behind Shanti's shoulder, and she nearly fumbled her glass. Only a few drops of the pale drink spilled out, and thankfully they landed on the wooden floor, not her clothes, or the lush fabric of the chair she was sitting in.

"I'm sorry," said Kayzark as he walked around the chair to where she could see him more clearly. "I didn't realise you would startle so."

"I just wasn't expecting you," stuttered Shanti, feeling embarrassed. *Does it look like I'm trying to be some sort of sneak? I hope he isn't offended.*

"Is your partner not coming? Is there something wrong with our proposal?" Kayzark's eyes flicked around Shanti, examining the empty space. She grimaced.

"No, we decided that Keema would do better to explore the city itself than the jungle. That way we learn more between us both." Shanti hoped that this explanation would do. She felt awkward discussing her wife with this man, who was effectively a stranger to her.

"So long as this is no sign of displeasure?"

"Not at all, I am still very keen to find out about your operation, and to see why you think you will be so successful so quickly."

"Very well. Come, I want us to be on the water before noon," smiled Kayzark, offering his hand out for Shanti to hold as she rose to her feet. She looked around for somewhere to place her glass and a servant materialised with their hands out to take it.

"Oh, thank you," she said as she passed it over, but they were gone already.

Kayzark led her out of the back of the building, to one of the small private landings on the canals that she had been able to see as she walked through the streets of Chechezuk. It was made of broad stone and low enough that small waves and ripples bouncing through the canals washed up onto it occasionally. There was a long thin boat tied front and back to wooden posts at the landing, and a short woman with thick curly yellow hair stood in the back. She had a sharp nose, but a broad smile, and she had a similar broad figure to Kayzark himself.

"Good morning Ekurk," said Kayzark as he swung one leg over into the boat. It swayed and wobbled and Shanti frowned. It was much narrower than the boats she had ridden in Gorduum. The ferries on the mighty river Nataat were much larger and steadier than this slim boat.

"Come along, it is stronger than it looks," chuckled the woman at the back. Shanti blushed as she stepped over, gratefully taking Kayzark's hand again as she got her balance and sat down facing him.

"I'm sorry for the awkward position," he said. He

had sat down near the feet of the woman, leaving the front of the boat for Shanti. "You'll have to turn if you want to watch where we are going, but it keeps the boat balanced better this way."

Ekurk nodded at Shanti and then unhooked the rope behind her. It had been looped over a tall thin extension of the canal-boat's stern, shaped to resemble a large feather or crest that stretched up to the height of Ekurk standing at the rear. It was carved into deep sharp ridges that made Shanti think of waves, or a face. A servant walked out of the building, across the landing, and undid the rope at the front of the boat, then spun around and vanished back inside. Ekurk placed both hands around a tall pole leaning against the side of the boat and pushed. The muscles in her arms bunched and shifted as she fought to bring the boat to motion. Her eyes narrowed with focus, but then she pulled up the pole and angled it forward and pulled again. Soon they were sliding along the canal smoother than glass.

Shanti was amazed at the way Ekurk was able to guide the boat around corners and through small spaces with ease. She felt like a fish, slipping along through the water's currents. Even when the canal met another waterway, and other boats were slicing along, Ekurk didn't seem to adjust her speed or her course, and yet the boats never even came close to colliding.

Some of the canals were just like the ones Shanti had already seen, just as broad as the streets that the pedestrians were using, broken up by landings leading into other buildings, or passing under the small humped bridges that Shanti had been crossing. But some took her into the private canals that the streets didn't overlook. These were much tighter spaces, with buildings that nearly touched overhead. Shanti could reach out and run fingers along the algae soaked wood that held up the structures on either side of her at the same time. Kayzark laughed again.

"We're nearly out of the city," he told her after they had been travelling for nearly twenty minutes. "Then we will transfer to a more appropriate vessel for the voyage out to the orchards."

Shanti nodded and wondered what the journey to the orchards might entail. She was excited to see what sort of vessel Kayzark was going to treat her with next!

The end of Chechezuk came much faster than the edge of Gorduum had. There, the city had dwindled, as buildings grew shorter, smaller, and less frequent, until eventually a traveller would admit that they were in farmland and not Gorduum anymore. Here, the last building rose out of the water alongside the canal, and then their thin boat shot out from the gap between it and the next building, floating across metres of open water. Shanti could see the last building of Chechezuk behind them like a cliff that they had just escaped, towering over the dark surface of the water.

On the far side of the water was the jungle, confronting Shanti with its size. She had assumed that the jungle everyone had told her about would be similar to the forests that surrounded Graama, and where she had spent so much of her childhood playing. But these trees were nothing like that forest. The jungle was dark and full of shadows that clustered below the broad hanging leaves of the trees that made it up. From the narrow boat, Shanti could see the trunks of the trees rise from the water in spiralling twisting piles. Algae and moss covered them in a soft green coat. The jungle was thicker and darker and more menacing than she had expected.

Though the trees reached at least two stories into the air above the water, they were so broad, and their roots and branches dipped and curled so low, that Shanti felt as though she would be able to walk between them as though through small bushes. As though she might run her hands across their green tops, just like she did when walking through the long grass of the fields in Graama. The water between city and jungle carried more waves than the canals, as there was more space for them to build and rise, but the jungle broke them down again, and the waters in the dim space beneath the trees looked still.

"It's stunning," she breathed. "I've never seen anything like it."

"It's an impressive jungle for sure."

"One of the other passengers on my ship from Gorduum said he had come to explore the jungle and find new groves that haven't been found before," said Shanti. Now that she could see the land that Rahit had come to explore, she wondered how he and his wife were doing. She could not imagine that it was going well.

Kayzark laughed in rolling bellows.

"Someone from Gorduum came to explore the jungle?" He cackled again. Shanti turned and saw him wiping tears away from the corner of his eyes as he tried to stem his laughter. "Excuse me, please. It's just that I always find the confidence of foreigners amusing!"

"Is it dangerous?"

"Is it dangerous!?" Kayzark bent over as the laughter burst out of him again. Standing behind him and moving with a long smooth motion to push the boat along with her pole, even Ekurk grinned at the question.

"Did you hear about the alligators yet?" he asked. Shanti nodded. "They are the biggest threat I would say. As in, the physically biggest thing that can kill you. But there are snakes, snapper fish, poisonous frogs, jagger thorns, and even the fisher hawks will consider marring your face if you look at them wrong." Kayzark smiled, and the look in his eyes was one of cruel amusement. "Yes, the jungle is no place for anyone who doesn't understand what they are taking on. Is it dangerous!" he repeated and his shoulders shook in amusement.

Shanti turned back to look at the twisted trees as Ekurk turned the boat and pushed them to the right, following the edge of the city, floating halfway between civilisation and the wilds.

Shanti stared at the jungle as Ekurk poled the narrow canal-boat around the edge of Chechezuk. It was so close, and so unlike anything that she had ever seen before. Brightly coloured birds swooped out of the dark trees and then curved through the air until they dived back into the foliage.

The water that wrapped around the city was not very deep. Ekurk was still able to use her pole to move them along with ease, and soon they arrived at some sort of inland port. It was made up of a broad open platform with many much larger boats tied to it. At the back of the wide wooden dock was an archway between two buildings and Shanti could see a small glimpse of the streetlife beyond. Behind them other boats slipped in and out of watery passages between the buildings.

Ekurk guided the canal-boat to an open space on the edge of the dock and then tossed a loop of rope over a wooden post. Kayzark motioned for Shanti to get out of the boat first and then followed, carefully holding on to a bollard carved into the shape of a squat person poking up out of the deck. He stood up and coughed as he straightened his clothes and then lifted his broad hat onto his head.

"Thank you Ekurk," he said with a nod then smiled at Shanti and motioned for her to follow him. She slapped at an insect that had landed on the back of her neck. He led her to another boat, this one much larger than the one that Ekurk had brought her here on. It was broader as well, with a front that curled up like the edge of a scroll and a very low wall around the sides. If not for the large mechanism at the rear of the boat, Shanti would have called it a raft. The tangle of metal gears and plates that took up the end of the deck was as tall as her shoulder, and looked heavy enough to sink the boat. Shanti wondered how safe it would be to travel onboard this vessel. Four people stood at the rear of the craft, wearing the same simple clothes as the servants who had waited on her and Kayzark in the large business rooms. They kept their eyes low as Kayzark and his guest walked on board.

A thin man with a shaved head and a short cropped orange beard stood near the rear of the boat, holding on to a long pole that jutted forward from the mechanism. Two broad shouldered guards, a man and a woman, were at the front of the boat, watching everything around them with narrow blue eyes. Both wore their hair long, pulled back into tails high on their skulls. The man nodded at Shanti as she walked alongside Kayzark, but the woman didn't stop searching for danger. Shanti's host sat on one of three broad backless chairs in the middle of the craft and waved at the one beside him, so Shanti sat in it.

"This is much more suitable for journeying into the jungle. These two will help keep us safe, and that lot back there," he said, jerking a thumb over his shoulder, "are much faster than a pole. Let's go!" he called to the man holding the long pole.

At a signal from the man, the group of servants reached out and took hold of long handles that jutted out from the mechanism. They each began rolling the handles forward, like they were rowing. The handles turned huge wheels inside the mechanism and Shanti could see gears and cogs begin to spin with more and more speed. In the middle of the machinery was a huge wheel covered in flat paddles, and as the gears and cogs flew, the wheel began to move. Slowly at first, but then faster and faster, the paddles rose dripping with green water. The boat slowly pushed away from the dock and headed toward the darkness of the jungle.

27

———

Shanti wondered how the broad flat craft would manage to manoeuvre among the twisting roots of the jungle, but as they approached she realised that there was an open passage between the trees. It felt strange to think of the space that opened up as a river, when there were no banks, and the same water spread out under the trees at its sides with no land in sight, but she had to assume that was what it was. A river-like depth where the water ran through the jungle, leaving a broader gap between the trunks and allowing the craft from Chechezuk to splash upstream. Within moments the city was hidden by curtains of thin dangling branches covered in tiny green leaves. The only sounds were the clacking of the mechanism and the rhythmic splash of its paddlewheel.

"How far from here are your orchards?" she asked.

"About an hour," sighed Kayzark. He shuffled on his seat. "Best get comfortable. Do you play Intrigue?"

He dug a pouch out of a box that was sitting by his chair and opened it up to reveal a set of small carved wooden tokens in light and dark wood. They were hexagonal and had different animals carved on the top, in a sharp simple style. When Shanti told him that she did not know how to play, he smiled and told her that he would remove many of the pieces from his side so that she would have an advantage. One of the guards frowned when Kayzark beckoned but then sighed and brought over a simple table to set between their chairs.

Kayzark explained how each of the pieces moved and then they took turns placing the animals on the table and moving them along the edges of each other. Soon Kayzark had trapped Shanti's crested lizard. She recognised it as one of the lizards that roamed through the city immediately, despite the stylised nature of the carving. As she retrieved her other pieces, alligators and snakes and hawks according to Kayzark, she asked him why the lizard was the piece she had to protect. He shrugged.

"Tradition I suppose," he grunted and then they began another game. "Jungle knows they are annoying animals usually." This time Shanti was just about to move her hawk across from one side of the pieces to the other and trap Kayzark's lizard when he shifted a snake that she hadn't noticed and completed his own trap. She smiled.

"This is fun! I nearly had you!"

"You did!" agreed Kayzark. He waved away an insect that was beginning to buzz down to the brim of his hat. "But I don't have any alligators or snapper fish."

"I'm very lucky," said Shanti with a carefully straight face. They both laughed.

The game filled much of the next hour, but Shanti also spent some time admiring the jungle around them. Although the view was all very similar from minute to minute, Shanti found each tree, each pool of water fascinating and engaging. The whole jungle was so different from the tall straight forest near Graama that she had grown up running beneath, or the broad and cultivated fields that grew outside Gorduum.

A snake dangled from the branches of a tree in long loops. Shanti gasped and pointed it out to Kayzark but by the time he looked the snake had gone. Kayzark said that it may have just been vines, but Shanti was sure it had been a snake.

Then the craft moved around a bend in the river and Shanti saw what must be Kayzark's orchard.

It was a building, although fortress might be a more appropriate way to describe the wooden edifice that rose up from the dark still waters that spread between the trees. A clearing in the jungle had been filled by the structure, although Shanti couldn't tell whether it was a natural clearing, or whether the twisting trees had been pain-stakingly felled and removed in order to create the space.

There was a fence wrapped around the outside of the area claimed by Kayzark's operation, built of tall thin poles almost a hands-width apart and held together by horizontal beams behind the posts. Water slid between the poles with barely a ripple. Standing at the top of the fence were figures wearing broad hats, mere shadows beneath the grey cloud filled sky. One of them raised a hand as soon as Kayzark's craft rounded the trees in the river. One of the guards onboard raised their hand in return, holding their arms at strange angles.

"The signs let the guards know that it is us. They'll be getting a telescope out to examine us as well, you should wave."

Shanti turned back to face the distant compound and raised a hand to her shoulder and shook it slightly, feeling self conscious. There was a glint of light from the fence and then one of the figures waved back. She stuck her hand down quickly.

As they approached, Shanti tried to get a sense of what lay beyond the fence, but could only see steep roofs with wooden tiling on them. With a closer view of the fence, she found that it was shorter than she had thought at first as well. They moved alongside the fence, turning to follow it to the right until they found a sliding gate that had been pulled to one side. Once they drew level with the opening, the boat turned to the left and went through the gap into the compound. The gate was pulled shut behind them by a system of ropes and pulleys. Water sluiced around the wooden gates, sending low ripples scudding across the water in and outside the compound. They died and settled much faster than Shanti expected. She looked up at the walkways along the inside of the fence, and her eyes widened. There were a lot of guards here.

"Why so many guards?" she asked, placing a hand over her mouth.

Kayzark grunted in surprise. "Because if someone came out here and took my orchard, they'd make a lot of money?"

"How could someone take your orchard?" Shanti asked. "Doesn't it belong to you?"

"Yes, but if they got rid of my guards, maybe it would belong to them. Who would argue?"

Shanti shook her head slowly. *What a strange system,* she thought. *Surely everyone knows when something belongs to someone else. It doesn't just magically belong to a new person without following some sort of rules?* Shanti knew that thieves existed, but they were the exception in society, not living by the system that everyone else agreed to. *That has to be the case, right?*

One of the guards was walking over a shoddy wooden dock to their boat. It pulled up to a mooring post and the guards onboard moved towards the edge to greet the newcomer. He was carrying a long heavy spear with two broad tips at one end that gleamed like butcher's knives. Shanti found that her pulse was beginning to race, even though she knew that she had done nothing wrong. *Maybe he is going to do something wrong,* she suddenly thought. *Maybe I have been kidnapped, or worse!* She recognised the old fears that were rising to the top of her mind and began the exercises she used to slow her breathing, trying to calm the frantic thoughts before they overtook her.

The guard raised his hand at the occupants of the vessel and then frowned as he looked at the water around it. He jabbed the double pronged spear into the water once or twice, swirling it around as though he was stirring a cup of tea.

"Did you see one?" asked Kayzark from the comfort of his stool.

"Not as such sir," replied the guard without

taking his eyes from the water. "But there's one that's been following boats in through the gate over the last week or so, and we haven't managed to get the blasted thing yet."

"You've managed to scare it out, but not spear it?" Kayzark sounded annoyed.

"Sir, if we tried to corner it, we'd end up damaging the fence!" protested the guard. He pressed his spear down again. This time it hit something solid just beneath the water's surface.

The water erupted as a massive creature like a tree trunk with small arms and legs jammed onto its sides flipped into the air, spinning and thrashing to knock aside the spear tip that had driven into its back. The guard was shoved backwards by the spear's shaft, and the wooden pole bent then popped out of the creature's back with a spurt of blood, before rolling along the deck and slipping between two loosely attached boards. The creature slammed onto the deck by the guard and Shanti saw its mouth open, stretching wider and wider until it looked like a pair of scissors with jagged teeth and bright yellow flesh around the outside. It snapped shut, barely missing the guard's leg as he shouted for help and tried to scramble away.

The two guards on Kayzark's craft stepped forward and pulled out their weapons. One muttered a prayer of sorts, pushing his hand forward with thumb and two fingers extended. "Alligators be calm."

Kayzark himself was still sitting on his chair. "What are you waiting for?" he yelled. "Open the gate and let it loose!"

The gate began to rattle behind them, and other

cries and shouts began to echo around the compound. People came running towards the small dock, all carrying a variety of implements to fight off the creature. One man caught Shanti's attention immediately. He was tall and strong, with the slim taut muscles of someone who used them hard everyday. His head was bald and Shanti couldn't help but compare his pale skin to a skull. She shivered as she wondered whether the gigantic creature would kill him. He was carrying a spear of his own, with a long broad blade on the end.

Shanti didn't think any of them could be effective against the monster though. The first guard's spear had gouged a bloody hole in its back, but that didn't seem to have slowed it at all. The creature coiled and whipped from side to side, its ridged tail alone longer than anything anyone was carrying with them.

It made a sound like a gurgling hiss but then turned and dropped off the edge of the deck with a crash of water, and vanished beneath the surface. Within moments, the ripples had spread and died and the water looked still. Shanti couldn't bring herself to lean over the edge of the craft to examine the water, but she would have sworn that it looked peaceful and empty even now, though she knew that beast must be hiding just beneath the surface.

"Is it out yet?" called Kayzark to the guards on the fence. The one nearest the craft shrugged and then cupped their hands around the mouth to call out an answer. The powerful looking bald man glared at the water, as though he could clear the water with the strength of his anger. Shanti wondered how he would deal with the creature. By the look of his shoulders shifting as he moved the haft of the spear in his hands, he might stand a chance. She released a breath that she didn't realise she had been holding.

"We'll wait until we see sign of the alligator outside, but without the Water's help there's no way to be sure whether it's the same one leaving or another one from out in the jungle," came the call from the guards high on the stockade. Shanti was thankful for Felldan's lessons, which allowed her to understand much of the Zukian being spoken around her.

"Muck the thing," growled Kayzark, mostly to himself. "Very well!" he called out. "Tell everyone to stay well clear of the edge of the dock until we get a better idea if it has gone!"

He waited until his guards motioned him forward and off the craft, then headed over to the guard who had dropped the spear. That man was standing with hunched shoulders and he was panting and gulping over and over again. Kayzark stood next to him and put an arm over his shoulders, remaining there until the other man took a deep breath and nodded. Kayzark nodded too, then slapped the man on the back in an encouraging manner and returned to Shanti. She looked at the water for a long time before darting across the open space between the craft and the deck.

"I don't blame you," he said. "Alligators are a huge problem. That's part of the expense of the tuft, of course."

"Of course," breathed Shanti. She couldn't believe how close she had been to something so devastating, and her hands were shaking. There had been no blood, but the panic that had struck her body stirred memories that she was always striving to leave behind. She shivered. *I never sent that letter home,* she realised. *And now my family will have no idea where I am or what will happen to me. They don't know about Keema.* She felt as though ice was seeping through her body.

28

"Training people is some of the expense too, traditionally speaking," Kayzark said once they had walked through the collection of buildings that made up his compound and reached the far end. They stood on the walkway at the top of the fence, staring out at an area of the jungle that Kayzark had claimed as his own. The leaves on these trees were paler than the rest of the jungle, and their branches thinner, but the twisting roots and tangled canopy were the same. Shanti slapped at the back of her arm, squashing a large bug that had just tried to bite into her skin.

"When we first found the grove and started encouraging the younger trees, we'd hire people to go out on skiffs and climb up the trees to gather the pods," explained Kayzark. He pointed to a deck just inside the fence at this end of the structure. A series of tiny thin boats were pulled up onto the boards, their surfaces peeling.

"You don't use them anymore?"

"We don't, but the other orchards still have to. The cost of training someone to use a skiff, sail out through the dark water in the orchard, avoid the alligators, climb the tree, choose ripe tuft to put in the waterproof sacks, fill up the skiff fully, and get it back here was eye watering, I can tell you. And that was before some of the mucky ingrates began demanding we pay them more money!"

Shanti looked out past the fence at the trees. Their pale leaves made the orchard stand out from the jungle around them. *Demanding that you paid them more money? It sounds like a really difficult job.* Shanti found that the thought of Kayzark being angry at the workers who had to work in such a dangerous place made her feel nauseous. *Surely they deserved enough money to make such a dangerous job tempting?* Her stomach rumbled. But she didn't want to offend this man, especially not while she was out at his private fortress. Despite the glow of the midday sun behind the clouds, and the wide open deck that they stood on, Shanti felt an old familiar fear crawling up her back. She shook her head and swallowed hard.

"Could I see some of the workers? After all, I am here to ensure that your process is as promising as we were told. If we are going to come to any agreement, that is."

"I understand. Unfortunately, it will be very difficult," said Kayzark. The broad man turned and sighed. "Most of our workers are already in the orchard for the day and they won't be back until nearly night. You might catch a glimpse of a few workers in the nearest trees if you are extremely lucky."

"Could we not go out to observe them?"

Kayzark chuckled. "I shall put it this way: Have

you noticed that our fence only goes so far? It ends here?" He gestured at another gate in the fence, slightly smaller than the one they entered through. It opened into the small lagoon that held the worn out skiffs. "It encircles our equipment, and our warehouses where we bundle the tuft ready for transportation. But we don't fence the orchard itself."

"Yes, I see that. I assumed it would be too expensive to build a fence all through that entire space. Is there another reason?"

"The jungle protects the orchard." He pointed overhead. Circling in the sky were the silhouettes of three birds.

"What are those?"

"Fisher Hawks. They're violently territorial, so even a large, well-covered intruder will have to try and fend off their talons from gouging their eyes. You've seen the alligators already, and there are many other creatures in the waters that make unexpected intruders extremely short lived." As Kayzark spoke, his eyes shone and Shanti felt her stomach clench.

"So your workers had a point," she said carefully. "It's extremely dangerous out there?"

Kayzark grunted. "Yes I suppose. We certainly found it got harder and harder to employ anyone. They'd insist on living in town and wanted us to provide transport out here everyday and..." he trailed off, shaking his head. "Anyway, we came up with a better plan."

"Better?"

"Come with me."

He turned around and climbed down a ladder leaning against the walkway they stood on. Once he had reached the main deck again, he led the way towards the nearest building. It was narrow, trying to use up as little as possible of the limited space that the soggy landscape allowed. This was the main building that Shanti had been able to see from outside the fence, tall and with a sharply ridged roof. Kayzark reached the broad double doors first and pushed them open. Shanti followed him inside.

Shanti paused at the threshold, waiting for her eyes to adjust to the dimmer light inside, though she was relieved that tall thin windows split the wall at regular intervals. The room wasn't as dark and confined as she was worried that it would be. Inside was a large space where walls had clearly been torn out, remnants of them poked out of the roof and floor in some areas. *Strange, surely people would be tripping over those all the time. Otherwise Kayzark would have finished the job,* Shanti told herself.

Lining the space were dozens of cages. Each was a few metres long and filled with old branches and twigs. As Shanti followed Kayzark into the centre of the room, Shanti looked into the cages, trying to figure out what was inside. She caught flashes of orange, but every time that she turned her head to focus on the colour, there was nothing left to see. Thin leafy branches shook as she walked by.

"What is this?"

Kayzark beamed and spread his arms. "This is how we will corner the market!" He walked over to the nearest cage and banged on the thin metal struts. Inside, a dark green lizard like the ones that Shanti had seen around the city jerked from its position on one branch and scuttled behind another.

She could see its dark eyes peeking around the wood, watching them.

"The lizards?" Shanti didn't understand.

"Yes indeed! They don't require us to pay them, they swim through the water to the orchard much faster than the workers used to pole the skiffs, and they can gather far more in the same amount of time!"

"So, it isn't as dangerous for them? Are they used to the jungle?"

Kayzark shrugged. "Some of them die, but they're only animals."

The knot in her stomach twisted again. "How do you get them to do it then? If it is dangerous, surely they would try to get away?"

"They would," he admitted happily. "But that's the secret we solved." He thumped the top of the cage again, and the lizard inside ducked out of sight completely. "You see, the mucky little creatures have been all over Chechezuk for its whole history, but no one ever figured out where they came from. It turned out one of my employees found out where they nest! The lizards mate for life and protect their eggs fiercely, so that's what we have in these cages."

"You have eggs in the cages?" Shanti was confused.

"I mean, sometimes, but more importantly, we have the mates in the cages. This one's partner is gathering tuft in the orchard as we speak."

Shanti leaned over the cage and looked in, trying to find the lizard that she had seen. Its dark green scales and long thin tail helped it blend in with the foliage that had been used to fill the cage.

"And they understand that they need to collect

tuft for you? Surely most animals would just think their mate is dead?" She was obsessed with exploring the full meaning of this bizarre set up. She must have misunderstood some part of it, there must be something she was missing that would help it all make sense to her.

"They are remarkably smart! You can train them to do just about anything, with the right motivation! There was one occasion where some of them tried to stop the collection, but we simply showed them the punishment and they got back to work." Kayzark folded his hands over his belly, his fingers interlaced like machinery. "So cheap and so fast. The other tuft investors would love to have an orchard as effective as ours."

"But you don't let them have any of the lizards, or tell them where the nesting site was," said Shanti slowly. She was getting a full picture of it all. Kayzark smiled like a proud older sibling.

"I thought you looked like a smart girl! You have it exactly!"

"Can I take another look at the orchard?" Shanti wanted to get out of this shadowy place as quickly as she could. She couldn't shake the image of a single eye peering at her from behind a branch.

"Yes, surely. I will see if we can spare a telescope as well, that might help you catch a glimpse of our workers in the trees."

Back at the gate by the unused skiffs, Shanti took the telescope she was offered and held the cool metal to her eye. She saw a wobbling tree in clear focus and concentrated on holding the metal tube as still as she could. As she brought her trembling hands under control, she saw a lizard with much more orange than green in it's scales. The creature was creeping down a curled treelimb, with a heavy black sack tied around its shoulders. She tracked it as it climbed down. When it reached the roots she watched as it paused to rummage with the sack and then examine the water carefully. It walked slowly in, creating almost no ripples at all, and then Shanti watched its orange head slip along the water.

A distant scream made her pull away from the telescope. One of the hawks in the sky above the orchard was plummeting towards the canopy. It slipped into the leaves, creating no disturbance. If she hadn't been watching, she would never have been able to say where the bird had gone or whether there had been a bird there at all. She kept her eye on the trees, waiting. Eventually it came flapping back out of the branches, wings beating, something long and orange clutched beneath it. The shape flicked and twisted, clearly trying to escape but the bird flew higher and higher and Shanti had to look away.

I watched it happen, she thought. *That creature was working in such a dangerous place, because this man has found a way to threaten and manipulate these animals, and one of them was just taken by a bird, and all I did was watch. I watched.* Shanti thought of the readings she had given, standing at the rear of the Tide's Daughter. She could feel tears pricking at the side of her eyes, but she didn't want to make Kayzark angry so she sniffed and squared her shoulders.

"Is this all of your operation?" She knew that she had to get a full picture of what was going on here, in order to understand what role she and Dunin would be taking in it.

"There's only the threshing-house left to show you. Come on."

Kayzark led her to another building and opened the door. Inside the building was one wide room, filled with rows of low tables. Piles of tuft covered the tables, and Shanti could see pod casings and branches tangled in the material. Standing by the tables, with their arms rummaging in the tufts, were even more of the lizards.

"What happens here," she said. Her voice felt as fragile as a spiderweb.

"The lizards deburr the tuft, removing all the extraneous materials that get in the way. We don't bother spinning it, I haven't found a way to train them to do that yet."

"But if you could?"

"Then we absolutely would. We could charge even more for spun tuft by the bale!"

Shanti nodded.

"Thank you," she said to him. "I think you have shown me enough to know what we are getting ourselves into." She made sure to smile as she spoke. He smiled in return, and then led her through the threshing-house to a door on the far side. As they walked through, Shanti was sure that the lizards were watching her with their black eyes. Everytime she tried to look back at one of them there was no evidence that they were watching, but she felt sure. At the far door sat the bald guard she had noticed earlier, though he wasn't carrying his broad spear now that he was inside. His eyes burned brightly above a thick fiery beard.

Once outside the wide building, Kayzark led her back to the paddlewheel boat. He took the long way through the compound, showing her the storage warehouse. Large rectangular packing crates were stuffed with the material and then bound closed with thick twine and stacked.

The ride back to Chechezuk felt quiet. Kayzark was sipping on a tall glass of yellow juice and offered one to Shanti. She accepted, but it was not finished by the time they reached the dock where Ekurk was waiting to pole them back into the canals between the buildings.

29

Shanti walked back through the streets to the Plaza and wished that Keema had come with her to the orchard. She felt sure that her wife would have been able to help her understand how she was feeling. A lizard had crawled halfway up a building on the edge of the Plaza and Shanti stared at it until it finally scuttled up and over the roofline out of sight. *Does it know what is going on? Did it ever work out there in the orchard? Would it even care, it's just an animal. Right?* Was the way Kayzark kept the lizards restrained and put to work any different to the way Keema treated her horse?

She wanted to go to Temple. Sitting with the community that she had found in Gorduum would have settled her nerves and calmed her down. The older folk would have shared the wisdom that they had learned over years, the youth would have brightened her with their optimism and jokes. She and Keema could have sat together, surrounded by a blanket of the well-being that could exist in the world.

What well-being is there for those creatures

though? What would Priest Komom have told her to do? How would she have reacted to the way Kayzark was treating the lizards? Would she have chosen a specific reading to teach the parishioners how to react to this situation? Shanti wished she knew the Writ well enough to know what Priest Komom might have chosen for such a reading. She wished she could look through a copy of the Writ now, to see if she could find something that might help her.

Shanti walked unseeing through the Plaza, moving around the edge, looking in at each food stall without really noticing what they were selling. She wanted someone to come and tell her what to do. *Dunin wouldn't care, would he?* Her uncle would just want her to sign whatever documents were required in order to get the exclusive right to distribute Kayzark's tuft in Gorduum. Maybe that was all she needed to do here, mind her own business and then go home.

"There you are!" Keema's voice cut through the fog of confusion that had stuffed Shanti's head and it was as though a light had blossomed in the depths of the darkest night; pure, small and good. Shanti's heart leapt up her throat and pushed the tears that had begun to build up behind her eyes closer to falling as she gasped and turned to look for her wife. Keema was striding through the crowd, her smile wide and her eyes glittering.

"Keema," Shanti whispered and she threw herself forward and into Keema's arms, wrapping her own around the slim woman's waist. Keema's arms came around her and her fingers dug into Shanti's shoulders tightly and then began stroking her hair.

Keema's face was pressed down to the top of Shanti's head, her breath a breeze down past her ears.

"Petal, what's wrong?"

Shanti opened her mouth to begin explaining everything that had happened during the day and twisted her thoughts but then shook her head. It was too much, and now that she had Keema's arms around her, all that she wanted to do was get some food and then go back to their apartment. She lifted her chin up and kissed Keema instead, soothed by the warmth that spread through her body from their lips meeting, from the way Keema held her and the way she held Keema. Her muscles relaxed from a tension she had not acknowledged and then she stepped back and wiped her eyes with the back of her hand.

"Come on, let's get some dinner," she said. Keema nodded with worried eyes. "Did you find the park?"

Keema grinned and winked. "You'll have to wait to see what I found today!" She was as excited as a puppy.

Shanti felt her face relax as she smiled. "I can't wait for you to show me."

They went to a new stall and ordered some food, then went to sit down. Just as they had settled onto an empty bench and Shanti was going to ask Keema about the exploration of the city she had undertaken, someone else jumped onto the bench on the other side of Shanti. It was Arsook, the woman they had met the night before.

"Hi girls!" said the newcomer. "I was wondering if I'd see you here again! I rather hoped that I would."

"Hello again," smiled Shanti.

Arsook leaned in close and began talking about her work for the day without waiting to be asked. Apparently searching the jungle for good wood was a dangerous job, and Arsook described racing away from alligator nests, and avoiding swooping fisher hawks. When she felt that it would not be impolite, Shanti turned to see how Keema was doing behind her. Her partner raised an eyebrow and rolled her eyes a little, but she kept smiling as Arsook talked. Shanti turned back to the new girl and was glad to feel Keema's hand on her side. She put her fingers on top of Keema's.

"... got a good way from the city along some of the western streams and tributaries. Have you been to the edge of the city yet to have a look at the river? I hear that in other countries the rivers are better be-haved and you can see the ground around their main channels. That's not the case here! It's all the water of the river here, but we know where the river is and where the waters are feeding and flowing, by the grace of the Currents." She held her hand by her waist and twitched her fingers.

"I did actually," said Shanti, managing to break into the flow of words with a laugh. "I went out into the jungle and saw a tuft orchard. We went on some sort of paddleboat."

"Oh yes, those are good and reliable, though they can be a struggle to turn around the tricky spots. I imagine you stuck to the main river most of the way?"

"I believe so." Shanti thought about the wide space between the trees and realised that she didn't know if it was the main river or not. *How big is the main river? Could it be even bigger than the passage Kayzark showed me today?*

Arsook nodded and pursed her lips. "It figures. You've got to keep that wheel turning if you don't want whoever is working it to keel over from exhaustion, and so turning around corners takes a while. I share a paddleboat with my workmate, but it's only small so we can get around the roots easier!"

"Do you run the wheel? That looked absolutely draining!"

"It's a solid workout, but there are fringe benefits." Arsook pushed her loose pale sleeve up her arm, revealing lithe muscles that she flexed and shifted under her pale skin. Shanti reached over without thinking and then paused.

"Go ahead," grinned Arsook.

Shanti ran her fingers along the bicep as Arsook flexed again. It was so firm. The woman's skin looked even paler when Shanti saw her own fingers on top. She pulled away again.

"You are strong."

"Thanks," said Arsook, pulling her sleeve down again as insects began to hum closer in the evening air. "So how was the tuft orchard? I've gone past a few in my time in the jungle, but tuft trees tend to be crooked and the wood rots too easily once you cut down the tree or lop off a few limbs. I look elsewhere for my troubles, with the River's help." The woman held out her hand, palm down, at hip height, and moved it in a short curve to the side.

"It was big." Shanti thought back to the sight that had spread out before her through the jungle beyond the tall fence. The surface of the orchard in her memory was made of shifting and shimmering green leaves surrounded by the darker trees of the main jungle. But the tuft trees stretched to the horizon beneath a sky full of grey clouds that moved in reflection of the canopy. "I had no idea that it would stretch so far-"

"But it makes sense, tuft pods are not very big and so you need a lot of it before you can start spinning it into something useful," Arsook put in.

Shanti closed her mouth mid sentence and smiled. "Yes, it does. I was impressed at how much was done right there. They have living quarters, warehouses, pod rooms where they remove the tuft itself. It's a remarkable process." Shanti tried to make it sound exciting but just talking about what she had seen was beginning to make her feel like curling into a shell. She kept thinking of dark eyes hiding behind twigs and branches.

"It's great stuff the tuft industry," said Arsook. "Between the tuft and the carvings, we've got textiles and artistry provided for the world! There's nothing like us!" she grinned, her teeth shining white.

"We have beauty in Gorduum," said Keema from over Shanti's shoulder. "Our lights are exceptional and valuable."

"And vulnerable." Arsook shook her head a little and chuckled. "I've heard lights are magnificent things, but they are so easy to damage and destroy. I've lived my whole life never seeing one here in Chechezuk! How can that be so important for the whole world, if I've never found any in this great city? But art inspires people, and I provide for the artists." She grinned again.

Shanti pressed on Keema's fingers at her side. "Everywhere has something to offer to the world,

I'm sure," she said. "But I must admit that I found the use of lizards confronting."

"Confronting? Like, you were upset? By the lizards?" Arsook's eyebrows wrinkled as Shanti asked the questions and then her eyes widened. "Oh my goodness, you went to Kayzark's orchards? Wow, I've been hearing that he found a way to use the lizards! That's incredible! How does the cunning scoundrel do it?"

"It is clever I suppose," allowed Shanti, but she was surprised by the joy that had erupted from Arsook. It made her lean away from the young woman slightly. "But it was cruel too."

"Cruel? How can it be cruel?" Now Arsook leaned backwards. "Those lizards are everywhere, surely you've noticed them?"

Shanti nodded.

"They're as bad as the bugs, crawling along the walls, coming in the windows, always causing a nuisance. It's better for someone to put them to work making something valuable for our city than just kill the pests, you must agree."

"Kill them?" Shanti felt her jaw hang open. "Can't you just leave them alone?" This woman had acted so cheerful and fun loving. She had reminded Shanti of her brother Fellbin, still far far away in Graama. But now she was speaking so casually about the harsh treatment that Shanti had seen in the orchard. Did she not care about anything?

"We can," groaned Arsook. "But then we have to live with them getting everywhere." She rolled her eyes and groaned. "They make such a mess."

"They make more than a mess," interrupted a deep voice from nearby. Shanti saw it had come from a young man with a bald head and a huge bushy beard that was as red as blood. The moonlight shone off the skin of his head, but his eyes were as hot as his beard. His shoulders were broad and his muscles pressed at the cloth of his shirt. She lifted a hand to straighten her hair as he stepped closer. *Is that the man from the orchard?*

"I'm sorry to interrupt ladies, but I just have to say, those mucky things are much worse than critters making a mess. Those things destroyed my mother's home."

"Really?" said Arsook. "I've never heard of them causing any lasting damage."

"I can vouch for it, you listen to me," he growled. "A bunch of the sodden things turned up in my mother's house when I was younger. They just kept crawling in through the windows and from under the floors. We tried throwing them out, we gave to the Lizards' temple and to the Night's temple, we tried poison, we tried killing them. But they'd avoid the poison, and have you seen their claws? The damp things fight back something vicious!" He sat down with a thump on the far side of the table and hung his head. "They started getting so fierce that we had to leave. My younger brother was still in a cradle, and my mother was worried that they'd attack him. Foul creatures."

30

"See what I mean," said Arsook, turning back to Shanti. "Creatures like that, well, why not put them to work? I bet Kayzark is making a fortune by using them! What do you think..." She turned to the newcomer, waiting for his name.

"Ukuck," he answered. "What do I think about what?"

"I was at Kayzark's orchard today and-" began Shanti.

"I thought that I recognised you," the man interrupted. "So you saw how he found a way to make the muddy things worthwhile?" *He is the man I saw,* realised Shanti. "It is pretty remarkable."

"I don't think that caging the creatures is really a way to make them worthwhile," she stuttered.

"I mean, I see that you wish they were free, and it's very cute, in a soft hearted sort of way," Arsook said to Shanti. She put out a hand and rested it on Shanti's knee."But you have to agree, it's a much cheaper way to run a business."

Keema leaned forward to try and add her own thoughts to the conversation. "Is it really so bad?

Plenty of animals are used on farms, to go hunting, to pull carts."

Shanti could hear a question in Keema's voice but didn't know how to respond. Did her wife think that Shanti was judging Keema for using her horse, Breenar, to pull a taxi cart in Gorduum? She sighed. She wasn't going to be able to explain to these two why the sight had upset her so much, especially if Keema didn't understand. To be honest with herself, she wasn't completely sure why it upset her. She wished again that she had someone to talk to. Someone who believed in the Masked God.

"Do you know if there are any temples in Chechezuk?" she asked, trying to shift the conversation.

"What do you mean? There's plenty of temples." Arsook answered while Ukuck drank from a tall glass of beer.

"There are!?" Shanti sat up straighter. This was more like it! Maybe she had just made a poor assumption that no one here would know the Masked God. Maybe the sailors were not very dutiful, and that was why many of them had not known about them.

"Sure. The River, the Trees, the Sun, the Wind. Plenty of temples to them all. You've seen the carvings of them all too, I'm sure." Arsook took a bite of her meal.

"I'm sorry? Carvings of the wind?" Shanti didn't know what Arsook was talking about.

"Yes, the man with the thin arms and legs and long hair. That's the embodiment of the Wind. There's a temple of His just around the corner, do you want to go?" She looked confused.

"No, I meant a Temple to the Masked God," said Shanti.

"Masked God? Is that something you people from Gorduum have? What does a Masked God do?"

"They watch us."

"Watch you? Sounds creepy. The Wind spreads the seeds of the jungle, brings rain and freshwater, and moves our ships to the corners of the map." Arsook sipped from her cup. "I know the Wind helps me. What does a weirdo in a mask do?"

Shanti pressed her lips together. She felt Keema's hand press at her side again.

"Maybe we should go home?" asked her wife from behind.

"No, it's alright," answered Shanti.

"Didn't you say that you were tired from today?" asked Keema.

"Yes, I was," Shanti frowned and waved a hand over her shoulder, trying to get Keema to stop. "But I think I need to explain this properly."

Shanti leaned forward to explain how the Masked God inspired her, and the community she lived in. She told Arsook and Ukuck the stories that had made her so happy to attend Temple with her family in Graama. She tried to explain how talking to the priests in times of trouble had helped her sort out emotions and feelings in her mind. In return, Arsook and Ukuck explained the temples of Chechezuk, small places that a person might visit on specific occasions when they needed the support of some part of the world. The carved figures that represented the gods had no names, and were known by their influence on the world. The Wind, the Sun, the River, all could be asked for favours in the small temples, but regular visiting bewildered the inhabitants of this city. Volunteers often ended up keeping the temples maintained, but it seemed outside their experience that someone could be considered to work there.

As the night wore on, Shanti tried to convince them that regular discussion and sharing with others was a valuable thing to be doing in honour of her god, but they just laughed nervously. *I'm coming across as some sort of fanatic,* she realised. *They think I'm crazy about all this.*

She wished that they had known about a temple to the Masked God somewhere in this city. It was the only way she could talk to someone about her feelings and concerns. But she had to admit, as her eyelids grew heavier and her voice grew hoarse, that she shouldn't be surprised that there wasn't one here. There were no temples for the gods of Chechezuk in Gorduum after all. *But why had those sailors come to listen to my readings then?*

A lizard moved across the stones near their table, only visible in the darkness and flickering torchlight because of its movement, the mottled green across its back hiding it in the shadows. Ukuck swung a boot at it, nearly catching the side of its head, but the creature leapt sideways and raced away before Shanti could say anything. She bit her lip.

"I think it might be time to go to bed now," she said.

"Thank you for telling us about your life back in Gorduum," said Arsook, standing up with Shanti and reaching over to touch her shoulder. The pale woman smiled. "I have enjoyed finding out more about you."

Ukuck stayed where he was, but moved his hand in a small wave.

Keema stood up too, putting her arm around Shanti's waist. "Thanks for spending the evening with us. Maybe we'll see you again."

"I do hope so," smiled Arsook, her eyes on Shanti's as she slid her fingers through her hair, pulling it away from her face and over her ear.

Shanti stumbled as she and Keema moved through the dark streets towards their lodging. Her legs felt heavy and tired, and she was only kept upright thanks to Keema's supportive arm. The streets were nearly empty at this time of night, and the few passers-by that were there stared unashamedly at Shanti and her wife. She just wanted to get into bed, go to sleep, and see what the new day brought. Keema got her ready for bed and laid her down on the mattress.

"I thought you said you wanted to come back hours ago," Keema said as she got herself ready and crawled into the bed next to Shanti. "You needed to get some rest."

"But Arsook could tell me so much about this place," said Shanti with her eyes closed. She wanted Keema to stop talking and let her slip into the dreamless dark that was waiting for her.

"I spent the day exploring it," replied her partner. "I think I could have told you a lot of that."

"It's not the same," muttered Shanti. " You're always there."

"Oh, I am, am I?" asked Keema as Shanti slid away, unable to fight sleep any longer.

.   .   .

SHANTI LAY in bed as the morning sun began to creep in through the window. Her head hurt and she wondered if she had slept awkwardly. Her mouth felt dry and sticky. *I hope Keema is getting some water.* She rolled over and swung her legs off the bed, then sat on the edge of the mattress and smacked her lips. Shanti rolled her shoulders, and enjoyed the feeling of the sun beginning to warm her back. It was taking her longer than normal to rouse herself.

She got dressed and looked around, wondering what she might need for the day, what she should do with herself. She would have to let Kayzark know her decisions soon, although she might be able to justify waiting until tomorrow before seeing him. The idea of staying in this city was beginning to feel uncomfortable, as though she had just taken an enthusiastic mouthful of stew only to find the vegetables in it tasted old and soft. She thought it might be a good idea to return to the Tide's Daughter and see how soon she could use the return trip that she had paid for.

Where is Keema? Shanti opened the door to the room and looked around the small landing outside and then leaned over the bannister and down the stairs, all the way to the ground floor. Keema wasn't there, but Felldan was walking down the steps a flight below her.

"Hey!" she called out. He stopped and looked from side to side with a puzzled expression on his face. Then he looked up and smiled as he realised Shanti was speaking to him.

"Good morning! How is your business in Chechezuk going?"

"Well thank you," replied Shanti. "Have you seen Keema this morning? Is she downstairs there?"

"No, I haven't seen her." He paused and leaned around, clearly trying to see if Keema was somewhere he might spot her, but then shrugged and looked back up. "She doesn't seem to be here."

"Would you mind waiting a moment then?"

Shanti rushed back into their room and looked through the suitcases for something to write with. After pulling two light dresses out and shoving them on the bed, she found a small notebook tucked between her blouses. Then she had to keep digging until she found half a pencil wedged in an internal pocket. *I wonder what the luggage maker expected me to keep in that space,* she wondered as she tried to pull the pencil out of the tight pocket.

Armed with the pencil and a sheet of paper torn from the notebook, Shanti wrote a quick message for Keema and put it on top of Keema's suitcase, placing a sock on top to keep it from flying away. With that done, she dropped the notebook and pencil back into her own case, and nodded sharply. She glanced around the room, checking that she had everything that she needed, and then walked out, shutting and locking the door behind her. *Did Keema have a key for herself,* she wondered. She couldn't just leave their room with all their belongings unlocked though, and so she put the key back in her satchel with a frown and headed downstairs.

Felldan was standing in the small lobby that the three of them had entered through only two days earlier, leaning against the wall and looking at his fingernails. He looked up and a smile spread across his face as Shanti came in.

"Have you made a deal with your contacts yet?" he asked, stepping up next to her and leading her out into the street. Pedestrians pushed past, and a trio of insects buzzed down towards Shanti and Felldan immediately. He swung his arm overhead, scattering them.

"Not yet," she admitted. "My contact seems to be keen to come to an agreement, and it certainly looks as though he will be able to supply us with a lot of what we are looking for. My uncle would consider it a perfect situation."

Felldan offered her his elbow as they moved along the street. She accepted, laying her hand on his sleeve.

"You don't sound convinced though?"

"I just have some concerns." Shanti wasn't sure if she should say anything to this man. He had been a great companion during the long voyage at sea, but after her conversation with Arsook and Ukuck the night before, she was concerned that no-one else would understand why she wasn't jumping at the chance to get involved with this business.

"Like what?"

She sighed through her nose and pursed her lips, then looked sideways at Felldan. *Are you going to get all confused, like they did*, she asked him in her head. She began to open her mouth and then shook her head.

"Don't worry about it. How about you, how has your work gone?"

"It's gone very well actually! I might even get a bonus if this all comes through properly." Felldan grinned and it made his face light up like a star. "I've had a few meetings with different people yesterday and today I am ensuring that I'm ready for Zekeka's return trip. Are you going to be travelling on Tide's Daughter to return to Gorduum as well?"

"I am hoping so, but I was going to check when that might be. It sounds like we could go together. But first, can you come with me to the Plaza? Maybe Keema is having breakfast?"

"Certainly."

31

———

The Plaza was not yet as packed as it would become in the evening, but still a thick crowd moved amongst the tables and milled around the stalls. It took nearly half an hour before Shanti was sure that she had seen everyone in the area, and could be certain that Keema was not among them.

"She's not here," she said as she rounded the Plaza and met back up with Felldan. He reached out a hand to her shoulder and lowered his head so that he could meet her eyes directly.

"I'm sure she's around somewhere. She seems like a capable young woman, even if she isn't made for spending time on the sea."

"Yes." Shanti took a deep breath. She knew Keema was resourceful and intelligent. She just had to hold onto that, and keep doing all the other things that she needed to do. "Speaking of that, let's go and see the captain."

Felldan nodded but then sucked on his lips and smiled. "Before we get down to business, would you like a tour of the city? I'm in no rush, we can always go to the captain later."

Shanti's brow furrowed. "I don't know…"

"Come on, we can have a look for your friend and see the sights, and then go speak to the captain. If we don't bump into her, then I'm sure we will discover her waiting at the rooms, or in this plaza for dinner!"

"I suppose so," replied Shanti. *She's not just a friend though,* she added in her mind. *She's my wife, the woman I declared that I would spend my life with. Although, it might be worth it if I can find some temple hidden away in the city that the others didn't know about.* The thought stiffened her back and she felt a fire grow in her heart. *Yes, that's a great idea! I just need some guidance. I've been feeling lost and adrift in the city, but part of that was just because I am in a new place. All I need is to reconnect with the Masked God, and a Temple will do that. I can talk to a priest and they will help me understand whether or not it is right to work with Kayzark. Yes, that's my plan!*

As she followed Felldan out of the Plaza and down new streets, Shanti felt a fresh sense of purpose and direction that lifted her chin and brightened her eyes. Felldan led the way, with Shanti's hand on his elbow. First they headed towards the outskirts of the city. Felldan told her that was what they were doing, but she had to take his word for it as the look of the buildings around her didn't change. In Gorduum, the buildings grew smaller and the alleyways tighter as one neared the edge of the city, with the largest and most impressive buildings rising from near its heart, like the tall dirt towers of an ant nest. Whereas in Chechezuk it appeared that the city was unchanging, a repeating milieu of dark wooden one or two storey buildings, punctuated by the occasional three or four storey giant, none of which had many windows, though all bore elaborately carved scrollwork along the rooftops that rose and fell like a row of teeth. They moved through the crowd and over small bridges, and all the while Shanti had no idea whether they were making progress or travelling in circles.

Then they turned left and walked under a low arch, covered in angular figures that stared down with wide unblinking eyes at the people passing underneath. Beyond the archway the city stopped abruptly, leaving a wooden path along the outside of the last buildings. After that stretched the wide water of the channel that surrounded Chechezuk, that she had ridden over with Kayzark yesterday. And finally, still further out past the green water, covered as it was with small boats poling their way from one location to another, spread the jungle just as impenetrable as it had appeared the day before.

Now Shanti noticed dark dots lazily circling in the warm air high above the green leaves. Birds drifting on the currents over the jungle. Dark shadows that curled around the trees in the water made her think of the alligator that she had seen in Kayzark's orchard. She shuddered.

"Are you alright? I thought you said that you went into the jungle already?" Felldan lifted a hand to cover hers on his arm. He leaned closer with a concerned expression.

"Yes, I'm fine," she smiled. "I saw an alligator while I was out yesterday. That was quite a worrying creature."

"Oh, alligators." Felldan nodded, his face serious. "I wouldn't want to tangle with one of those things. How close was it?"

"Honestly?" Shanti looked around and then pointed at an old man walking in the other direction with a large sack over his shoulder. "About as close as that man."

"Blinded Eyes," swore Felldan. "No wonder you flinched at the sight of the jungle!"

"Thanks for realising that I'm not just a vulnerable little flower."

"No no, you're a petal, aren't you?" he grinned.

Shanti pressed her lips together and looked away. *He shouldn't say things like that.* She thought of the long path that they had wound through the city to get to this place. *Would I be able to return on my own? Could I hire a boat to bring me through the canals?* She didn't have any idea how much it would cost to do such a thing, and whether the Lagoon and Plaza were real names that anyone else would recognise if she asked for directions. *Maybe if I ask someone about Kayzark, they might be able to direct me back towards familiar streets?*

Before she could convince herself to pull away from Felldan he began leading her along the path outside the last buildings of Chechezuk. *I'll stick with him for now,* she decided, *but I must make sure that he knows not to call me that in future.*

Buildings rose alongside the path they followed, exactly the same as the buildings that lined the streets inside the city. Doorways cut regular openings in the pale wood, and some of the doors themselves were painted in bright colours. Near the roof might be a tall thin window with swirling scrolls carved into the shutters. The eaves were carved with similar shapes, some curling like plants, others jagged like broken wood.

"Why did you bring me out here?"

"Looking over the jungle is one of the things that makes Chechezuk different to Gorduum. What do you see when you are outside of that city?"

"The hills, the fields, the lights." Shanti closed her eyes and thought about the beautiful visions that lay outside her new chosen home. She stayed inside the city most of the time, but the view that lay just outside always made her smile and her heart lighter.

"Exactly. I can see by your face that Gorduum makes you feel at home. It makes me feel this way as well. So, does this look different? How does this view make you feel?" He spread an arm towards the jungle, leaning back slightly to look into the cloud-filled sky.

Shanti looked at the jungle and drew a deep breath. The smell of damp wood and water plants hit her nose, and normally she would have said that it smelt dead or decayed. But today was different. She felt it's dark odour move down her body and stretch through her limbs.

"It makes me feel calm and still," she said.

"Yes. It is so still. As though it never changes; Like a mirror."

They stood together, looking at the jungle as the crowd walked around them.

Finally Felldan shivered and turned back to the path.

"Also, you said Keema was looking for a park that you wanted to see? The one I was talking about is near here and I thought that perhaps she had found it. We might even find her there."

"That's brilliant, thank you!" Shanti was thrilled to hear that Felldan had brought her somewhere that might help her find her wife. They continued down the path and walked under the next archway on their right, back into the canyon-like streets inside Chechezuk.

Shanti looked at her feet as they walked through the narrow spaces between the buildings. Sometimes they followed pathways alongside the canals back into the city, but they soon emerged back out on the boardwalk that surrounded the city. Shanti knew that the inhabitants of the city must think that she stood out like spilled wine on a carpet, so she was pleased that they didn't seem to glance at her more than once as she walked by.

The paths of the watery city were much easier to navigate than the ones she was used to back home. There were no carts that she had to dodge around! In Chechezuk the canals carried all the cargo that would be carried by carts in Gorduum; from weary travellers resting their legs, to tall stacks of bound goods or barrels. Thin canal-boats poled along with cargo stacked high in their bows. Shanti was amazed that they didn't topple into the water.

But the other thing that kept drawing her eyes downward was the path itself. They were walking along broad stone cobbles that had been carefully laid in repeating patterns. However, she knew that the city rested above the waters of the river and estuary that flowed freely over this whole land. *How do they stay up,* she wondered. She started leaning over the canals when she had a chance, leaning out over the railing of the short, humped bridges to see the thick, wooden posts that held up many of the buildings. She could see that they were solid wooden structures, with little thought given to making the building pretty. The inhabitants clearly used their carving skills for decoration, while the buildings themselves remained mostly square structures set on thick poles that drove deep into the water and mud.

She was so caught up with the arches and dark, slapping, wet sounds coming from beneath the city, that she didn't notice that Felldan had stopped walking. He had to touch her shoulder to bring her to a stop on the pavement and then she looked back at him with a small frown.

"Look," he said, pointing to what lay before them.

Another space between the buildings opened mere metres ahead of Shanti. It was much bigger than the Plaza, and possibly the size of the Lagoon. She could imagine many ships sailing into this space and drifting through the waters. A broad stone path wound around the edge of the space and water lapping echoed from under the buildings. Unlike the other watery spaces that Shanti had seen in the city, here the water rolled in small waves up a grassy shore of an island in the middle.

The shore rose like the back of a great hairy green creature from the water: curved and smooth. Not much further than the water's edge, the first roots began to coil up from the ground. They were each huge round ropes of wood, gigantic loops that knotted around each other. This pile of roots tangled higher and higher, blocking out any view of the buildings beyond, until they suddenly changed direction, spilling out across the sky above like a ceiling. A ceiling of green with speckled light peering through.

Shanti stood with her head tilted back and her mouth open, staring up into the mutlicoloured canopy. Dark greens, browns, pale creams, vibrant yellows. It was impossible to say whether she was looking at branches or leaves, reflections or shadows, it was all one broad and shining canvas. The wind shook the leaves at one end of the tree and the movement passed among the branches in the same manner as a breeze might send ripples over a pond.

Standing in the presence of such a huge tree made her think of her childhood, playing in the forests around Graama with her brothers and the other children of the village. They would play chasing games, racing each other to be the one who could make it back to a particular tree stump or rock before being tagged by the others. They would skip through the creeks from stone to stone. Living in Gorduum, Shanti had not realised how much she had missed the forest, but this tree growing here made her want to return to those forests. The jungle beyond the edge of the city was a new place, totally unlike the forests she knew, but this tree, this was familiar.

32

———

"Is that grass on the island? I haven't seen any since we arrived here," Shanti breathed.

"Sort of," said Felldan. "It's swamp grass. It's actually a bit like a sea weed? It grows in the water and on this island it is sometimes exposed when the water level goes down."

"The water goes down?" Shanti was surprised.

"Of course. Did you think it is always the same depth?"

"Yes?" Shanti felt her mouth hanging open a little as she tried to think of how to shape her thoughts into actual words. "Why would the water level ever change?"

"The river is always shifting in Gorduum, why wouldn't it do the same here?"

Shanti thought back to the times she had stood waiting for river ferries on the docks of the Nataat in Gorduum. The first time she had waited on them, the water had been sliding across the top of the stone docks in a thin film that left her feet damp. Now that Felldan pointed it out, there were other times that she had not received such wet feet. Were those at the same docks or others? She realised that she had assumed that these docks were simply built higher. She wondered if her cheeks looked as red as they felt.

"What causes it?"

"The same as in Gorduum. The seasons can be drier or wetter, sometimes the river breaks the channel and floods other areas more than usual. Even the tides of the sea can push more water into Chechezuk at times."

"So, the waters are low at the moment?"

"A bit. That's why the grass is exposed."

Shanti stepped forward and began walking around the tree. Some of the inhabitants of Chechezuk were sitting around the space as well, dangling their legs off the edge of the path and over the water. They sat with their friends, laughing through conversations, or eating some food that they had brought with them. They all looked to be enjoying spending time in the shade of the tree, but Shanti couldn't believe that they were treating it so casually. She wanted to find a perfect spot to stare at the tree for hours, taking in every piece of it!

She clutched both hands to her chest and breathed out and smiled. Then her eyebrows creased.

"Do you see Keema?"

Felldan flinched and spluttered.

"Keema? I, uh…" He widened his eyes as he looked around, shielding his eyes from the sun for a moment, then shook his head. "No, I don't think so. I would expect her to stand out!"

"So would I." Shanti looked away from the light

reflecting off the leaves and looked around herself. "She really isn't here."

"Is that such a problem? Look at this place, isn't it amazing?"

"Yes." *But I really did want to see it with Keema. I wonder if she had already found it. Was she hoping to introduce it to me?*

"I love going to new places and seeing all the amazing things that exist in the world. Have you ever seen a tree this massive? I want to sit and stare at it all day! How does something like this even happen?"

Shanti looked over at Felldan, the way he was smiling as he stared at this tree. She could see that the people of this city probably just saw a tree, an extremely pretty one maybe, and a wonderful place to eat your lunch with friends. But Felldan could see how much more than that it was, just like she did.

It was something truly ancient, older than much of the city. She could see that in its size alone. *What things had it experienced,* Shanti asked herself. *What had happened beneath those gigantic shielding branches? What joys and disasters were still to happen under its observation?* No one else understood why she wanted to see the world.

"Yes, it's beautiful," she agreed.

"Look, you can see the lizards in the tree." Felldan leaned over so that he was alongside Shanti, putting one arm around her shoulder to steady himself and placing his head only a centimetre or two from hers. He reached out to point with his other arm, but she blinked and tried not to move away from him. She looked down the length of his arm and finger to see what he had spotted.

Indeed, a lizard was clambering up through the huge whorling roots of the tree. This one was a much brighter orange than the ones she had tried to watch in the orchard out in the jungle. It retained some mottled green patches, but they were quite small, and restricted to a few blobs of colour over its rear thighs and hips. She watched as it scrambled, limbs flicking out and up the bark of the tree, climbing higher and higher.

Then one of the green patches on its back moved, and Shanti lifted a hand to her lips. The patch shifted and it became clear that the dark green was a baby lizard that had been clinging to the older one. The smaller lizard shot off the back of its companion and disappeared along a thin leaf-covered branch.

Shanti found herself thinking about her younger brother, Fellbin. *How is he managing without me to support him or to calm down the neighbours when he tries to make fun of them or plays pranks on them?* In the last letter that her mother had sent to her, Shanti remembered that they had mentioned that he was spending more time with the local priest of the temple in Graama. *But that was one of his favourite tales to tell,* she reminded herself. If Shanti had been given a sweetcake every time Fellbin had huffed into the house, thrown himself into a chair, and declared that he had passed his day in quiet introspective discussion with the priest, then she would have been a very contentedly fed young woman. Had she been treated to a small coin if she had seen him out causing mischief those afternoons, despite his claims, then she would have been a much wealthier person as well.

But she had been gone so long, and she knew Fellbin could not be relied upon to provide the help that her mother needed in her store. Shanti's mother was a firm woman, with strong opinions and a way of bringing others into her line of thinking. But Fellbin was like a gust of wind, carrying leaves and feathers with it, with no way to tame it until it decided to settle of its own accord. Shanti had been the one who spent the most time at the store, helping customers and stocking shelves. She had been the one to go and speak to the neighbour whose meal Fellbin had tainted with strange spices or whose pet dog Fellbin had been teasing over the garden wall. Without her, were they managing?

Shanti watched the larger lizard as it followed the younger, marvelling at the way its bright orange scales vanished into the mottled light and dark beneath the leaves of the gigantic tree. How did these creatures manage in such strange surroundings? They had grown to live in the jungle, clearly, but now they found themselves surrounded by buildings, all hard surfaces and sharp angles, unlike anything that the lizards must have been used to. How did they thrive in such a place? How did the grown lizards take care of the younger ones, when dangers surrounded them? Dangers like a large man with pale skin, bright eyes, and a plan to make himself very rich. Memories of events years old filled Shanti's head and she felt as though she would fall to her knees.

"They're amazing aren't they?" said Felldan, breaking her train of thought. "I think they are the thing that I most enjoy about coming to Chechezuk."

"They are striking." She shook her head and swallowed deep breaths of air, blowing them out slowly between her lips. Her heart was still pounding. "And it seems that they can be trained to perform quite complex tasks."

"What?" Felldan laughed. "Complex tasks? I've seen them used for simple duties, but it was always a coincidence. You know, someone might keep one as a guard animal for their storeyard? But the lizard only wants to protect the yard because it considers the area to be its territory, not because it helps the people living there."

Shanti wasn't sure how much she should share. Kayzark had openly admitted to using the lizards in his orchard, and was convinced that his knowledge of their breeding grounds was what gave him the edge over any business competitors. That was the only thing that he had kept to himself during her tour. But would it be appropriate to reveal this information to Felldan? Clearly they were able to understand the complex task of gathering tuft, and also to understand the threat of what would happen should they try to disobey.

She felt her brow furrow as she glanced at Felldan. He was usually so full of information about this new place. She had quickly come to rely on his perspective. Was he like most of the people in Chechezuk, did they all think the lizards were so simple? Or had he not noticed something that was right in front of him? He had proven himself to be a remarkably useful friend while they were on the Tide's Daughter, and he was being a lovely guide now. She decided to give him some of her trust.

"In fact, Kayzark uses them in his tuft orchards. They gather the tuft and sort it."

"Are you sure?" He stepped away so that he could turn his face to her fully. His hand left her shoulder and Shanti realised that she had not noticed that he had left it there as they spoke.

She nodded. "Absolutely. I watched them do it."

"But that's incredible! How does he train them?"

"I rather think that his methods must be something of a trade secret. I wasn't sure whether I should reveal this much."

"Yes, that is fair." Felldan bit on his lip and looked slightly above Shanti's head, his eyes unfocused. "That is quite a feat," he murmured, mostly to himself. Then he sniffed and shook his head. "Still, none of this is finding Keema, is it? Shall we go somewhere else?"

"Do you have a good idea where to go?"

"I have some wonderful ideas of places to show you, " he laughed. "But whether or not your friend is there, I cannot say."

Again, he called Keema my friend. He has to know that she means more than that to me.

Before she could gather herself to say something, Felldan offered her his elbow and they set off past the crowds and out of the gigantic open space, filled by the monstrous tree. Felldan took four sharp corners in succession and led Shanti to a small dock over a narrow canal. Three narrow canal-boats were tied up here, and their polers stood on the dock, watching Felldan and Shanti with wide eyes. One of them leaned over to whisper in the ear of her neighbour, who covered his mouth while his shoulders shook.

I wonder if they have ever seen anyone who looks so different to them, Shanti wondered. She had to force herself not to giggle. *We must be a strange sight to those not expecting us!*

"Good morning," said Felldan in Zukian. Shanti concentrated to make sure she followed what he said. "We'd like a bit of a scenic tour over to Kezustar, if you would be so kind?"

An older woman with a wrinkled face but strong broad shoulders stepped forward from the three. She spat on the dock and then turned and waved them onto her narrow boat, pulling her pole from where it leaned in the water with two others.

"Thank you very much," Shanti said as she stepped onboard, hoping she enunciated the sharpness of Zukian correctly, and settled her skirts.

"No problem," grunted the woman. She narrowed her eyes at Felldan as he stepped into the boat as well. "It'll cost yer twenty though."

"Twenty?" Shanti was appalled. "How far is it?"

"It's not that far," said Felldan in their own language. "But I did ask for a scenic tour. I want you to see some of the bigger bridges. If she fulfils that, twenty is reasonable. Half now?" he directed the question at the poler in Zukian again.

"Sure," she nodded, and held out her hand. Felldan rummaged in his pockets and then gave the money to her. She tucked it away into a pouch slung on the front of her belt and then lifted her second hand to the long pole.

"Here we go," she said, and they were off.

33

———

The narrow canal flowed in a dark straight path between the buildings on either side. Shanti watched a pair of lizards scuttle sideways along the eaves overhead, always trying to get further from the boat below them, but never actually changing direction. This meant that, as the boat moved, the lizards had to dart forwards again and again. Eventually they must have grown too nervous and they ran up and onto the roof, out of sight.

The boat reached the corner and the poler leaned into her pole, turning the narrow craft to the right. The new canal was broader, and more boats were moving along its deep dark surface. More footpaths were visible now, between the buildings and occasionally coming out to the edge of the canal. No one looked down the few feet to where Shanti sat in her boat but she watched them, searching the pale faces of the inhabitants of the city. She wanted to see just a glimpse of the darker skin and eyes of Keema, and it was a wish that sat heavily in her stomach, like a stone. She just wanted to see her wife.

"Have you seen the bridges?" asked Felldan.

"Of course," replied Shanti.

"No, not just seen that there are bridges, or walked over them," added Felldan. He leaned forward to touch her shoulder and gestured at the short round bridge that they were about to pass under. "Have you really *seen* them?"

Shanti looked at the side of the bridge and felt her eyes widen. The sides of the railing were as heavily carved as the opening bridge that the Tide's Daughter had passed under a couple of days earlier. That bridge had been gigantic, stretching across a massive gap between the buildings that reminded Shanti of the Nataat river back home, whereas this bridge was short enough for pedestrians to jump over entirely. And yet the sides had been lovingly detailed with more of the figures that she had seen on the first bridge. These figures were different though, including an old man with impossibly wide shoulders and thick curling hair in his beard and on top of his head. She could tell that he was old because the wrinkles in his cheeks and shoulders were chiselled deep into the surface of the wood, and simple white paint had been used to colour his curls.

"Who is he?"

"One aspect of the jungle. He represents the endless history of the jungle. It was here long before Chechezuk was carved from its borders, and should the city ever fade away, he is the one who will guide the trees as they grow through its old buildings and paths."

"What's his name?"

"The spirits don't have names for themselves," interrupted the woman while she pushed her pole in a steady rhythm through the water. She spoke Gawaalti with a heavy accent, but Shanti was impressed. She hoped her Zukian was half as clear as this woman's Gawaalti. The poler sniffed and pulled the pole up, shifting it forward and planting it back down so that she could haul the boat along. "But people might call him the Old Jungle, or Time, or something of that nature." The woman lifted her hand away from the pole and curled two fingers into a hook, before grabbing it again.

They moved into the dark space beneath the bridge, listening to the thunk and clip of shoes as the crowd walked up and over their heads. Beneath the bridge the sound echoed grandly, but more impressive to Shanti were the carvings that she found.

"They carved the bottom of the bridge," she burst out, reaching up instinctively as though she might run her fingers across the ridges in the wood. Her voice sounded hollow in the strangely shaped space.

"Yes," smiled Felldan. "They knew people would see it."

This scene was made of long thin lines, and at first Shanti wondered if it was a pattern that had been repeated along the wood, a series of lines like a ladder or railway track. But then she began to notice the slight shift of the angles, the small incisions that curled into eyes and teeth.

"Alligators."

"Yes."

"Do they ever come into the city?" Shanti moved herself into the middle of the seat she occupied in the boat. Though she hadn't been close to the edge before, she suddenly wanted to make sure she was as far as possible from the water.

The poler laughed.

"Naw, they don't come in here. Too noisy, too dangerous."

"Dangerous? For those things? How could anything be dangerous for them?"

"They might be able to snatch themselves a meal from the canals, that's true" said the woman. Her eyes widened and her teeth grinned as she leaned closer to Shanti. Then her shoulders shifted as she pulled backwards on the pole. "But before long they'd be hunted down by passers-by, let alone the polers and sailors themselves. Them creatures learned a long time ago not to bother with the city water."

"There's nothing to worry about," said Felldan. He shuffled along his own seat and reached out to place a hand on Shanti's knee. His eyes looked deep into hers, and the light washed across his face as they moved out from under the bridge. Shanti blinked and looked down. She patted the back of his hand and he leaned back, removing it. But she could feel the shape of his touch on her skin, even through the cloth of her skirts.

THE JOURNEY through the city was a delight. Shanti found her gaze distracted by many carved figures, some huge and posed to hold up the bridges that they were carved into, while others were smaller than the lizards that crawled along them.

More than once they moved out into broad open

spaces of water and travelled away from one cluster of buildings to another.

"Why are the canals so wide here?" she asked Feeldan when they were halfway between the buildings in one such crossing. The space was far larger than the Lagoon, enough for Shanti to ask if the city had stopped and they approached a new one.

"The islands that the buildings are set on were far apart here," he shrugged. "There's more than a hundred islands beneath the city."

After one of these crossings, the poler let the canal-boat drift in a slow circle as Felldan pointed out landmarks.

"That's part of the Chechezuk house of learning. It's a bit like the university back in Gorduum, but much smaller."

The building was the same size as the others that lined the path alongside the water, but tall panels framed the entranceway. Even from the water, Shanti could see the thin figures that stretched up in the wood, carved with slow long curls, and sharp ridges that caught the dim light from the sun through the grey clouds overhead.

"Everything here is smaller than the university anyway isn't it?"

"I suppose you might say that," he agreed. "But this is more like a collection of people who happen to teach others for a fee. The University is a much more substantial organisation."

"Sounds the same to me." Shanti thought of her friend, the professor Darsat. He had worked at the University in Gorduum for decades, and in theory his job was to find out new and incredible things about the world and teach it to students at the university. However, Shanti had observed that he spent most of his time in his office, drinking tea and smoking his pipe, reading books and letters from other learned men and women around the world. He used to spend a large portion of his time out travelling the world to do his research about the stars, but now he was old and enjoyed his creature comforts more.

"In any case, I do think that the carvings around the entrance are quite stunning."

Shanti nodded. The figures stretched many metres along the panels, and they had been detailed with rich red and white paint. It made them seem powerful and lively. *It's interesting,* she thought, *that such strong colours don't make the carvings seem less real. I wonder why that is?*

There was a jolt as the poler jammed her pole down and halted the boat in its gentle rotation, then heaved her shoulder sideways with the effort of starting them towards another narrow canal. Shanti lurched and flung a hand out to steady herself. She felt something warm under her hand as she caught herself and pushed herself back onto her seat, then looked down. Her hand was placed on Felldan's thigh, the material of his trousers wrinkling under her fingers.

"Oh my goodness," she blurted out as she pulled her hand away.

"That's alright," he smiled.

They slid through the canal, heading into new areas of the city that looked different to those she had already seen. Here Shanti saw that the buildings still looked to be built of the same style, but their carvings were older. Dark patches of mould could be seen on some buildings, and the ridges of the carvings were weathered and soft. Shanti could tell by the movement of the sun's glow behind the clouds that hours had passed already.

Finally, they came to a lagoon surrounded by buildings painted deep red and covered with criss-crossed white lines. The figures in the carvings along the lintels of each were strong and clear, each building featuring only one of the figures that Shanti had seen elsewhere in groups.

"What are these buildings? Where are we?"

"These are the main temples," murmured the poler. She manoeuvred the boat up against one of the landings.

"This is one of the most fascinating areas of the city, in my opinion," said Felldan as he offered a hand to help steady Shanti as she climbed out. She clutched his fingertips gratefully, and held her skirts as she stepped across to the wooden platform. Once she was there, she kept a hold of his hand as he stood and stepped over as well, then she pulled her hand back and looked away.

"I know that you were so enthused about the Masked God on the ship," said Felldan. "And I also know that there's not many people who follow the Masked God here in Chechezuk. These are the gods that people follow here." He spread his hand and gestured to the buildings that stood all around them. "I thought, maybe, that you would find some solace in one of them? Or perhaps, if there are any temples of the Masked God in this city, that they might be somewhere here also?"

"Thank you," said Shanti. She meant it too. The fact that he had thought about what she was looking for here, not just the business that she was following up but the personal needs that she had, meant that she felt like someone in the city had really noticed who she was. It was as though the Masked God was working through him to bring her comfort. She reached out to his shoulder. "Really thank you. That means a lot to me."

Felldan smiled again, and his face was as warm as a summer's day.

Shanti walked slowly around the lagoon, intrigued by the people who filled the wide path. They were all dressed in the familiar loose trousers and shirts of the city, most of them also wearing the wide hats that were common here. But they moved much slower around these temples, pausing often to tilt their heads back with eyes closed, moving their lips and fingers as they mouthed silent prayers, accompanied by strange gestures.

"What is going on?" whispered Shanti, leaning in close to Felldan.

"I believe that this is how they ask for help from the gods," he replied, also in a low voice. "The gods here are not quite like the Masked God. They don't have names, they don't have books or songs that you are supposed to know. They are like..." He paused, searching for the right words. "They are like forces, forces that will affect your life and that you should try to make work to your advantage."

"How do they make the gods work for them?" Shanti found the idea confusing. The idea of making the Masked God do something was utterly wrong, and made her stomach clench. The Masked God watched and acted as they would, it was not for followers to give the Masked God guidance. *All we can do is to act as their Eyes, and ensure they see injustice and work through us,* she reminded herself.

"I think they speak prayers that ask for help from their gods, and they give offerings in the temples." Felldan pointed at an older woman walking into one of the temples with a broad ceramic bowl in her hands. A selection of dark purple and bright yellow fruits were bundled on the bowl. "She'll probably leave those in there." He looked up at the carvings over the temple's entrance, shielding his eyes with his hand. "That looks to me like the embodiment of the animals in the jungle. Maybe she needs some help managing animals?"

Shanti looked at the carvings as well. This figure looked much more ferocious than the others she had seen around the city so far, with large glaring eyes and sharp teeth in a wide mouth. Its fingers curled into hooks and it had a long coiled tail instead of legs.

"Are we allowed to go in?"

"I'm not sure, I've never tried. Come on!"

34

Felldan grabbed Shanti by the arm and jogged over to the door before it shut behind the old woman. He led the way inside, pulling Shanti behind him. The old woman turned to look at them as they entered, but her expression didn't change, so Shanti felt sure that they weren't breaking any rules.

She slapped Felldan on his shoulder. "Don't do things like that to me!"

He smiled back at her.

Inside, the temple to the strange animalistic figure consisted of a small room with an exceptionally tall ceiling. People were kneeling around the floor, and more figures and carved panels took up the walls. The only illumination came through a round window in the roof, meaning that it was difficult to see. As the only source of light, Shanti's gaze was drawn to the window, and she was surprised to see small dark shapes crawling in and out of an open pane. *More lizards,* she realised.

The old woman that they were following walked up to another old woman who was wearing a long pale dress with dark panels decorated in shining golden embroidery. *She seems important,* thought Shanti. The old woman spoke in a low voice and the woman in the dress pointed to an area at one side of the room. The old woman moved to that side, knelt down, and placed the platter of fruit on the ground beside her. As soon as she did, three lizards rushed out of the shadows and grabbed armfuls of fruits each, rearing up onto their hind legs in order to get a better grasp of the fruit and carry more. Shanti stared as they rushed back into the dark. *Did they just steal the food,* she wondered. *But no, no one seems surprised by this.* She had noticed that neither the old woman nor the woman in the dress reacted in any way to the appearance of the lizards. *Then what is going on here? Was the food an offering for them?*

She stood near Felldan, to one side of the entrance, and turned slowly, trying to find out where the lizards had taken the piles of fresh fruit. Eventually she caught a movement to her right and saw that the lizards were moving through a doorway, barely visible in the dim interior of the temple. The three lizards she had seen grabbing food from the offering, slipped around the door with their prizes, and another came scampering back into the temple. It raced over to a man dressed in a robe that was decorated similarly to the fancy woman, though with a slightly different cut to account for his round belly. The lizard climbed up his back and peered over his shoulder, a thick black tongue flickering between its lips. The man reached up and rubbed the snout of the lizard.

"I need to find out about this," Shanti said to

Felldan, putting a hand out to tell him to wait as she walked over to the man with the lizard.

"Excuse me," she began in her faltering Zukian. "Why do you let the lizards take the food?"

"Good afternoon child," replied the old man. His eyes were bright and kind, though the skin on his face was loose. He glanced over her foreign appearance and then clearly took pity on this stranger in his city by speaking as slowly as he could. "What are you asking about the lizards?" Even though he spoke carefully for her, Shanti could barely make out his words through the sharp tones of the language.

"I just saw some steal the food that lady brought in." Shanti pointed to where the woman was still kneeling, her hands flat on the floor in front of her and her head bowed.

"Oh I see! No, they aren't stealing the food. They work for us."

"What do you mean?"

"They perform simple tasks for us and it helps us manage a little easier."

"I didn't think people in the city could make them do that? I was told they can't be trained." Shanti watched the man's face, trying to determine if he was trying to trick her somehow. "Don't they just want to set up their nest and survive, like other animals?"

"Other animals help people in many ways. Where have you come from, that has no animals to help the people there?" He raised an eyebrow.

Shanti blushed.

"Yes, of course, we do. Only, those animals are

trained and tamed. These lizards don't seem to be tame."

"They are smarter than the average animal I would say, though the tasks they can undertake are simple. As to their own animal urges to survive, we have allowed this brood to make a nest in the storage room at the back of the temple. We leave them some of the offerings, and they help us with odd jobs."

"Can they do anything else?" wondered Shanti.

"Like what?"

"I don't know. Clean the windows?" Shanti leaned back and pointed up to the round window high in the ceiling, filled by a single pane of glass that was propped open. A lizard paused halfway through leaving through the gap and turned its wide eyes to stare down at her over its back.

The man laughed kindly. "I imagine that they could do the job! I have seen them in action for years and I feel that they may be smarter than most people give them credit for. But I believe that they don't want to do such drudgery any more than I do."

Shanti nodded and looked around. Despite the fierce carving of the spirit that had decorated the front of the building and towered over the people inside, Shanti felt a sense of peace that she hadn't noticed in Chechezuk before. It was quieter, more still, than the rushing streets and canals.

"Are you in charge here?"

"No," he shook his head. "But then again, no one is."

Shanti glanced down at his elaborate clothing and then back to his face. Her face must have shown her confusion because the man laughed and then continued.

"I have volunteered here longer than anyone, ever since my son was able to earn enough for me to stop working. The Alligators have done well by me in my life, so I came here to pass on that fortune. No one is in charge, but I suppose I know how it all works better than the others."

"Is everyone a volunteer?"

"Of course. What spirits would force someone to do their bidding?"

Shanti paused as she licked her lips.

"Sir, I hope that this doesn't seem rude, but do you know about the Masked God?"

"Ah, I thought you looked Gaawalti. Am I right?"

"Yes, I grew up in a small village in the north."

"Of course. Yes, I have heard of the Masked God before. Occasionally travellers come through and ask me about them." He tilted his head to one side and raised an eyebrow. "Are you going to ask me if I believe in the God now?"

"No." Shanti knew that was not what she needed to know, and she knew that the idea that this man, in his own temple, in a city that didn't seem to know the Masked God at all, would be a follower was ridiculous. "But I would like to know if you do know of anyone who is a follower?"

The old man's brow creased.

"It's just that I am feeling disconnected," Shanti continued. "I don't feel as comfortable as I would like here in this city, and I know that talking with others who know the God would help."

He clucked his tongue and reached out to place a comforting hand on her shoulder.

"I wish I could give you a more helpful answer," he said, squeezing softly. "But I don't know of any followers of your Masked God here. You are not untethered though. You are surrounded by people who you can make connections with, and the gods fill the air and water. You are surrounded," he repeated the phrase and Shanti could tell that he thought it was meant to make her feel better. *Perhaps it does give him a sense of belonging,* she thought. *I can imagine how that might work for the people here, who believe in spirits of everything around them. But it just reminds me that no one else here understands things the way that I do.*

She nodded at the priest and took a step back. A hand moved onto her shoulder from behind and she turned to see Felldan standing behind her. His eyes were full of concern and he reached out with his other arm to gather her into a hug. She lowered her face to his shoulder and sighed.

"Is everything alright?" His breath tickled her ear and the back of her neck. Shanti nodded. She squeezed him in return and stepped out of his arms.

"There are no temples. At least, none that he knows about, so they will be hard to find if they exist." *That hug was nice,* she realised after she got over the shock of how close Felldan had been to her. *It's the only thing that gave me a feeling of connection all day.* "I think we can stop looking for that."

"Okay." Felldan put his hands on his hips and looked around the dim temple. Lizards still moved along the walls and through the shadows. "Shall we go then?"

"Please."

Outside on the edge of the path, waiting for a boat to come close enough that they could hail a ride back to the more familiar side of the city, Shanti saw more of the lizards. They would appear in the water near the massive, wooden posts that held up the path, posts slick with dark algae. A small ripple or flicker of movement revealed the location of a lizard faster than she could spot them against the mottled colour of the wood, even despite the bright orange sections on their skin.

As she watched, they would swim out and around the posts, some following the edge of the lagoon to a distant goal that she could not distinguish, others carrying baskets and bags on their heads. She glanced up along the street. No one else noticed them at all, though, many of the pedestrians had destinations in mind, and were clearly focused on getting where they were going. Very few were standing so close to the edge of the path like she was.

"Come on," said Felldan. He was standing with one foot in a new boat, his hand extended to help her aboard. "It's probably time that we went to see Zekeka again."

They made their way through the streets and back to the Lagoon, then up the gangway on the Tide's Daughter. Tozan was in his usual position, but he simply nodded at the pair as they reached the top. Shanti was about to follow Felldan across the deck when she paused and turned to the old mate.

"Have you seen Keema here?" she asked him.

He frowned and shook his head slightly, as though he wasn't sure what she had meant, so she repeated the question, adding "You remember her? My wife? She had cobblefeet?"

"Yes of course," grunted the old man. He sniffed.

"Nope, haven't seen her onboard or walking the paths anywhere near us."

"Thank you anyway," said Shanti as she moved over to catch up to Felldan. *Where are you Keema?*

They were heading towards the door at the rear of the ship when it swung open and an extremely tall thin woman stalked out. Her mouth was set in a grimace and her long legs swung in huge strides out of the hallway. When she saw Shanti and Felldan, she paused and bowed her head slightly.

"Forgive me, I'm not usually so foul faced," she murmured as they bobbed their heads to her. Then she straightened and pulled her lips into a tired smile and strode to the gangway. Tozan began to open his mouth, but she lifted a pale finger on one hand and jammed it towards his face so hard that he flinched. He closed his mouth again.

"What do you suppose that was about?" asked Shanti. Felldan shrugged.

They walked into the small hallway that led to the captain's office and Shanti gritted her teeth. Felldan paused at the door and she stepped away from him before she realised what she was doing. She drew a slow deep breath through her nose and waited until she had managed to release it just as slowly before she allowed herself to step closer to him again. He turned his head to her as she did, and his eyebrows drew into a puzzled crease for a moment, but then he smiled at her and knocked on the captain's door.

"Yes what? Come in, come in," replied Zekeka from inside. Felldan pushed open the door.

35

───────

The captain was less happy than usual, wearing a crinkled forehead and dark bags beneath his eyes. Shanti tried not to stare, as the blue-ish colour looked so unusual on his pale face. "Oh it's you two. I wasn't expecting to see you both at once. What do you want?"

Felldan motioned Shanti over to one of the chairs bolted to the floor in front of the captain's desk. As she sat down, he answered Zekeka.

"My business is concluded, and I wanted to know when you were going to be ready to ship out back to Gorduum."

"You're finished already? I'm only halfway through the nonsensical forms that this bloody city has found for me to fill in." The pale captain waved a hand over the desk in front of him and grimaced. "I thought avoiding this sort of fishguts was the whole reason to get into business with someone on land. They do the paperwork, I carry the goods!"

"Is Kayzark not treating you properly?" asked Shanti. This was an important insight that she would need to consider as she decided whether or not she and her uncle would work with the man. Zekeka pressed his mouth closed and then she saw his tongue lick slowly across his lips. His eyes twitched.

"Kayzark has absolutely upheld his side of our arrangements," he said after a moment, slowly and carefully. "He has fulfilled the expectations that he was supposed to and he has actually gone further than he had to. As a business partner, he is definitely not cheating me in any way." He breathed out heavily through his nose. "But I cannot convey to you how much I loathe paperwork."

The captain leaned back in his chair and turned his eyes back to Felldan. "You're ready then? I should be able to leave in a day or two, assuming this all gets sorted through and we load up the hold full enough. How about you come back each morning, and I'll let you know whether we have a time to sail, or whether you should check on us in the evening?"

Felldan nodded. "I'm staying nearby, and I don't have much to collect. That suits me."

"Good." Zekeka picked up a pencil from where it lay on his desk and began chewing the end as he looked down at the papers that were strewn before him. Then he frowned and looked up. "You're still here?"

"Good afternoon Captain," began Shanti. "I had some questions myself."

"Oh." Zekeka put the pencil down again. "I hadn't... go ahead."

"I think that I will be able to get my business with Kayzark completed in the next day. Can I assume that you will give me passage back to Gorduum as well."

"Of course." Zekeka blinked. "Oh, I hadn't actually thought about it. Yes, you have return passage, but we will need you to check when we sail. We can't wait for you to wrap things up, so you will need to make quick decisions if you're still thinking when we are ready to go."

"You gave me return passage, but cannot wait for my business to conclude?"

Zekeka sighed and drew a hand down over his face, rubbing at the skin. "It's the same for everyone on every ship. We leave when we leave. If you decide to stay for your business, fine, but we have to keep moving. Kayzark should be able to arrange another berth if you need one."

Great, thought Shanti. *No one ever wants to give me time to think about what is going on, or let me have a chance to decide on the best course of action. It's always "Decide now, act now!" and blind anyone who is concerned that poor choices might be made.*

However, what she said was, "Fine, I will be sure to come and check in the mornings. One more thing sir."

He nodded.

"I was wondering if I might be allowed access to the copy of the Masked God's Writ that is being stored onboard?"

"The Writ? Why?"

"Because I have not been able to see any other followers while I have been in the city, and I'm feeling low. But I am sure that if you would allow me to take a reading, I would soon recover my optimism."

He chuckled once. Then he nodded.

"Yes, that would be fine. However, you will need to come and read in the cabin. I don't want that book being carried around Chechezuk and lost. It's a valuable possession."

"Why are you carrying it back and forth over the seas if it is so valuable? I had thought perhaps you were going to sell it here in Chechezuk?"

"What would we want with a book about someone else's god?" asked the captain. "No, it belongs to a companion of mine, whom I sometimes see in certain ports. She values it immensely."

"Should you have let me use it during the journey here?"

"Perhaps not. Are you asking me to change my mind and restrict you from it?" Zekeka raised an eyebrow and leaned closer.

"No, no!" Shanti stood up quickly. "May I read it now?"

Zekeka waved a hand dismissively. "Certainly. Find Tozan to unlock the doors for you. I'll see you regularly until we leave." He returned his attention to the papers on the desk and Shanti took the chance to leave before he did change his mind. Felldan followed.

As they left the hall and moved over to speak with the mate, Felldan whispered to her.

"Are you really going to sit with the book for the rest of the afternoon? It's already pretty late." His brow was furrowed.

"Yes, I really think I need some time to think about what is going on with everything related to this deal before I decide what I am going to say to Kayzark when I see him tomorrow. I have to consider what my uncle wants, and what would be good for him, as well as how I think the Masked God would want me to choose." She took a long slow breath through her nose. Every word that she said was making her feel more calm, more in control of her situation. She hadn't fully realised just how much she felt as though she was losing that control.

Felldan frowned and then pushed a hand through his hair and looked around the deck of the Tide's Daughter.

"Okay. I suppose that I could come in and read over your shoulder, or-"

"That's kind of you to offer," said Shanti as the man paused momentarily to consider his options. "But I will really be okay by myself. I think it would be useful for me to have some time alone to contemplate the Writ."

"Oh. It's just that I thought we'd had a really nice day." He stepped closer, and Shanti felt her pulse quicken. "I thought we could spend the rest of it together. Get some dinner maybe." He reached out one hand and took Shanti's fingers in his own. She lowered her head and pulled her hand away.

"That's very sweet," she stammered. "But I think I will read the Writ. It's important to me."

Felldan leaned down so that he could peer beneath her brow, looking deep into her eyes with his large brown ones. His lips thinned slightly, but he sighed and nodded.

"Hopefully I'll still see you later in the Plaza then?"

Shanti nodded.

"Alright. I hope you find what you are looking for in there." He walked away across the planks, lifting a hand to wave at Tozan as he moved past and down the gangway. Before Shanti could think, Felldan had vanished into the swirling pedestrians on the dock.

Was he trying to say he wanted to spend more time with me? As though he was courting me? Shanti lifted her hand and curled her fingers tighter. She could still feel the warmth of his fingertips where they had held hers. It had been a long time since she had been the recipient of such attention and it left her feeling slightly shaken, as though the Tide's Daughter was once again out in the rising swells of the ocean, and it had begun to fall away beneath her. Her stomach was lighter and her balance unsure.

He knows that I already have a partner in Keema, Shanti thought to herself. *Doesn't he?* She thought back over some of the things that Felldan had said and done while she had known him. He saw them arrive together, and how they moved through the city together. But Keema had disappeared today, and had been trapped in the bunkroom during their time at sea. *Perhaps he doesn't really believe it. That's why I have to keep telling him that she is my wife. But why wouldn't he believe me, when I've told him so many times?*

Shanti walked slowly to Tozan as she tried to sort through the jumble of thoughts that had scattered through her mind. He smiled as she approached, and the unusual expression stood out on his face like a full moon in a midnight sky.

"What?" she asked suspiciously.

"I can see what's going on here," he smirked.

"Young man caught the attention of a young lady, has he?"

"Not really," she said quickly, her brow creasing. "I seem to have caught his attention, but I don't think he understands my position at all."

"Oh?"

"It's just that I've told him about Keema, he's met her, he knows that we are married. But I get the feeling that he is just ignoring that, because it is inconvenient to him."

Tozan grunted and his face slowly lost its wrinkly smile.

"In any case, I have other things that I want to be thinking about right now." She focused her eyes on Tozan and smiled brightly. "The captain agreed to let me have access to the Writ, providing I read it in the cabin. Would you mind?"

Tozan led the way back into the cabin where it was kept, unlocked the small cabinet that contained the Writ and left Shanti by herself. She sat down at the same table that the passengers had dined around so many evenings during the voyage. Now the room was dark and quiet. She felt her breath grow faster and her fingers began to shiver in the quiet darkness, until she moved to a small box near the door and drew out some materials to light the room's lantern with its strangely thick glass. As the light wobbled through the cabin, Shanti was able to bring her hand under control, and slow her breathing.

Then, she settled herself back at the table and ran her fingers along the leather cover of this copy of the Writ. The surface felt smooth and cool, though it was ridged where the letters had been stamped into the material, and the surface held minute burrs that pulled at her skin like an insect walking across her arm. She turned the pages and wondered what part she should turn to, where would be a good place to begin. She knew that some people would open the book at random and believed that fate would somehow guide them to the right page, but she had seen how repeated use often creased the spine of a popular book, and she wondered how many followers used the Writ in such a way, constantly finding themselves reading the same story over and over.

Shanti felt that focusing on one story in such a way, and having to try and find a way to apply it to any situation, would only serve to stunt a follower in their appreciation of the Masked God. Shanti believed that she wanted to bring the compassion and protection of the Masked God to the world, and the only way she could be sure that she was succeeding would be to try to fully understand how the God reacted in any situation.

She flipped slowly through the pages, wondering if a word might stand out. She reached the end of the book, closed the front cover, and then lifted it, turning the pages into an extremely slow waterfall of white, speckled with black ink. By the time she reached the back cover the second time, she knew that she was floundering.

36

———

I need some sort of guidance, *she told herself.* *What is it that I really need from the Writ right now?* She wished that there were others here for her to talk to. It was always much easier to figure out what was happening in your own mind when others guessed and got it wrong. The impulse to say "No, not at all, what I meant was..." was a wonderful way to resolve one's own muddled musings.

I'm confused because Felldan has suddenly acted like more than the friend I thought he was, she decided. *And it was unexpected, and it has befuddled me. However, what I really need to know is what the God might think of Kayzark and his operation. That's more important right now.*

It was clear that Kayzark had created a successful tuft orchard, and that he would be able to produce plenty of the material for a long time to come. From a strictly money-making perspective, this was an easy decision. Work with the man, be his contact in Gorduum, and gain the benefits for as long as he could control the lizards better than any of his competitors. But that was the problem, the way he treated the lizards.

Shanti had immediately felt as though something was wrong with his treatment of the orange and green creatures, and the more the large man had spoken, the stronger that feeling had grown. It didn't seem right to hold creatures like that in such conditions, to knowingly threaten their mates, their nests and their eggs. This was what was causing the fluttering on the back of her neck, the tightness in her stomach, Something was wrong here.

The pages of the Writ fluttered past, slipping from under her fingers and falling open. She felt as though she was hoping that the book itself might be able to point her towards a passage that could help her. She paused, and the word "merchant" stood out from the page.

Kayzark is a merchant, she thought. *Maybe this will be about how merchants should behave?* She skimmed back along the page, searching for the beginning of the reading. When she found it, she began reading forwards in earnest.

It didn't take long for her to realise that this story was not going to be the thing that she needed. While it was about a merchant who was mistreating others, it turned out that the merchant was defrauding her customers. She would make false claims about her goods, and sneak underweight measures into large orders. The Masked God eventually appeared in a mirror, the God's golden eyes staring out of her own face, and she was brought to her knees in fear. Though her heart remained hard at first, the Masked God's eyes began to consume her vision all through the days, first as glimpses of golden light in reflections of the merchant's own face, but then through the eyes of everyone she saw upon the street. Eventually the mask, the solid unchanging face of the God, would hang before her at all hours of the day and she could no longer see what she was doing.

Finally, when faced with the never-ending accusing gaze of the God, she realised that she was betraying the Masked God and changed her ways, becoming generous and giving more than she received.

Shanti leaned back in the chair as she reached the end of the reading. The light flickered across the wooden walls of the cabin as she rubbed her forehead. *A pretty story, but it doesn't really tell me anything about whether or not I should feel bad about Kayzark and these lizards. I mean, Keema has a horse and what is so different about that? She keeps Breenar in a sort of trap, Breenar can't go anywhere without Keema letting her out. So, maybe it's fine to use the lizards for the harvest.* Shanti tried to ignore the little voice in the back of her head saying that perhaps Keema shouldn't have been keeping Breenar all this time.

She flicked a few more pages through the Writ and wondered how late it was getting outside. Would Zekeka kick her off the ship if she didn't leave? She wondered whether she would want to stay on board, but quickly realised that the room she had with Keema was much more comfortable. She thought about the small warm bed, with its piled blankets, and how safe she had felt curled up under those covers with Keema. *Where is she?*

The Writ was open and she was letting her finger drift down the page, when she saw the larger writing that indicated the beginning of a reading. With her thoughts still wandering, she began to read.

This reading talked of a time shortly after the Masked God had left the Village, back in the early days of the world. The villagers had learned to look out for one another, to be the God's Eyes, so that they no longer needed the God to pass judgements and resolve disputes for them. The God was free to travel throughout the world, and to help others.

Shanti recognised this beginning, it was one that she had seen in many other tales from the Writ. They were sometimes referred to as the Wanderings, as they were a series of stories about the God's travels. Most of them described how the God had arrived somewhere where there was disharmony and anger and mistrust. Because the God was no part of the quarrel, they were asked to provide judgement, as they had back in the village. And as they had in the village, their solutions and pronouncements could be difficult to understand but were always rooted in deep justice.

This one began in the same way, with the God walking in on a woodworkers' camp. The large strong workers were sitting in front of a quickly built hut, waiting while a pot of stew was being boiled. As usual, the God introduced themself to the people, and the people gave the God their stories. However, there was no quarrel this time. The God sat and ate the stew with the workers, who talked among themselves and then quickly fell asleep.

The next day, the workers set off into the thick forest, carrying axes, saws and ropes, ready to carry out their work. The God followed them into the shadows beneath the branches.

Shanti frowned as she continued reading. The Writ described the forest as dark, with old dead branches covering the ground, snapping beneath the heavy step of the workers. No birds sang from the trees, and the Masked God clutched at their shoulders for warmth, shivering in a cool breeze that wrapped past the wide trunks.

The God arrived in a clearing where two of the workers were chopping down trees. Together the workers swung their axes into the trunk, biting out chunks of wood with the sharp blades. They worked like a machine, each wrenching the axehead away as the other slammed theirs in. Eventually the tree could no longer stand, and the call to keep clear rose in the still air. The tree ripped through the branches of those around it and crashed to the ground in the clearing. Then the two began moving along the trunk, clearing away branches with smaller hand-saws. The Masked God stood at one side and watched.

Finally, the workers wrapped ropes around the trunk, and some of the nearby trees. By wrapping the ropes back and forth, they were able to create a way to haul the massive trunk through the forest, dragging it metre by exhausting metre until they reached a shallow path that they could roll it down, until it plummeted into a river. They would send it down the river to where other workers could collect it and prepare it for use. The two began walking back to the clearing, placing their hands on one trunk then the next, looking for the perfect next choice.

The Masked God watched all this with hands held behind their back. Their eyes glowed softly, and the expressionless mask stared forward, as white as clouds, but as still as ice.

At the end of the day, as the sky grew dark, the workers stretched their backs and groaned as their muscles ached. They swung their axes up onto their shoulders, wrapped their ropes around their torsos, ready for the long hike back through the woods to the rundown shelter that they were living in.

The Masked God stepped forward.

"Are you finished?" the God asked them.

"Yes," they replied, quick and quiet. They would not spend more energy than they had to.

"Will you return with seeds later?" asked the God. They still stood with arms held behind their back, but now the mask tilted sideways.

"Seeds? No." replied the workers. They waited to see if the strange newcomer would ask them any other questions.

The Masked God nodded and then stepped aside, watching as the workers set off through the darkening woods.

Shanti paused in her reading. The cabin was silent and she felt quite alone in the room. The wood of the ship creaked as it settled and eased itself against the ropes that held it to the docks, lifting and falling in the small swell that travelled through the city to the lagoon.

This was unlike any other story of the Masked God that she had read before, and she didn't recall ever hearing anyone else talk about it. Usually there was a problem that the people in the story had been unable to resolve, and the Masked God arrived to impart their judgement, always with compassion, but also detachment, leading to justice even when it was difficult. That was why the priests read the Writ, to give examples of the many problems that the Masked God could help solve. But no one had a problem here.

Sometimes the story described people who could easily explain the problem, but they had no power to change what was going on. The God often arrived through someone who could affect this suffering, even in a way that was less obvious than one might have thought. But no one was suffering an injustice here. She returned her focus to the Writ.

The Masked God waited in the clearing, looking at the shattered trunks of felled trees all around. It was possible to follow the path of the workers by these tree trunks. The older remains were weathered and beginning to be claimed by thin creepers and fungi from the undergrowth. The workers had begun close to the river and then followed the best trees deeper into the forest, leaving a path of open canopy behind them.

The Masked God walked over to the last trunk that the workers had felled and placed a hand on the bark. The Writ recorded their words, as they spoke out loud, though Shanti wondered who could have heard what the God had said.

"Sometimes people are doing what they can in their world, working as hard as they can to keep up, and they don't realise that something is missing. I am the Eyes that see what they do not. We are here to make a difference where we can."

The God reached out into the air and seeds fell from the branches around them, spiralling through the air and into their hands. The seeds piled up, moving like insects swarming around the God, in a way most unnatural. Then the God walked along the barren path that led back to the river's edge, seeds spilling from their hands and burrowing into the soft earth.

When they reached the river, the seeds were gone, and the God turned to follow the river until it wound its way past the workers' camp. The God walked back to the camp, where all the workers were asleep.

Shanti took a deep breath. *We are the ones who see what others do not,* she repeated to herself. *We are the ones who must make a difference.* She felt a sense of warmth fill her chest, and she wanted to smile slightly. There was a quiver of fear in her stomach, but she knew that she was right. This story was exactly what she needed to hear from the Masked God. If she saw something wrong, she did not need to punish or judge, but she must make what difference she could. *Dunin might not like it, but I can't work with Kayzark, not with the way he imprisons and threatens those animals.* The resolution she felt was like a heavy door swinging open, revealing a well-lit path with a golden field at the end.

But the story didn't end there. Shanti kept reading.

The God was standing beneath the trees by the workers' camp, watching the dark shack, listening to the low snores that came from within.

"It is one thing to ease suffering when we can," the God said to no one. "But if we can bring an end to the root of suffering, we must."

As the workers slept, the God walked through the camp. They reached out and touched axes and tools stacked in corners and leaning against the walls. As their fingers passed over the tools, black rust spread across the metal surfaces, and rot softened the wood. The tools were ruined within seconds. Then the God walked back out into the forest and continued looking for places that did not know the gaze of the Masked God.

Shanti closed the Writ. *If I can bring an end to the root of suffering, I must.* She put the Writ back in the small cupboard that held it and hurried out of the cabin. The sky was much darker above the Lagoon and she smiled at Tozan as she rushed down the gangway and onto the docks.

"Did you find what you needed?" called the old man from behind her.

"And more!" laughed Shanti, spinning to wave farewell and then turning back to run towards the arched lanes that would lead to the Plaza.

Who can I get to help, she wondered as she ran, ignoring the startled looks of pedestrians as she passed. *What will I need? A boat, obviously, but how could I get in?*

She brushed small biting insects away from her face as she entered the Plaza and slowed down to look around. *Felldan should be here somewhere,* she thought. *But where?*

She turned slowly, and moved aside as other passers-by grumbled that she was blocking the path into the plaza.

"Sorry," she murmured, then returned to her search. *He got the skewers last time,* she recalled. *Maybe he's over by that stall?* But she could see no sign of him.

There was a loud yell from her left and she spun around, mirroring many others in the plaza. A small man with a thick beard was dancing on the cobbles, jabbing out his elbows to either side, and kicking up his feet. It appeared that he had knocked over a long bench near him, and was now ignoring the glares from patrons eating their food nearby. Shanti smiled. It was Gudan, her smiling, gambling companion from the Tide's Daughter. She began to walk over towards him.

As she approached, Shanti saw that Taadin was standing with a worried look on his face near his husband, his bald head reflecting some of the firelight that illuminated the plaza. He had his broad hands clutched together in front of his chest, and his lips were drawn into a frown.

Gudan however, continued to dance and grin, motioning for others to join him, and cheering as some people started clapping a rhythm for him, keeping time for his dancing.

"Taadin!" called Shanti from a few tables away. When the large man turned to her she had to cough and ignore the way the glares of nearby diners turned to her. She rushed up to her former cabin mate. "I see you have been having a great time in Chechezuk?" she laughed.

"Some of us have," he murmured in response, still watching Gudan, who was now spinning and simultaneously bobbing up and down. A musician with a small stringed instrument had started strumming and laughing along with the dance.

"Is he alright?"

"He's fine. He's just been having a good day. He made a lot of money and thought it would be a good idea to spend it on drinks."

"And how are you feeling about this celebration?" Shanti hadn't heard the large man speak much, as he usually kept to himself on board the ship. But she got the impression that he sometimes found it overwhelming when his partner began to act loud and boisterous. She sympathised.

"I only had one, and then I stopped." Taadin sighed. Shanti reached up and patted his broad shoulders.

"Sometimes it can be difficult to cope with the way those we care about behave," Shanti commiserated, though she found it hard to keep a smile from her face. "Keema loves playing darts back in Gorduum, and I have spent many night watching her take it all very seriously."

Taadin nodded with pressed lips. "What you say is very true."

"Now that I have crossed ways with you both," began Shanti carefully, "I wonder if you might be able to help me out?"

"I'm sure we would love to, but I cannot guarantee that he will be of any help until at least tomorrow evening now." Taadin raised an eyebrow and gestured at Gudan.

"How familiar are you with Chechezuk?" asked Shanti anyway.

"Somewhat. We have been here a few times."

"Do you know how easy it might be to get a boat?"

"Nothing easier." Taadin barely glanced at her. "They travel the canals constantly. You just wave them over if they seem empty, very easy to find."

"Yes, but I don't think they would be keen on my plans, and I need them to come out into the jungle, not just transport me through the canals."

Now Taadin did turn his head. Shanti bit her bottom lip as the large man looked closely at her, her eyes narrowing slightly. "Into the jungle?"

She nodded.

"So, you really just want the boat, no poler? Would you do the poling or paddling yourself, do you think?"

Shanti's discomfort was increased by the way his large face looked at her with curiosity but no judgement. She chewed her lip a little harder and then nodded again.

Taadin sucked in a deep breath through his nostrils. "That is trickier. Let me think on it." He turned back to Gudan, who was slowing down now, a film of sweat on his forehead. "What are you up to?" he asked without looking at Shanti.

"Something important."

"Hello you," said a soft voice from behind Shanti. She turned, a smile spreading across her face as she anticipated who the voice might belong to, but blinked when she realised that Arsook was the one who had spoken.

"Oh. Hello! I thought you were someone else, sorry." Shanti shook her head to clear her confusion.

The young woman hummed sceptically, but then smiled. "I'll forgive you this time." She stepped forward and hugged Shanti. "I was hoping that I'd find you here again. How have you been- Who's this?"

Arsook stepped forward to stand next to Shanti, keeping an arm across her shoulders, and looked at Taadin. He nodded back at her.

"My name is Taadin. The dancing fool who is finally going to sit down is Gudan."

"A pleasure to meet you." Arsook's accent was stronger than it had been the night before. Shanti wondered if she should move Arsook's arm from off her shoulder. But the other woman's body felt close and warm next to her. "How do you boys know this lovely lady?"

"We were on the ship with her." Gudan threw himself onto a bench in front of them, his eyes shining bright and his cheeks flushed. "That was exhilarating Taa, I wish you had joined me!"

Taadin put a hand on top of Gudan's on the wooden table, then leaned down to kiss the man's forehead.

"You are clearly having enough fun for both of us," he said, though he was smiling now.

"How about you Shanti, keen to come and have a bit of a dance?" Gudan's chest was swelling and falling as he caught his breath. Shanti laughed and shook her head.

"Thank you, but I need to have something to eat, and I have some plans to make for tomorrow."

"Why, what's happening tomorrow?"

Shanti considered how to answer Gudan. She knew that she had to do something about Kayzark's orchard, but she didn't think that the people in the city would understand why. Could she answer him more directly with Arsook standing next to her like this? She was feeling quite awkward with Arsook still laying an arm along her shoulder, but would it be too rude to lift it away? She hadn't even opened up fully to Taadin when it had just been the two of them in conversation.

Arsook! Shanti nearly squealed as she realised that the solution to her problem had walked up alongside her.

"I've been wondering about heading out into the jungle," she said. "But I really need to get a boat of my own."

Arsook squeezed Shanti's shoulders. "I have a boat, you know."

Shanti turned to look at the woman directly now. Her face was close, and her eyes were large.

"I do know, but I didn't want to presume." She tried not to let the excitement she had felt with her realisation taint the way she spoke.

Arsook licked her lip slowly, a mischievous smile growing on her face. "Would you like to use my boat tomorrow would you?"

Shanti felt a ball of guilt in the bottom of her stomach. She knew that she was encouraging Arsook now, only to use her for the boat and her own ends. She hoped that it wouldn't hurt Arsook.

"If you don't mind?"

"What for?"

Shanti paused and glanced away. "It's a bit personal," she said, hoping that the comment would keep Arsook from asking any more questions.

"I like personal," said Arsook, stepping forward so that she was now holding Shanti closely, body to body. Shanti felt a shiver slip down her spine. *I don't think Keema would approve of this,* she thought, trying not to pay attention to Arsook's face so close to her own. *But if Arsook is more willing to let me use her boat, then maybe I can muddle through a little bit longer.* She lifted a hand to Arsook's side. Her fingers were shaking and she hoped that Arsook simply took it for nerves, not fear.

"I spoke with some of the other passengers on the way to Chechezuk, and they talked about the valuable resources in the jungle. I would like to have a go at finding some myself." Shanti felt like an idiot as she spoke. *This isn't going to work. Arsook is going to realise that I am just trying to trick her into letting me use her boat, or she's going to insist on coming with me and that is going to ruin everything.* The hair on the back of her neck was standing on end.

"Shanti, what's going on?"

Shanti leapt away from Arsook as though the woman was made of fire. She flung her arms out and could feel that her eyes were stretched as wide as they could, and her cheeks felt cold as the blood drained out of her head.

She turned slowly, with a heavy rock in her stomach. Keema was standing behind her, barely a table's length away.

"What's this?" asked Shanti's wife, with wide eyes and a hanging mouth. She was glancing back and forth between Shanti and Arsook. Shanti began to shake her head. *Why am I not saying anything,* she thought. *I'm still not saying anything. Why can't I make words come out of my mouth? Oh Keema!*

Arsook stepped forward beside Shanti and put a hand on her shoulder. "What's the problem, love?"

Keema's eyes narrowed like a cat in an alley and she pulled her lips back from her teeth. It would be possible to claim that she was smiling, but Shanti knew that she was not. "None of your business, you trash peddler."

"Hey, watch your tongue!"

"Keema, I can explain..." Shanti managed to say, but the words sounded as hollow as they felt. *By the God, she must think that I was trying to connect with Arsook for real. How else would it have looked? But I can't explain myself in front of Arsook, I still need that boat!*

"Keema, I think you and Shanti should go and speak together." Taadin had stepped forward as well, and Shanti found that his massive presence was actually reassuring.

"Yes, please can we go and-"

"I don't think I want anything to do with you right now," snapped Keema, jabbing a finger at Shanti. She sniffed and lifted her arm to her face, scrubbing the back of her sleeve across her eyes. She spun on her feet and dashed away.

38

"Keema!" called Shanti. She felt as though a cold hand was squeezing her heart in her chest, and her throat was tight. "What have I done?" She stared down the street after her wife, the woman she had been with for years in Gorduum, who had shared the new adventures of her life beyond Graama.

"You've done nothing darling," said Arsook, squeezing Shanti's shoulder again. Shanti flinched away. "Hey! It's alright, these things happen."

"I didn't mean for it to," muttered Shanti.

"Did I see Keema?" Gudan's voice was slurred as he rolled forward on the bench. "How is that little scoundrel doing?"

Shanti couldn't take it anymore. She ran into the dark streets leading away from the plaza.

As her feet smacked onto the narrow cobbled path, Shanti tried to bring her thoughts to order, but they darted across her mind like minnows in a pond. Names flashed to the front of her vision, Keema, Felldan, Gudan, Arsook. She felt her heart pounding but ignored it, as she ignored the pressure that was building in her temples. Her face felt flushed.

She dodged around the few pedestrians on the streets at this later hour, rushing straight back to the lodging house that she and Keema were sharing. She nearly knocked over the old man by the counter, who shouted after her as she ducked through the curtain to the back and began climbing the stairs two at a time.

As she reached the top of the stairs, the burst of fear and panic that had carried her finally lost its hold on her muscles and she slumped to the wall, forcing herself to continue climbing up the stairs out of sheer will. She wanted to catch up to Keema and try to explain what had happened. She had no idea what she was going to say, or how she would clarify things to her. Would Keema understand that Shanti needed a boat? Or would she still judge Shanti for trying to make insinuations to Arsook that she wasn't going to follow through on. *Oh no,* thought Shanti managed to pull herself to the landing outside her room. *Maybe I already went too far for Keema?* She remembered the feeling of Arsook in her arms, and the thought was momentarily pleasing. *Maybe Keema saw how close we were and already thought I had broken trust with her?*

With her pulse pounding in her ears and hot breath tearing at her throat, Shanti leaned on the door to the room they had taken and pushed. It was locked. Snuffling and sniffing, she fumbled for the key and then pushed the door open and walked through. The room beyond was empty.

After she had sat on the edge of the small bed and cried for as long as it took for her to calm herself down, Shanti straightened her shoulders. She swallowed and sniffed and tried to bring herself back under control.

It's okay, she told herself sternly. *Keema loves you and you love her. This is a bad night, but it's nothing that you won't be able to sort out once you find her and talk to her. That's all that is needed here, is a chance to talk to each other.*

As she pulled out a handkerchief from her luggage to blow her nose she thought back to how Keema had been behaving since Shanti had suggested coming to Chechezuk at all, let alone that they might travel together. She remembered how Keema had been less than enthusiastic, and how she had been worried about her horse, and her business. *Maybe this was a bad idea for her.* She felt a knot grow tighter in her belly. *I'll just have to admit that to her when I find her,* she thought. *I'll tell her that I hadn't really acknowledged how much of a big deal it was for her to join me in this journey. I'll have to tell her I really appreciated it.*

Shanti thought of only the night before, when Keema had been so much quieter than usual. *She felt left out,* Shanti realised as she stood and began to make her way back downstairs. *She didn't feel like she should have come along, she didn't think I needed her. But I do.* Shanti sat, staring between her feet at the floor beneath them. *Why would she think that I don't need her?* Shanti thought about her discussion with Gudan on the Tide's Daughter. He and Taadin had held a massive wedding, with all their family, and they had proclaimed their love to the world for all to see. What had Shanti arranged for Keema and herself? Nothing so dramatic. *Does Keema think that I didn't value our wedding? Does she think that I don't value our marriage?*

Still sniffling and trying to bring her tears under control, Shanti sat up. She wrapped her hands around her stomach and breathed in and out slowly, each shuddering breath bringing her closer and closer to feeling calm. It was like she had been in a storm, with winds and lightning colliding all around her, pushing her to and fro, but now the storm was passing. The air was quiet, although the distant thunder would not yet let her relax.

Eventually she stood up and smoothed her skirts, then lifted her hands to tidy her hair back into place around her head.

"I can't just stay here and wish for the world to get better," she said out aloud, hoping that the sound of her voice would make her feel more convinced by herself. "Nothing changes if I don't step out to make it change."

She walked out of the room and down the stairs, heading back towards the Plaza, and the woman that she knew had a boat.

THE PLAZA WAS FILLING up as the night settled in, though clouds of large buzzing insects were gathering. Braziers dotted amongst the tables and benches were burning fistfuls of herbs and incense, large leafy branches that released a pale sweet-smelling smoke as they smouldered. The smoke made Shanti squint, but kept the insects from swarming too thickly in the plaza itself. She slapped at one that had landed on the back of her arm and then began to push her way through the crowd, looking for Arsook.

After moving halfway around the Plaza she had found no sign of the young local woman. However, she did find Gudan and Taadin still entertaining themselves. Gudan had dug out his dice and was trying to teach a new game to some locals. He swayed as he spoke, holding out a finger as he tried to make a point, but the way his hand spun through the air made his audience chuckle. Shanti wondered if he was as drunk as he was acting. He had been so loud when he was singing and dancing before. She remembered that he had been quite cunning while playing games in the bunkroom under the Tide's Daughter's deck.

Taadin was leaning against a wall behind his partner, letting his gaze sweep across the audience. Some of the locals were beginning to dig through their pockets for loose coins, dropping them to the ground by Gudan whose mouth spread into a shining smile at the sight. Shanti stepped around the game to speak to Taadin.

"Did you see where she went?" she asked.

"You were the one chasing her," was his reply and for a moment Shanti was confused. Then she realised that he had assumed she was asking about Keema. She coughed.

"I couldn't find her," she admitted, trying to pretend that she had indeed been asking about her wife. She coughed again, lowering her gaze. "Did you see where the girl I was talking to went as well?" She tried to sound as casual as possible. She didn't want Taadin thinking that she was going behind Keema's back. *Even though, in many ways, that is ex-*

actly what you are doing, spoke her voice deep in the back of her mind.

Taadin raised an eyebrow before he answered. "She hung around the Plaza for a little while, trying to encourage my man to try some of the local drinks."

Shanti looked at where Gudan was trying to pick up the dice for a second time, after missing them entirely the first time.

"She had some success with that?"

"Yes, more's the pity." Taadin pursed his lips and tightened his crossed arms. "Why are you asking about her then?"

Shanti tucked a lip over her lower teeth. "I need a boat, to be honest, and I know she has one. But Keema got the wrong idea."

"Are you sure she got the wrong idea?" said the tall bald man slowly.

"Do you think that maybe she understands then? Maybe she's not too upset?" Shanti lifted her eyes and her shoulders rose too. She could feel a smile tickle the corners of her lips.

"No," snorted Taadin. "Are you sure that what she thought was happening isn't the truth?" Taadin's soft question was like a dagger in her heart. He leaned back against the wooden wall.

Shanti lowered her gaze again.

"Wasn't Felldan here as well?"

"Yes, he was." Taadin sniffed. "He moved on pretty quickly after the rest of you vanished. I think he only really had one thing on his mind, and neither Gudan or myself can help him with it."

"I think I'm going to keep looking around. I really need that boat."

"Shanti," said Taadin as she turned away from him. When she looked back, his dark eyes were wide and his forehead wrinkled with concern. "I hope you sort things out soon. Try to talk to who-ever it is you need to talk to so you both understand what's going on. Don't expect them to magically un-derstand what's going on inside your head otherwise."

"Is that how you two do it?" she asked.

"I don't think Gudan has any more idea than the rest of us of what is going on inside his head," laughed the huge man. "But yes, it is what we do."

Shanti nodded. "I will make sure I talk to Keema."

Taadin held up a hand, palm facing Shanti. "Talk to whoever it is that you need to talk to. I'm not judging who that might be."

Shanti snorted, and then moved off into the crowd that filled the plaza.

The crowd was thick this evening, the benches full of people sitting and eating or drinking. Songs were being sloppily sung from all around, and the different melodies were creating a remarkably pleasing harmony. It was impossible to make out any one tune or lyric, but the sound was a jumble of happiness and joy.

Shanti looked closer at each knot of people that she passed, hoping that she would find Arsook or Keema before she circled around the entire Plaza. But as she came back to the start of her circle she was disappointed to hear Gudan's laughter cracking out of the crowd before she had seen any familiar faces.

Then she saw Keema.

Keema was standing near the game, talking to Gudan, who had stood up from his position on the cobbles. He had a hand on her shoulder and was stretching his other out across the game below as though he was about to fall down. The people he had been dicing with watched him talking to Keema with blank expressions.

Standing next to Keema, close to her, with an arm around her waist, was a young woman from Chechezuk, with long yellow hair that was bound in a thick plait that fell to her waist. Shanti reached behind her back and grabbed the end of her own plait. Keema's arms were wrapped around the woman's shoulder, and her head was tilted towards her. Shanti could see Keema's jaw moving as she spoke and then Gudan leaned back, laughing. He clutched his stomach with both hands and then dropped himself to the pavement again, ready to return to the game.

Keema turned to the woman in her arms and Shanti stopped as she watched her wife lean in and kiss this other woman. Shanti wanted to look away, but it was as though some magic was forcing her to stare at the display. Her stomach felt like ice and her limbs grew instantly numb.

Behind Keema, Taadin's eyes reflected the fires in the braziers. He was looking directly at Shanti. She roughly brushed aside the tears that were bursting from her eyes and spun around, running out of the Plaza and not stopping until she was back in her room, buried beneath the blankets. As the tears kept coming, she grabbed some clothes out of Keema's luggage and held them close to her.

For the first time since she had unpacked in

these lodgings, Shanti heard noise from the next room. A soft thud as someone stepped across the creaking floorboards, the rustle of bed clothes as they settled down. She stared at the wall, imagining what she might see if she was able to see through it. Felldan had the room next to her and Keema, she remembered. She hadn't noticed him moving around or making noise any of the other nights that they had spent in their room. But now she was acutely aware that he was there, a few metres away, and still clearly awake.

The darkness of the night pressed in through the windows.

39

S hanti lay in her bed as dawn began to eke its way down the walls. She could hear the skittering sound of a lizard somewhere on the roof. She rolled over, trying to hide her face from the light, and caught her arm in a loop of cloth. She frowned and pulled it away, flinging it to the ground beside the bed. It was one of Keema's shirts.

Shanti buried her face in her pillow and considered what she could do now. *I suppose I could just go home,* she thought at first. *Maybe it's time to just get out of Chechezuk and all the troubles and confusion it's causing me. Gorduum is much less confusing, and I have friends there.*

She drew a deep breath and stretched her neck. *I could just sign whatever deal Kayzark wants for me, and be done. Zekeka will be sailing soon, I'm sure. I could just go home.*

How would Keema get home, asked a curious voice from the back of her mind.

She shook her head and sniffed, squashing the thought as quickly as she could. *That's not my problem, she's the one who should sort out those details.*

What will you do if she ends up on the same ship home then? The icy feeling returned to her stomach.

I suppose I would just have to make do. Besides, Keema got sick while we were sailing, surely that would happen again. She rolled over onto her back and pressed a hand to her stomach. She felt it tense with an involuntary clenching, as though she was about to throw up. The feeling passed as she tried to settle herself. *And then I would be at home, back with my uncle, with a lucrative deal on paper. How could I turn any of that down?*

She sat up and rolled her shoulders, stretching out the tightness and stiffness that had gathered in her muscles overnight. She closed her eyes and appreciated the feeling of her muscles loosening and shifting. She tilted her neck to one side and then the other, groaning as a sharp clicking sound accompanied her bones settling into another position. Then Shanti opened her eyes. Directly opposite her face, on the wall of the room, was a mirror, set up to help lodgers with their dressing. The sun had just passed by the lip of the mirror and its golden light burst off the clear glass like a blossoming flower. The angle was exactly right for her face to disappear into the beaming golden light, neck and jaw vanishing beneath the sunburst, as though her eyes were blazing with molten fire.

Shanti lowered her eyes to her hands, clutched in her lap as she sat on the edge of the bed.

You are only thinking about yourself, she admonished herself. *Up until you saw Keema last night, you were thinking about others, those who don't have someone to speak out for them. Your uncle will help you.*

Felldan, Taadin and Gudan all seem nice enough to help you. If the worst comes to the worst and you must flee from Gorduum altogether, you could find a place to stay with your family in Graama. But these creatures have no one to save them.

The voice in her head sounded different now. It had grown deeper, richer, like someone standing in a deep cavern, with the reverberations of their voice reinforcing and building into something even stronger.

You know what you should do. The Masked God watches through your eyes. The Masked God brings justice for those who are not seen. You know what must be done.

Shanti stood up. She wondered if the voice was just her own conscience and deep thoughts, reminding herself that she had already made a promise to do more than just sign a document and sail away from this. Or had the God actually spoken to her? She shook her head. Either way, it didn't matter. She knew that she was going to do something about the orchard.

She rose and got dressed, packing all her belongings into her suitcase as quickly as she could. She finished rolling up her dresses and stockings, tucking them into the case and then lowered the lid, tightening the straps and locking the clasps. She pulled on the lid and nodded to herself when it remained firmly closed. She leaned back on her heels and looked down at the case, running her fingers along its worn old leather.

I'm going to need to be ready to go, she thought to herself. *Today is either going to go very well, in which case I'll want to get out of Chechezuk as soon as I can, or it's going to go very poorly, in which case it would be rude to leave the room in a state where someone else would have to clean it.* She wondered whether keeping the room clean was the sort of thing that the Masked God would expect, or whether she was trying to live up to the expectations of her mother and father. She snorted through her nose. *As if they will ever know what I am getting up to today!* Shanti lifted a hand to her mouth. She had thought of a ship ride to Gorduum as going home. She had considered going to her family as Graama as needing a place to stay. *When did she decide that home was no longer the place she grew up? What had turned the city into her home?*

Shanti sought out some paper and sat down to write a letter to her family. It didn't take as long as she had feared that it might. The things that she wanted to tell them were not complicated. A sense of tightness in her shoulders lifted as she wrote and she knew that it was the right thing to do. She only wished that she had done it earlier.

Then she looked to the side, where Keema's case was still sitting.

The lid was flung open and Keema's trousers and shirts were spilling over the sides and strewn along the floor. She slowly reached out and picked up one, rubbing her fingers together as they pressed either side of the material. She lifted the shift closer to her face and let the soft material run across her cheek. Shanti remembered the feeling of Keema's shoulder under the material, pressing on her cheek as they held each other, the feeling of Keema's fingers running through her hair.

She sighed and picked up the clothes. Then she stood up and moved around the room, collecting any small objects that belonged to her or Keema. A wooden hairbrush with short blunted wooden bristles, a slim round silver container that contained a small amount of makeup for her cheeks. She tucked all the objects into Keema's suitcase and then paused again. She pulled the makeup container back out and worked to unfasten her suitcase so that she could tuck it in there instead.

I hope Keema doesn't find any trouble out there. She sat on the edge of the bed and considered her feelings. She knew that it was true that she still didn't want Keema to suffer simply for arriving in the city alongside herself, but there was a small part of her, a sour knot in her stomach, that found the idea of Keema getting a scare appealing. Although Shanti wanted her wife to get out of Chechezuk and return to her life in Gorduum, she also hoped that somehow the universe might punish Keema for her betrayal of Shanti's trust. She rubbed her hands down her face. *No. I mustn't be like that. The God would not approve.*

But maybe the God would? Shanti wondered what the God might think of a woman who was kissing someone else, when their wife was worried and looking for them. Perhaps it would be right for Shanti to provide the justice that the God would want meted out? But even as the thoughts flickered through her mind she knew that it was wrong. She knew that the God wouldn't be working through her to provide justice to Keema, it would just be her own desire for some sort of revenge.

Instead of making any further plans, Shanti picked up her suitcase and walked out of the room.

She dragged her luggage all the way back to the Lagoon and up the gangway to the Tide's Daughter. The long thin plank bounced beneath her feet, reminding her of the way the entire ship had shifted and moved while they were at sea. *Not long to go now,* she hoped.

Tozan stood at the top of the gangway with his usual frown and his usual crossed arms. He nodded at Shanti as she walked past, barely looking at her. She just smiled to herself as she headed across the deck. She did notice that there were more sailors aboard than she had seen the last couple of times she had returned to the Tide's Daughter though. She glanced sideways, watching as they scrubbed wood clean, untied and retied thick lengths of rope around stout wooden pins along the rails. Some of them glanced up at her in return, and a few smiled in recognition or gave her a quick nod before returning to their tasks. She felt a flutter of hope in her heart. *If Zekeka is leaving today then I might have a chance of getting away with this!*

Shanti moved into the hallway and gritted her teeth as she felt her muscles tense in the small dark space. She blew slowly through pursed lips and shook her head a little, trying to relax her shoulders, then knocked on the captain's door.

"Yes? Come in."

Shanti pulled her suitcase in behind her. Zekeka smiled from behind his desk and motioned her to the immobile seat opposite him.

"Welcome back Shanti," he said. "I am pleased to see you so promptly, as we had discussed."

She nodded.

"I see you have your suitcase with you. Is there anything else you require in the city, or is everything onboard now?"

"I have some errands and meetings I was hoping to complete today, but all of my belongings are here now."

"That's perfect!" He smiled wide. "We are planning to be ready to leave late this evening. The tide will be high and falling, and we should have finished loading cargo." He looked at Shanti with wide eyes, waiting for her response.

"Good, great," she stammered. "That feels so sudden?"

"Yes, it probably does, but that's how things are. We sail in, we seem to have to sit and wait and talk for days and days, then all of a sudden we must be on the move. Still, you should be ready for us?"

"Yes. You say that the Tide's Daughter will sail in the evening?"

"Yes, well after dark. The pilots will help us avoid damaging buildings as we go," he chuckled.

A double edged sword, though Shanti. *Leaving later in the evening means I have plenty of time to do what I need to do, but it also means that there will be more time for someone to chase me or even catch me.*

"Shanti?" Zekeka had raised an eyebrow. "Is something the matter?"

"No, no!" She shook her head sharply and made sure to smile back at him. "I was just making sure I will have time to get back before sunset. And I have a letter here." She took out the folded piece of paper. "If I don't make it back in time, could you see that it reaches my uncle Dunin?"

"Surely!" He took the paper and placed it on the desk, leaving one hand resting on top of it. "Now, unfortunately, I will have to organise a lot of things to ensure we meet the tide, so if you don't mind..."

"No, of course." Shanti stood up, narrowly avoiding cracking her knee on his desk, and grabbed her case.

"Tozan can stow that somewhere for you I'm sure." Zekeka was already looking down at the papers on his desk. Shanti managed to hold back a laugh but then moved out of the office. *That was easy,* she said to herself. *Now, I hope the rest of my plan goes even half as well as that.* She felt more at ease now that the letter was in safe hands as well.

Outside she went over to Tozan.

"The captain suggested that you might be able to put this somewhere for me?" she said, after coughing slightly to get his attention.

"Surely you could put it somewhere for yourself." He stood with crossed arms, looking back at her.

"Just, down in the cabin I suppose?"

"No, don't go down below deck!" Tozan snapped. "The sailors are restowing all the barrels and crates that they've been loading, and we still have plenty to get onboard! You'll be more underfoot than a silted shiprat! Give me the sodden thing." He reached out and took the luggage from Shanti. She tried not to laugh at his face, which was grimacing, although she had realised by now that the mate was actually much more obliging than his attitude had suggested.

"Thank you very much for doing that, I would hate to cause a problem for the crew."

He grunted and nodded.

"I have some meetings to attend, so I will leave you all to get things ready, and I will be back before sunset. You won't be delayed on my account."

"Glad to hear it," he growled.

As Shanti began to walk down the gangway she saw someone else rushing around the lagoon path towards it. The figure strode with elbows jabbing out to either side and her face was dark and thunderous. It was Lorku, the snooty wife of Rahit, who they had shared the cabin with during the long trip to Chechezuk.

"Lorku!" called out Shanti as she lifted a hand to wave in greeting. The other woman skidded to a stop and blinked up the gangway at Shanti. She lifted her own hand to shield her eyes from the early sun and then lifted it a little more to wave back.

"Shanti?" asked Lorku. She stepped closer to the gangway, barely noticing the glares she was receiving from others walking along the path who had to alter their steps around her.

"Yes, it's me! I thought that you and Rahit were going deep into the jungle? I'm surprised to see you back here already." Shanti reached the bottom of the gangway and stepped forward to give Lorku a hug. The other woman felt bony and stiff, as though she had tensed herself up as Shanti leaned forward.

Shanti stepped back and tilted her head a little. "Is everything alright?"

Lorku blinked and her mouth wobbled open and closed, and then she swallowed thickly before shaking her head. "No, not really."

"Is Rahit okay?"

"I think he will be."

"What? Oh my goodness, what happened?" Shanti reached forward to scoop Lorku's arm into her own and then began walking towards a sheltered alcove between the buildings nearby. Lorku glanced back at the Tide's Daughter for a second and then allowed herself to be drawn on.

"It's just that... this jungle... It's worse than anything Rahit had possibly dreamed up! He never thought that it would be... He certainly never told me that it would... By the God." Lorku was muttering, half to herself, as they moved. Shanti tried to pat the older woman's hand in a comforting way, but it wasn't clear that Lorku even noticed.

"Why don't you start at the beginning. You two were buying some equipment and heading out into the jungle straight away, wasn't that the plan?"

Lorku nodded. "Yes, straight out."

"Did that go well?"

"Yes, we found what we needed." Lorku went on to explain that Rahit had found them a decent sized boat that even had a shelter built onto it, big enough for them to live in, as well as resources, supplies, food that would last, and even some weapons to defend themselves, "because who knows what sort of monsters are out there in those watery trees."

Shanti remembered the way the guards at Kayzark's orchard had panicked when they had realised that the alligator was inside the heavy stockade that surrounded the buildings. She nodded fervently.

"That was probably a good idea. This sounds promising!" Shanti smiled but then looked closer at Lorku, noticing the tiredness that puffed around her eyes and the way she slumped against the wall as though she was barely strong enough to hold herself upright. "So, what went wrong?"

Lorku groaned. "Do you know how huge this jungle is? And there's no way to know which way you are going, because it's all just thick dark water and piles of looping roots, beneath an endless canopy of leaves!"

"I've seen it," admitted Shanti. She was beginning to wonder how she would find her way to the orchard. It was just along the main channel of the river, wasn't it?

"Exactly, so you know! It's a labyrinth made of living trees."

"But, you had supplies? And besides, Rahit said that your plan was to go and explore, didn't he? You don't need to have a destination in mind for that." The man had been convinced that he could find pockets of raw materials, whether they were mineral, plant, or animal, that the local population had not. He was sure he would be able to fill up his boat and come parading back to Gorduum as a much richer man in no time at all.

"Yes, we were not aiming anywhere in particular, but we kept getting lost and turned around in the river."

"What do you mean?"

"I mean what I said, we would be turned around.

We would be trying to make our way into the jungle and would end up popping out beneath the trees and facing the edge of Chechezuk again."

"Perhaps the currents are difficult," wondered Shanti aloud.

Lorku snorted. "Quite. And the few times that we did manage to get any reasonable distance in, we would be chased off by others."

"What others?"

"Others trying to make money. They would yell at us in their incomprehensible language, and some even threw javelins and loosed arrows!"

"Hidden Eyes," Shanti swore. "That's very serious! Is that what happened to Rahit, is he hurt?"

"No, the old fool. He's still convinced that we should return but I've had enough. I want to get back home to Gorduum and return to my mother's house. He can drown in this swamp for all I care!"

Shanti raised her eyebrows and blew softly out through her lips, her cheeks puffing up. "It's that serious?"

"He's trying to replace me now, hoping to head out before the heat of noon. As though some boat-hand helping him through this murky wetness would be a replacement for the loving wife he's been with for the last fourteen years!"

"That's terrible! Being replaced so casually makes you think that they never really cared about you in the first place, doesn't it?"

"Yes, exactly, as if the blinded man never really saw what he had with me!"

Shanti felt her throat tighten. "How did you know it was enough?"

"What do you mean?"

"How did you know that it wasn't worth trying to discuss things with him any more?"

Lorku narrowed her eyes. "When he stopped listening to me, I knew that I had to think of what I wanted, because it was clear that he wouldn't!" She glared at no one in particular, her frustrations and anger at Rahit overflowing onto her face. "Do you think the captain will take me home?" She jerked her head in the direction of the Tide's Daughter. "I don't know if I'll be able to cover the cost of my passage..."

"I'm sure he can arrange something. Maybe your family could pay him on your return?" Shanti bit her lower lip and looked up at the sky above the building that they were hunched next to.

Would Keema listen to her still? She wished that she was as certain as Lorku. It would be so much simpler if she could complete this task and then return to Gorduum on her own. But she felt such a strong desire to talk to her wife, to try and find out what had gone wrong. Would Keema think of what Shanti wanted, what Shanti needed?

But there was no time to spend on that right now. She had an important task to complete before she could think about her own needs.

"I'll be back later and I can help you try to convince him. In the meantime," she spoke carefully, with glittering eyes. "In the meantime, where is Rahit now?"

After getting directions from the older woman, Shanti walked quickly over to the Plaza. Her stomach was rumbling, and although she didn't always eat a large breakfast, she had a feeling that she was going to need as much energy as possible for the busy day that she had planned.

As she waited in line, tapping her foot and with her hands clutched around her elbows in front of her, she looked around the crowd of people in the Plaza. As always, it was quieter in the morning. There were very few musicians walking around, seeking small coins for their skills, as she saw in the evenings. People with insular faces took their food to the tables and benches and sat to eat methodically and quickly, before rising and heading out of the Plaza. There was none of the usual hum of conversation, none of the laughter and smiles.

Then Keema walked over towards her.

Shanti felt the muscles up her back stiffen, and her neck grew tight. She had to remind herself to release her breath.

"Hello Shanti," said Keema, with her face low. She set her case behind her so that it wouldn't fall over and jammed her hands into her pockets. She rocked back and forwards on the cobbles, without once lifting her eyes.

"Hello," replied Shanti. She waited for the other woman to say something.

"How are you doing this morning?" Keema asked.

"I am fine. I have a busy day today."

"Oh? I thought you would be done with all your meetings by now?" Keema glanced up, though she didn't meet Shanti's eyes. A small smirk was trying to establish itself on her cheek.

Shanti pulled her arms tighter and stared at Keema without speaking. The other woman sighed.

"I guess, we should talk."

"I don't know if we need to," replied Shanti. "I think I saw how you feel about things last night."

"You saw how I...? Oh. You saw me back here?" Keema's face fell again. "What did you see?"

"Does that matter? You didn't seem to care at all." Shanti could feel an angry flower beginning to uncurl in her chest and the heat of it was seeping into her arms and building behind her eyes.

Keema was frowning and crossed her arms. She kicked at the stones beneath their feet.

"I guess I didn't think you would notice," she muttered.

"Wouldn't notice?" snapped Shanti. "You thought I wouldn't notice you kissing someone you didn't even know, while I was worried that I had hurt you?"

"You appeared to be very interested in Arsook the last time I saw you." Now Keema did look up, her own eyes flashing.

"And so it was okay for you to go running into the arms of the first woman you saw?" Shanti could feel rawness in her throat. The heat of the angry flower that had blossomed inside was trying to burst out of her and it was taking all her strength to keep it under control.

"No. Yes! Not really. But I had no idea that I was hurting you! You haven't spoken to me in weeks, you barely spent any time with me in this city. You keep finding new people to be with, so why shouldn't I?"

Shanti felt her mouth open but her breath was caught and she couldn't speak. *How could I have spent more time with her!? She spent the whole sea voyage to Chechezuk on a bed, and then we've had meetings and business to attend to. Besides...*

"I've spent every morning and evening with you!"

"You've spent that time near me, yes. But you haven't been with me. You've been with them." Keema glared at Shanti.

Shanti turned around. The flower in her chest was wide and straining for the sky. *I don't need this right now,* she snapped to herself. She began to walk away, with a hungry stomach. I have a huge day ahead of me, and I shouldn't have to deal with her accusations. *I didn't even do anything, she was the one who did something wrong!*

"Shanti!" Keema called out to her. Shanti ignored her and strode out a random street. She stomped along the path until she reached one of the small arched bridges that passed over the canals and then paused to lean on the carved railing.

Shanti waited. She didn't know what she was waiting for, but she looked down at the dark water of the canal below her feet as she waited. A canalboat poled past, with a young man and woman squeezed next to each other in the middle. They looked up at her with bright eyes and she saw the woman lean in to whisper something in her partner's ear. He chuckled and slipped an arm around her shoulder, pulling her close.

Shanti sniffed and stood up, turning to look back along the path to the Plaza. She saw no one she recognised along the way.

41

———

Back in the open space of the Plaza, lined with stalls and filled with wooden tables, Shanti turned slowly, giving her eyes time to search as fully as they could. When she had passed them twice over the scene, she lifted a fist to her chest. He heart felt as though it was about to shrivel into ash.

"Shanti?" said a deep man's voice from nearby. Taadin was walking closer, his brow creased in concern. "Are you alright? You rushed off last night." He paused and pursed his lips. "At least two times that I know of."

Shanti began nodding and then felt her face fall and so she buried it in her arms. She felt Taadin's massive arms fold around her like a blanket.

"Shhhh," he murmured. He patted her back. "Are you alright?"

"She didn't... I left but she..." stammered Shanti into the darkness of his shoulder. Her face was hot and wet.

"Yeah, I know." he said.

"You do?" she sniffed as she leaned away from him, scrubbing her face on the back of her sleeve.

"Not at all, but it made you feel better, didn't it?"

She laughed and then sniffed again.

"Where's Gudan?"

"Here," groaned a figure slumped at a table not far from where she stood with Taadin. Gudan pushed his head higher on one arm and turned raw red eyes towards her. He tried to lift a hand to wave a greeting but the movement made him blink and then grab at his stomach as he doubled over.

"Oh dear," said Shanti. "Should we do something?"

Taadin shook his head. "All we can do is wait with him. Eventually the poisons will work their way through his system and he'll be back to his usual self. In the meantime..." He shrugged. "We just put up with this mess."

Shanti giggled again.

"Like you should do with Keema?" he asked carefully.

Shanti's shoulders stiffened. "You think I should wait out her mess?"

He sighed. "Or maybe you get the poisons out while she's waiting for you?"

"What!?"

He lifted his hands defensively. "I don't know! I don't know enough about what's going on with you two. But I know what I saw last night."

"So do I. I saw her run away from me. I tried to find her, to talk to her, but she ran away, and then she broke my trust. When I ran away, she didn't follow me."

"I don't think she knows you ran away."

Shanti tried not to let her thoughts and feelings show on her face. She could feel the harsh angry flame that had grown inside tempering down already. But she didn't want to forgive Keema. She closed her eyes, and a vision of her partner, with her arms around someone else, with her lips pressed against someone else's, burst across the darkness behind her eyes. She shook her head slightly as a tear began to work its way out of the corner of her eye.

"But she was kissing that girl, that stranger."

"I think she may have felt that you started that. Regardless, she sent that girl away not long after I last saw you."

"She did what?"

"She actually spoke to Gudan and myself about it. She said she was making a mistake and she didn't know how to fix it."

Shanti didn't know how to respond to this. What would she say to Keema if she saw her again? Could she forgive her? The flower burned in her chest still and her anger refused to consider the idea, but now there was a cold rain washing its way through her limbs and she didn't know what would be left when it was done.

She kissed Taadin on the cheek, patted Gudan on the shoulder, ignored the feeble groan he emitted at her touch, and left the Plaza. She still had a task to complete today.

Lorku had been telling the truth. Shanti found Rahit at a dock, still lying on the large boat in a daze. She was shocked by the appearance of him after only a few days in the jungles around Chechezuk.

His eyes were pulled wider than was natural, and his lips were cracked and dry. His cheeks and neck looked lumpy and discoloured, and when he lifted an arm slowly to acknowledge Shanti she could see that the same rash was spreading along his arm.

"Are you alright?" she asked as she carefully climbed across the railing onto the boat. It was large enough to live on, but much much smaller than the Tide's Daughter. There was a low cabin at the rear with only a single small door for any passengers to use. There were no windows. Shanti couldn't imagine that it was large enough to fit more than a thin mattress or two, and she began to understand why Lorku was ready to leave.

Further towards the front of the boat was a contraption similar to the one that had propelled Kayzark's boat, but instead of a huge single wheel that dipped into the water, here it was two smaller wheels, one on either side of the boat. There was a seat set near the mechanism.

At the front of the boat, the prow rose up into a narrow fin, eager to slice the air as the boat moved forward, just as its hull would slice through the waves. From alongside, the fin was broad with a rectangular shape, but with ridged carvings that wound in spirals inside the outer edges.

Rahit nodded and ran his tongue across his lips, flinching.

"Yes, I will be okay," he replied in a rasping voice. "I keep licking my lips instinctively and it hurts every time." He chuckled and shook his head.

"Lorku said that you'd been severely bitten in the jungle, but I had no idea it was this bad. Did something happen?"

"It had been bad enough as they followed us around," he replied, waving a hand to disperse two of the large insects that had buzzed closer while they spoke. "But then we must have sent the boat over a nest or something. A giant cloud swarmed out of nowhere and covered us!"

"How come Lorku was okay?" asked Shanti. She tried not to stare at the marks that covered the man.

"She managed to get under a blanket while I tried to get the boat away and squash as many of them as I could." He sniffed. "So, you saw her. Do you know what her plan is?"

"I think she is going to go back to Gorduum," admitted Shanti. "Didn't she say as much to you?"

"Yes, she did, but I had hoped that she was kidding." He slouched back onto a bench near the small cabin at the rear of the boat. "Why did you come down here? To tell me that she was leaving?"

"Are you sure that you don't want to leave yourself?" Shanti moved over to see him more clearly. "It looks like things are going much harder than you realised."

"I had such a grand plan!" he declared, lifting his arms into the air above him, fists clenched. "I know that this could work!"

"But is it really more important than her?"

His arms lowered slowly to the bench by his sides. One hand rested on his stomach and he stared at the sky.

"You really think I am going to lose her, don't you."

"I think you already have," said Shanti quietly. "But if you go after her, if you show her that your plan is not as important as she is, maybe she'll take you back?"

"Do you know what it is like to have something this important in your life?" He sat up now and looked at her with a face twisted by anguish. "I know I can do this, I'm sure of it! But I can't keep her if I do it. What sort of price is that? Why would she do this to me?"

Shanti thought about what Keema had said earlier. Keema already felt as though Shanti had been leaving her behind, as though she was being left out. Maybe that was how Lorku felt, as Rahit kept pushing on with this expedition into strange lands, into swarms of insects.

"Maybe it's not always about what she does affecting you. Maybe you need to start being more aware of how you are affecting her." Shanti waved a hand at a single insect as it flew past her ear.

"Maybe. I'm just not used to it I guess."

"It's important. After all, she is important to you isn't she?"

"Yes. She's more important than this." Rahit gestured at the equipment that he had gathered on the small deck of the boat. "But what do I do with it all?"

"I have an idea about that," said Shanti carefully, biting her lip to keep herself from smiling.

She felt as though Lorku and Rahit were just like her own parents. Though trials might cause them to bicker and argue, really they had a deep love for each other, and they wanted to support each other. Her father Neeran made sure that Auga had enough time to run her store and keep the accounts, and in turn Shanti's mother doted upon her husband. When times were tough, Shanti had heard them arguing in the living room while she lay in her bed upstairs, but by the time she came downstairs in the morning they were always holding each other and smiling again. She knew that it was the same here. Lorku had come to support Rahit in his goals, and she had tried as long as she could. Now Rahit just needed to open his eyes wide enough to see that he had done what he could but it was time to support her.

Within half an hour, Rahit had cleaned himself up and gathered the belongings he would need to return to Gorduum into a massive canvas sack that he slung over his shoulder. He shook hands with Shanti and then stepped off the boat with a skip in his step that suggested he was feeling more positive about his destination than he had first thought. Shanti waved as he left and then turned to examine the boat she now controlled. *How do I make this thing go?*

After studying the large mechanical device, Shanti was able to figure out what she had to do. It was actually obvious enough once she took the time. She sat down on the broad seat next to the contraption in the middle of the boat, settling down onto the shaped wooden chair. Rahit had left a thin piece of material folded up on the seat as a kind of cushion, but it was not very effective. Shanti had to shift every few minutes as her muscles pinched against the solid seat.

She slipped her feet into the pedals that were mounted in front of the seat and took hold of a pair of long thin handles that were attached to the wheels at the side of the boat. With a deep breath and a muttered prayer for the Masked God to watch over her and keep her from drowning, Shanti began to pedal.

It was easier than she thought, and her feet moved in small circles on the pedals while the wheels splashed softly into the water alongside the dock. However, even though the wheels spun rapidly, the boat itself did not. Shanti felt as though the boat was making faster progress due to the winds and currents pushing it out into the water than it was from her efforts. Nevertheless, she continued pedalling, twisting the handles to direct the large wheels on the sides of the boat, steering the boat towards her goal. Slowly, inexorably, like a cat on a hot summer afternoon, the boat began to head down the short canal to the wide water that surrounded the city.

Shanti didn't look at the people walking along the docks as she pedalled, but she could see from the corner of her eye that many of them were out pacing her. *How did Rahit do it,* she wondered. *How did he get this boat moving with Lorku onboard and everything?* She couldn't think of any way that he would have been able to get more out of the boat than she was.

After much longer than she would have liked, she was out in the open expanse of water between the city and the edge of the jungle. Narrower boats were slipping through the water and past her, with their polers raising an eyebrow at her meagre efforts. They were all heading towards a large dock on the outside of the city, opposite a clearing in the thick trees. *That must be the main channel's entrance,* she told herself. *I'm sure that it looks like the one Kayzark took me into.*

She heaved on the handles and sighed as the boat began to slowly curve towards the distant channel. She gritted her teeth and kept pulling, hoping that she wouldn't end up accidentally running into the huge roots that rose up beneath the jungle canopy. Those twisted trees were coming up fast.

"Shanti!" called a voice from somewhere behind her.

42
___

Shanti couldn't turn around, as she was too busy trying to keep control of the large vessel. She turned her eyes sideways, trying to see who had called. A narrow canal-boat came up alongside her, and the poler reached out to grab the side of Shanti's boat so that they would stay in position.

It was Keema.

"Why are you here?" spluttered Shanti.

"I know that I've done wrong, but I do care about you. I wanted to show you that I cared. Taadin told me that you were trying to get a boat, but by the time I managed to get this one, I saw you trying to pedal this massive thing out into the jungle." She slapped the railing that she was holding on to. "Wouldn't this canal-boat be easier?"

It would, thought Shanti, though she would hate to admit it to Keema right now. The anger she felt was still bright and raw. But her conversation with Rahit had made her think about her own situation. *Maybe I have been ignoring what Keema wants, and I have simply been expecting her to keep up with me. I shouldn't be surprised if she has had enough and wants to retreat somewhat.*

She absolutely broke my trust! came the angry justification in her mind. Her emotions flared and she felt her face grow hard.

She did, was her response to herself. *But I don't have to ignore that. Maybe I just need to begin by acknowledging my own role.* She took a deep breath.

"Yes, I think that boat would be much easier," she grunted. She lifted her feet from the pedals and clambered off the seat. She looked around the boat before she moved closer to Keema's boat though. *What will I need?* She picked up a heavy wooden club with a handle tied in leather strips, a wooden spear with three narrow tines at the end, and a long thin coil of rope. Then she picked up a broad bladed paddle and threw it over into the canal-boat as well.

"What exactly do you think we need all that for?" asked Keema.

"You'll find out later." Shanti stepped over into the canal-boat, pausing as it swayed beneath her footsteps. "For now, can you take me down that channel over there?" She pointed over to the empty space in the trees.

Keema's forehead creased in confusion, but she began pushing the pole through the dark shallow water.

"I thought that you were just trying to travel around the city quickly. Why do we need to head out into the jungle? I saw that you took your stuff out of our room already, are you planning on staying here instead of going back to Gorduum?" Although she managed to keep the worry out of her voice,

Shanti could see by the tilt of her wife's eyes how scared she was that Shanti might stay here.

"No, I just…" Shanti licked her lips, wondering how much she should tell the other woman. "I have something I have to do. I've been thinking really hard about what the Writ tells us about the Masked God."

"Oh? Did you see something? Something that the Masked God should fix?"

"I saw something."

Keema laughed. "You've always been the God's Eyes, watching out for us all."

"I hope so," agreed Shanti. "And now I have to act."

"You don't think that you should leave it for the God to work out?" Keema grunted as she stuck the pole forward and began pulling it back along the length of the boat. "Does it have to be you?"

"If it's not me who rights this wrong, how can I be sure that anyone else will?" Shanti could feel strength in her shoulders as she clenched her fists. This purpose was going to drive her on.

Keema got the boat moving faster and soon they reached the gap in the trees where the main river channel emptied into the waters under Chechezuk.

"It's a lot deeper here," Keema said slowly. "I don't think this pole is going to work anymore."

"Time to use this then." Shanti lifted up the broad paddle that she had thrown in from Rahit's boat. She shuffled in her seat halfway along the canal-boat, gripped the handle at the end of the short paddle and then stuck it into the water. Just as she began pulling through the shining surface of the river, Keema put a hand on her shoulder.

Keema moved forward and took the paddle from Shanti with a smile. "You'll need to save some strength to do what the God needs you to do. Why don't you let me do this bit?"

Shanti nodded and moved to the back of the canal-boat. She watched Keema's back as the woman pulled the paddle through the water and then lifted it out and shifted it to the other side of the narrow boat. She paddled two or three times on each side, and then swapped over, keeping the canal-boat on a straight course deeper into the darkness beneath the jungle trees.

She turned up, thought Shanti. *She could have left me here. I would have expected her to leave me here. She acted awfully, she hurt me. But at least she is here now.* Even now, looking at Keema the morning after an evening that had shocked her thoroughly, Shanti did feel a sense of comfort that Keema was with her. It made her feel a little bit sick, swirling that nausea with the anger and hurt that was still flowing strongly through her system. *What do I do now?*

They moved along the river for an hour, with nothing to look at except the passing trees and the slowly uncurling ripples that stretched across the slick surface of the river.

"I am sorry Shanti," Keema said, as the shadow of a bird darted across them.

Shanti was watching the sky, dark grey clouds hanging low. She didn't speak.

"I've been feeling really unnoticed by you. Like who I am isn't really important. I know that it's no excuse for hurting you. I just lost myself."

Keema paddled on in silence for a while.

"Will you forgive me?"

She didn't turn around.

Shanti kept watching the sky. She nibbled on her lower lip. She studied the back of Keema's head, the sharp spikes of black hair that she loved to run her fingers through jutting out in all directions. She watched as Keema's muscles shifted beneath her shirt as the woman paddled them deeper into the jungle.

"I am sorry that you have felt that way," Shanti said slowly. The water of the river slapped against the edge of the canal-boat. "Especially the parts of it that were my fault." She thought about how she had encouraged Keema to leave her horse behind in Gorduum, to abandon the work and friends that she knew for such a long time. She remembered Keema lying sick in the bunks of the Tide's Daughter for weeks as they sailed across the sea to this city. "But I don't know if I can get over what you did. It showed no consideration for me or my feelings."

"I know." Keema's head lowered and she kept paddling.

They continued to follow the river around broad curves. Each time Shanti would reach down to clutch the handle of the large baton that she had grabbed from Rahit's boat. But the river was empty, and the large stockade of the orchard was not in sight.

"Fancy seeing you out here in the jungle!" called a voice from far behind them, the sound thinned by the damp air. Shanti spun to face in the direction of the call, her eyes wide.

Arsook was standing at the front of a long triangular boat whose pointed prow lifted up and out of the water, jutting metres ahead of the hull. It ended in the familiar rectangular fin that so many Chechezukian boats had. From this distance, Shanti couldn't see the carvings in that fin, but she knew that they would be there.

As Shanti felt the blood drain from her face, she looked over the rest of Arsook's boat. It cut along the river faster than she would have thought such a small boat could move. She hadn't been watching for any one to approach them from behind, a mistake that she only now recognised. At the rear sat a heavily muscled man with a blank expression on his pale face. His red hair fell in long shaggy waves down his back and he wore no shirt. His muscles shone like well-polished marble, even in the scant sunlight that reached him from the overcast sky. He was leaning back in a long seat that was set on top of a set of interlocking metal cogs and wheels, like the contraptions that were on both Kayzark's and Rahit's boats. Another wheel of paddles was connected behind him. Two long handles reached forward alongside the seat and his arms gripped them tightly as he pedalled and the wheels spun.

Arsook was carrying something long and thin, like a pole that the boat polers used to propel the canal-boats through the narrow waters in the city. Then the tip of it caught the sunlight, revealing a thin needle-like shimmer of metal at the end of the shaft, and Shanti swallowed. *It's some sort of spear,* she thought.

In front of her, Keema had stopped paddling and sat with shoulders tensed. She had barely turned her head at all.

"Hello Arsook," called Shanti. She ran swallowed as a trickle of sweat passed down the back of her neck. "How are you?"

Arsook laughed loudly, the sound echoing briefly in the trees and causing a flock of small dark birds to launch themselves into the air.

"I'm fine! I was a little confused when you disappeared so quickly last night though, by the Stars! Why did you leave me?"

Shanti was very aware that Keema was sitting in front of her.

"I had something important to do." The long boat was coming closer and closer. Shanti began to worry that Arsook would realise what she was doing. *Don't be silly,* she admonished herself. *Not even Keema knows what you are doing. This is fine, just get her to leave again.*

"What is more important than me?" asked Arsook as her boat thudded softly into Shanti's. She grinned and set the haft of her spear on the bottom of the boat. The large man at the back turned his wide eyes to Shanti and Keema, but otherwise showed no sign that he was aware of anything happening in the world around him.

"Just something I had forgotten, I had to try and deal with it straight away."

"Did you manage to get it sorted?"

Shanti remembered the feeling of seeing Keema with the other woman and the unsettled sleep that she had endured. "Not really. Things got better this morning."

Keema sat a little straighter.

"I guess you've got work to do though, so we'll just leave you to it," said Shanti, leaning forward as though she was about to tap Keema as a signal to continue paddling.

"I do, but I'm much more curious why you are all the way out here!" Arsook leaned forward with both hands on the spear, resting her weight on it and letting her face move even closer. Her eyes were wide and piercing.

"We just thought we would go and see more of the jungle before we leave. It's a special place." Shanti hoped that implying she was operating out of naive curiosity would be enough to assuage Arsook's own.

Arsook narrowed her eyes. "It's a dangerous place. People don't generally come out in such a small boat with no way to defend themselves. The alligators can knock over a boat like yours in moments, though the Currents forbid." She leaned closer again, shifting her fingers on the spear.

"I suppose that we didn't think about that," said Shanti. She could feel the wooden club lying next to her foot.

"How about we escort you back to the city. I'd hate to see you get hurt out here."

"No, I think we'll be okay."

"Do you." There was no question in her tone. "I think I might have to insist."

43

"Does it really matter?" Shanti could feel her blood racing. Her forehead was throbbing. She felt flashbacks to a dark room and the dark hallway outside it, memories of shadowy figures grunting and yelling in the night, the flash of a knife. This jungle was such a different place, lit by a few shafts of pale sunlight leaking through the treetops. But here she was again, stuck in a situation where she wanted to make the world better, and trapped with people who might try to hurt her for doing it. "Couldn't you just go about your day, looking for wood and things, and let us go?"

"It is also my job to check on people out here in the jungle." Arsook's smile had gone now. "I just hoped that you weren't going to be one of those problems. It's a shame, you have such a beautiful smile." She leaned back and lifted the spear.

"I'm no problem," blurted Shanti, leaning away from the other woman. "How is this your job?"

"She's like some sort of guard for the place," said Keema over her shoulder. "I assume she's out here to stop foreigners from taking advantage of the things that are here in the jungle."

"Why didn't Rahit mention this?" Shanti was genuinely confused. "How do you know about this?"

"I just put two and two together," shrugged Keema. "Isn't it clear that she's some sort of enforcer. Did you never run into any of them in Gorduum?"

"What? No, I never saw any "enforcers" in Gorduum!"

Keema chuckled.

"Of course not. You're well behaved."

"Rahit?" interrupted Arsook. "Is that the old fool who arrived on the Tide's Daughter with you?" She snorted. "The biggest problem he was going to cause was clogging up some waterway with his corpse. But you look determined." She straightened her shoulders, loosening her muscles. "Now turn that boat around." She lifted the spear.

Shanti looked at the needle-thin tip, spiking forward towards her. Her blood felt like ice and every breath made her shiver. She leaned forward and placed a hand on Keema's shoulder.

"Get us out of here," she said.

Arsook's face twisted into a snarl, and she jabbed the spear forward directly at Shanti. Shanti screamed and leaned backward. The tip shone as it raced towards her but then was smacked aside. Keema's paddle had swung through the air before Shanti could think to defend herself, crashing into the thin shaft and sending it sideways so that the narrow spike impaled in the wood at the side of the boat instead of Shanti's chest.

Arsook's face was twisted in anger. Shanti was shocked. She had never expected that the young woman who was so interested in talking to her could be such a dangerous individual. For a moment her thoughts were flooded by the realisation that, again, she had allowed herself to think that someone was safe merely because they were kind to her and talked to her as if she were interesting. Only a few years earlier, when she had met Keema, a young man who had taken her out to a lavish ball and pursued her around the streets of Gorduum had turned out to be a vicious individual, capable of murder. How had she found herself in the same situation now? Shanti's muscles were frozen by the sudden familiar feeling that Arsook had evoked in her.

Keema leaned further over, pressing the spear down with the broad blade of her paddle, and stretched down to grab the club by Shanti's feet. She roared as she swung it up and nearly thumped the weighty piece of wood into Arsook's face, but the pale woman released her spear and dodged backwards just in time.

Keema grabbed the spear and pulled it onboard and then tried to start paddling away, further out into the middle of the river. Shanti reached forward slowly and picked up the spear, clutching it closely across her chest.

"Thank you Keema," she said.

"What are getting us into Petal?" yelped Keema as she dug into the river's surface with the paddle.

The boat shifted sideways and there was a dull hollow wooden thunk. Shanti looked around and saw that the long upturned prow of Arsook's boat had nudged them as she pursued them, though the woman was unable to reach out to their boat yet.

Her hands were empty. *Perhaps she has no more spears,* though Shanti.

"Do you think I can get us away from her?" shouted Keema. She tore at the water passing by beneath them.

Shanti looked around again. The huge man sitting above the gears and wheels at the back of the other boat still wore the same bored expression he had earlier, but his thick legs were pumping the pedals with no sign of discomfort. The wheel in the water behind blurred as it spun, splashing water in a great spray behind him.

"No."

"Then what in the blinded Eyes of the God are we going to do?"

Shanti gripped her hand around the shaft of the spear that they had ended up with. She looked back over the boats at Arsook, who was shrieking incoherently at her and Keema. *Could I stop her?* Shanti shifted her grip on the spear, testing the weight of it, looking at the distance between the boats. *There's no way that I could really stop her,* she admitted to herself before lowering the spear.

Keema paddled them out further into the middle of the river. Eddies coiled in the dark water around them and branches drifted past, waving their twigs into the air, the final leaves clinging to them like survivors of some catastrophe at sea. Another thunk signalled that Arsook was still right behind them.

"Here, grab this!" yelped Keema, shoving the club backwards with her foot. Shanti lifted it carefully, laying the spear down at the bottom of the hull.

"What's your plan?"

"I've had to take shortcuts through the alleys before, but I don't know if this is going to work out the same! Keep us off the biggest roots!" Keema hauled on the paddle and the long narrow boat shot into the gigantic coiled roots on the far side of the river. Shadows washed over them as they left the relatively bright sky over the river channel. Now smaller branches poked out of the water at odd angles. Vine loops passed over their heads as Keema kept plunging the paddle forward and pulling back.

There was a loud crash from behind them as Arsook's boat ran into some of the heavy roots. Shanti turned but then Keema yelled, "Stay focused! If we can't keep off the roots we'll be as stuck as them!"

Shanti spun forward and pushed out with the club, managing to lever them away from one of the roots just before they smashed into it. The wood ground against the side of their boat and the vessel creaked ominously, but held.

"I don't think they'll be broken up, but I think their boat is harder to move around."

There was a hideous grinding noise from below Shanti's feet. "I don't think anyone else is stupid enough to come out into the jungle in a canal-boat!" she yelled over the sound.

"I guess we'll just have to show them how it's done!"

They bounced away from more of the roots, and Shanti began to see creatures in the low boughs that hung overhead. Ragged curtains of leaves and vines drooped from the branches, and snakes lifted their eyes to watch the two women as they passed. Birds screeched at them or took to the wind with a battering of wings. She was sure that they rode the boat over the top of an alligator at one stage, but perhaps it had been a semi-submerged log.

Eventually, with her heart still pounding, and sweat freezing in the rushing wind, they manoeuvred their boat out of the trees and back into the main channel of the river. Shanti fell forward and threw her arms around Keema's shoulders, pulling her close and pressing her lips to the hair on the back of Keema's head.

"You got us through, thank you so much!"

Keema lifted a hand to pat Shanti's arm where it hooked around her neck.

"You're welcome Petal. Can you tell me what in the world is going on yet?"

Shanti sighed and smiled to herself.

"I decided to release the lizards."

"What? What lizards?"

"You've seen all the lizards that live around this city, right?

Keema nodded.

"It turns out that Kayzark has trapped dozens of them in his orchard and is using them to harvest the tuft. That is how he is going to make so much money and become such a big influence on the trade."

"That doesn't seem too bad. Why do you want to sabotage it? Weren't you going to make some sort of business agreement with him?" Keema sounded confused.

"It's all about the way he does it. The lizards are hard to train, but he found out that if he keeps their mates and eggs and young in tiny cages, and kills them if the workers get out of line, then the lizards will do whatever he wants."

Keema paddled on in silence for a moment.

"If they respond to such threats, doesn't that mean..."

"It means that they understand the threats." Shanti's throat felt thick. "That's what made me start thinking about it. They aren't just animals, they know what's going on. They understand brutal threats like that."

"That is horrifying," said Keema, nodding slowly. "But are you sure this is the way to handle it? Couldn't we just tell him that you don't want to take the deal and leave?"

Shanti shook her head. "I spent a lot of time thinking about this. I read through the Writ. I'm sure that this is what the Masked God would want."

Keema turned around to face Shanti. The boat slowly began to spin on the surface of the river, pushed by the current.

"It's a ludicrous idea," she smirked, but then her face grew serious. "And I'll follow it through with you, as far as you want to go."

"Thank you," grinned Shanti. Keema smiled and then turned back to her task and Shanti studied the back of her head. *How much has she managed to do for me, even when I haven't asked. She got it wrong and hurt me sometimes, but she says that she is sorry.* She resolved to use their time journeying up the main channel of the river to try and sort out her feelings. Maybe she could decide how to treat Keema by the time this task was done.

At least, I hope it's the main channel, thought Shanti as she looked left and right. *I have no idea if this is the same river, or which way will lead us back to the city.*

Shanti and Keema followed the river around two more corners in the trees and Shanti began to worry that they were completely lost. She was sure that they would find themselves back at the city before she knew it, or worse, lost in the massive jungle with no sign of anyone ever. She thought of the alligators that lurked beneath the still water and shuddered.

Then they rounded a bend and she breathed easier as the stockade that marked Kayzark's orchard appeared in the distance. But then a knot began to tighten in her stomach.

"How do we get inside?" whispered Keema over her shoulder.

"I haven't really thought about how to do that," admitted Shanti in a normal voice. "And you don't need to whisper, there's a long way to go yet." Shanti let her eyes drift along the top of the stockade. "They have lookouts. Maybe we should go into the trees again."

"Alright. Help keep us off the roots."

For the second time, Keema steered the narrow boat to the side of the main river channel and into the narrow confines of the monstrous tree roots. Shanti leaned over the edge, pushing her club against the strangely smooth trunks and reducing the bang and thud of their boat hitting them. The twisting maze through the trees made it extremely difficult for them to move quickly.

"Do you think she will have followed us?" asked Shanti softly.

Keema shook her head in front of us. "I wouldn't think so. She can't be sure which way we went, or why. But I'm glad to know that Zekeka is leaving

Chechezuk tonight. I assume that's your plan as well?"

"Yes. I was hoping to do this today anyway, but when I found out that today would be the last day the ship was at the lagoon, I knew I had to act."

They moved on without speaking, accompanied only by the slosh of water moving around them and ripples washing through the tangled roots. A bird called from somewhere in the distance, muffled by the thick leaves overhead. Its song trilled and spiralled around itself in a series of chirps and whistles and then cut off just as abruptly as it had started.

44

———

Shanti listened to the birds in the trees and pulled in a deep breath.

"Keema, I'm sorry for all of this."

"What do you mean?"

"I'm sorry that I dragged you along to this place. I didn't realise how much it was asking of you. You had to basically abandon your work for months, just to support me on whim."

"It wasn't a whim. You always said that you wanted to see as much of the world as you could. I've thought that you were going to leave Gorduum so many times over the last few years that I've stopped counting."

"You have? I've never considered leaving before."

"You haven't?" Keema sounded truly shocked.

"No! I would be heart broken if I had to leave and not see you for weeks or months or, the God forbid, years. What if you went back to your old life? You were pretty happy before you met me."

"You know, I was." Keema paused in her paddling and turned to look over her shoulder. "But it was nothing to how I feel knowing that you are waiting for me at the end of a long day at the reins. Even my worst days are brighter than the ones I had before, with you in my life.

I've been terrified that you were finally going to realise that our marriage was some foolish youthful misadventure, leaving me behind to go out into the world. That's why I couldn't let you go here on your own. That's why I've been so upset that you don't want to be around me."

"Why would I think that our vows were so shallow?" asked Shanti, though she felt a rock in her stomach. She knew why Keema might feel that way. Gudan had pointed it out on the Tide's Daughter. Why hadn't she considered what Keema was thinking more often? Why hadn't she just asked?

"We got married so quickly. We didn't even have your uncle there, and I know family is so important to you. You haven't taken me to Graama to meet them." Keema paused, keeping an eye on the fortress downriver from them. "I can tell that it's not really what you want."

"It *is* what I want. *You* are what I want," replied Shanti, her heart glowing. Then it felt a stab of icy cold. "That's why I was so shocked when I saw you kissing that girl. I felt like you had decided to go back to the life that you knew worked." She hung her head. "Especially when you were here, somewhere that you didn't really want to be, somewhere you didn't know the streets."

Keema sighed. "I am so sorry I did that. It was a terrible thing to do, and I have no excuse. But I want you to know that, while it has been hard to be here with you, there was no way I was going to let you come on this journey without me."

Shanti leaned forward and rested a hand on Keema's shoulder. "I love you."

"I love you too."

Before they could say anything else, a lizard burst out of the foliage in the branches above them. It broke thin twigs and knocked leaves loose. When it noticed them in the boat below, it froze and tilted its head at an unnatural angle to stare at them with one bulging brown eye. It had large spikes running down the middle of its head, which grew longer and softer over its shoulders and then shorter again. The middle spikes looked like thick threads of hair that were dangling over its forelimbs.

Its face was a bright orange, nearly yellow, that faded behind its round cheeks to a duller shade, and then the rest of its body was deep green. From where Shanti was sitting in the boat she could see that a bulging leather satchel was slung over its back that appeared to be so full that it was about to burst open.

"Look!" cried Shanti.

"I see it," said Keema. "What in the world is it wearing?"

"That's one of the workers at the orchard. That's what it uses to collect tuft and bring it back to be threshed and bundled."

"By more of the lizards, like you described?"

"Exactly."

They looked back at the lizard. None of the three moved.

"And you think they know how dangerous it all is?" asked Keema.

"Yes." Shanti looked at the lizard's face. Its eyes were wide and unblinking, and a thin whip of tongue slithered out then back into its mouth. And yet she was sure that it was considering their presence more than it would think about any other animal in the jungle. She was sure that it recognised them as people, in the wrong place, and was trying to figure out if they were related in some way to Kayzark and his workers.

"Do you think there is any way we can prove it?" asked Keema.

"I can try," said Shanti.

She cupped her hands around her mouth and called up to the lizard, trying to be loud enough for it to hear her, but not loud enough to be heard through the jungle. She had no idea how far away the guards and lookouts of the orchard were.

"Hello lizard," she called, using the simplest words in Zukian that she could remember. "Can you understand me?"

The lizard stepped forward on all its limbs, long thin fingers clutched at the wood beneath it.

"I am here to help."

The lizard kept looking at her.

"I want you to be free. I want your families to be free. I want you all to be free."

The lizard wobbled on its legs, back and forth, and then leapt forward and disappeared through the leaves around it. Despite the bright colour of its face, it had vanished from their sight instantly.

"What did you say?" asked Keema.

"I asked if it could understand me, and tried to tell it that we were here to help."

"I'd take that as a no," said Keema, looking at the empty branches left by the lizard's departure. "Come on, I think we are pretty close to the orchard."

Keema guided the narrow boat slowly forward, turning around one large cluster of roots and then jamming her paddle into the crannies between the thick roots. Shanti leaned over to help bring the boat to a halt as well.

"Look," hissed Keema.

They were not at the edge of the jungle yet, but Shanti could see where the trees stopped only a dozen metres or so ahead of where they were. The light was brighter there, reflecting off small ripples in the dark water. A further dozen metres over that water, the thick stockade of the orchard rose up from the shimmering surface.

As she had noticed during her previous visit, Shanti could see that the poles were not tightly packed together. There were gaps between each, and someone inside would be able to look through and see them relatively easily. She looked up. Although she couldn't see any of them, she knew that the lookouts would be standing on their walkway near the top of the stockade.

"Now what?" asked Keema.

Shanti sat in frustration wondering what to do. She had been operating on impulse, driven by the goal that she knew she had to pursue, and rushing to achieve it as she knew time would be short. But now she had reached the point where she didn't know what to do next.

Movement to their left caught both her and Keema's attention. A lizard was scuttling down the looping root of a tree right on the edge of the jungle. It paused at the bottom, centimetres above the water, and cocked its head in a variety of directions, looking down at the water, out at the stockade, and back. For one brief moment, Shanti was sure that it looked back towards the jungle, directly at her. Then it dropped into the water and slid under the surface.

At first she and Keema could see no sign of the lizard, but then its head poked out of the water. The creature's scales were a stunning orange and yet its shape vanished in the sunlight glinting off the surface. A pair of angled ripples slid out behind the lizard's head as it propelled itself through the water, making a sinuous motion to slip forward. Shanti was amazed at how quickly the creature was able to move.

"If we could swim like that we'd have no trouble at all," muttered Keema.

The lizard reached the stockade and turned to swim alongside the tall posts to the left. It reached a low gap in the fence where the poles above were supported by a thick structure that left an opening below. The opening was just at water level, and occasional ripples slapped against the dark wood above. The lizard ducked under the surface. A few seconds later they could see a glimpse of it clambering up to the deck inside the stockade.

"That's how the lizards get in. That gap would have to be tiny, far too small for us to get in."

"Good, I'm glad you've at least crossed one option off the list. So how many options are left?" asked Keema, turning her smirk at Shanti with a raised eyebrow. Shanti stuck out her tongue in return.

"We can come up with something. I just need to get inside, because I know where the lizards' cages are. Once they are open then they should be able to swim away pretty easily."

"And how do we escape?"

"I haven't really thought about that."

"Because the rest of the plan is so well detailed." Keema shrugged her shoulders. "Shall we try to move around and see if we can see another way in?"

"Probably."

But before they could start moving, more lizards came rushing down from the shadows beyond the gap in the stockade. They plunged into the water and shot through the gap before poking their heads out of the water on the outside. Two began swimming to the right at speed, splashing and whipping their long tails out of the water and back down. Shanti thought it was strange that they made such a scene as they moved through the water, when she had seen many of these lizards swimming so smoothly previously. The last one moved more slowly, following the same waving motion as the earlier lizard had done, moving to the left of Shanti and Keema. It reached the jungle and climbed up onto the roots and scampered into the branches.

"Blinded Eyes Shanti, look!" Keema reached back and grabbed Shanti's hand. She pointed sharply out to the right.

A hefty log lying in the water beneath a large root arch had begun to drift out from under the cover of the trees. *What is she talking about?* As it reached the brighter space beyond the canopy's shadow, Shanti realised why Keema had reacted so strongly.

Oh! It's one of those alligators! Shanti leaned back slightly, even though the creature was far away from herself and Keema. What she had thought was dark heavily-ridged bark, became clear as heavy scales and spiked skin. The light reflected off a single eye like a ball of glass. Most of the creature was hidden beneath the water, but Shanti remembered the bulk that she had seen when she came to the stockade earlier. Her blood ran cold and she tried to pull herself further from the edge of their canal-boat. *That thing is bigger than this entire boat,* she realised. *If one of them had decided to try and knock us over at any point on our way out here, we could have done nothing to stop it.*

There was a scratching noise from above them. Shanti turned and saw a lizard leaning out over them, close enough for her to touch. She recognised the bright orange face. It was the same lizard she had seen earlier.

"You're back?"

The lizard turned its head so that the side was pointing at Shanti, and its eye ticked from one angle to another as it looked her over. Then it scurried face first down the branches until it was crouching on the roots near them, just above the water, and just out of their reach. It paused, totally still except for the slight billowing of its chest as it breathed,

"Does it think we are a threat or something?" asked Keema.

"I don't know," breathed Shanti.

Back across the water, the splashing from the other lizards had grown louder and when Shanti looked back at them she could see that their movements had grown frantic as well. The massive alligator still appeared to be drifting like a log through the water, but it was clear that it was heading towards the lizards.

Shouts came from the top of the stockade and

Shanti crouched down as though the movement would hide her. Keema leaned back closer to her as well. The shouts were distant and agitated, making it difficult to determine what they were saying. *Have they seen us,* panicked Shanti.

There was movement at the top of the stockade. Shapes started running to the right. The lizards vanished around the curve of the stockade and the alligator began to move faster, ripples showing how its massive broad tail was undulating to drive it further through the water. Soon it vanished around the corner also.

45

The lizard waiting on the root next to them thumped its foot loudly. Shanti and Keema turned back to it. Once it was sure that they were both looking at it, it slid off the root into the water, and began swimming directly for the gap it had come out of.

"Does it want us to follow it?" asked Keema.

"No, it couldn't possibly," said Shanti automatically. *But maybe it is,* she realised as it paused in the water and spun its eyes back to stare at them. Shanti felt disconnected from herself, as though someone else was speaking, though she recognised the sound of her own voice and could feel her mouth moving. "Maybe we should just assume that it does?"

They pushed forward from the roots, Keema carefully paddling so as not to cause splashing. Shanti used the club to help as much as she could until they moved beyond the roots. Then she felt exposed and couldn't help but look up to the top of the stockade. Grey clouds overhead made it hard to see into the dark shadow of the stockade. Nothing was moving there.

Shouting and banging began to echo back from the main gate into the stockade. Shrieks split the jungle air like nails driving into wood and Shanti flinched each time, wondering if one would be the sound of a lookout spotting them.

To her shock they made it across the water without drawing attention, pulling the narrow boat in tightly against the stockade and hoping that it would not be spotted by anyone looking out from above them.

The lizard that they had been following paused in the slim gap, its long limbs and strange fingers gripping the structure above and its rear legs hidden under the water. It looked as though it was holding the space open. Its angular face was turned towards them and its string-like tongue flickered across the scaly edge of its mouth.

"Still think that gap is too small for us?" asked Keema.

"I mean, yes? But I think this lizard thinks that we will fit."

Shanti moved to the edge of the boat, catching her breath as it rolled in the water. She blew out a breath and then hopped over the side while clutching the rail. She prepared herself to plunge deep into the water, holding her breath and tensing her muscles against the sudden rush of cold, but was pleasantly surprised to feel her feet sink into a layer of mud when she was little more than waist deep.

"It's so shallow!" she squeaked.

"Shanti, you remember that we just saw a gigantic beast of a creature swimming through this water?" Keema was staring at her with wide eyes.

"All the more reason to move quickly," responded Shanti. The thought had actually slipped from her mind in the heart-racing moment of finding a way past the stockade, and now Shanti's nerves began shivering. She moved forward to the gap, where the lizard was watching and waiting.

She lifted her legs onto the lower half of the structure and groaned a little as she felt the slippery algae that grew on the wooden supports. She reached out to hold the upper structure as well. The gap between the two was just as small as she had thought, barely as long as her forearm. There was a soft splash behind her and she hoped that it was the sound of Keema joining her. *Do I have any better ideas,* she asked herself and then she ducked down and under the gap, pulling herself forward.

Beneath the water Shanti found the world was dark and silent. The shouting that had been all around them above the surface vanished. As she pulled herself blindly forward she began to worry that she would not find the end of the entrance, and that it was far too small for her to turn around easily in this narrow space. She opened her eyes, hoping to see a destination, but the water was thick and murky and she could see nothing.

An orange shape bobbed closer. The lizard was staring at her beneath the water, barely twenty centimetres away from her face. It whirled in the water like a dancer and sped away from Shanti, so she pulled herself after it. Just as her lungs were beginning to burn, she realised that the water above her refracted a silvery light. *Please, let that be the opening I need!*

It took all of Shanti's will not to suck a huge

gasp of air down as soon as her head broke the surface. She wanted to stay as quiet as possible. The distraction near the entrance to the stockade couldn't keep all the lookouts occupied for long, and she was going to need to be careful not to be caught before she had managed to release the lizards.

Shanti looked around. She was in a small pool surrounded by wooden decking just inside the stockade wall. When she turned around, she could see through the narrow gaps in the posts to the water outside. *That passage felt so much longer while I was in the water.* She placed a hand on her chest and tried to control her breathing.

Flights of low stairs led a metre up from the pool in semicircles like the seats in a theatre, until they reached the main floor level within the stockade. She put her hands on the edge and pushed herself out of the pool, then lay on the deck staring up at the sky. Water drained out of her hair and clothes and she shivered as the cool air began to trace the exposed skin of her hands and creep down the back of her neck.

Keema stood up in the pool and began sucking in air through her nose. She was clearly trying to stay quiet as well. After a second she moved over and pulled herself up to sit on the edge next to Shanti.

"We made it inside," she gasped. "Now what?"

Now that she was inside the stockade, Shanti could get her bearings. To her right was the long long workhouse that lizards would be chained inside, threshing the tuft that had been collected by the others. Beyond that was the taller building that housed the cages. Shanti remembered that guards were posted all around.

"Now what? Now we go into the workspaces. There will be people trying to stop us," she warned Keema.

The other woman frowned.

"Did you bring the club along with you?"

Shanti bit her lip. "No. We'll have to think of something before we get there."

The lizard who had led them inside was standing on the steps nearby, reared up on its hind legs, with its body curved up to leave its arms free. It took a wobbling step towards the workhouse and then stopped again. Shanti nodded. "We'll find something. Come on, let's act quickly."

The small group moved through the buildings cautiously. The sounds from the far end of the complex had quietened now, and Shanti assumed that the guards and lookouts had driven off the alligator. *I hope that those other lizards are okay,* she thought. *I can't believe that they were creating a distraction for us!* She had realised that there was nothing else that could explain their behaviour. They were instructed to head straight out into the orchard and collect the tufts, with threats of violence against the mates and young that were kept locked up inside. Swimming around to the front of the stockade was not part of those instructions at all. *And the orange faced one was so good at swimming, surely that calamitous method the others had used was deliberate, done to attract the attention of the alligator. They couldn't possibly swim like that naturally!*

The trio reached the door to the workhouse and paused. No one had stopped them yet and Shanti was sure that she had seen plenty of guards during her earlier visit. The lizard that they were following stood outside the door, with one long fingered hand resting on the handle. Its eyes swivelled back to look at Shanti.

"This is one of the problems they have," said Shanti as she realised why it was watching her. "They can't open the doors easily, certainly not quick enough for a rescue or escape." She reached out to the handle. "Maybe we can bluff our way through?" she asked, looking back at Keema.

The other woman shrugged. "What's the worst that could happen?"

"They kill us as intruders and leave our bodies in the swamp water."

Keema blinked and licked her lips. "When you put it like that... Do you have a better plan?"

"None come to mind," said Shanti and she turned the handle and pushed the door open.

The room was as wide as she remembered, full of rows and rows of tables lined up. Lizards were hunched over each one, running their long fingers through the thick white puffy tuft and pulling out burs and fragments of detritus and then flicking it to the ground. Their thin fingers were nimble and the small claws at the end helpful for hooking on to the imperfections that needed to be removed.

Standing next to the doorway was a large man with broad shoulders. He frowned as Shanti and Keema stepped inside and placed a hand on the heavy wooden club that swung by his hip, hanging from a loop of leather. He grunted and said something to them in the spiky language of the city. Shanti blinked. She was a novice and had missed enough of his words to have not the slightest clue what he said. The man narrowed his eyes and then spoke in a thick accent. "Who are you?"

"Just friends of Kayzark," beamed Shanti, pulling her lips into as big a smile as she could manage. She wasn't sure what she needed to do next, but she knew she needed to convince him not to grab that club and use it to stop her and Keema.

"Oh yeah? Why isn't he here with you?" The large man turned his gaze to the empty doorway behind them, just as Keema pulled it shut.

"He's on his way, he was just inspecting the workers coming in from the actual trees."

"You are so wet?"

"We slipped while getting off the boat."

The man nodded, but then his forehead crinkled in confusion. "Workers? What workers?"

"Oh, I mean them," said Shanti, pointing over at the lizards.

The man laughed, and it was a short nasty noise. He rubbed his nose with one huge hand. "Workers, yeah right! These silty creatures are our workers!" He chuckled some more, his large shoulders bobbing up and down like boulders tumbling down a hillside. But he turned away, and Shanti breathed a little easier. *Where did that orange faced lizard go?*

She moved over to the first of the tables. The lizard working at the table didn't even look in her direction, its hands just kept passing over and through the tuft, then pushing the pale pile further along the table. Other lizards worked on the clumps that were pushed their way and then passed them along, multiple sets of eyes and hands ensuring that the final pile of tuft at the far end of the room was as clean and soft as possible. Shanti looked at the chain that locked the lizard into position.

It was finely made, small but black and solid. The end of the chain split into a pair of shackles that were fastened around the lizard's rear legs. There didn't appear to be a keyhole in the shackles and Shanti wondered how they were kept fastened. She leaned closer.

A voice spoke behind her and Shanti straightened immediately. She turned, trying to slow down so that she didn't appear suspicious. A short broad woman with light yellow hair cut short and spiky was walking over towards her.

46

———

"Hello," said Shanti. She waved a hand back towards the first guard that they had come in past. "He said it was okay to have a look around."

The second guard glanced back towards the first. He was leaning against the wall near the door, but it was clear that he had seen Shanti come in and was unconcerned. The woman narrowed her eyes and pressed her lips together but then sniffed and turned to walk away again.

Keema walked up next to Shanti. "You got away with that for now, but they are going to get suspicious when that guy you mentioned doesn't come in. What do we do?"

Shanti looked down at the shackles again. They were held in place by a thick bolt of metal that screwed through the curve of a chain link and connected them to a metal plate on the floor. The screw had a heavy set of wings built in. *So, all it would take to open the shackles and get out would be to unscrew that bolt?* Shanti was confused. *Why don't they just undo their shackles and get out of here?* She looked around the room. There only appeared to be the two guards.

"Keema, I think I'm just going to start releasing the lizards."

"What?" Keema tried to keep her face calm, but her eyes widened and Shanti could see how her whole face tensed up.

"Once I get a few out they should be able to release the others, and when there are more of them out, they should be able to overwhelm the guards. There are only two of them after all."

"That's not exactly a very well thought through plan, Shanti," hissed Keema. Her eyes were full of panic. Shanti felt a sense of ease in her body though, as though she was floating in a gentle pool with sunlight warming her from above.

"The God is watching us," she said, and she bent down to the lizard. It twisted to watch what she was doing as she reached out to its leg. She grabbed the metal bar, set her fingers to the wings on the end of the bolt, and twisted. It didn't move at first, the metal was jammed shut. Clearly these shackles were not undone often. For a second Shanti wondered if the lizards were expected to simply remain at the tables even when they weren't working.

"Hey, what are you doing?" a voice called out from behind her but Shanti didn't pay it any attention. Instead she pulled at the bolts and threw the shackles aside.

"Open some more," she urged the lizard, but it sat in the seat staring at her with no expression. *None of them have any expression*, Shanti realised. She didn't have time to dwell on the lizard's reaction, so she shuffled further down the table and began un-bolting the next lizard.

"What is she doing?" yelled the voice, closer now.

"She's just getting a close look at their legs, she needs to see if they've been well taken care of, in case she does want to buy some." Shanti was grateful for Keema's quick witted answer.

"What?"

"That's why she's here, she thought she might buy some of these creatures to work for her, but they'll need strong legs."

Shanti dropped the pair of shackles that she had just undone and gave the lizard a push. This one responded better. It watched what she was doing but as soon as it's legs were free, it leaped onto the table and slid and banged across the tuft, kicking white fluff into the air around it that began to fall like snow. All the other lizards stopped what they were doing and watched it go.

"She let them go!" The voice was angry now, and Shanti hoped that Keema would be okay. She could hear scuffling behind her but she didn't dare look around now. She moved on to the next lizard. *Why aren't they helping me,* she thought in a panic. *They should be undoing more of these shackles!*

As she worked on this set of leg shackles, Shanti turned her head to see what had happened behind her. Keema had grabbed the arms of the stout woman who had been questioning her. Keema was holding on to the other woman's wrists to stop her grabbing the wooden club at her side, but the angry determination set on the guard's face made Shanti fearful. The woman's arms were thick and strong, and she was managing to move even though Keema was still holding her, though she moved slowly.

As though in a dream, Shanti watched as the guard by the door came rushing up. She could tell that he was rushing, by the way he moved his arms and legs, but to her eyes he moved extremely slowly. Nothing Shanti did could speed up time, and she watched as he began to raise the club he had been holding. His mouth was stretched open in anger, and his eyes glowed. The club swung down like a felled tree, crashing onto the side of Keema's head.

Keema fell to the ground and rolled. Shanti shrieked and her throat clenched hard enough to stop her breath. *I can't stop now,* she thought, her mind tumbling words over itself as she tried to focus though tears were bursting from her eyes. *I have to get them out.* She pulled out the bolt and dropped it.

This lizard didn't run for the other side of the room like the other ones had. It jumped over Shanti, lightly scratching her shoulders with its long claws as it moved directly over her, and launched itself at the guards. They yelped and cried out as it crawled over their clothes and bit their exposed skin, leaving small bloody gashes on their noses and the backs of their hands. They swatted at themselves, trying to hit it. Another lizard jumped onto the guards from behind. It was the orange faced one who had led Shanti and Keema inside. The God only knew where it had hidden itself while they tried to sneak in, but Shanti was thankful that it had joined in the rescue.

Just as she pulled another set of bolts loose, one of the guards managed to grab a lizard and fling it away from the humans. It slammed into the wall and lay on its side, panting through a half opened jaw, staring at the ceiling. Shanti gritted her teeth and kept moving down the line as the lizard she had just freed joined the fight with the guards.

The lizards kept them occupied while she managed to release another two or three, each rushing to jump onto the large humans and give her time to release more. The still-chained lizards were eerily quiet and still, staring at the woman who moved amongst them.

Shanti turned just in time to see one of the guards grab a lizard by the tail and swing it around his head before releasing it headfirst into a wall. The sound it made when it struck the wall was horrifying and Shanti jerked her head away.

She was nearing the end of the first table, but there were many many more to go. These guards were going to be able to brush off the lizards eventually, probably faster than she could release them. She needed to do something to stop them and give her time to release the others. She stood and looked around her, but could see nothing to use as a weapon, to bring down the guards.

One of the lizards was finally doing what she had hoped they would do, helping her release the others. Its skin was a much paler green than the almost black darkness of most of the others, its scales and spikes were small and soft. It reached over to the wings on the bolt of its neighbour's shackles but its long thin fingers struggled to get a strong enough grip to spin the metal. *That's why they couldn't help or free themselves,* Shanti realised. *Their fingers don't really work for this sort of task.* She moved past the lizard and began undoing the next. She was able to release three more lizards before the first managed to undo the bolt on the lizard it was helping. Most of them dove into the twisting mass of tails and long thin limbs that were scuttling all over the guards, tripping them, nipping them, scratching them.

Shanti hoped that the guards' shouts and yelps weren't going to be loud enough to alert anyone else. *No time to worry about that right now, I have to get them all loose as fast as possible!*

More of the lizards had begun helping each other now, and Shanti stood to face the guards. They had both fallen to their knees and she could see hints of red blood beneath the scaled bodies that wound over them, scarlet glimpses that stood out even more on their pale skin. Shanti walked closer, carefully edging around the guards so as to not be struck by them as they thrashed about wildly.

The other reason that she stepped carefully were the bodies of many lizards that lay around on the floor. The lizards had jumped into the fight against the guards, and must understand what a chance they had to escape in this moment, but the fact remained that they were so much smaller and weaker than the powerful humans that they were attacking. The guards' clubs, hands, and heavy boots had left many lizards sprawled across the floor, blood leaking from their poor broken bodies. Shanti wiped the back of her hand across her cheeks, trying to scrub away the residue of the tears that had dried there, only to feel fresh hot wetness fall from her eyes.

One of the guards thumped to the ground and the lizards scattered off them immediately. Shanti watched as the guard tried to roll over, and then fell back onto their front on the wooden floor. The number of cuts that covered the figure made it impossible to tell which of the guards it was. Shanti could feel the heat of her tears turning to anger.

The other guard slumped down as well. Shanti poked them with the toe of her shoe. She was surrounded by a wide circle of lizards, all with the same expressionless face, staring down at the guards lying before them. Now Shanti saw the orange face that she had quickly grown to recognise, the lizard who had found them in the trees. The lizard had been struck hard enough to turn its head violently on its shoulders, and its eyes were closed. The narrow scaled chest was still, drawing no breath where it lay on the floor near the wall.

"Well done to you all," said Shanti in Zukian. She ran the tip of her tongue across her lips then caught her lower lip in her teeth. "I'm so sorry that this happened this way." Shanti's shoulders fell and she clutched her arms around her middle.

A man's face appeared in her memory, dark and stern, with a cleanly shaved bald head. His eyes were fierce, but even without a smile, the face exuded a sense of safety. It was the look of a strong man who used his strength to protect those around him. A man she had barely known but who had lost his life helping her years ago. Shanti squeezed her eyes shut and tried to ignore the memory as her heart burned and her muscles tensed. *I'm bad luck,* she thought quietly. *My stupid ideas just get people killed. I should learn to leave things alone. It's none of my business.* Her throat felt as though something was wrapped around it, pulling tight.

No, came a voice from deep in the back of her

head. She couldn't tell who it was, but it didn't sound like her own thoughts. Was it the memory of Darsat back at the University in Gorduum, or his wife Dulku, lending her the wisdom of their years in the world? Was it thoughts of Keema, stepping forward to support Shanti when she was doubting herself?

It felt as though warm golden light was pressing against the inside of her eyelids, and she felt a soothing presence spread out from her head and down her back, letting her shoulders lift back to their usual position. She drew a deep breath and felt cleansing air fill her lungs.

You are stepping in where you are needed, said the voice. *Someone must watch over those whom others ignore.*

Shanti shuddered but managed to swallow and step away from the guards. They were severely wounded but the lizards couldn't kill them. She wondered if she should tie them up and began to look around the room for anything she could use.

The shackles were the only things that looked like they might be suitable, and so she fetched as many of those as she could. She had to look at Keema as she did so, but Shanti didn't pause until she had secured the guards. They groaned as they felt her passing the thin chains around their wrists and ankles. Then she went back to look at Keema.

47

K eema was still breathing, thankfully. There was a large welt growing on the side of her head just above her eyes. Shanti reached out and let her fingers drift across the injury, but still Keema moaned and flinched away, her eyelids fluttering.

Shanti looked around the space. The guards were lying still. Lizards stood and crouched all around, watching her with their strangely bulging eyes. She stood up.

"We can't stop now," she said. "We need to let out the rest of your families. But we will need a way to draw the other guards away." *I wonder if they really do understand what I mean,* she thought.

She walked over to the wall and lifted down a lantern. After unscrewing its top she was able to snuff out the wick inside. She swirled the lantern and heard the sloshing of oil inside. She smiled and looked at the piles of tuft that were strewn along the tables.

Soon, Shanti was crouched behind a set of crates. She assumed they must be filled with bundled and tied bales of tuft. She had managed to drag Keema over to this low hiding space and then go back for the two guards, pulling them to another space where she hoped they would be unable to call attention to themselves. Then, she lit the threshing-house on fire, and now she was waiting for a chance to run across the empty deck to the tall building that contained the cages, and eggs, of the lizards that she had released. The lizards had vanished out of the room as soon as she had opened the door, and she hoped that she had understood her plan of entering the cage-house.

Feet pounded across the wooden deck. Shanti crouched lower, not daring to peek around the edge of the crate yet. She looked down and could see through the gaps in the planks below, down to the black surface of the water that lay like a slowly shifting sheet of silk barely a metre below the deck. Shouts and screams accompanied the new guards as they arrived at the tufthouse.

Shanti smiled to herself. Between the lantern oil that she had poured into several pools through the room, and the piles of tuft that she had pushed into place, she was sure that the fire would be spreading much too fast for them to bring under control. *So long as they can't get it under control in the next thirty minutes,* she told herself, *that should be long enough for me to do what I have to do.* She rose to her feet and began walking quickly towards the cage-house.

She had to leave Keema behind. The other woman had groaned and fluttered her eyelids as Shanti dragged her to the mediocre hiding spot behind the crate, but Keema hadn't roused fully. After the crack on the skull she had taken, Shanti was worried about her, but Keema was breathing and right now that was all that Shanti could do.

She couldn't see any lizards anymore either. She was surprised that they had managed to disappear so thoroughly across the empty wooden deck and its few buildings.

At the door to the cage-house, Shanti paused to catch her breath. Her heart was quivering like a small bird in a cage and she felt light headed. She could feel the cool metal of the handle under her palm. *If I wait too long, one of the others will see me out here anyway. I have to get inside.* She pressed down on the handle and stepped through.

It was darker than she remembered in the cage-house, and quiet. She felt as though something must be watching her, outlined as she was against the daylight beyond the door, and so she began to pull the door closed behind her. It jammed and there was a strange hissing sound. She glanced back over her shoulder and saw lizards crawling in around the doorframe, from above and either side. One of them was clearly glaring at her.

"Sorry," she blurted and then felt her cheeks flush at the strangeness of the moment.

The room was quiet. Shanti began to walk forwards to the cages. All around her, shadows on the floor began to roll as lizards moved with her, some of them as thick and long as logs, others smaller than her forearm.She knew that many of them had orange coloured splotches among their scales but, as it had in the forest outside, the colour helped them blend into mottled patches of daylight leaking in through cracks and around shutters.

At the first cage, Shanti examined the door carefully. The cage was held shut by a large padlock, heavy and dulled from constant handling. She leaned back and pushed her fingers through her hair as she tried to think of a plan. From the floor all around her, blank reptile eyes stared up at her, tiny pinpoints of light reflecting off them.

"I'm not sure what to do," she muttered. "I don't have any tools to break the padlock..." She looked over the rest of the cage, wondering whether she would be able to find a better way into it than through the door. But the mesh that stretched around the small enclosure didn't appear to have any clear weak spots that she might be able to work on, even if she did have a crowbar or some other tool to try and break through with. A tiny lizard was rearing up inside the cage, leaning on the mesh and watching her.

"I'm truly sorry," she said to it. "I just don't know what to do next. I assumed that the God would help me." She lowered her head, feeling the darkness of the wide room piling over her and pressing down on her. She wanted to drop to her knees and let the darkness hold her there.

A board creaked behind her.

Shanti turned around and lifted her hands, terrified that a guard was about to jump at her and crack her own skull. *If they decided to get rid of me and Keema, they could do it out here.* The thought flashed through her mind like an alley cat chasing a mouse, sharp and fast. *They could just dump us into the water and we'd be gone.*

But the figure that had made the noise wasn't just any guard. It was a solid young man with square shoulders and a thick red beard covering his chin.

His eyes glowed as he looked at Shanti and she recognised Ukuck. The guard who had scared her in the Plaza, and who had come running to drive off the alligator by the gate.

"What are you doing?" he snapped, his face twisted and fierce.

Shanti swallowed heavily as she saw his muscles tense.

"I... I'm just..." Shanti wished that she could think as quickly as Keema. But instead she found her mouth wavering as she desperately tried to imagine a suitable explanation to soothe Ukuck's suspicions. *What will he do to me,* she panicked as her heart started pounding.

The man stuck a pale finger towards her. "What are you doing with our property?"

"They aren't property, they are intelligent living creatures, and you should all be ashamed of the way you are treating them." Shanti heard her own voice reply, but didn't remember thinking of any of the words before they were spoken.

"You've lost your mind," he declared and then he turned and ran towards the door.

"No!" Shanti shrieked. *If he gets out of the door and alerts the other guards, they will quickly overwhelm me even if the lizards try to help! Why couldn't he try to hit me, I might have been able to dodge out of the way then!*

Before he could reach the doorway, lizards rose up from the floor like a wave. They launched themselves off the walls towards him, from dark shadows that Shanti hadn't realised that they were hiding in. He was covered instantly, and toppled to the ground.

Shanti ran over to him and found that he was lying on the ground perfectly still, staring at the ceiling, with his lips wobbling. Angry tears slid down the sides of his head and his mouth was a tight line.

"You've been working really hard for Kayzark," she began quietly. His eyes didn't move, though she could tell that he was listening to her. She watched his strong arms shift, testing the weight of the lizards, and then saw his pale skin pricked and dimpled by claws. "And I know you don't like these lizards. But you're wrong about them."

Shanti sat back on her heels and looked around the room, looking at the rows of cages in the dark. She leaned forward again.

"In any case, it looks like you're in charge of keeping them in these cages today. So, you must have a key to the padlocks. Right?"

His blue eyes bore into hers while lizards moved across him like a blanket. A few light red lines showed where they had scratched him before he wisely chose to remain still. He carefully nodded and began to move his arm, then winced as a lizard nipped the skin on the back of his hand.

"Let him move, slowly," she told the lizards in her poor Zukian. She was no longer surprised that they responded to her speech, although from the way the man's eyes bulged out as they began to move off him, he was. Did the local people never even try to speak to the lizards? She was fairly sure that they must threaten the lizards in that language. Perhaps that was all they had ever tried.

Ukuck moved his hand into his pocket and drew out a small ring with a few keys hooked onto it through the large loops at their ends. He held it up towards Shanti. She snatched it out of his hands and began to move back over to the cages.

"Don't let him stand up," she added as she left, and she smiled at the rustling sound of the lizards crawling back onto top of him, and the sharp gasp as he sucked in a breath.

Once back at the cages, Shanti tried the keys in the heavy padlocks, soon finding the one that fit. She twisted and sighed with relief at the loud clunk that the lock made. She pulled the door open and the tiny lizard inside jumped out immediately, skittering through the crowd of lizards to one at the far corner. Shanti was expecting them to hug each other for a moment, but they didn't. Instead their thin ribbon like tongues slipped in and out of their jaws much faster than usual. Their faces still bore no expression, and they just faced each other for a while.

"I guess that's how you celebrate," she muttered as she moved on to the next cages.

Opening them all took a long time. Each opened door was followed by lizards standing facing each other, tongues flickering, and more would go to stand on Ukuck where he lay near the door. The shouting outside was getting louder, and Shanti hoped that they hadn't found Keema. She began to worry that they might have brought the fire under control, and that some of the guards would be returning to the cage-house soon. There were so many cages left to open. Her shoulders were beginning to ache from the repetitive motions of lifting and twisting the keys in each lock.

A massive roll of thunder rattled the walls and nearly knocked Shanti off her feet. The lizards all ran in small circles and then froze, staring at the ceiling with their odd sideways manner.

"What was that?" she snapped, and then she ran

over to the door. She carefully pulled it open a little and peeked through the gap.

Across the open deck from her, the threshing-house was a mountain of red flame, with thick clouds of black smoke billowing out and stretching up into the sky. Her heart sank into her stomach and she lifted a hand to her mouth. *How did the fire get so bad so quickly?* She spun around and shut the door, and then leaned on it. *Are people going to die? At least they are too busy to come and find out what I'm doing. Oh blinded Eyes, will I have enough time?*

48

———

S hanti rushed back to the cages, working as fast as she could. The lizards were on edge around her now. She could feel the energy from them throbbing in the room. They were waiting for her, but they wanted to get away from the stockade now.

Why aren't any guards coming in to release the lizards, Shanti suddenly wondered. *They have all these creatures in cages, surely they should be coming through to release them before the fire spreads to this building.* The realisation that the people working in this orchard would absolutely not be coming to take care of the creatures that they had trapped and forced into working for them made Shanti's anger swell in her belly. She frowned and kept opening cages, faster now. *I owe those monsters nothing,* she decided. *This is the consequence of their cruelty. I hope no one dies, but I have to do what has to be done.*

There was another crash from outside the cage-house. Lizards began to move towards other doors and windows, working in teams to lever open the shutters. They began to trickle out, leaking away like water in a broken bowl. Shanti moved faster, but kept looking over her shoulder at the guard lying beneath a stack of lizards. Already there were barely half the number of lizards on him as there had been moments earlier. She could see his face, how his eyes were hardening as he watched her.

She opened the last cage and spun around, ready to race out of the cage-house and retrieve Keema. At the same time, Ukuck rolled over the floor, flinging the few remaining lizards off his figure as he moved. He rolled over one of them and Shanti couldn't help but let out a short scream as the creature lay still after the man had moved.

"You monster!" her words burst from a tight throat.

"You're an idiot," he snapped, glaring at her. He reached over to the door. "Wasting your time on these silty beasts! They're no good for anything except work. And I think maybe that's the best you should hope for as well!" He opened the door and stepped out.

Shanti started running towards the door. Her best chance was to escape before the guards he summoned could stop her getting out. She wondered if the lizard gap in the stockade would be shut now, or whether she would be able to get out that way still. The thought of dragging an unconscious Keema through the submerged gap was a block of ice in the back of her mind, but she saw no alternatives.

The lizards remaining in the cage-house poured through the open doorway after the man left, like a swarm of insects scattering after a child lifts a rotten log in the depths of a forest. Shanti joined them in their flight. Once she left the doorway she froze at the scene she found before her.

The threshing-house was still a giant inferno, with figures silhouetted against the flames desperately flinging buckets of water in an attempt to quench its roiling mass. But other structures were burning now as well, and patches of the deck had caught, creating holes that emptied into the blackness of the water below, ringed by orange lips that drew wider and wider.

Ukuck was only a few metres in front of her, but even as she watched, a section of the deck beneath his feet gave way and he plummeted through it. He grabbed the edge of the wooden planks and hung, armpit deep into the hole. Sparks flickered on the edge of the decking, small flames licking at the wood and extending the gap around him.

Shanti heard him yell, but couldn't tell what he was saying. *At least he doesn't seem to have caught the attention of any guards,* she thought to herself, relieved. Lizards rushed past the man, and she was glad to see that they were ignoring him completely. *Should I pull him out,* she wondered. She looked around the deck, checking that no one had noticed her, as she moved slowly towards the man where he dangled over the water. His feet were just able to flick up a few drops from the surface of the water below as he kicked them fruitlessly.

There were figures shouting and rushing around the burning buildings and across the deck that was covered in rising embers. None of them looked in her direction, as far as she could tell. She reached the man and stood over him. His eyes were wide and panicked. She sniffed and crossed her arms.

"Will you behave now?" she asked.

Before he could answer, a shape made of scale and muscle erupted from the still black water beneath him, rising up around his legs like a sack made of pale scaly leather. Shanti was able to look into the glass-like black eye of the gigantic alligator before it crunched its jaws shut around the man's midriff and pulled him down into the water. Ripples rolled out across the water's surface.

Shanti realised that she could hear a woman's voice screaming in one long loud breath of terror. After listening to it for a moment, she was shocked to discover that it was her own voice. She tried to make herself quiet, but her mouth wasn't responding to her thoughts. She tried to lift her hands to physically push her mouth closed, but her arms wouldn't obey her thoughts either. It took immense effort to push against her frozen muscles hard enough to actually raise an arm and then to press up on her own chin. She managed to make herself silent but the raging river of ice and molten fire that was pumping through her body kept her lungs panting and she began to shiver.

Shanti stumbled away from the now empty hole and staggered against the crates where she had left Keema. She looked around the side of the crate, ready to burst into tears if the other woman wasn't there.

Thankfully, Keema was lying exactly as Shanti had left her, one ankle tucked beneath the other and an arm dropped uncomfortably over her face. Shanti leaned down and pulled on Keema, trying to lift her up and hoping that the other woman would be able to stand on her own feet now. Keema's weight pulled Shanti sideways and she nearly fell down. She groaned and then heaved Keema up and into a position where Shanti would be able to roughly manoeuvre her. Step by difficult step, Shanti began pulling the woman back toward the low stairs that surrounded the lizards' pool and its narrow exit from the stockade.

How am I going to get her out through this tiny gap, Shanti thought as she moved closer to the pool. Each step was an effort that required shifting her grip around Keema, trying not to let the woman's head fall into too awkward a position. She grunted as she struggled not to drop her.

I suppose I could try and tie her to myself as I try to get out, and just pull her along behind me? No, that is a silly idea, she remonstrated herself. *Keema would just breathe in all the water and drown well before I was able to get her out the other side. And on top of that, it was a difficult space for me to get through on the way in, trying to do it with the weight of Keema at the end of a rope pulling on me...* She shook her head, as though she were arguing with someone else rather than herself. *No, I can't do it that way.*

Maybe if I swam through myself and then pulled Keema through on a rope? But, no, I couldn't make sure that she didn't get the rope tangled around her in a dangerous way, and she'd probably still drown. It's not like I could pull her through much faster that way. Shanti had reached the edge of the pool and felt her teeth begin to chatter as she looked down on the dark waters that shifted with small swells.

What if one of those beasts is under there?

The water rippled and something moved in it. Shanti stepped backwards, and caught the back of her heel on Keema's leg which sent her tumbling onto the deck, sprawled across the other woman. Shanti lifted herself on her arms in time to see one of the orange and green lizards scramble up and over the side of the pool. It crawled right up to stand on Shanti's chest and looked down at her face from mere centimetres away. She was shocked at how light the lizard was while it stood on her. Three more came out of the pool and stood around her.

The first lizard crawled off her and then the whole group moved a metre or so away, heading back into the midst of the burning buildings inside the stockade. They all paused again and turned their bulbous eyes back to Shanti. She hauled Keema back up into her arms and began staggering after the lizards. Satisfied that she was following them, they moved forward again.

The lizards led Shanti in a winding path through the burning buildings. She winced as heat from the flames billowed out of windows and stretched up into the thick black smoke overhead. More than once she was sure that she heard panicked voices from inside the buildings, or saw the dark shapes of figures in the water below the half-destroyed plank floor. Reflections of fire traced orange lines that slid and spun across the surface of the water. The smell of smoke and burnt wood stuffed her throat.

The lizards doubled back more than once, taking Shanti the long way through the chaos.

"This woman is really heavy," she tried to tell them at one intersection. "Wherever we are going, can we just go straight there?"

One of the lizards looked back at her and then they all turned and marched back the way they had come. Shanti moaned but followed and then heard shouts and footsteps rush by the intersection they had just abandoned.

"You know what you are doing I guess," she said to the lizards. For creatures that she was sure had no recognisable expressions, they certainly looked as though they were smirking at that moment.

The lizards led her around the back of another smaller building that was so far untouched by fire. Thick black smoke overhead made the passageway behind it difficult, dark and small. The weight of a body in her arms in such a confined space started visions and memories tumbling forward from the back of Shanti's mind. She paused and sucked in a deep breath through her nose, but the smoke made her cough and splutter. *Focus,* she thought to herself, with her eyes closed. *You're going to be okay. Keep moving.*

She managed to slide her feet along in the dark, bumping into small piles of ropes or discarded tools and stepping around them. As she reached the far end of the alley, she caught up to her lizard escorts. One of them glanced back at her, but otherwise they remained still, looking out across an open space on the deck.

Beyond the corner of the building stockade workers were running back and forwards, trying to make sense of the chaos that had engulfed them. Fire was spreading slowly out along the deck and licking up the posts of the stockade wall. Shanti watched as someone dove over the stockade and heard the splash of them hitting the water on the outside. They must have decided that it was a safer way down than the fiery stairs, or jumping metres onto the hard wood of the deck. She remembered the creature that had grabbed Ukuck from right in front of her and she shuddered. She hoped she wasn't left to make any such choice between solid wood, fire, or teeth in the water in order to escape this stockade.

Some of the workers were trying to shout orders, and arrange for water to be carried up to the buildings, but each bucket tossed into the flame vanished into steam before it made any difference to the inferno.

Most of the figures were trying to find a way out of the stockade. It looked as though the main gate was jammed, or perhaps the people who were required for it to be opened had already fled. Maybe the mechanism could only be operated by controls that were currently deep inside the flames. In any case, teams were hauling on ropes looped around the gates posts, or trying to use oars and lengths of wood that they had scavenged to lever the gate open. Others were hammering on the stockade itself with a motley assortment of scavenged tools, hammers and axes and more that they had scrounged from somewhere in the facility. She heard them calling prayers to their spirits over the roar of the fire.

"Smoke clear!"

"Time go back!"

"How are we going to get out?" Shanti asked the lizards. She was ready to believe that one of them might even answer her now.

However, the lizards made no response, no indication that they had even heard her. They stayed still, absolutely motionless, watching the noisy whirling scene before them.

49

There was a cry of triumph from Kayzark's workers as the gate groaned a metre open. Immediately, the people who had been working to open it dropped their equipment and ran to the widening gap. A couple jumped into boats moored nearby and began trying to steer them out of the gap, but most simply dove into the water and began swimming.

Shanti shivered as a dark shape rose up amongst the swimmers and then rolled across one, before vanishing under the water. Screams began to echo across the empty deck. Some of the figures who had been running towards the gap now stopped and darted away from the water's edge.

"Come on, there's so much going on that they won't care about us," she said to the lizards, and began pushing past them. They moved out of the shadowed space alongside her. As she had said, none of the figures trying to get out of the gate paid any attention to her as she approached. She began running her eyes along the edge of the decking, trying to spot a boat that she would be able to use.

One of the lizards ran ahead, leading the rest past two small boats and one much larger one. Shanti tried to follow as quickly as she could, wondering why the lizard had not stopped at the first vessels.

An older man came running past, clutching at his cheeks and scrubbing fingers through the scraggly beard that grew there. He turned at the sight of the lizards.

"What? How did they get out? Is this their fault?"

There was a crash from the buildings as a roof caved in. The man turned around at the thunderous noise and Shanti rolled Keema into the bottom of the boat that the lizard had chosen. Then she held her breath and jumped over the small watery gap from the deck into the boat herself. By the time the man who had spotted them turned back, the lizards had leapt over into the boat with Shanti. They began scrabbling at the ropes that were looped over stumpy wooden posts in the decks, holding the boat still.

"Where are you going?" he yelped.

"Anywhere else, " she said as she grabbed the pole that was lying along the middle of the boat. Once the ropes were pushed up and off the posts, she used the pole to push away from the edge of the dock. The lizards began pulling the ropes into the boat. The man stood with his jaw gaping.

"How did you get them to do that? They're just clumsy creatures."

Shanti snorted and stuck the pole down, using it to push off towards the gate. The man suddenly realised what was happening.

"No, wait! Take me with you! Fire spare me!" He

jumped down into the water. It was much deeper than he had expected and his face went beneath the surface for a moment before he bobbed back up, spluttering. "Help me!"

"Good luck!" called Shanti, and she kept pushing forwards.

There was a thick cluster of boats at the half-opened gates. Workers had realised that this was their best chance of getting through the gate without being caught by the alligator that had made its presence known. Many boats were a finger's width from sinking under the weight of so many bodies crowding onto them, the occupants of the boats flinching away from every splash as though it was an alligator launching towards them. Paddles, poles and oars tried to pull the boats forward, but they wallowed like cows in mud.

As her own boat drew closer, Shanti began to worry. If someone from one of those lumbering craft tried to leap over to her own boat, there could be trouble. *How will I get past them?*

The lizards tumbled around each other to the prow of the boat and dove into the water. A few of the people scrabbling against each other on the boats pointed and stared at the lizards as they swam by, but in the darkness of the thick smoke, and with fire cracking and roaring around them and walls collapsing, there were bigger things to worry about. Shanti pushed a clenched hand to her stomach, waiting in terror of the alligator rising up in the water, those monstrous long jaws crashing around one of the creatures that she owed so much.

But no alligator appeared from the murky water inside the stockade, and the small arrow-shaped ripples of the lizards' passage moved out past the overloaded boats and through the half-opened gate.

Shanti leaned on the long pole that she was using to control her small boat, heaving forward to try and stop it from approaching the workers of the orchard. More of them were watching her now and she wanted to crouch down, as though she would be able to hide alongside Keema in the bottom of the boat.

Shouts from the lead boats drew the workers' attention away and Shanti turned to see what was going on. The small ripples made by her lizards were shooting back in through the gate, slipping past the wallowing boats that they had only just swum past on the way out. Behind them the water rose in a ridge, like a sheet of satin being torn apart, reflecting glittering red light back toward the people on the boats. The wave broke and spilled aside, revealing an alligator, massive and scaled, its eyes dark black orbs that blazed with hunger.

Shanti gasped at the sight of the brute, but the lizards swam straight for the boats clogging the gate and then turned aside, heading back to her. The giant creature was not nearly so nimble, and its broad back smashed into the first of the boats, setting the vessel rocking in the water. Waves curled over the railing and water began to flow easily into the boat, so low was it riding due to the number of people who had clambered onboard. They began to shriek as they realised that their boat was sinking, and some at the back dove off and tried to swim back for the stockade deck behind them.

The other boats started trying to paddle backwards as well, and Shanti felt as though she was going to throw up when she heard a terrified scream suddenly cut off. The alligator thrashed through the water and Shanti was sure that blood was spreading.

Another of the creatures erupted from the water alongside one of the retreating boats, launching itself up and latching onto the shoulder of a man standing at the edge of the boat. He screamed and toppled into the water with the alligator. The boat he was in lurched from one side to the other. Water began swamping this boat too. *Two of them! I had never thought that there were two of them here!* Shanti tentatively poked at the water with her pole. *What if there are even more of them?* Her boat looked awfully small.

The lizards slipped out of the water and back into the boat, watching the carnage with their usual blank expression.

"What have you done?" asked Shanti. The devastation was horrifying. They looked back at her then turned their heads towards the gate. *They're right,* realised Shanti. *I have plenty of room now.*

With the alligators attacking anyone who had fallen into the water, and multiple boats getting in each others' way, there was plenty of space for Shanti to guide her boat through the gate now. She tried to ignore the sights and sounds of the stockade workers' plight as she managed to pole her way out into the waters of the jungle.

As she moved the boat out towards the deeper water of the main river channel, she was also drifting out from under the heavy black ceiling of smoke that the fire had unleashed. The sky was still its usual grey, but she could see that the glow of the sun was far down towards the horizon now.

The day had passed much faster than she had realised.

Further out in the open water, the lizards began to get agitated. They would turn to her and open their mouths, pushing their strangely bulbous bright pink tongues forward. She was sure one or two of them made a hissing sound.

"I don't understand," she said to them eventually.

One of them started looking into the sky and then jumping from one side of the boat to the other. Another stared at the stockade that was falling behind them and then ducked down behind the low railing of the narrow boat.

"Are you worried that someone can see us?"

The lizards all stopped what they were doing and looked at her.

"I don't know what to do about that." Shanti shrugged and poled the boat further. "Following the river is how I get home."

As one the lizards all turned to look at the trees that lined the main channel. Shanti looked at the trees as well.

"It's harder to move the boat through there."

The lizards didn't move. Shanti sighed and lowered her shoulders.

"Alright."

No sooner had they reached the thick roots of the trees, then Shanti noticed a shape on the river, heading towards the stockade. She turned to watch the shadow as it approached. It grew larger until she was able to see that it was a boat. As she pushed her own boat further between the roots, she realised that it was Arsook again. The woman was standing near the long pointed prow of her boat, one hand on the jutting rectangular fin and her stern face locked on the burning structure. Shanti shrank down into her boat and watched Arsook leading her boat towards the stockade, that giant of a man in the back propelling them forward on the paddle mechanism.

She must have seen the smoke in the sky, thought Shanti. *I need to get out of here. She'll catch me far too easily in that thing.*

Shanti hauled on the pole in her hands, moving the thin boat beside the thick roots that jutted up from the water, marking the edge of the jungle. She tried to find a way to move into the roots and hide amongst them while still heading away from Arsook as fast as she could. The tangled mass made it extremely hard to do both. As she moved, the lizards jumped off her boat and started climbing up into the foliage overhead. Shanti leaned back to watch as the lithe creatures vanished among the branches and leaves.

"You can't help me get back to Chechezuk?" she asked plaintively, leaning on the pole for a moment.

One of the lizards turned to stare back at her, and then raced off along the branch it was standing on before disappearing in a rustle of heavy green leaves. The only sound she was left with was the hollow slap of water on the side of Shanti's boat.

"Alright. I guess you helped me more than I had really expected just by getting me out." With a deep breath she continued shoving the pole through the water and pushing the boat along the edge of the main channel.

The current drew her downriver much faster than Keema had been able to paddle them up it.

Keema had been forced to send them among the trees more often also, whereas Shanti was trying to go as fast as she could and so stayed closer to open water. Her arms were beginning to ache so much that she thought she would have to stop and hope that the boat might just float back into the city, when she finally saw the outer edge of Chechezuk's wooden buildings appear between a gap in the trees.

"I don't know how you did it," she gasped at Keema, who still lay unconscious in the bottom of the boat. "I feel like my arms might snap off at any second, but you got us all the way out to the orchard." Shanti turned to look back upriver. A black cloud rose above the treetops and smeared out across the grey sky like artist's charcoal.

50

They moved out from the channel and began to approach one of the broad docks that spread out like a skirt floating on the water around the city. Some boats were heading past them out into the jungle, with people pointing at the dark cloud as they went, but many more were going about their day's work without regard for the black column. Shanti wondered if fires were common, or if the people just preferred to keep to their own business.

The sky was dimming as the sun began to set, and Shanti saw the beginnings of evening groups forming in the streets. Musicians had started playing, some of the pedestrians walking by were holding drinks and food. Occasionally one would pause and sing along with the musicians.

Shanti tied up the boat quickly, not paying any attention to the loose knot that she was relying on. She only needed it to hold long enough to pull Keema out of the boat and lay her on the wooden path. She knelt down next to the other woman and ran the backs of her fingers down Keema's face and past her cheek. The thin woman was breathing slowly but she looked ashen.

"What can I do with you?" asked Shanti. She looked up and noticed the hastily averted eyes of many passers-by. *I'm not going to get much help out of them, clearly.* She clenched and unclenched her fists, trying to get some blood pumping through her muscles. Then she knelt down again and pulled Keema up into a sitting position. She leaned down and wrapped her hands around Keema's waist and then pulled the woman over her shoulder and tried to stand up.

Shanti could feel her legs wavering but she gritted her teeth and held firm. *I can do this,* she told herself. *Keema got me out there, she supported me when I was alone, I can be here for her now. It's no worse than shifting sacks of flour in my mother's store!* She ignored the stares that were more openly directed her way now, and began walking steadily but slowly along the path.

Soon Shanti realised that carrying Keema was much worse than shifting sacks in the store. There she might have to heave the sack around, but she could drop it if she had to, and the distance it needed shifting was never much more than a few metres. With Keema over her shoulder, Shanti was going to have to walk a long way before she might reach somewhere safe.

With every step Shanti felt out of place and vulnerable. She was sure that each person that they passed knew that she had done something terrible out in the jungle, or that Arsook would rush up behind them any moment and declare her a criminal.

Shanti wasn't even sure that she didn't deserve it. Step by step, she struggled on.

A middle aged woman with her long red hair tied up in a pile on the top of her head, streaked with threads of grey and silver, turned and began to walk closer to Shanti with a frown on her face. Just as she opened her mouth and lifted a raised finger, there was a shriek from the other end of the street. The woman blinked and turned to see what was going on.

A group of pedestrians were scattering away from a building, looks of confusion all over their faces. Some stopped and turned around once they were clear of the building, others kept running.

"What the-" snapped the woman.

Then lizards began crawling out of the doors and windows of the building. There were so many of the creatures that they soon completely covered the walls and hid the structure beneath their bodies.

"What are they doing?" muttered the woman and she rushed away from Shanti to get a better look. Shanti kept walking. Shanti staggered past the crowd that was forming and saw the lizards were carrying things out of the building. Furniture, clothing, all of it carefully carried out and left on the path outside the front door.

"That's my stuff you sodden animals!" yelled a bald old man who was standing closest to the door. He shook his fist at them as three lizards carried out a wooden stool between them, and then he took a step closer. Immediately a group of the larger lizards slipped in between him and the working lizards, rising up on their rear legs and spreading their forelimbs wide, displaying the long black claws that jutted from each long thin finger. Their faces remained as blank as always, but their intentions could not be more clear. The old man stepped back again and clutched both hands to his head.

"They're taking over my house! What am I supposed to do now!? Someone help!"

Shanti turned her eyes lower and kept walking, grateful for the distraction from her own unusual behaviour, but also wondering what the lizards were doing. Why were they kicking the man out of this house?

More shouts began to rise from around the city. The lizards were emptying other buildings, driving out the human occupants. Lizards were also streaming out of the attics and nests that they must have been hiding in around the city, abandoning the dark cramped spaces that they had been living in until now.

As Shanti kept walking, trying to focus on moving her legs one after the other, she had to ignore the rising shouts and crowds that were forming. *What have I done,* she wondered. *Is this my fault? The lizards in the city had been quite content before today, is it a coincidence that I helped free the ones trapped in that orchard and now they seem to be rising up in the city itself?* She couldn't believe that it was a coincidence, but she also had no energy left to work out what the connection was. One foot ahead of the other she headed for the Lagoon, where she hoped that the Tide's Daughter would still be waiting.

As she walked through the Plaza, Shanti had to pause, wobbling with the weight of Keema on her shoulder pressing her down. The Plaza was in an uproar, with lizards crawling through the stalls and shopfronts, walking under tables with wraps and meat dangling from the small stubby teeth in their jaws. Some people were screaming and waving objects at the lizards, trying to drive them out of the plaza, while others were staring in disbelief or huddling against walls to avoid the creatures. Shanti tried to adjust Keema on her shoulders and kept walking.

She felt as though she were walking through a long dark cave. Everything around her was fading away into shadows as night fell, and the sounds were becoming muffled. Her heartbeat thumped a rhythm that she found herself walking in time with. Far ahead of her was a small bright space, the only thing she could really see. Finally, that tiny space filled with the familiar sight of the gateway to the Lagoon. Although her heart lifted, Shanti focused on continuing to move. With the end in sight, it wasn't time to stop.

She walked into the Lagoon. Sailors were working with no concern for the noises of the city. Shanti wondered if they would react differently once the lizards reached this place. Then she wondered whether the lizards would be interested in coming here at all.

She approached the gangway to the Tide's Daughter and placed a foot on it. The long narrow piece of wood sagged under her foot and bounced worryingly. She looked past its edge to the water a couple of metres below, then swallowed. No alligators had appeared in Chechezuk, but even a fall into empty water in her current weary state could see her struggling to swim to the surface, dragged down into the depths with water-logged clothes and aching muscles. She slid to her knees and guided Keema to the ground next to her, before bowing her head and crying, heavy hot tears.

A hand reached down to rest on her shoulder and she looked up. Tozan was standing over her, his eyes hard and his mouth set in a stern line. But he reached down and scooped Keema up into his strong arms.

"Come on girl, up you get."

Shanti pushed herself to her feet.

"Let's get you both settled below. We're heading out soon." He sniffed and glared over her shoulder at the sounds coming from the city. "By the sounds of it, there's no better time."

Then he turned and carried Keema up the gangway without a second glance at the water below. Shanti followed, feeling as though she were about to lift off the ground and float away into the sky; she had become so used to the weight that she had been carrying. Tozan led the way down the steps and through to the passenger cabin. He laid Keema on one of the lower bunks and looked around. There were three other people sitting at their bunks, reading by the dim greasy light of the thickly glassed ship lantern that was lit to one side of the room. They glanced up but soon returned to themselves. One frowned at the sight of Keema, but it was a look of concern, not judgement.

"These are the last passengers," announced Tozan as he stood up. "This one's had a bit of a turn, but she should be alright soon. We've only a few things to stow and then we should be riding the tide out of this city within the hour." He nodded at the other passengers and left.

Shanti sat down beside Keema on her bed and brushed her hair out of her eyes.

"Come on Sunshine," she whispered. "After all this, you need to be okay." Shanti was feeling off balance, as though she was walking along a narrow path of numbness and tiredness, but a great pit of fear lay to either side, and she might fall in at any moment.

51

Keema murmured and turned her head. *Is that more colour in her cheeks,* Shanti asked herself, touching them lightly with her fingertips.

"Would you like to play cards?" asked one of the other passengers after long quiet minutes spent sitting in the room. The passenger was an older woman, whose skin was much darker than the people who lived in Chechezuk, though not as dark as Shanti's. Though her face wore many wrinkles, her eyes sparkled. Shanti shook her head. "How about coming above deck and we can watch the ship sailing out then? I thought coming into this lagoon was very impressive, I suspect the journey out will be also."

"Perhaps," said Shanti slowly. "I am worried about my wife though."

"I can see that," said the older woman. She stood up from her bunk and walked over to stand by Shanti. "She seems to be sleeping now. What happened to her?"

"She was in a bit of an accident." Shanti didn't

want to reveal too much to a stranger, no matter how friendly they were being.

"I see." The older woman watched Keema for a minute. "Whether or not she is doing well now, there isn't a lot that you can do for her. Come on, let's watch the ship leave."

"No, I can't." Shanti had spent weeks leaving Keema behind. She had not paid attention to her wife's worries about leaving Gorduum. She had spent time with other people while Keema was suffering by herself. She had let her own decisions and feelings guide everything that they had done in Chechezuk, even down to the rescue today. Now Shanti had to show Keema that the other woman was actually as important to her as she claimed. She held Keema's hand. "I have to stay with her."

The older woman smiled softly. "When she wakes up, I would love to have you both join me on deck to watch. I'm sure she will be alright soon."

The woman left the passenger cabin and Shanti watched the light from the lantern dancing on the side of the room. Keema turned on the bed, mumbling. There was a knock at the door.

Tozan entered quietly and handed a small folded piece of paper to Shanti.

"The captain thought you might want to deliver this yourself, seeing as you made it to the tide," he muttered, and then left the room.

She turned the paper over in her hands, smiling as she realised that she was on her way home. She could send the letter when she got back to Gorduum, letting her parents know that she was married and apologising for not inviting them. It told them that she would visit as soon as she could, and she knew that taking Keema to see her family was all she would work towards now.

Shanti wasn't sure how long she sat waiting with Keema before she fell asleep, but the exhaustion and excitement that had carried her through the eventful hours of the day drained out of her, and she sank to the mattress and into a dreamless sleep.

When she awoke, the cabin was dim and quiet. Snores rumbled from the bunks on the other side of the room, but the lantern was still burning. Shanti rolled over and twisted her back and neck, groaning at the solid stiffness that ached as she tried to move her protesting muscles. Bones clicked as she shifted from the awkward sprawled out position she had been lying in.

She sat up and looked around the cabin. It was still and quiet. She recognised the old woman who had spoken to her earlier lying in one of the bunks, breathing softly in her sleep. *We must be far from Chechezuk now,* thought Shanti, *for her to have come back down. The only view now would be endless darkness of the ocean at night.*

There was a movement by her side and Shanti looked down at Keema. Mumbling and twitching turned into fluttering eyelids that opened into the beautiful bright eyes that she hadn't realised she had missed. A flush of cold relief washed through her.

"Sunshine? Sunshine, can you hear me? Keema?"

"What's- Where are-" Keema tried to sit up but then groaned and clutched the side of her head and fell back onto the mattress. "Oh mercy, I can't think."

"You're safe. We're safe. We got out and we're on the Tide's Daughter right now. We're going home."

Keema blinked some more. She opened her mouth but Shanti shushed her, suddenly conscious of the other passengers still lying nearby. Even in sleep, Shanti didn't want to risk that they might overhear what she had done.

"We did it. We did what we had to. And now we go home."

Keema reached out and took Shanti's hand, squeezing her fingers weakly.

"I can't wait to be at home with you," said Shanti.

THE NEXT MORNING, Shanti helped Keema walk up onto the deck. Keema's cobblefeet, coupled with her injury, meant that it was a laborious process. Shanti had to keep an arm around Keema's waist, who had to lean heavily on Shanti's shoulder. Pausing to rest often, and allowing Keema to hang her head low and suck in deep breaths of air, meant that they were able to make it out to the main railing of the ship and look out over the rolling waves.

Felldan was standing at the railing already, leaning on it with his arms crossed. He smiled when Shanti and Keema arrived next to him.

"I'm glad to see that you both made it," he said. "The city was in a complete uproar last night, I had become concerned that you might have got into trouble!" He winked at them.

Shanti blushed. *If he only knew what sort of trouble I had caused!*

"I didn't see you in the cabin," she said.

"I've spent most of the night talking with Zeke-ka." Felldan turned his face out to the ocean again.

"Really? Why?"

"It's all part of the job. So, how shall we spend the day today?" He turned again, leaning his elbow on the railing and facing them fully. "Do you want to keep doing your readings for the crew? Perhaps we could see if we can find Kechak, she might teach us something new about life on the boat?"

Shanti became more aware of her arm, and the way it sat against the curve of Keema's waist. She pressed her fingers into her wife gently, relishing the feel of her shirt. Shanti turned to look at Keema. She bent her head and kissed her wife, pressing their lips hard against each other, and she felt Keema's hands pulling their bodies closer too. It was as though the two women were trying to occupy the same space. Shanti only knew that she couldn't let Keema get so far from her again.

They pulled apart, smiling awkwardly at each other. Shanti licked her teeth.

"What do you want to do, Sunshine?"

Keema laughed and then her eyes widened and she leaned out over the railing. She hung there for a second, waiting to see if her stomach would betray her, and then looked back at Shanti.

"I don't think I can stay out here long. But I would love some company in the cabin. Maybe we could play cards."

"I love that idea, but I don't have any cards," admitted Shanti.

"I've always got a deck somewhere," grinned Keema.

"It's a date," smiled Shanti in return. She glanced

back to Felldan. "I might see you later. My wife and I are going to relax."

Together she and Keema began making their way to the stairs below decks. While she held onto her wife's elbow to support her slow steps down the steep stairs, Shanti took one last look around.

Ahead of the Tide's Daughter, the sun was lifting its way above the horizon. They were travelling home, into a new dawn, and Shanti smiled as she thought about what she and Keema could build once they were there. Maybe it was time to visit Graama? They could recommit their vows to each other, with family present, as they should have done the first time. It would mean that Shanti could finally check up on her brothers as well.

The sun moved higher, pushing back the darkness of the night and spreading red and gold light into the world.

THE END

Keep informed of any new writing by Aaron, by signing up for his Mailing List at: bit.ly/3kLKaaG

ACKNOWLEDGMENTS

The first person I need to thank is Carla. I thought that Shanti had already had enough of an adventure in Where The Fields Grow Light, but she kept asking me questions about what happened next. Before long I was asking those questions myself and When Hidden Eyes Grow Dim is the result. It doesn't include all the answers I came up with either.

As alway, Steff is far too generous with her advice and support. Such a successful author should have better things to do with her time! I couldn't have got this book halfway done without her. You can check out her books at www.steffanieholmes.com

I relied on the support of two friends to edit this novel.

The first was Kat who always does an amazing job even if she doesn't always get to the end of my manuscripts... Any problems you noticed were my fault, not hers.

The second was Emma, who brings a level of attention to detail that puts me to shame. If there's any professionalism in this book, she has provided it.

All of you who read my previous books and told me that they weren't awful, thank you for that encouragement to write more.

And finally, always, huge love to my wife Andy

who has taken me on so many adventures that I couldn't help but feel inspired to write parts of them down. It was her love of lizards that inspired a lot of this book! Which I suppose means I owe her something of an apology for how they were treated in it...

ABOUT THE AUTHOR

Aaron Dick is a teacher living north of Auckland in New Zealand with his wife, their two daughters, and a small menagerie of household animals. They all love when his eldest daughter visits too.

He grew up as a voracious reader of science-fiction and fantasy, often to the annoyance of his unheeded family. Becoming an author was a childhood dream, alongside being a palaeontologist, or a rock star.

His stories have featured in a collection of New Zealand short stories inspired by Grimms' Fairy Tales and in the gothic art and lifestyle magazine Nocturne.

You can read both of these stories for free, and keep informed of any new writing by Aaron, by signing up for his Mailing List at: bit.ly/3kLKaaG

You can also find him on Facebook at: fb.me/AaronDickNZ